POP-WHITE

GO DOWN HARD

GO DOWN HARD

CRAIG FAUSTUS BUCK

ISBN: 1941298702
ISBN 13: 9781941298701

Published by Brash Books LLC
12120 State Line #253
Leawood, KS 66209

www.brash-books.com

AUTHOR'S NOTE

I would like to warn my readers that they are about to enter a world of situational punctuation. All apparent errors in traditional punctuation are mine by choice, having overridden my rigorous copy editor, not to mention the *Chicago Manual of Style*. In this book, I sometimes eschew the grammatical canon to use punctuation as a composer might use rests, to indicate cadence. I hope this practice doesn't annoy the purists as much as it worried my editor, and I trust this disclaimer will anesthetize the pain.

ONE

Eve whispered to Adam
Have some fruit from our yard
It'll fire up your blood
For when we go down hard
Lord have mercy
   Gonna go down hard

—Lana Strain

I look through the spyhole. Gloria has a bottle of gin in her hand and a pair of cuffs hanging from her belt loop. A deadly combination.

I open the door. "Evening, Lieutenant. You got a warrant?"

"Here's your warrant." She grabs the back of my head and sticks her tongue down my throat. I'd like it better if she didn't taste like Cheetos.

She walks in followed by her dog, Runt, who's not too bright but gets by on his looks. The strapping whelp of an Irish Setter and a Rhodesian Ridgeback, I suspect his red coat is the inspiration for Gloria's dye job.

Gloria gives me that crooked grin that always gets to me. It's the coy curl that promises exotic pleasures if you're lucky enough to have those lips engage just about any part of your anatomy. I've known more than a few guys who mistook that grin for an invitation and got decked. Gloria throws a mean left hook.

She heads into the kitchen for ice. I hear the clink of those steel-chain positive swing-through bracelets with every sway of her hips. She wears them in a cuff pouch at work, but tonight she's accessorizing. At the station, a cop might absently pick up the wrong set of cuffs from time to time, but Gloria doesn't have to worry about hers since they're powder-coated hot pink. They're also back-loading for fast closure, the kind of closure I could have used when my marriage collapsed.

I watch her pour a fist of gin. Five eight and lean, she has on the same pair of jeans she wore sixteen years ago when we first met at the academy. I've been married and divorced since then, but they still fit her, even if they used to be a bit looser, lazier in the thigh. She looks damn good.

"Still seeing the boyfriend?" I ask.

She cups her hands and pushes the lever of the ice maker with her knuckles.

"Why? Are you jealous?"

About a half dozen ice cubes spit onto her palms, but she can't catch one. They scatter across the floor like cockroaches in a blast of light.

"Just making conversation." I grab a beer from the fridge.

Gloria picks an ice cube off the floor and throws it in her glass. She only has room for the one cube without causing the booze to overflow, so she leaves the rest to melt on my linoleum. I debate picking them up but decide it's a bad precedent.

The boyfriend is a dentist she met at a Baptist church. Not that she's religious, but she loves gospel music. He calls her his girlfriend; she calls him her Baptist with benefits. Gloria is philosophically opposed to monogamy. As she puts it, "If we were wired to be monogamous, the honeymoon would be a lifestyle, not a phase." The Baptist doesn't like it, but his only alternative would be to live without her, and she's an addiction that's tough to kick.

For more than a decade, she's been my best friend, except we sometimes wind up in the sack. Or on the kitchen table. Or on the floor. Or just rammed up against a wall somewhere. That doesn't happen with any of my other pals. Not that I'm complaining. Sex with Gloria is wild and thrilling and sensual and full of surprises, even after all these years, but it can also be unrelenting. If the woman tracked her orgasms, she'd need an Excel spreadsheet. Friends shouldn't give friends performance anxiety.

Gloria takes a hefty slug of gin. "I've got a present for you," she says.

"What did I do to deserve a present?"

"Nothing yet, but if you're a bad boy, maybe I'll give it to you."

She moves in and kisses me again. This time she tastes like gin. A big improvement. I slide my hand up inside her blouse to feel her nipple trying to punch through her bra. She's already primed.

"It involves Lana Strain," she says.

My heartbeat spikes. Lana Strain was my adolescent wet dream, that perfect goddess who stamped the mold for my ideal woman. In concert she was high-voltage all the time, a blues-rock Tesla coil. Her songs exploded out of her with dead-on pitch sanded rough by too much smoke and rye whiskey then torched with raw emotion. Her heart-wrenching delivery left me burning to rescue her from the demons in her life, to make it all better for her, to wrap her tight in my arms and comfort her, preferably naked.

Then, when I was seventeen, some douchebag saw fit to splatter the back of Lana's head across her million-dollar Lichtenstein.

I was a four-point-oh heading for the Ivy League, a swim-team star, a party animal, invincible, immortal, at the top of my game. Nothing could take me down, not even my father's death six months before. I'd managed to ride out that trauma on a wave of denial, but a second wave never came when Lana got shot and

I needed one bad. The night they broke the news, I sat crying in my room, listening to *Lana Live at the Hollywood Bowl* over and over. Or was I crying for my father? I used to think I knew. These days I'm not so sure.

"What's this present got to do with Lana Strain?" I ask.

"You want to find out? Let's see how bad you can be."

We migrate toward the bedroom, entwined like tango dancers. Runt makes a halfhearted attempt to herd us back into the kitchen, knowing he's about to be ignored for a while, but when his efforts fail, he pads off to my office to sleep on his favorite sofa. He's been chewing on it for months now, slowly ripping it to shreds. At first that upset me, but then I just gave up. Once Runt's pea brain settles on a project, nothing can stop him.

Gloria rips off my clothes with a sense of urgency. She's ready to rock. I take my sweet time, savoring her, button by button, inch by inch, opening her up like a Chinese puzzle box. It drives her nuts. She heats up, I back off. She cools down, I crank up. It's an excruciating equilibrium.

I work her this way for maybe twenty minutes, until she sounds like an amplified asthma attack, then I pull out the stops. She wails, she howls, she growls, then she goes off like a rocket. Multiple stages.

I'd like to take responsibility for satisfying Gloria, but she's as easy as a bottle of Coke—just shake and pop the top, and she starts spurting; my finesse is just for show. Still panting, she turns the tables and devours me like a rabid beast. A highly skilled rabid beast. It doesn't take me long to detonate but she doesn't stop, she just slows and teases to keep the after surge going on and on. Nice.

Gloria flicks my ear with her tongue, still breathing hard. "You ready for your present?"

"Sure." I guess I was bad enough. And we didn't even use the cuffs.

Our clothes are scattered across the floor. She rolls over and finds her blouse. She pulls a thin chain from her pocket. It has a little gold half heart on it with a jagged edge. It's the kind of pendant that comes in a matched pair for best girlfriends or maudlin lovers to fit together like puzzle pieces so that their heart can only be complete when they're together.

"You can't keep it," she says, "but you can have it for tonight."

I try to take it, but she closes it in her hand. "Uhn uhn," she says, shaking her head. "No hands."

She drops it in her crotch.

"Are you telling me that was Lana's?"

"Probably. But no one ever saw her wearing it."

As I lower my head to retrieve my prize, she adds, "Until they found her body."

TWO

It's not even eight, but the view through my office window already shimmers in the heat from the dew baking out of the San Fernando Valley floor. I'm supposed to be writing five hundred words for the *Enquirer* about a sixteen-year-old girl who managed to stab the spike of a compass through her geometry teacher's chest and into his heart. What do I really know about this girl?

My eyes flit to Lana's pendant, which now hangs from my desk lamp. I grab a pencil and start to sketch it as my mind strays from my work. What do I really know about Lana?

I force my thoughts back to the job at hand. I put down the pencil and turn my eyes back to the screen. Despite nine outstanding queries, this stabbing story is the first assignment I've landed in two weeks. I need the money. I need to focus. What do I really know about this girl?

What do I really know about any woman? They use you up and throw you out, that's what. I type, *Fuck you, Holly.*

My mood sinks just seeing my ex-wife's name on the screen. She was the love of my life when we tied the knot. I'd just become a cop and was riding high. Four years later I watched another cop do something he shouldn't have. I turned a blind eye. Holly thought I was better than that. I wasn't. Things kept sliding downhill from there. It took her a year to divorce me. Two months after that I left the department. The rise and fall of the Nob Brown empire.

Gloria walks in, buttoning her top.

"Sleep well?" I ask.

"What are you doing up so early?"

"What do you think?"

"Writing."

"You should have been a detective."

"How's it coming?" She glances at my screen.

"Not too bad. If you don't mind starving for work and drowning in debt."

She swivels my desk chair and sits facing me on my lap. Her freckled brown eyes stare into mine. I feel like she's poking around inside my head, opening drawers, peeking under rocks.

"You okay?" she asks. "You've seemed a little down lately."

"Haven't you heard? Down is the new up."

She gives me that grin and presses her lips to mine. The kiss is soft, uncharacteristically gentle for her, unsettling. She pulls away and I feel like she's picked my pocket, even though I can't find anything missing.

"I need to drop Runt off before work," she says. "I've been saving something special for your birthday, but I think I'll give it to you early, maybe get your motor running."

She plucks Lana's necklace off my lamp and walks out with Runt on her heels.

Two hours later I watch Gloria close her office door to spare me the prying glares of the detectives in the bullpen. I don't have too many friends left on The Job anymore.

Gloria sits down behind her battle-scarred desk, which is so tight to the wall she has to lift her feet over the seat of her chair to get her long legs into the kneehole. That's the only configuration that leaves room in front for a folding chair to accommodate visitors. Steel. Unpadded. God forbid I should get too comfortable and overstay my welcome.

A glass nameplate on her desk is engraved with an LAPD Detective badge beside the name Lieutenant Gloria Lopes, which rhymes with "hopes," even though she's descended from an Argentine. I guess the culture didn't stick.

She pulls an eight-by-ten glossy from a bulging file and it immediately curls into a cylinder. She hands it to me and I stretch it taut. The image is like a sucker punch.

Lana Strain's body sits dwarfed by the wall-height painting. Her brain has exploded across the canvas of the *Dotted Babe*, the perfect spacing of Lichtenstein's half-tone dots disarrayed by the spray-painted blood. I have to take a deep breath to keep my stomach at bay.

The crime-scene photos were never released, so the faded still life is not just a shock but a revelation. Lana slumps against the bottom of the painting like a life-size rag doll, her Streamline Moderne body vacuum-packed in a black halter dress of dotted swiss. I've pictured her dying in jeans and a camisole top, in sweats, in leather, in tight T-shirts, in torn T-shirts, in wet T-shirts, in men's dress shirts, in shorts, in slit skirts, in bikinis, in teddies and, of course, in nothing. But fifties vintage never crossed my mind. Dotted swiss just doesn't seem right.

Lana looks drunk with her head twisted at an awkward angle, chin on chest just above that half-heart pendant. Her face is covered by an onyx wave of silky hair falling slightly open at the part to reveal one eye, a startling mosaic of greens and golds. Her other eye is hidden beneath her hair, but I doubt much of it survived the bullet's entry.

I can feel Gloria watching for my reaction. My primal love for Lana outlived her gruesome murder, outlasted my adolescence, persisted through many a romance, and survived the carnage of my marriage—and Gloria knows it. She knows me too well. She's waiting to see some eruption of emotion like a Roman lusting for a gladiator's blood. I don't give her the satisfaction.

"The shot heard 'round the world," I say softly.

She allows a smirk.

The colors of the photo have yellowed with age, the reds faded more than the cooler hues, turning bloodred into a pale tangerine. I can see a vanity in the background, but everything on it is too blurred to be recognizable. Something that looks like an open umbrella, maybe a lamp. Something that looks like a human head, maybe an oval mirror.

"Too bad about the painting," says Gloria. "I wonder if they ever got the bloodstains out."

Some cops just don't get it. "Why would they want to? A good story just jacks up the price. *Dotted Babe*, now in red."

"You don't think like a cop anymore," she says.

Under the harsh light of the ancient fluorescent fixtures, Gloria's red mane looks amber, like my eyes, though she says they're hazel.

"Ever find the gun?" I ask.

"No."

I lay the eight-by-ten like a priceless papyrus on her desk and lean my six-foot-one frame back in the rigid chair. I feel a bump where it hits my back. Someone must have kicked a dent in the steel. Gloria can have that effect on people.

"I loved her voice," I say. "Reminded me of Janis Joplin, only Lana Strain was better built."

"They both died drunk."

"They both lived drunk. What do you expect?"

During my high school years I had the famous swimming pool poster on my wall where I could see it from bed, the one where Lana's arms and legs covered just enough of her body to make the poster legal to sell to minors. Her piercing, carnivorous eyes haunted my dreams. Now I have a new image to haunt me.

My gaze drifts back to the photo, again curled into a scroll. Twenty years later and I still can't believe Lana's dead. In every city she toured, she'd go to blues bars in parts of town the cops were scared to drive through. She'd get drunk and start brawls.

She should have been shot in one of those. That would have been a death in character, a death with flare. Getting shot in her Laurel Canyon bedroom wearing dotted swiss was too suburban middle-class for Lana Strain, too mundane. It just wasn't her style. I find it hard to swallow, as if someone covered up the truth about how she died.

"I know you've been slobbering over her since you were old enough to jerk off, Nob, so happy birthday."

Gloria uncurls the photo, slips it back into the several hundred pages of file, and pushes the engorged folder toward me.

"You don't use three-ring binders for murder books anymore?"

She shrugs. "I took it apart so it wouldn't be so obvious. Keep it organized."

"You're letting me take it home?"

"Like I said, you're looking depressed. With the twentieth anniversary coming up, maybe you can sell a retrospective. Maybe a gig will perk you up. I worry about you."

I can't help but smile, amused. "You worry about me?"

"Go ahead and laugh. But no one knows you like I do. Not even Holly. I know when you're in trouble. And that worries me. You know I love you."

"You must if you're willing to put your badge on the line."

"It's my good deed for the decade so don't make me regret it. I can only check the book out for seven days so I want it back in six. And don't use any direct quotes or descriptions. Background only. You never saw this file."

"Thanks."

"Don't mention it. And I mean that literally."

"I'll have to tell Mel."

"No one else." Gloria knew my assistant Melody before I did and knows she can trust her. "I'm counting on you to not be your usual fuckup."

"I'll do my best."

I reach for the yellowed file, half-expecting it to sear my hand. The overstuffed folder looks almost bronze, like it was baked in an oven, the edges so well thumbed they feel soft to the touch. It may be two decades old, but it's still the hottest unsolved murder of the twentieth century.

For a Lana Strain worshiper who makes his living as a true crime writer, this is gold bullion, a guaranteed magazine piece, if not a book and maybe even a movie. I can't help but savor the irony that the first love of my life has returned from the grave to save me from the financial divorce havoc wreaked by the second.

Gloria pulls a plastic shopping bag from her garbage can and hands it to me so I have something to hide the file in. I wrap it and tuck it under my arm.

"I owe you one."

"Don't worry. I won't let you forget it."

As I leave the station I pass from conditioned comfort into one of those unforgiving LA days where the summer sun makes you feel like an ant that some kid is broiling with a magnifying glass.

I head down the street, hugging the building to catch its small skirt of shade, savoring the heat of Lana Strain's file on my forearm. It occurs to me, for the first time since Holly dumped me, that I've got something to look forward to.

THREE

I walk into the house carrying Lana's file and a pound of fresh-roasted Ethiopian Yirgacheffe beans, still warm from the roaster in the coffee store half a mile down the road. I'm almost high from the aroma, and my gait is syncopated by the Lana Strain tune in my head. Then I spot Melody Elvinstar, deep in meditation, sitting in the lotus position on the oak desk that used to be my father's. At four foot six, maybe seven, eighty-five pounds, she's small enough to fit on my blotter. My head music stops hard like someone scratching the tone arm across an old LP.

"I'm not paying you to contemplate your eyelids."

She opens her eyes, russet and annoyed. "Do you mind?"

My gaze drifts from her knobby knees to a Post-it on my monitor. "What's that?"

"Shhhhhhhhh." She closes her eyes.

I drop Lana's file on the desk with a resounding thud.

Her eyes snap open. "Was that really necessary?" She swivels off the desk.

"It's my next story. It's heavy." I peel the Post-it from the screen and read it. "I phoned in for messages. You forgot to tell me my agent called?"

"I'm sorry, okay?" She says it impatiently, like it's my fault. "Your ex-wife called, too."

"I wonder who has worse news."

My agent hasn't called with good news since the day he offered to represent me. And I'm not sure that news was so good.

Melody drops her head to stretch her neck, and her straight dyed-black hair falls across the left side of her face, a curtain shaped like a shark fin. She cuts the right side shorter. She cuts it herself. I know she's hovering somewhere near thirty, but her skin could be a teenager's if you overlook the death's-head tattoo on her left bicep.

I pick up the phone and punch my agent's button. Since the advent of speed dialing, I've managed to forget every phone number I ever knew.

I'm pretty stoked about the Lana Strain piece. It could have a shot beyond the *National Enquirer*, maybe landing in *Vanity Fair* or *Rolling Stone*, with extras in *Salon* or the *Huffington Post*. Especially if I can uncover something new. Like her killer. The thought makes me yearn for those adrenaline rushes I used to love when I was a cop.

There's the brass ring of a movie deal, or at least a cable movie to rejuvenate the career of some forgotten star. Maybe one of the Olsen twins, probably the anorexic one.

"Berger Bergen Agency." I don't recognize the voice. Charles runs through receptionists like six-packs at a Super Bowl party.

"Nob Brown for Chuckles."

"There's no one here by that name."

"Charles."

"Oh. Hold on." I guess brains weren't high on the job requirement list. Chuckles has his priorities.

I wait, tapping the drum solo to "Wipe Out" on my desk. She comes back. "He's on another line. He'll get back to you." Click. I wonder why I bother to call.

My eyes drift back to Melody. She's just sitting there, cross-legged on the office chair like a pipe-cleaner Buddha. "You're supposed to be doing research."

"I'm clocked out," she says, irritated by my insinuation.

I don't have a whole lot of moral authority here since I've never paid her. I deduct her paltry salary from the nineteen and some odd thousand dollars she still owes me for finding her brother George. He'd wandered off from rehab in a delirious state, and it took me two months to track him down to a Venezuelan prison where he'd been locked up by the government on a trumped-up charge of espionage. More than half of what she owes me went to bribe a rummy army captain who was greedy enough to betray the revolution for one night. Once back in the States, George managed to stay on the street for about two months before landing back in jail, this time in Tehachapi, for dealing crank. Thus I have a part-time assistant.

"You old enough to remember Lana Strain?"

"Sort of. I was about seven or eight when she was killed. My folks used to love that song she wrote about the chick who was obsessed with her own stalker."

"Some Asshole's Watching Me Tonight." The title takes me back to 1991, the first time I saw Lana live. She debuted the song that night. The performance replays in my head, a pristine recording:

> There's someone loves me more than you,
> He shows me love more than you do.
> He cares for me the way you should
> He'd die for me, I know he would
> Love's in his eyes, they shine so bright
> Some asshole's watching me tonight.
>
> I've glimpsed him passing by my door.
> I've seen his shadow on the floor.
> I've seen his eye glint through the wall,
> Just where the vent holes show it all.
> Love's in his eye, it caught the light
> Some asshole's watching me tonight.

Melody pulls me back to the present. "Wasn't there some connection between that song and her murder?"

"No one knows. In the song, she entices him to have sex, then when he climaxes, she sticks an ice pick through his gleaming eye."

"Très romantique," she says.

"No one even knows if he was real. She could have made him up for the song. She never said. This would be a huge story if I could find that out."

"What about the case of the fatal compass?"

"I'll get to it."

I pick up the phone and call Danny Samo, my editor at *Playboy*. At least he was my editor for the one story I've managed to sell them so far. It was about a neurosurgeon who had to drink to keep his hands from shaking.

After wading through *Playboy*'s voice-mail system I finally get Samo on the phone. He doesn't recognize my name. Not a good start. I remind him I'm the ex-cop who wrote the alcoholic brain surgeon story. Luckily, he remembers the story and apparently liked it, so he's open to a verbal pitch. I tell him I have access to hundreds of pages of unreleased information about Lana Strain's murder, including the murder scene photos, which I can describe but not release. Since the twentieth anniversary of her death is coming up, *Playboy* should reopen the case and send intrepid reporter Nob Brown out to review the record and solve the crime. Even if I fail, it's still got sex, drugs, and rock 'n' roll. He likes the idea. Not only was his father a big Lana Strain fan, but *Playboy* once offered Lana Strain ten grand to pose nude. She declined, but only because of a scheduling problem.

"I'll tell you what," says Samo. "I'll pay you twenty large if you nail the bastard who did it."

"And if I don't?"

"I'll pay you three."

"You've got to be kidding. It's the same amount of work either way."

"You're welcome to take it to *Hustler*."

"Come on, Danny. Make it five, at least."

"Take it or leave it."

I take it. It's a buyer's market. He says he'll send me a contract and cover expenses. I hang up and turn to Melody.

"Decongestant junkie?" She sounds like a corrupted download or, as they used to say, a broken record.

"I'll get to it. In the meantime, why don't you start on the Strain piece. Cruise around, see what you find. I'll need contact info for her family, band members, friends, whatever names you can get from the case file."

"Contact info might be hard to come by. The celebrity thing." She climbs off the desk and stretches by pulling one leg up next to her ear while balancing on the other. She does this all the time, but it never fails to amaze me.

"Do the best you can. And see if you can find any media reports on who stood to gain from her will and how much. Her lawyer was some guy named..." I check a scratch pad on my desk. "Gary Cogswell at Benchley Nugent. See if he's still there. If not, track him down."

"Don't you have a friend who works there?" She switches legs. I think "ambidextrous." I try to come up with the analogous leg word. I used to know it.

"Not anymore, but he used to. Swims in my lane at the Westwood Pool."

To stay fit I'm a masters swimmer, which sounds highfalutin but just means you have to be older than nineteen to join. That's how I met Jack Angel.

"I'll give him a call," I say. "We're overdue for a dog day anyway."

"A dog day?"

"Lunch at Pink's." The very thought makes my mouth water.

"Do you have any idea what they put in those dogs?"

"Yeah. Flavor."

She switches legs again. What the hell is the word for that?

"And rat shit," she says with her characteristic disdain for any food that's cooked faster than wheat grass can think.

She finally finishes her balancing act. It's not until she has both legs on the floor that I realize I've been tense, as if I've been watching a trapeze artist without a net. I let my breath out and the word comes to me: ambicrural! My dad would be proud.

"I'll worry about my diet; you worry about tracking down Lana Strain's family. She had a couple daughters, Ginger and Sophia. They were thirteen and fourteen when she died. Father was Billy Kidd. I guess he still is."

"That name rings a bell." She opens a file on her laptop and starts a to-do list.

"Guitar legend. Big heartthrob at the time. Still tours."

Melody furrows her brow. "I think my mother was really into him," she says.

"And I seem to remember there was some issue with the inheritance. Maybe ten years ago. I don't remember the details, but there was a lot of money turned up missing. There could be a motive for murder in there somewhere that the police didn't know about at the time of the investigation."

She writes it down.

"There was some kind of investigation, too. Lana's father was accused of something. Maybe plundering the estate? Let's try to track him down, too."

"I gotta pee."

I give her a wave of dismissal and she heads to the john. I figure I'll make a quick call while she's gone. No sense wasting the time. Of all the people I want to speak to for sixty seconds or less, my ex-wife tops the list. I punch her speed dial on my cell. After four rings, she picks up.

"Holly, it's me."

"Oh." I've only said three words and she's already disappointed. "I just stepped out of the shower. Can I call you right back?"

"No. I gotta run." I'm not sure why I say it. I guess I like the idea of making her drip. Not that I have any interest in talking to her naked, though with her miniature Barbie body, that *is* her best look. More like I'm hoping she'll catch a chill. I'm not a vengeful guy; I wouldn't want to hurt her. But I wouldn't mind giving her a little sniffle for old times' sake.

"Mel said you called. What do you want?" I ask.

"What do you think?" she says.

"I'm shocked."

"You're overdue, Nob. I've got a mortgage to pay."

"I'm waiting on some payments. It's not like I get a regular paycheck."

"Why do you make me do this? You know I hate to be like this. Neither one of us wants to get Jerry involved."

The thought of her scum-sucking lawyer gives me a gas pain. She's a deputy DA. Why can't she be her own lawyer?

"I'm expecting a check from the *Daily Mirror* any day now. *Hustler* owes me, too."

"Oh, Nob." She sighs. I imagine her ivory skin covered in goose bumps, the sparse hairs of her arms sticking up like cactus spines, her brows furrowed beneath her natural-blond bowl-cut bangs. "I'm going to have to call Jerry. You're not giving me any choice."

"Go ahead. He'll come over, I'll hit him, he'll sue me, then *he'll* have your money."

"You're never going to grow up, are you?"

The good thing about these conversations is they reinforce the thought that splitting up wasn't all bad. I hear Melody flush the toilet, and it reminds me that the flapper needs replacing again. Rubber parts don't last long in LA. The smog eats them up. I make a mental note to pick up a new one. One more errand to put off.

I promise to do what I can and hang up. I feel like shit not being able to pay my debts on time, as punitive as they may be, but all I can do is try.

Melody walks back into the office and settles in front of the monitor, oblivious to the view through the window behind her. It's one of those rare LA days where the sky is blue, not brown, and punctuated by a few puffs of white clouds. From my bungalow in the hills of Sherman Oaks, the view across the San Fernando Valley is often filled with smog so thick that you can't see the Santa Susana Mountains, fifteen miles away. But at the moment, the air is crystal clear, and I can see not only the Santa Susanas, but the Santa Ynez Mountains another fifteen miles beyond. It's glorious. No wonder so many people want to live here.

"Lana Strain and the Brothers of Libation," says Melody. "Six gold records, two platinum."

I look back at the monitor to see an interminable search-engine list slowly loading.

"Rockin' band," I say. "Lana on vocals and rhythm guitar, Billy Kidd on lead, Don or Dan something on bass, and a black chick drummer named Boom-Boom Laphroig." God only knows from what dark mudhole of my rat-eaten memory that little tidbit erupted.

"See? You do have some recall left." As if I need Melody to rub my nose in my own mortality. Lana Strain's killer did that for me years ago. It's about time I returned the favor.

FOUR

"I'm a lawyer, Nob, not a crook."

"Like there's some big fucking difference."

"That's a bit cynical, don't you think?"

"The case is twenty years old, Angel. The client is dead. No one cares about the ethics."

We step up to the window, and I order for both of us.

"Your turn," I tell Angel.

"You're the one wants the favor. You pay for lunch." He gives me that smug Jack Angel smile, and I think this guy looks pretty good for his age. He's got to be sixty, but his teeth are sparkling white. I used to think it was the contrast against his black-coffee skin, but he told me he had them lasered. Must have cost him a grand or two. And his blue pin-striped Hugo Boss suit probably cost more than my car. But he's still gaming me for a four-dollar dog.

"I haven't seen any favor yet." But I reach for my wallet anyway. I pass a couple Hamiltons through the window.

"Well, I don't work at Benchley Nugent anymore, so I don't have access to any files, even if I was willing to show them to you."

"I don't care about files. I'm getting her probate docs from the county."

"So what do you want?" He grabs a couple napkins to blot the sweat off his brow. The city may be ten degrees cooler than the Valley, but it's still ninety-five.

"A couple weeks before she got popped, she kicked Hubby out of the house," I say. "You gotta figure she'd want to, maybe, I don't know…modify her will?"

"I don't do wills."

"Just introduce me to the lawyer who did, okay? He sees I'm a friend of a former colleague, maybe he'll deign to talk to me." I take my change and step aside so the next person can order.

"If *I'm* not willing to tell you anything, why should he? Besides, they've got three hundred lawyers, most of whom came since I left. I probably don't even know the guy."

"You were both there at the same time. Name's Gary Cogswell."

Angel couldn't have been more shocked if I'd swung a chicken into his face. "You're kidding, right?"

"I guess that means you know him."

"You don't know who Gary Cogswell is?"

"Just tell me."

Angel grabs another napkin and runs it up his forehead and over his thick mat of silver curls, as if his sweat were some sort of wet-look gel. To my surprise, it seems to work. If I tried something like that, it would turn my dirty-blond hair into a grease mop.

"Don't you read the papers? He's Vlad Bakatin's consigliere."

Now the chicken hits me. "Vlad the Impaler?"

"What other Russian has a consigliere?"

"That's some gig."

"Not exactly a career path they taught us at Harvard."

"He went to law school with you?"

"Oh yeah. Me and Cogs go way back. We were summer associates together at Benchley Nugent; then after law school they hired us both. The pay was fantastic and the paralegals smokin'. So what if it was tax law?"

"I take it he didn't like it as much as you did."

"He liked the paras all right, but that was about it. I remember one time, he got drunk and nibbled on the earlobe of the head of HR. She filed a complaint."

"That why he left the firm?"

Angel laughs. "God no. They buried that one."

"Then why?"

"I know you're going to find this hard to believe, Nob, but some people find estate planning boring. Cogs was going apeshit. He was a star fucker. He wanted glamour."

"Russian gangsters are glamorous?"

"He was an adrenaline junkie."

The counterman hands us our dogs. I look around. No tables. We find a place to lean against the stand, hovering near two women who are just finishing up—a middle-aged matron in an Ann Taylor dress with her hair sprayed into a helmet shape and her biker daughter sporting a Harley jeans vest and a crew cut.

"I remember the day he got the idea," Angel continues. "I mean, he could get pretty wild after a half dozen Cuervo Bulldogs. I watched him dive off a fourth-story balcony once, into a swimming pool. Almost made it, too, except for one foot. He still limps pretty bad from that one. But this one afternoon he was stone sober. Completely insane, but sober. He says he's thinking about asking Bakatin for a job. I say, 'The man murders people, Cogs.' He says, 'You know he doesn't murder people, Angel.' I say, 'Let's not get technical. He orders people to murder people.' He says, 'Who says? *USA Today*? I haven't seen him get convicted of anything.' I say, 'Don't be a moron. We both know what he does for a living.' But he has his mind made up."

The ladies stand up and we grab the table.

"So he makes me drive him over to some kind of social club on South Fairfax. Says he read in *Time* magazine that Bakatin operated out of there." Angel bites into his jalapeño dog and drips about a pint of chili into his cardboard tray.

"I say, 'What are you going to do? Hand Vlad a résumé?'"

Angel takes a sip of his Yoohoo. A drop of the chocolate drink dribbles down his chin and he has to wipe it with the back of his hand to protect his tie.

"I tell him, 'You want to rub shoulders with criminals? Be a defense attorney. You're too short to be a consigliere.' But he wants to be Robert Duvall in *The Godfather*. How tall is Duvall, anyway? You know, sometimes they make short actors stand on boxes so you never know."

He scoops up some chili with his fingers and plops it on top of his jalapeño dog before taking another bite.

"You don't just walk up to a capo and ask for a job application," I say. "Guys get killed for less." I bite into my dog and the natural casing makes that satisfying snap.

"He'd already done Bakatin's estate at Benchley Nugent, so he had a leg up on the guy's financial situation. Maybe he leveraged that."

"Mobsters have tax attorneys?"

"The smart ones do, at least since Capone got nailed by the IRS."

Angel's head starts to sweat from the jalapeños. He wipes his forehead with his napkin and unknowingly smears mustard on his brow. I don't say anything.

"You got a number for Cogswell?"

"No way I'm giving it to you."

"Come on, Angel. I bought you lunch."

"Kiss my black ass. The guy's mobbed up."

"I'm not going to ask him about his day job. This story's yesterday's news."

"You want to meet him? Find Bakatin's social club, and you'll find Cogs. He'll be the smallest guy there. The one with the limp."

FIVE

I have a fake Eames lounge chair in my office. I know it's fake because the real ones don't recline and mine does. Another clue is the three-grand price difference. I'm in it, fast asleep, when Mel traipses in and throws open the curtains. Daylight hammers me awake.

"Working late or up early?" she says.

I have a vague recollection of slipping out of bed and sneaking back to work around two a.m. The last thing I remember was Runt chewing on the sofa but he's gone now, so I assume Gloria left early to take him home before work. The back of the sofa looks like someone blasted it with a shotgun. The upholstery is shredded and stuffing is strewn everywhere. Runt's job is complete. I'll deal with it later.

"Up early," I mumble, trying to shake off the sleep. "Finally finished the *Enquirer* piece a couple hours ago."

I groan and stretch, and Lana's file slides off my lap, spreading papers all over the floor.

"Smooth," says Melody.

She makes no move to pick anything up, so I drag myself out of the chair and start collecting the scattered file.

Melody watches me grunt every time I bend over. "You really had a thing for this chick singer, didn't you?"

"Lana Strain wasn't just some chick singer. She was God. And then she got shot. It was like Elvis's death all over again, except this time I was already born. A whole generation facing mortality for the first time at exactly the same moment. This story could tap all of that. It could be huge."

"It's old."

"So's the Bible, but the older it gets, the better it sells. If I can find something new to make this story sing, it could kick-start my career."

She looks at me like a doctor trying to figure the odds on a tough diagnosis. "Your mother called today, didn't she. Whenever you start talking about improving your lot in life, I know she's been pulling your chain."

"This could turn into a movie deal, okay? I could make some real money for a change. Pay Holly off. Buy my car a new clutch. Give you a raise."

Melody coughs up a laugh. "I'm not holding my breath."

I stoop to grab a few pages and feel my back start to tighten. I try to stretch it out by arching backward as far as I can. At least an inch.

Melody bends over backward, somehow contorting herself to operate the mouse behind her head like a sideshow freak.

"There's plenty out there about Lana Strain and Billy Kidd," she says, "but I'm having trouble finding much on the other band members. You have a real name for Boom-Boom Laphroig?"

"No. I searched for her but only found band references. And she's not on Facebook, at least not under that name. But there's a reference to her in a Brothers of Libation fan group. Someone named Kate Dreyfus apparently went to Beverly High with Boom-Boom. I put in a friend request."

She clicks a bookmark for a site called LanaLives.com.

"I did find something else that might interest you. You being a dirty old man and all."

"I'm not that old."

She hits the back button twice, and I watch Lana Strain begin ever so slowly to coalesce on the screen in crappy resolution.

Lana's hairline comes into focus, then her eyes, her nostrils, her luscious mouth. My eyes lock on her lips—naturally plush, long before collagen injections. Then the process freezes up just below her neck. Fiber-optic demons. "What is this? DSL?"

After another twenty seconds in dog years, the image of Lana Strain finally comes into unpixeled view. It's a candid photo that looks like an outtake from the shoot that produced my old swimming pool poster. She's lying naked on her back on the concrete deck against the backdrop of the turquoise water. I remember lusting after those breasts in my teens, tracing them with my finger on her CD covers, studying their vivid curves as they molded her tank tops into adolescent fantasies.

Even with Lana supine, their resistance to the flattening force of gravity is impressive. And silicone-free. My eyes are drawn to the sparkle of sunlight reflecting off a bead of sweat on her belly.

Melody busts me with a smirk. "What is it with men and tits? You want a magnifying glass?" Her sarcasm could eat through steel, but I'm immune. Her opinions of movies interest me; her opinions of me don't.

"Spare me the lecture. If she had a dick, I'd stare at that, too."

Melody stands and drops into the splits, just because she can. In her other life, she's a dancer.

An animated title scrolls from left to right: "Fun with Dick and Jane Productions Presents *Cybersex with Lana Strain!*"

I stare dumbfounded as Lana sits up, live as she ever was, not much older than she was twenty years ago, black hair flowing, green eyes witching, looking finger-lickin' good in a dental-floss bikini.

"Hi," she says in that unmistakable smoke-tortured, whiskey-strained, honky-tonk, sex-drenched voice. "I'm Lana Strain and I've come back from the dead, streaming live just to get you off."

I hear Melody chortle at me, but I can't take my eyes off the screen long enough to send her a decent glare.

The dead chick continues, "You can call me toll-free, or just type your pleasure on your keyboard, and I'll do anything you want, right here, right now. No fantasy is too filthy for me because I've got nothing to lose. I'm already dead. For just four ninety-five a minute, you can have the time of your life, if not mine."

She reaches behind her neck to untie her bikini strap.

"How do they do that?" I ask.

"I don't know," Melody says as she unbends herself. "The second coming?"

I ignore the pun as Lana starts playing with her top, enticing me with the promise of exposing her breasts. As she approaches the point of revelation, the video teaser ends. Her image just stares at me, animation suspended, poised for my money. In a way I'm glad. There's something decidedly unsavory about being baited by a corpse. On the other hand, it's so perversely absurd that I can't resist. I sit down and hit Enter.

"Remind me to call *Wired* magazine," I say. "Maybe I can talk Frank into a piece on this."

"Sure, Nob." As if I'm rationalizing, which I probably am.

A little window comes up with a revolving logo. Something loads, and there's Lana, frozen in time, waiting for me to click on a button marked "Cum On In."

After swearing that I'm eighteen and that viewing pornographic material is legal in my state, I come on in. The next screen asks me to download some free software. At ninety-five cents a minute or twenty-four ninety-five a month, I guess they can afford to give it away.

I'm no technowiz, but I know how to point and click, so I do. I agree to a lengthy list of terms that I don't bother to read, probably signing away my privacy, my identity, my car, and my firstborn, but at least the video conferencing software installs itself without crashing my system.

I type in a user name and password. Duly registered, I give this random porn site my credit card number, despite the probability that they'll sell it to every hacker in the Czech Republic, and I'm finally ready to meet the star. One more click, and the clock starts ticking on the transaction.

A live-feed video window opens up, and there's Lana, completely naked, bronco-riding a vertical vibrator the size of a Louisville Slugger. She looks like a woman-shaped popsicle.

"Push the button," Melody says. I feel uncomfortable watching this in front of her.

I push the "Talk to Lana" button and get a banner that tells me my ninety-five cents a minute doesn't include direct conversation with the fantastic phantasm, it just buys me a seat to watch her fulfill someone else's fantasy. I've got no complaints. After all, it's not every day I get to see a corpse do a three-sixty on a piano leg.

But if I want to communicate my own fantasy, either on the phone or through my computer, I have to pony up another four ninety-five a minute. I punch the button to enter the direct-contact queue.

"How the hell am I going to explain this on my expense report?"

"Charge it to health insurance," says Melody. "Sexual dysfunction treatment."

I ponder this as I wait. After another two minutes the caller before me achieves happiness and hangs up. It's my turn. Everyone else is apparently being satisfied at the ninety-five-cent level.

"Hi, I'm Lana," she says in her Jack Daniels voice. "What's your name?" She can talk to me, but I have to type my response.

I punch in "Nob."

She laughs when she reads it.

"What's your fantasy, *Nob*? Or should I call you Big Nob?"

"I just want to talk to you," I write, correcting two typos along the way. At four ninety-five a minute, it finally strikes me why high school typing might have been a good idea.

"What kind of talk, you naughty boy?"

"Just talk."

"For another two ninety-five a minute, you can call me on the phone," she says.

"It's not about sex," I peck. "It's about your murder."

"Sorry, honey. But this is a sex line." To make her point she climbs off her vibrator, spreads her legs and, lacking a speculum, uses her fingers to simulate a gynecological exam.

If this is supposed to arouse me, it isn't working. Don't get me wrong: I like a naked woman as much as the next hetero guy. But I'm supposed to be working. I guess it's ground-in ethics from my days on the force. It's like the amputee thing, where you can still feel the limb after it's gone. That's my badge. Sometimes I can still feel it tucked over my waist, pushing against my thigh, plugging into my nervous system like a pacemaker, making my heart beat faster, pumping up my muscles. Then I wake up.

"Want to see me deep-throat an English cucumber?" she asks.

"For seven ninety a minute," I type, "I should get to talk about whatever I want."

"Not on my server, asswipe."

"She knows your real name," says Melody.

Lana punches something on her keyboard, and my screen freezes. It strikes me as odd. Not that women and rejection haven't gone hand in hand in my life, but I didn't think it was supposed to happen when you're paying for the companionship. I watch my screen, waiting for some sort of invoice, but instead it goes blue with white letters. The dreaded blue screen of death. I'm aglow in the luminescence of Windows irony: "Fatal error."

Melody smiles. "That went well."

"I don't know what I expected," I say. "What would some porn actress know about Lana's murder anyway?"

"I doubt she's an actress," says Mel. "She looks too much like Lana Strain. It must be some kind of CGI thing."

"But we were having a conversation. You think a porn site can afford the kind of special effects that can make a live actress look like somebody else in real time?"

"They've got this newfangled thing called research, Nob. You ought to try it sometime."

I pull up Bing because I've heard that Google is kind of prudish when it comes to porn, and I don't need a censor right how. "Cybersex with Lana Strain" pulls up more than three hundred thousand hits. I'm about to cry from overload when I notice a "Related Searches" list on the side of my screen: Celebrity lookalike porn.

I click and there, in the listing, is "How do they recreate Lana Strain?"

I cruise to the question.

"Well?" says Melody. "Was I right?"

I give her one of those looks reserved for softening the blow when you tell your child there is no Santa. "Our bat girl's secret isn't CGI, it's DNA. She's Lana's daughter."

SIX

mpersonating your dead mother doing live porn. I'm thinking there's got to be a commandment against that as I walk down Van Nuys Boulevard and into one of the few five-story buildings built before the local specific plan imposed height restrictions. I found the place by doing a Whois search on "Cybersex with Lana Strain" to find the web-address registration contact information, but that doesn't mean it's accurate or current.

There's a building directory in the shoebox of a lobby but Fun with Dick and Jane Productions, Inc. isn't on it. I guess if I was in the porn business I'd keep a low profile, too.

I check the suite numbers: 101, 102, 201, 202, 301, 401, 402, 501, 502. Doesn't take a genius to see the hole in the pattern. I step into the elevator and punch three.

The door closes to reveal purple Sharpie graffiti on the inside, a cartoon drawing of a woman blowing two men at once. The caption reads: "Two heads are better than one."

I ponder this deep philosophical thought as the door opens. I step into the middle of a short corridor with an office at each end.

Number 301 belongs to the Ocularists' Guild. I'm impressed that they know where to put the apostrophe; most businesses get that wrong.

The door to 302 says "D&J Modeling." Pay dirt. I walk in.

The reception area is about twenty feet square with a decrepit sectional wrapping one corner. The black Naugahyde decayed long ago, revealing a spiderweb of white backing through the age cracks. A cheap oak coffee table that must date back to the seventies holds a selection of automotive, soft porn, and gossip magazines, all at least two years old.

By the couch is some sort of potted fern that seems to have taken over the entire corner of the room. Must be a lot of moisture in the air. The opposite corner is piled high with boxes full of DVDs, as if they've run out of storage in back.

The highlight of the décor is a wall covered by framed DVD box covers with bad puns for titles. There's a whiteboard above the couch that has female names organized in a schedule by two-hour blocks. Names like Trixxxie and Roxxxi and Classy and Swallow. I look at the time and see that "Ginger," who I assume is Lana's daughter Ginger Strain, is currently online or on camera or up to bat, whatever you want to call it. I also note that her hours appear irregular with the exception of Wednesdays, where a column of red Xs implies that she's unavailable. I wonder why.

Opposite the couch is an oak desk that matches the coffee table, and behind it sits a receptionist transferring handwritten invoices into QuickBooks. Short black hair. About thirty. Olive skin, maybe Middle Eastern. He's dressed up in a sleek black sport jacket, pale-yellow shirt, and gray slacks. His tie looks yellow striped from a distance, but when I get closer I realize the stripes are rows of SpongeBobs lined up like dominoes. The realization makes me wonder whether it's time to have my eyes checked.

"Can I help you?"

"I'd like to see Dick or Jane," I say.

His eyes narrow. "Who are you?"

"I'm a writer. I want to give your website some free publicity."

"Who do you write for?"

"No offense, pal, but I don't pitch to receptionists."

I'm surprised his eyes can narrow even farther, like one of Zeno's paradoxes, getting ever halfway closer to being closed.

Then the door opens behind me, and a woman walks in and barks, "Robert! Bring me Arthur's contract!" She's taller than

I am by a good three inches, and I'm six one, maybe two on a good day, so she's up there. Willowy, graceful. She breezes past us, looking fine in what must be a twelve-hundred-dollar dress. She swings open a door to an inner office.

"You Jane?" I ask.

She swivels on toe, like a ballerina, to look down at me. "And you are?"

"Nob Brown."

"What kind of a name is that?"

"Mongolian. You got a minute?"

"Why should I waste my time with you?"

"I'm funny."

"Not so far."

"I'm a writer. I'm writing about a murder."

Her left eyebrow rises half an inch. "Murder?"

"Just give me a couple minutes. Everybody loves a good murder. It'll be worth it for the amusement value if nothing else, and it could get your site a mention in *Playboy*."

She breaks into a hearty laugh. "Okay, Mr. Nob Brown. I'll give you two minutes to win me over." She flows into the office, leaving the door open behind her as an invitation.

Her office looks like a display in the back of an Office Depot: a bunch of cheap generic furniture arranged to look like an executive office by a seventeen-year-old stock boy who's never been in one. Jane looks far too sophisticated for the environs. Then I notice the movie poster behind her. It's Jane, a few years younger. Different hair. Wearing nothing but heels and a translucent purple strap-on. The film was called *Cheeks Asunder,* starring Vajayna. Very classy.

She follows my gaze and laughs as she sits in her black vinyl executive chair and rocks back. "What's the matter, Mr. Brown. Never seen a CEO portrait before?"

"They're usually wearing a watch."

She holds up a diamond Rolex that must have cost fifty grand. "Here it is. And it's ticking."

"I'm here about Lana Strain."

"What about her?"

"She's no longer with us."

She deadpans, "Does anyone else know?"

"I'm supposed to be the funny one." I feel an itch on the arch of my foot and try grinding my shoe into the ground to scratch it, but it doesn't work.

I say, "I want to know how come she's pole vaulting on your website if she's dead."

"I'll let you in on a little secret, Mr. Brown. That's not really her."

She winks conspiratorially, and I wonder what she'd do if her false lashes snagged shut.

"You think maybe there's something a little sick about pimping a daughter to play her dead mother?"

She laughs. "It's about eyeballs, Mr. Brown. She attracts them."

"Maybe she's attracting the eyeballs of her mother's killer."

She laughs again. "You *are* a funny man."

"Well, here's the punch line. I've got a list of all the people questioned by the police regarding Lana Strain's murder. You let me cross-check my list against your subscribers, and maybe we can find Lana's killer, get you a few brownie points with the cops."

"Sweet little Ginger draws thousands of paying customers to our site every day," she says. "All kinds of people. Doctors, lawyers, candlestick makers, murderers, whatever. They're paying customers and I, being an advocate of the Bill of Rights, am determined to protect their privacy. It's a promise we make in their registration agreement."

"You're claiming the moral high ground here?"

"I'm sure a lot of unsavory people shop at my local market, too, but that doesn't make the milk go sour."

I shrug. "Maybe it would be better if I took my suggestion to the police."

She holds up that sparkly Rolex. I wonder if it was a gift or a purchase. "You've failed to amuse, Mr. Brown. Your two minutes are up."

I check the time on my cell phone as I leave. Three thirty-eight. Lana's shift is over in twenty minutes. From what I could gather in chat rooms, most of these places have girls broadcasting from home, but Dick and Jane has a reputation for "quality," i.e., they care about lighting and sound, so their girls work out of the studio.

I get into my stick-shift '91 Legend—once a luxury car, now my comfort food—and drive around the block. I pull into the alley and pick an empty parking lot behind a Thai restaurant. There's steam coming from the roof vents. Smells like garlic and fish. They don't open for two hours, but they're already cooking.

I choose a spot that lets me see through two chain-link fences into the lot behind Dick and Jane's building. I watch and wait.

At 4:04 the back door opens and Lana steps out. I know she's really Ginger, but the likeness still takes me by surprise. I assumed she used makeup or something to look so much like her mother, that when I'd see her in real life she'd look different, but no. She's the spitting image of Lana, only with her head intact.

She's wearing a stretchy tube dress, slinky, clingy, cut low on top and high on the bottom to show off what she makes her living with. Too explicit to be sexy, at least to me.

She gets into a fairly new, black Honda Civic and takes off. I let her get fifty yards down the alley then pull into her wake.

I follow her down Van Nuys to Ventura, then east to Laurel Canyon where she heads over the hill into Hollywood. We wind through the fabled wooded canyon where the likes of Joni Mitchell, Frank Zappa, the Mamas and Papas, Crosby, Stills, Nash & Young, and the Byrds once lived and played.

About halfway up the canyon, she turns onto a narrow, winding street called Weeping Glen. Another quarter mile, and she pulls into a driveway. I recognize the address from Lana's file. The murder scene. I park a half block away and watch Ginger get out of her car and head up the steps toward a wood-shingled two-story geodesic dome surrounded by trees.

She flips through her keys until she finds the right one. I try to imagine what it must have been like for her, thirteen years of age, coming home from school to this same house and finding her mother's brains sprayed across the *Dotted Babe*. I wonder if she unlocks that memory every time she unlocks the door.

SEVEN

feel like a gangbanger stuffed into my first suit to mislead a jury. I wait nervously in the fading light, squeezing my finger into my collar to give it a yank, hoping to admit some airflow behind my tie. No such luck.

The peephole finally goes dark. She's looking at me. I drop my hand and wonder if my hair is combed. I should have checked the mirror sometime during the half hour I just spent in my car screwing up the courage to knock on this door, but it didn't occur to me until now. My hair usually sprouts a cowlick by noon, oddly never in the same place. It's a mystery of nature. A forensic lab tech named Edsel once told me I should tame it with "product," but I have no idea what that means.

I hear the bolt clack open, and my heart steps up to a mambo as the door swings in a few inches then catches on a security chain. I'm staring into Lana Strain's astounding eyes, only they're looking back from her daughter's face.

"Yes?" With only one word, her voice whips up my heartbeat. She sounds just like Lana with that dusky timbre of whiskey and smoke. The precious libidinous cravings that died with Lana so long ago are suddenly resurrected, but they're fleeting. She looks like Lana, yet she doesn't. It's discomfiting. There's some indefinable flaw in the re-creation, something that whispers "imposter," something Madame Tussaud got wrong.

"I'm sorry to just show up unannounced like this, but I didn't have a number or an e-mail address. My name's Brown. Nob Brown. I'm a freelance writer, working on a retrospective on your mother for *Playboy*. I was hoping we could chat for a few minutes. I mean, if it's convenient. If this isn't a good time, I could come back or meet you somewhere."

"And just what sort of writer might you be, Mr. Brown?"

"Magazines, mostly. Crime stories."

"My mother's been dead for twenty years. Why would you write a story about her?"

While Lana was pure southern wildcat, Ginger seems more southern belle, only without the accent. Graceful, polite, yet shy and wary. Not at all what I expect after seeing her raunchy slut performance on the website.

"She had a big influence on my life," I say. "I'd like to see her killer brought to justice."

This seems to interest her. "And what makes you think you can succeed where so many others have failed, Mr. Brown?"

"There were a lot of people involved who might not have felt comfortable opening up to the police in those days. There were a lot of drugs around. Sometimes the passage of time loosens tongues. People have things bottled up that they're relieved to let out. Or they just feel freer to talk about others they're no longer in touch with."

She doesn't seem convinced. I change tack.

"Besides," I add, "Your mother's music just went up on iTunes. The timing of this story couldn't be better to promote sales. I'm assuming you share in the royalties."

This argument seems to bear weight. "You have some sort of credentials, I suppose?"

I pull my wallet from my back pocket. "I've got a card here somewhere." I rummage through until I come up with an old business card from *Crime Time* magazine. They'd printed them for me once, hoping I might recruit some cheap talent at some Mystery Writers of America event. Afterward they'd deducted the printing costs from my paycheck. I hand the card to Ginger.

She reads it and laughs. "I never even heard of *Crime Time*."

"It's big in England. Web-only these days, but like I said, this piece is for *Playboy*."

She assesses me warily, presumably weighing the publicity value. I give her the kind of pleading look that a five-year-old might give his mother as he's begging to keep the kitten. I can be cute when I have to.

"I don't think so," she says, then starts closing the door.

"There's a possibility that your mother's killer is the same person who looted your inheritance." The door freezes for a moment, then reverses direction.

"All right." She releases the security chain and waves me in. Even this simple gesture reminds me of Lana. She's changed into a pair of denim cutoffs and a simple spaghetti-strap top. It's a much more appealing look—suggestive, not revealing.

My mind tries to reconcile a confusion of visions—Ginger on a stick, Lana by the pool—hot, unwholesome images that make me feel like the inside of my skull is sweating. I need to get a grip.

Ginger leads me into the living-dining room under the dome ceiling. The place feels like a tree house, with windows all around looking out over a circular veranda into the tops of the sorts of trees that Holly used to bring to life for me. She'd tell me what they're called, what the Indians used to do with their bark or their leaves, what sort of climate they prefer, what their flowers look like, what sorts of animals they house. These days they're just trees.

We sit down on a semicircular couch, and I rest my reporter's notebook on the ship's-hatch coffee table. Ginger leans back, and her eyes lock on a mirrored disco ball that hangs from the ceiling of the dome.

"I always hated that ball," she says, "especially when Mama turned the spots on to spray the walls with those hokey spangles."

A blinking red light reflects annoyingly from dozens of tiny mirrors on the ball. It's the message light from an ancient answering machine on the side table beside her. It looks like the same recorder that was here the night Lana died, the one referenced several times in the murder book. Ginger grabs the power cord and yanks it from the wall socket, knocking a narrow, plaid pleather address book from the table.

"My father refuses to redecorate," she says as she gets up to retrieve the address book. She sits back down, absently thumbing the pages. "Can I ask how you found me?"

"I found your website." I regret it as soon as I say it, but she doesn't even blush.

"I hope it didn't shock you."

"I'm not easily shocked."

"Did you like what you saw?" She says it softly, toying with me. But it feels like an act. Trying for coy but achieving awkward.

"I'd be lying if I said no, but that's not why I'm here."

She smiles as if relieved. "Ask away, Mr. Brown."

As I reach for my pen, it snags my pocket and falls. I reach down to retrieve it, and my hand accidentally brushes her bare thigh. She starts as if she's been zapped by a defibrillator. Her smile disappears like a popped bubble. She scoots away from me on the couch, suddenly nervous, staring at her hands, avoiding eye contact. Some mental switch has been flipped. The silence is abrupt, uneasy.

I end it. "You wouldn't happen to have any water, would you?"

"Where are my manners?" Still shaken, she gets up and heads past a dining area through a swinging door, the kind you can open in either direction with your back when your hands are full of plates.

I try to make sense of what happened, but there's a definite disconnect. Here's a woman who brazenly unfolds her genitalia to the world, who performs the most private acts imaginable for public consumption, yet she shrinks at an inadvertent touch like a homophobe at a gay orgy.

I pick up the address book and open it. Most adult scrawls require some interpretation to read, but Ginger's cursive is strikingly legible, like a script font or the writing of a prissy preteen girl.

I leaf through to the Ks. There's a number for her sister, Sophia Kidd, and another for Billy with a "c" beside it, presumably his cell. I copy them both, wondering why Ginger took her mother's last name while her sister kept her father's.

I hear a fridge close and replace the book where it was. Then the kitchen door swings outward and Ginger walks through, cracking the seal of a small bottled water.

"They say tap water is purer," she says, "and the carbon footprint of these bottles is awful, but I'm a creature of habit."

She hands me the bottle and sits down again, this time beyond arm's length, her eyes darting around the room as if checking the shadows for hidden assailants. She appears to be on a hair trigger.

"You were saying?" she says.

"Why don't we start with your father." I click my ballpoint like a cheap hood cocking his gun.

She laughs as if I've made a joke, only it's the kind of laugh you hear from the back ward of a mental hospital. "You sound just like my therapist."

I smile. "I understand Billy lives here with you."

"Daddy still lives here, more or less. He's on tour nine months a year—he calls it the nostalgia-neuralgia circuit—but this is where he drops his dirty laundry."

"But he wasn't living here when your mother was…"

"Murdered, Mr. Brown. Go ahead and say it. I've spent years seeing Dr. Karl in order to deal with it; I might as well get my money's worth."

"Your father had already moved out when she died, right?" I still avoid the M word. Despite her assurances, I'm afraid of setting her off again.

"That's right. He was staying in some cheesy residential hotel in Hollywood while they were trying to sort things out."

"Why'd she kick him out?"

"I don't know. I mean, I know what they wrote in the tabloids, but Mama and Daddy never talked about that stuff to us, so who knows if it's true? Sure, they used to fight all the time, but it was always over some little thing that made no nevermind. Sophia and I used to wonder what they were so angry about; the fights seemed so petty."

Our attention is suddenly drawn to a huge bobtail rat scampering across the room and under the kitchen door. I'm surprised that Ginger doesn't start.

"Oh, that's just Sven," she explains. "He must be hungry. Come on."

I follow her into the kitchen, and she motions for me to sit in a retro chrome and red vinyl chair as she opens the fridge and grabs a small log of something that looks like goat cheese.

"The first time I saw him I jumped right up on the counter," she says. "If I trained for a year I doubt I could do that again, but he scared me right up there."

She cuts a small wad of cheese and places it in front of a hole in the baseboard beside the stove.

"Daddy came running out with his toothbrush in his mouth when he heard me scream. Sven was long gone, but he'd left a turd on the floor, and Daddy said he was a Norway rat. You can tell by the blunt little ends. Roof-rat droppings are pointy like a football." Her words are chatty, but there's a sharp edge to her voice. A bad actress trying to play normal.

"Billy Kidd just happened to know that?"

She moves to the sink and washes the soft cheese off her fingers. Several times.

"Oh he knows a little about everything. That always amazed me when I was a child. There's nothing he knows a lot about, but he's got this vast store of random facts, like a big mental junk drawer. Impresses the heck out of the groupies."

She turns off the tap, but it keeps dripping. I'm guessing the washers haven't been replaced in a decade or two. Maybe I'll get her some new ones when I buy the new flapper for my toilet.

"I'd like to meet him," I say.

"That shouldn't be a problem. He's always looking for new souls to bring to Jesus."

"I thought he was into Scientology."

"That was three revelations ago."

Sven pokes his head out of the rat hole, whiskers dancing to capture the scent molecules erupting from the cheese. We watch him dash for it, grab it, and scurry back into his hole. Show's over. Ginger smiles like a child. I ponder the meaning of a porn star who adopts a wild rat, Norwegian or otherwise.

"How did you feel about your father moving back in so soon after your mother's death? I mean, she'd just kicked him out a few weeks earlier."

"Nobody thought twice about it, at least not that I knew of. I mean, he was the only parent we had left."

"I understand your father moved back in just hours after the crime scene was released."

"Oh no. Some columnist reported that, but we didn't live here for quite a while. First it was the investigation. Then after that, Daddy had to get the bedroom cleaned up and painted, get a new bed. Then we had to lay low for a couple more months until the reporters drained away."

"It must have been hard on you and your sister with your father being one of the prime suspects."

She laughs, her disturbed demeanor suddenly gone, its disappearance as bizarre as its arrival had been.

"We knew he didn't do it," she says. "If he had, he'd be doing Hawaiian Huna rituals every night or lighting candles or going to church or biting the heads off live roosters. You may not know from week to week what he believes in, but one way or another, he's a deeply religious man."

"Do you think he had anything to do with your inheritance problems?"

"I'd call 'problems' an understatement. When I turned twenty-five I gained control of my trust and found it pretty much empty. They did an audit, but they couldn't find anything wrong. I just know it all wound up in Gary Cogswell's pocket, but he's the Einstein of covering his ass. He claimed Daddy used up the money to raise me and my sister." She laughs. "If that was true, we would have been raised in a palace and dripping with diamonds. Of course, Daddy loses track of any number that exceeds his fingers, so he was no help."

"What about your mother's father? Wasn't he involved?"

"I don't want to talk about Grandpa Nate."

"But…"

"I said I don't want to talk about him."

She grabs a cuticle in her teeth and tries to strip it off then winces as she draws blood.

EIGHT

Nathaniel Strain stands stock still, gripping a one iron, staring at the dimpled ball before him. He shakes his head back and forth, but his pupils are laser-locked on that golf ball like olives on toothpicks.

"So you're a writer?" he says.

"You may get an argument here and there, but that's what I'm considered by most of my friends." I wonder why I don't just say yes.

I think I'm getting hypnotized by the pendulum rhythm of his jaw. I want him to look at me, but I don't want to come out and say it. People have a tendency to clam up when you say things like that.

The Quonset hut that houses Strain Fabrication is all function, no style. The corrugated-steel arched walls set the tone. The air is laden with the acrid smell of molten flux and the pops and hisses of blowtorches. Strain's office itself is just a sheet-metal box, maybe eighteen feet square, jammed into a corner of the cavernous space, with a door and no lid. What little furniture he has is crammed against the walls to make room for the Astroturf putting mat and electric ball-return cup.

Strain has Mark Twain's eyebrows. He appears unusually fit and trim for his age. He must be close to eighty, but he looks closer to sixty. His silver mane could have come from a Clairol commercial, but his face is too odd for a model's. His eyes bug out, and the top of his nose caves in where it meets his brow, making his profile appear almost inside out.

He stands with his side to me, backlit by a bare bulb suspended on a long cord from the vaulted ceiling. From this angle, I can see the bulb shining straight through the sides of his cornea, making his eye gleam.

"Whom do you write for?"

I always hate this question. "Magazines mostly. I freelance."

"I see." He says it as if he knows all he needs to know in order to write me off as an unemployed hack. I feel my interview floating down the gutter, seconds from the sewer. But he surprises me.

"Okay," he says. "I'll talk to you. Would you like to know why?"

"I wouldn't mind," I say.

"Because you're not from the *New York Times* or *Time* magazine. The mainstream media was merciless to me and my family when my daughter was killed. They were vultures, hyenas, nothing but carrion eaters, hiding behind the mythical cloak of objectivity."

His head swings are really annoying me now. I have to force myself to concentrate on what he's saying.

"The tabloids, the rags, the fan magazines—they were the ones that mourned with us. They loved her. They were kind to us. So I'm willing to talk to you, Mr. Brown. It's the least I can do."

"Much appreciated, Mr. Strain."

"You don't mind if I do some golf exercises while we talk, do you?"

"You're the boss." I wonder whether he's exercising his neck or his focus.

Strain has the air of a man who thinks a navy blazer, red bow tie, and gray wool slacks make him look informal. In fact, it makes him look like the cover of the *AARP* magazine or maybe *Power & Motoryacht*. His sort of dapper seems out of place in this blue-collar proscenium, but this is where he hangs his skipper's cap every day. I make a mental note to have Melody look into his background.

"Why don't we start with your relationship with Lana. Were you close?"

"Of course. She was my only child. My baby. We saw each other every week, talked on the phone almost every day."

His tone is mannered, patrician. Not a trace of the Texas Badlands where Lana was born. More like Connecticut or Massachusetts.

"The day she died you left a message on her answering machine," I say. "Didn't sound too loving."

The only evidence of family in the room is a sixteen-by-twenty framed photo on the wall, which, I notice, includes neither Lana nor her mother. It's a black-and-white portrait of a much younger, broadly grinning Nathaniel Strain with his foot on the bumper of a vintage midfifties Morgan convertible roadster, holding the keys aloft like a triumphant big-game hunter who'd just bagged the thing with a single shot. Almost incidental to the picture are Sophia and Ginger, two preadolescent bystanders sitting on the running board looking bored. Something about the photo nags at me, but I can't put my finger on it.

"We had our disagreements, like any other father and child. She inherited my temper, so when we crossed, it wasn't pretty. But we always made up."

"Except the night before she died. I understand she threatened to cut you out of her will."

The one eye I can see doesn't deviate from the ball, but it tics as if someone had pricked him with a pin. "She'd make idle threats all the time. Never carried through."

"What about the girls? How did they get along with Lana?"

His chin continues to swing without falter. "Lana tried to be a good mother, but she wasn't exactly suited for the job. I tried to teach her, but she didn't want to hear it. What sort of discipline can you teach young girls when both parents are on the road nine months of the year? That's why all hell broke loose after she died."

"Is that when the girls stopped speaking to each other?" I ask.

"That's right. Soon after they started family therapy with Sophia's boyfriend."

"Her boyfriend?"

"Well, he wasn't her boyfriend at the time. That didn't start until he dumped her as a patient. At least that's what I've been told; Sophia and I aren't very close anymore. But personally, I wouldn't trust Karl Lynch as far as the end of my nose."

"Why is that?"

"Lana dies. Billy takes the girls to Lynch for family therapy. Within a month, the girls stop talking to each other and don't ever talk to each other again. They split out into separate therapy sessions, but the eminent Dr. Lynch keeps seeing them both, which I understand is a violation of professional ethics. Flash forward twenty years, and one of the girls is barely functional and back in therapy with him while he's shacked up with the other one. Do you see anything there that suggests competence?"

I'm shocked to learn that Sophia lives with Ginger's psychiatrist, but I keep it to myself.

"Ginger seems pretty functional to me."

"You're very charitable, Mr. Brown, but the truth is she's sick, and Dr. Lynch hasn't helped. Do you remember the McMartin case?"

"Sure. How could I forget it? Psychologists brainwashed forty-one preschool children into believing they were sexually molested by teachers doing satanic rituals. It was a huge frame-up."

"Well, he was one of the framers. That quack knows how to get into people's heads and twist them all around. Lynch is the reason Ginger won't talk to me anymore. That sick bitch won't even let me in the door of my own daughter's house. She's got serious mental problems because of him. You can't believe a word she tells you. She lies like a rug."

I'm stunned. He calls his own granddaughter a sick bitch? Mental problems? Lies? The interview is veering wildly off course.

"Do you know what she does for a living?" he asks, as if to cinch the final strap on her straitjacket.

I ignore his question and crumple the list of my own, tossing it into the mop bucket he uses for a trash can.

"What makes you say she's a liar?" I ask, trying to reclaim the reins.

"She's been making up stories since she was a child. I have no idea what she told you, but I can guarantee it's not true. She's always making false accusations."

"What sorts of accusations?"

"She accused Billy of verbal abuse. She accused Lana of beating her. She accused Lana's friend Claudine of stealing jewelry. She actually attacked Sophia over some squabble the girls refused to talk about."

"How do you know the accusations weren't true?"

"The girl was a nut case. Still is."

"What did she accuse you of?"

His jaw twitches, and his head finally stops. He turns to face me for the first time, and the gleam disappears as his steel-blue eyes turn almost black.

His biceps tense like he's on the verge of a one-iron shot to my temple.

"Nothing."

NINE

I t's almost six by the time I get home. I walk into the office to find Melody in the midst of a sneezing fit.

"You okay?"

"We've *aaahuu* got to *aaahuu* get that *aaahuu* sofa *aaahuu* out of here!" I guess she's allergic to the stuffing Runt pulled out. She sneezes all the way up the steps as she helps me carry Runt's sofa up to the street.

Back in the office, she continues to sneeze, so I open the windows, and we head out to the deck to talk while the office airs. Melody opens the spiral-bound pad she uses for notes and runs down a list of messages.

"Frank at *Esquire* replied to your e-mail and said he needs to see a written proposal to make any kind of deal on the Lana Strain piece."

"A written proposal?"

"That's what he said."

"In other words, forget the A-list, I'm not even on the B-list over there."

"Next, Ginger Strain called. You've got an interview with Billy Kidd tomorrow afternoon at the house."

"Bless her heart. I didn't think she'd come through."

"Why not?" She gets something in her eye and pulls the lid down to tear up and rinse.

"She just seemed a little preoccupied last night. I didn't think she'd remember."

"So much for your judgment. Speaking of which…" She pulls a certified letter from her notebook, holding it gingerly by the corner like a bag of dog shit she doesn't want to touch. Must be from Jerry.

Jerry has been Holly's friend since high school and when I started dating her, he came with the package. He was married to Trudy at the time, and the four of us used to double-date. He and I hit it off pretty well and wound up playing fast-pitch softball together every Monday night. A lot of beer under the bridge. Somehow, when he represented Holly in our divorce, all that camaraderie disappeared like dry ice in a hot skillet.

I open the letter to find an ultimatum. I call Jerry's office on my cell and get bounced from his receptionist to his secretary before he finally comes on the line.

"As your friend, Nob, I'm sure you can appreciate how hard this is for me."

"How much are you soaking Holly for in order to steal my house?"

When Holly left me, the house was our only serious asset. She wanted to sell it, I wanted to stay in it, so we made an arrangement that I would buy it from her on time. I took over the mortgage and agreed to send her rent every month in order to pay off her half of the equity with interest. Unfortunately, she bought a condo beyond her means, relying on my monthly payments. Her safety net was my LAPD salary, but a couple years later I quit the force. Now, when I have cash-flow problems, she does too. Makes us both edgy. It's a bad situation all around.

"Holly wanted you to know that, as a charitable gesture, she is giving you until noon on Friday to provide what you owe her before I file a motion to sell the house. I counseled her to file immediately, but you know Holly: big heart. I, on the other hand, have little patience for deadbeats."

"Deadbeats?" I blurt. I wanted to stay calm, but Jerry knows my buttons. "I give her all I can, Jerry. I can't help it if the freelance market is going down the tubes. People are reading less. Newspapers and magazines are dying in droves, in case you haven't noticed."

"That's your problem, Nob. Don't make it Holly's."

"Well, how about this, Jerry? When we worked out our divorce, I was employed and had a regular income. The mediator based the alimony on that. If you take this back to the court, I'll have to request a modification of the agreement due to the changes in my financial situation. Does Holly know about that?" I silently thank Angel for giving me this bit of advice in the locker room.

"Of course," he says, but somehow I doubt we'd be talking if she did. Knowing Jerry, he's giving her the hard sell so that he can be the hero and maybe get into her pants after all these years. She'll never find him attractive, but his ego obscures that fact, much like his belly does his penis.

"I can't give her what I don't have. End of story."

"You think I enjoy talking to you like this, Nob? You think this is the apex of my day? It's conversations like this, day in and day out, that makes me hate my work."

"My heart bleeds for you."

"Take out a second mortgage, Nob. Judges hate deadbeats."

"Fuck you too, Jerry." I hang up.

"Eloquent as usual," says Melody.

I put the conversation behind me. "Anything else?"

She checks her list.

"Oh yeah. Gloria replied to your e-mail about Vlad the Impaler. He apparently hangs at some bar on Fairfax in Little Ethiopia."

This doesn't surprise me. Little Ethiopia used to be a Russian community until about a decade ago when the Ruskies migrated north to eastern West Hollywood to avoid ethnic diversity.

"This bar have a name?" I ask.

"The Odessa Club."

TEN

I open the door slowly. It takes a few seconds for my eyes to adjust to the dim light but I can make out a roomful of shadowy figures, most of them built like Bulgarian weightlifters. From the door a blade of midday sun cuts to the back of the room, hitting Vlad the Impaler like a spotlight. A thin string of sauerkraut dangles from his mustache as he glances up from a plate of pirogies to watch me walk in. He looks like he weighs north of three hundred pounds, so the small fortune he must have spent on the custom tailoring of his Italian silk suit is pretty much wasted. But it makes me conscious of my own suit—sixteen years old, cheap, worn, and wrinkled. I'm in running shoes. No tie. The Odessa Social Club is filled with slack-jawed, beer-bellied Slavic gangsters, and they're all dressed better than I am.

Between the cops and the Feds, they've tried to nail Vlad Bakatin for murder, racketeering, smuggling, prostitution, gambling, weapons, and knee surgery without a license. He's been charged twelve times, tried three, never convicted. They should have clocked him on a no-smoking violation. The place reeks of tobacco.

I scan the rundown restaurant, size up the dozen or so men who sit drinking, smoking, and playing cards, then head toward the back, toward the capo's table. Of course, I don't get there. Big Ugly Guy and Bigger Ugly Guy stand up from opposite sides of the room and close ranks like two steel doors slamming shut. The Great Wall of Russia between me and the boss. They left their butts in their ashtrays, but smoke still curls from their noses.

Big Ugly Guy speaks. "This is private club."

"I'm just looking for Gary Cogswell. Name's Brown. Nob Brown."

I can see Bakatin's curiosity stir like a sleeping dog opening one eye. I hand Big Ugly Guy a business card and am somewhat surprised when he actually glances at it. I wouldn't have guessed he could read.

"Mr. Cogswell don't like unannounced visitors." He rips my card and lets the pieces fall to the floor.

"Nobody does," I say. "But we all get 'em every once in a while."

"He don't."

"I'll tell you what. Why don't you let me ask him? If he doesn't want to see me, I'll go."

Bakatin blurts out a single laugh then goes back to his pirogies.

Bigger Ugly Guy clenches his fists, waiting to spring if the smaller tank makes the first move. I tense, thinking there's a chance these galoots are going to mash me to a pulp. Maybe this wasn't such a good idea.

"Let him come." The quiet order cracks the tension like a sledgehammer. I peer past Big Ugly Guy and lock eyes with The Impaler. I break into a sweat.

Big Ugly Guy glares at me, but we both know he's not going to do anything. Bigger Ugly Guy reaches out and pushes my arms up to frisk me. I stand as if crucified, waiting for the minor humiliation to end. The Ugly Twins separate and I walk through the mountain pass.

"I'm sorry to bother you, Mr. Bakatin...sir. I'm looking for Gary Cogswell."

Bakatin's thick brows rise like a drawbridge. "What for you want Cogsvell?" He looks into my eyes, and I feel like he can see everything there is to know about me.

"Remember Lana Strain? The singer?"

"Maybe."

"She was murdered in 1995."

"You don't look like no cop."

"I'm not. I'm just barely a writer."

"I don't like reporters."

I can feel excitement in the room, as if the alpha wolf is about to throw a scrap into the hungry pack.

"I'm not a reporter. I don't do news, just human interest. For magazines."

"What that got to do with Cogsvell?"

"I'm doing a story on Lana's murder. In his old job he handled her estate. I thought maybe he'd be willing to talk to me about her. It's no big secret he works for you now, but my story has nothing to do with that."

I've been trying to ignore the sauerkraut that still clings for dear life to Bakatin's mustache, but the effort proves too nerve-racking. "You've got a thing," I say. I indicate the mirror-image spot on my own face.

The Russian capo stares in disbelief for a moment. It seems as if everyone in the club is holding his breath. I know I am. Then Bakatin bursts out with something in Russian that sounds like "Hooey!" and breaks into an uncontrollable laugh. Everyone else in the club laughs, too. I have no idea what he said, but I smile along. He wipes the cabbage off his face and calls out, "Leon! Bring da man a dople."

The bartender jumps into action at the espresso machine.

"You know what's a dople?" The Russian accent makes the Italian sound Yiddish, but I'm not about to correct his pronunciation.

"Italian, isn't it? Double espresso?"

"Da. It's a habit I was gave by my Italian comrades in New York. You know why I order you a dople?"

"No."

"To remind you, you got two *yáytsa*."

"That's one I don't know."

"It's Russian for those two what you got between your legs. It's your yáytsa what you don't want to wake up one morning, find stuffed in your mouth, capeesh?"

He turns his hand and moves it back and forth as if cupping some testicles. He reminds me of Captain Queeg on the stand, except the balls he's rolling are mine.

"I mean no disrespect, Mr. Bakatin. I just thought maybe Cogswell might be here."

"Let us pretend, for sake of entertainment, I am the sort of *zadneetza* what had a need for such a person as your friend Mr. Cogsvell. What for would I be telling you?"

Leon arrives and places an espresso on the table in front of me. The word "neurotoxin" crosses my mind.

"Look, I'm not here to make trouble for anybody, especially me. I was just hoping he could answer a few questions, that's all. The murder is twenty years old, he's not a suspect, so it's not like he's got anything to hide."

"Everybody got something to hide."

"I don't."

"Of course you do." He says it like a threat, like he could find out with a car battery and two alligator clips before he even finishes his dople. "And if you think Vlad beliefs you really are after writing old, cold story, you are bigger fool than what you look."

Bakatin's laser eyes burn into mine. I sense that he expects me to start shaking or maybe twitching. While nothing along those lines is outside of the realm of possibility, I manage to resist the urge.

Then he smiles again, like he's just kidding. "You maybe have card?"

I look woefully at the scraps on the floor. "Not anymore."

The Impaler laughs again. "Cheap *ublyoooduk* only carry one card!" The others howl at this heady demonstration of wit. "Not to worry, Mister 'barely a writer.' We will tell Comrade Cogsvell you was come to visit."

Somehow I don't find this reassuring. "Thanks. And thanks for the dople."

He says nothing, so I stand and start toward the door.

"And Mr. Nob Brown," he says.

I stop and turn back, praying that my trembling legs don't give out on me.

"No worry about no card. If Cogsvell want to talk, we will find you. At that we are very good."

ELEVEN

M elody's on the deck with her laptop when I get home.
"How'd it go?" she asks.

"He wasn't there, but I met his boss."

She looks stunned. "Vlad the Impaler?"

"Yep. He bought me an espresso. A dople." Then, in my best Bakatin impression, "You know what's a dople?" I come off sounding like Boris Badinoff.

"Lemme guess. A synonym for attempted suicide?" She sets her laptop down and stands, putting her hands on her hips to twist back and forth.

"I was just trying to find Cogswell."

"And you risked your life to do that because..." She motions with her hand as if trying to lure a puppy out from under the bed.

"I didn't risk my life; I was just looking for the guy and Bakatin happened to be there."

"I don't suppose you used an alias."

I can tell she's thinking I pissed off the Russian mob and bought her a ticket to Collateral Damageville.

"I asked Bakatin to tell Cogswell I wanted to talk to him about Lana Strain, that's all. It's not like I'm writing about anything Bakatin's involved in."

"You asked The Impaler to be your errand boy?" Those are her literal words, but her tone of voice makes them sound like *It would have been smarter to drive a four-inch machine screw through your eye.*

I shrug, nod, and shuffle my feet.

"And you told him you wanted to talk to one of his thugs about a murder?" It's a different question, but the same tone of voice.

"He's not a thug," I say defensively. "He's a lawyer."

"What a relief." The tone is getting repetitive.

———

An hour later, I glide up the driveway of the geodesic dome house that guitar legend Billy Kidd and his daughter Ginger Strain share with Lana's ghost.

My nerves are still jangling from my little coffee klatch with Vlad as I climb up the redwood stairs to the second-story deck and ring the front bell. Ginger answers the door and invites me in. The gloom of the murder didn't weigh on me the first time I was here, but it grows geometrically as Ginger leads me downstairs toward the bedroom where Lana was shot.

At the end of the hall she waves me into the master where Billy Kidd reclines on his king-size bed. The *Dotted Babe* hangs beside him, floor to ceiling, powerful and dramatic. No sign of bloodstains. I wonder what it took to clean them off. My eye sweeps the baseboard, drawn by the morbid prospect of seeing a speck of blood that might have somehow evaded decades of Central American cleaning ladies. I don't see any.

"Daddy, this is Nob Brown, the writer I told you about." And to me, "I told him how much I enjoyed talking to you."

This surprises me.

Billy doesn't acknowledge my presence. He just stares through cheap drugstore readers at the ridges that run down his cracked nails.

"How have I offended thee, O Lord," he intones in his famous Kentucky-fried baritone, "to be burdened with such mis'able nails and a godless daughter?"

God doesn't answer right away, but I'm guessing he'll speak through Billy in tongues the next time they're both in church.

Now fifty-five, the aging "bad boy" looks strangely androgynous in a once-elegant mauve satin robe covered with faded embroidered roses. His feet are shod in violet polyester-fur slippers with a spray of lavender feathers around the ankles. His long gray hair is pulled straight back in a severe ponytail banded by a black leather strap with an Indian nickel snap closure. By the looks of it, a retired cock ring.

Ginger sits on a stool by the bed where she must have been giving her father a manicure when I'd rung the bell. The sight of this living, if fallen, legend—whose guitar riffs still grab me, who once lived with the sexiest woman on earth, who let a groupie give him a blow job onstage at the Fillmore without missing a beat—elevates my mood.

Billy lounges like a king, surrounded by his Bible, his antique aqua-blue Princess rotary phone whose nightlight dial still glows after forty-some years, his box of Ultra Soft Kleenex, his See's assorted chocolates, his current issues of *Rolling Stone*, *Billboard*, *Sports Illustrated*, and *Pentecostal Evangel*, and his miniature poodle.

"I'm not godless, Daddy, I just can't see thinking about children right now." That voice again. Just like her mother.

Ginger applies some Dry Kwik to the metallic gold enamel on her father's nails. Both of his hands show the tail ends of intricate dragon tattoos that peek out from the flowing sleeves of his housecoat.

"I want to see grandkids before I croak."

"Hang out in the park on Sundays. You'll see lots of grandkids."

The graying legend turns his steel-blue eyes to me. The whites are shot through with a crazing of arteries from years of drug abuse. He looks at least ten years older than he is, just the opposite of his father-in-law.

"You got any young'ns?" he asks.

"No," I say, thinking about Holly. We'd been trying to have kids when I left the force. We'd been trying for three years with no luck and no explanation. It didn't sink our relationship, but it wore the hull pretty thin.

The dog gets up and wanders across the bed to sniff at Billy's nails.

"Hosni, you get away," Ginger chides. "Don't you remember last time when we had to use nail polish remover on your nose? That wasn't fun now, was it?"

I almost expect Hosni to reply, but instead he trots back to his spot by Billy's pillow and lies down again.

Lana's presence pervades the air, a poltergeist searching for her long-gone parietal lobe. I wonder how Ginger can sit in this room. I wonder how Billy can sleep here.

"You listen up, pumpkin," says Billy. "You're one hot little chicklet, just like your mama, may she be jammin' with the Lord. You should use them assets to get some hot dog to slip a ring on 'at finger of yours and knock you up before you get too old to go forth and multiply. I wants to see you fill your God-given purpose on this earth and be happy before you die and go to Hell."

"You of all people should know that family doesn't always mean happiness."

"What about the 'Hell' part?"

"I'm not getting born again, so forget about it." She turns to me. "Ever since he went Pentecostal, he's been on me about getting born again, like the first time wasn't bad enough."

"Sweet Jesus of Nazareth, please forgive my baby sinner."

Ginger sighs. "Mr. Brown came all the way up here to ask you about Mama, not to listen to your sermons."

The aging rocker takes a deep breath, as if girding for the moment he's been hoping to avoid. "All right. Let's get it over with."

"Let's start with Lana's death. After all these years, you must have a theory about who killed her."

"No fuckin' idea. Maybe the Asshole from the song."

"Do you know who he was?"

"A lot of folks think he was supposed to be me."

"Oh, Daddy," Ginger chides. "Don't be ridiculous. He called that night."

"On the phone?" It's a stupid question, but the shock stunned my brain. The police tried to find him, but they couldn't even verify that he existed.

"He talked to Mama." She blows on her father's nails. "Almost a year before she died."

Billy picks up the story. "We was in the livin' room, talkin' about some new licks when Lana grabbed a call and just kind of froze on up. Sweet Jesus, she looked like she seed Armageddon its own self, pop-eyed as a wild hog with rabies. He said somethin', and she said fuck you and hung up."

"How did you know it was the asshole?"

"She told us," Ginger says.

"I 'bout ripped Lana's head off, God rest her soul."

"I don't understand."

"He weren't just callin' outa the blue. She knew the fucker."

"Did she tell you that?"

"Didn't have to." Billy looks me right in the eye, and his expression hardens like fast drying cement. "She never wrote no song 'bout nobody she ain't fucked at least once."

TWELVE

By the time I leave, Billy has taken a shine to me. Don't ask me why. He's famous for impulsive infatuations, but they're usually for new cults or causes. Today's craze is me. For whatever reason, he has convinced himself that I'm the only writer he can trust. He vows to help me with my story in any way he can and, when I'm finished, to let me be his official "autobiographer," a word he mistakes for ghostwriter. I take his promises with a grain of salt. In my experience, rock stars tend to treat promises like groupies: easy to make and quickly forgotten.

On my way home, I swing by the Iliad on Cahuenga, one of the few extant used bookstores in the Valley, to check for any Lana Strain biographies I don't already have. I don't find any. But my eye falls on a book called *Born to Use* by Vern Senzimmer. The name rings a bell. I pull it off the shelf and read the back cover. It's *a self-published autobiography* by a guy from some grunge band called Sticky White. That's where I know the name from. I don't remember their music, but I do remember rumors that Lana was sleeping with some guy from that band behind Billy's back. According to the barely literate blurb, Senzimmer was the love of Lana's life. I read the first few pages. The self-indulgent style aspires to stream of consciousness but reads more like a trickle. I spring for the fifty cents to buy the thing anyway.

When I finally get home, the sight of the shredded sofa on the street reminds me that I have to call Sanitation in the morning. I check the mail. Still no probate records from the county, but there's a kill fee for a *Hustler* piece they rejected three months ago. Three hundred simoleons. It won't cover what I'm supposed to pay Holly by the end of today, but it'll pay my water and power this month. I walk into the house, wondering if I'll still be living here this time next month. There's one message on my voice mail. I punch the one key to play it, praying it's not Jerry.

"Nob, it's Ginger. I need to talk to you. Can you meet me tomorrow at Solley's Deli around three?"

She sounds upset. I wonder what happened in the hour since I left her. I call back to find out and get her voice mail. I RSVP that I'll see her at Solley's.

There's some day-old coffee left in the pot, so I pour it into an ice cube tray and stick it in the freezer. I can use the cubes to chill some iced coffee tomorrow. It's an old trick I learned from Holly to keep iced coffee from getting watered down. She apparently learned it from my mother, who never bothered to teach it to me. Ma can be sexist that way.

I brew myself a fresh pot and take a mugful into the living room to settle down on the couch with a photocopy of one of Lana Strain's journals. She wrote hundreds of pages that I'm trying to wade through, ever on the lookout for motives.

You'd think a successful lyricist and larger-than-life rock star would fill her diaries with lush descriptions, intimate musings, and lurid details, but Lana was disappointingly sketchy.

Had lunch with Bosco today. Ordered the Caesar. She said I shouldn't because of the garlic. I told her Bozo wouldn't care, he smells like an ashtray anyway. She said she wouldn't mind getting into his pants. I told her to feel free, but I know she won't because he put the make on her last year, and she had to smack him with a tambourine to get him off her. She just said it to make me jealous because Gomer wants to fuck me. Like I'd give his skinny ass the time of day.

And so on. The nicknames are annoying. I've figured out that Bozo is Billy, and I've got a few theories about one or two others, but that's all so far.

After an hour in Lanaworld I hear a key in the door, and Melody walks in carrying a brown bag filled, I'm sure, with unspeakable things made of tofu called *faux* something or other. I'm wrong. She reaches into the bag and pulls out a silicone vagina.

"That supposed to be lunch?"

"It's your friend Vajayna," she says, "from Fun with Dick and Jane. It's an exact replica. Someone actually made molds of the folds. I bought three of them. From three different sex shops." She reached back into the bag and pulled out some sales slips. "Here's your receipts."

"You expect me to pay for those?"

"There's nothing like a chick buying fake pussy to get a porn dealer talking. You want to bitch about the cost, or you want to hear what I found out?"

My reply is to take the receipts out of her hand.

"Shockingly," says Mel, "Jane is her real name. Last name Porter. Grew up in Bakersfield, did a little modeling then came to the big city to break into acting."

"These sex-toy salesmen knew all this?"

"Everybody knows everybody in that business. It's like one big happy family."

Melody lifts her leg straight up and touches her ankle to her ear. She's wearing a short plaid skirt that falls immodestly onto her shoulder revealing her black leotard crotch, but it doesn't faze her. She stretches like that for a few seconds, then rests the heel of her Capezio jazz shoe on my brick mantel. She holds that pose as she talks.

"When Hollywood didn't come knocking," she continues, "your girlfriend connected with a guy who directs porn flicks, and before long she'd parlayed a negligible gag reflex into stardom and her own production company. The boyfriend didn't last, but the production company took off, mostly due to the success of one of her many porn sites."

"Ginger's?"

"Bingo. There are hundreds of thousands of porn sites out there, most of them indistinguishable from each other. But what Ginger does is unique. She's got that necro-rock-star-fetish thing going, and it's been making a lot of money for Jane Porter."

Out of curiosity, I hit the keyboard and Google around for tidbits about Jane. Ten minutes later I hit on a five-year-old article from the *LA Business Journal* that someone scanned and uploaded to a porn chat room. The headline reads, "Porn Meets Rock and Earnings Roll."

I read it and whistle.

"What?" says Mel, switching legs.

"In 2010, the profits from LanaLives.com surpassed Danni Ashe's best year."

"Who?"

"You never heard of Danni.com?"

Mel looks at me like I'm speaking Icelandic.

"I interviewed her once for a *Penthouse* piece. She was the only woman to ever appear on the covers of both *Juggs* magazine and the *Wall Street Journal*. She practically invented Internet porn."

"How much money are we talking about?"

"At its height, Danni.com was estimated to be worth thirty million dollars."

Now it's Mel's turn to whistle.

THIRTEEN

I spend the next morning on my deck overlooking the inversion layer that holds the smog down on the Valley floor. The few wisps of clouds offer scant cover from the merciless sun. The only thing more aggravating than the weather is Vern Senzimmer's book, which I've managed to almost finish.

From beginning to end, it's a gaping yawn. He spends two hundred pages describing egocentric tales about his struggles with addiction to weed, speed, coke, crack, heroin, tequila, Lana Strain, and tater tots.

"I got tired of her whining," he writes, "and told her I didn't want to see to her anymore, didn't even want to talk to her, but she wouldn't listen. She called ten times a day, day after day, begging me to take her back."

It makes me want to throw up. You'd think he was Hugh Jackman spurning a stalker, even though multiple sources, including Lana's journal, confirm that Lana was the one who did the dumping. So am I reading the denial of a drug-addled mind? Or the regurgitation of bitterly sour grapes?

I have trouble keeping my mind from wandering to Holly. I wonder if she'll actually kick me out of my house. I'm sure that's exactly what Jerry's campaigning hard for her to do. Does she hate me enough to go through with it? Do you have to love someone to generate that much hate?

I identify with Senzimmer. We were both dumped. And I suspect we were both floundering in love, though he doesn't seem willing to admit it. According to Lana's journal, she just got bored with him. I'm still not sure what Holly's excuse was. It's not like I cheated on her or hit her or stopped loving her. She said it was about my ethical deficiencies, but I always felt that was an intellectual smokescreen for some other failing on my part. I wonder what it would take to make me despise Holly as much as Senzimmer seems to despise Lana. Would losing my home be enough?

Why can't all relationships be as simple as the one I have with Gloria? No demands, no expectations, just a loving friendship. If I'm in a jam, I know she's always there for me and vice versa. Love without strings. It's a beautiful thing. In terms of sex, we keep it flexible. Gloria thinks monogamy is absurd and contrary to human nature. I disagree. So if I'm not dating anyone, our relationship includes sex. If I am, it doesn't. When I was married to Holly, for example, Gloria and I stayed tight, but sex was off the table. After my marriage fell apart, on those rare occasions when I dated a woman more than once, Gloria respected my feelings and laid off until my fling was over. And flings are all I've had since Holly. I don't envy the women who date me. Between Holly and Gloria, the bar is set pretty high.

Somewhere in my reflections on relationships I've fallen asleep. I wake up a half hour later to find the pages of Senzimmer's book soaked in drool. How appropriate. I retreat to my air conditioning, pour the dregs of this morning's coffee in a glass and throw in a half dozen cubes of frozen coffee. While I give it a minute to chill, I call Angel.

"Well if it isn't Nob Brown! I'm sure you're bearing good news or money, because even you couldn't have the balls to call for yet another favor."

"It'll just take a minute. Relax."

His trademark sigh precedes his words of resignation. "Lay it on me."

"If they file whatever it is Jerry wants to file today, are they going to get my house?"

I hear him chuckle. I must have I missed the joke.

"They can try," he says. "Have the sheriff seize your tax returns, garnishee your bank account, cause you grief, and give you a hard time. How much do you owe again?"

"Two Gs," I say, thinking he probably spends two grand on hairstyling every month, and I can't even scrape that much together to save the roof over my head.

"Well, you'd think a judge would be hard-pressed to kick a man out of his castle for two thousand dollars. On the other hand, you could draw some judge who just caught her hubby in the sack with the babysitter, and she might use you as her whipping boy."

"I thought justice was blind," I say.

"Only the statue," says Angel.

I take a sip of iced coffee. It tastes great.

"So what do I do?"

"Any chance of getting the money together?"

"I'm waiting on a few writer's fees," I say. "But they're mostly for a few hundred bucks apiece, except for one from *Hustler*. But it could be another two, three months before I see it, and I need something to live on."

"Ever hear the phrase 'saving for a rainy day'?"

"Sure. It means scrimp to save a nest egg so you have cash to pay the lawyers when you get divorced."

"Point taken," he says. "Look. Just try to stall them. Tell them your tax records are disorganized, and it'll take some time to pull them together."

"And that'll work?"

He draws air audibly through his teeth to express his doubts. "It's free advice, Nob. You get what you pay for."

We wrap up the conversation. I hang up and set the timer on the stove so I don't lose track, then I go back to my journal readings.

At two o'clock I jump in the shower.

I check the mail before I leave. No money and nothing from Jerry. I guess that's a good omen, since he hasn't called and there's been no sign of a process server. I wonder whether Angel's threat worked, or Holly just postponed, or the papers are at the court but I don't know it yet. Knowing Jerry, it's the latter.

Solley's Deli is about five minutes from my house, but I rarely eat there, not because they're in a rundown shopping strip on Van Nuys Boulevard, but because they think they're on Rodeo Drive in Beverly Hills. Eight bucks for a loaf of rye bread?

Three o'clock is a little early for dinner, even for the blue-plate-special crowd, so the place is practically empty. There are a few elderly couples scattered randomly in a sea of booths and a big guy in a Gators cap sitting across two stools at the counter, snapping his head back and forth like he's in the front row at Wimbledon, looking for a waitress. No sign of Ginger.

I grab a menu and take a booth by the window to watch for her.

A waitress asks me what I want, calls me Hun. I consider making an Attila joke then decide it's not funny. I order a coffee and tell her I'm waiting for someone. She tells me they're out of the kishka and the short-rib flanken. I tell her there's a guy at the counter wants to talk to her. She walks off, not toward the counter.

I take advantage of the wait by calling three-one-one. A city operator puts me through to Sanitation to order my large-object pickup, but the line is busy. I hang up and look back at the parking lot. No Ginger.

My coffee comes fast, but I'm into my fourth cup by three thirty and I've polished off the complimentary pickles and still no Ginger. I'm beginning to worry. The waitress is giving me sideways glances, making me feel conspicuous, so I order a five-dollar smear of lox spread to give her something else to think about. I try calling Ginger's cell for the third time, and I get her voice mail again. I remember the desperation in her voice when she left me the message about meeting, sounded like she'd been crying. My worry grows. When the waitress comes back with my food, I tell her to pack it to go. Something smells fishy and it's not the lox.

I walk down the street to Fun with Dick and Jane, hoping to find her there. Same graffiti in the elevator. When I step out, I see the door to the suite. It's ajar. Music from the *Psycho* shower scene starts up in my head, violins screeching to a driving beat. I pull my shirttail out of my pants and use it to avoid leaving prints as I push open the door. It swings wide to reveal nothing. Literally.

The place is stripped clean. No art, no Naugahyde sectional, no whiteboard, no framed DVD box covers, no desk, no coffee table, no magazines, no giant potted fern, no Jane, no Robert, no SpongeBobs. I walk through into Jane's office. Not even a dust ball in the corner. My worry turns to dread.

I decide to try some of the other tenants, see if there's any juicy gossip running around. My first stop is the Ocularists' Guild next door.

The door is unlocked, so I walk in. It's not a suite like Dick and Jane's, just a ten-by-fifteen box with a window overlooking the alley. A Rubenesque woman on the far side of her fifties looks up at me through turquoise butterfly-shaped glasses whose lenses make her eyes look like ET's.

"I know," she says. "I have two eyes."

Her glare is intensified by her thick lenses. She has painted-on eyebrows that match the copper of her hair and follow the undulating curve of her glasses. Her pink-glossed lips are framed by frown lines that make her pout look like a permanent fixture.

"I wasn't going to say anything."

"Sure you were. Everybody does. They assume you work at the Ocularists' Guild because you have a glass eye. Like it was a condition of employment or something."

"Actually, I was going to tell you how impressed I am by your correct usage of the apostrophe in Ocularists'."

This cracks her frown. She almost smiles and then blushes and pretends to brush a piece of lint off her shoulder to avert her eyes.

"What can I do for you?" she asks.

"I was wondering if the suite next door might be available for lease. It seems to be empty."

"I wouldn't know."

"I'm surprised to see the place empty," I say. "You'd think management would put a 'for lease' sign up before a tenant was moves out."

"They made smut, you know. Of the filthiest kind. Management was not the primary skill for which people in their business are known." The copper eyebrows rise for effect.

I life my eyebrows, too, to encourage her to keep talking.

"You don't need to be Columbo to see the stupidity of hiring a pornmonger to manage a building," she says, "but the landlord doesn't seem to care. You can't imagine the sorts of perverts they brought flouncing through the building. I'm sure you saw the graffiti around. But 'management' seems to be gone now, so good riddance."

"So if I'm interested in leasing, I should talk to the owner," I say.

"What sort of business are *you* in?"

"Manufacturing," I say. "Silicone toys."

Before she thinks too long about this, I ask her for the owner's name and number.

Her face resumes the pout as she pulls the contact up on her computer and copies it onto the back of one of the Guild's business cards.

"Thank you so much," I say. "Perhaps we'll be neighbors."

She replies with a humph. Her phone rings and, when she picks it up, I walk out.

———

I drive up to the Van Nuys Civic Center, just a half mile north. As a cop, I often had to testify at the Van Nuys courthouse, and I remember that the parking attendant in the Braude Building went off duty at four o'clock. It's well past that now, so I park underneath and take my chances that some overzealous DOT engineer doesn't have me towed.

I walk across the street to the county recorder's office. In the mornings, the lines snake out the door, but at the end of the day, I just stroll right in and find only one person in line ahead of me. It's irritating to have to wait at all, but it's easier to go in person than it is to find ownership records on the Internet. State law prohibits the posting of home addresses online and, to avoid potential errors, the county recorder doesn't post commercial addresses either. With so many stars in residence, LA is full of stalkers. Why simplify their job?

I finally get up to the window and find out that Dick and Jane's building is owned by a company called Kocibey Development.

I call Mel on my way back to the garage and ask her to see what she can dig up on Kocibey.

I get home twenty minutes later to find her doing downward facing dog.

"Any luck?" I ask.

She replies without breaking form.

"Kocibey's at the end of a long and winding paper trail that leads nowhere. Just a string of mysterious shell corporations. I looked into individuals named Kocibey and found a few on Facebook, LinkedIn, phone books, and such, but didn't find any that had apparent ties to construction or real estate or even finance. I did, however, discover an Ottoman vassal named Kocibey who founded a city by the same name in 1240 AD"

"I think the thirteenth century is a little far afield."

"How about the eighteenth century? That's when the Russians renamed it Odessa."

The light bulb flashes above my head. "Fuck me."

"What?"

"Bakatin's place," I say. "It's called the Odessa Social Club. He must either own or have a piece of Fun with Dick and Jane. That explains why he'd use them to manage his building."

"You're saying Vlad's in the porn business?"

"Wouldn't you expect him to be? He is, after all, The Impaler."

FOURTEEN

I try Ginger's cell again. Still no answer. She sounded desperate the last time she called, and now she's been MIA for three hours. I decide to head up to her house. If it wasn't for my fear, the drive into Laurel Canyon would be a breeze. Opposing traffic, on the other hand, is frozen in time. I have to wait two minutes to make the left turn across it onto her street. The two minutes are interminable.

I wind up Weeping Glen to find colored lights in front of the dome house. Cop lights. Spinning, flashing, glaring, bad-news cop lights. There must be a half dozen black-and-whites up and down the narrow street, blocking it off. There's a forensics van, too. But what really gets my attention is the county meat wagon.

I park and walk up the hill, feeling slightly nauseated. There's yellow crime tape around the house and a couple of rookies standing guard. I ask one of them what happened, and he tells me to please stand back from the tape, sir. I'm about to tell him to eat shit when I see Detective Rafer Dumphy walk out the downstairs door in a polyester satire of a suit. Maybe that's why his friends call him Dumpy. It's been a while since he's seen the inside of a gym, and he carries his extra poundage on a frame that would be about my height if his posture weren't so pathetic. Hard living is writ large across his face in rheumy eyes and a swollen, reddened nose. He sees me and smiles. It is not a friendly smile.

"If it ain't the cub reporter," he says.

Dumphy's a pretty good cop most of the time, but we busted a crack house one time, and I watched him pocket a couple grand from a pile of confiscated cash. He offered me some but I refused, and that soured our friendship forever. I agonized over what to do, but he was waging a costly, heart-wrenching custody battle for an out-of-wedlock daughter who was dying of Hodgkin's disease, so I gave him a pass. I rationalized my inaction by calling it a victimless crime. Almost half a million dollars still made it to the evidence locker, so it's not like Dumphy's skim undermined the prosecution of the crack dealers. But they might have gotten off if I had exposed him. Another rationalization. I left the force soon after.

"What's going on, Dumphy?"

"Some reason you can't wait for the press release like everybody else?"

"I'm a friend of the family."

"Brown, I got news. You ain't got any friends."

"I just want to know if Ginger's okay."

"Ginger?"

"Ginger Strain. She lives here. With her father."

"Well I don't know, bright boy. Lady in there ain't in any shape to introduce herself."

"Let me take a look."

He doesn't like it, but even he understands the advantage of making a positive ID. He nods to the rookie, who lifts the tape for me to duck under. Dumphy leads me up the outer stairs and around the deck to the kitchen door and tells me that's as far as I go.

There's a vestigial odor of natural gas in the air as I peer into the room and let my eyes adjust to the bright light from a stand of floods the forensics guys set up to illuminate the shadows. There are two lab techs in there now with purple gloves, blue paper booties on their shoes, and matching surgical hats on their hair. One of them bags the trash for logging in the lab while the other goes over the kitchen table with a tweezers, collecting and cataloguing any visible hair or fibers. After the body is removed, they'll vacuum the scene for trace evidence.

The two oven doors are open.

A body sits on one of the red vinyl chairs, slumped over the kitchen table, head lying at an awkward angle on a straw place-mat, staring lifelessly at an empty yellow teacup with a blue leaf pattern. I feel my stomach pitch. There's no mistaking those green-gold eyes.

FIFTEEN

At seven o'clock I decide to skip dinner and crawl into bed. Ginger's death is a kick in the head, yet another in a vicious cycle of losses.

The thought of her committing suicide stirs up sour memories of my father's death.

Then there's my marriage, or lack thereof. Every time I look in the mirror I see myself through Holly's eyes, a vision of profound disappointment. I hear the woman I loved telling me she can't live anymore with a man she doesn't respect. As time passes, the pain changes in nature, but not depth. I carry it with me everywhere, hoping I'll never need it again but holding it close just in case. Kind of like always packing the gun you used in a failed suicide attempt.

And of course there's that dark, empty place where my badge used to be.

These thoughts lace in and out of dreams as I thrash in and out of sleep. I'm consumed by the vision of Ginger's face on the table, her eyes dull like Lana's one eye in that crime-scene photo. I can't get it out of my mind, but I can't get it in there either. A square peg in a round hole. Lana: murder. Ginger: suicide. Could the cause be twenty years removed from the effect?

I try to imagine a teenage Ginger, coming home from school, dropping her backpack by the door, skipping down the stairs to find her mother's head splattered around the bedroom. It had to redefine her experience of pretty much everything for the rest of her life. A reincarnation without having to die, a retooling of the self, an imagination remodeled. Every thought, every feeling from that moment on must have taken off from a different launch pad, a deeper, bleaker jumping-off point.

Did she retreat behind a wall of denial? A protective curtain of delusion? Or was she smothered by the harsh carnage, over-powered by the nauseating reality? I can't begin to fathom, but I obsess about it anyway. I can't shake the guilty suspicion that my questions led her back to that place, to some black hole from which death seemed a relief. The timing is just too suspicious to be coincidental.

I replay our conversations in my head. Did I trigger some fatal train of thought? Upend some hidden memory? She seemed fine except for that one moment when my hand brushed her thigh and she closed up like a sea anemone. Could that tiny emotional nudge have triggered an emotional landslide? According to the coroner's preliminary estimate, Ginger died on Thursday, four days after we'd met. Was that enough time for her to spiral into oblivion?

Gloria walks in. "Get your ass out of bed, Nob."

"How'd you get in?" I ask. I'm still in that Kafkaland between dreams and reality, so it doesn't occur to me that we traded keys years ago.

"I blew the butler."

"Well, you can leave the same way."

I look at the clock. It's only 9:17. It feels like the middle of the night.

"You're either getting out of bed, or I'm hauling your ass down to the station."

"On what charge?"

"No charge. You're a material witness."

"To a suicide?"

"You were in her datebook, Nob. At the time of death, you were supposed to be with her."

"So what?"

"So were you?"

Through my mental smog an image starts to form. An image of me doing a perp walk. "Go away," I say.

"What happened that afternoon, Nob? Were you with her when she died?"

"Am I under arrest?"

"Get your sagging ass off the sheets. I already brewed up a pot of black."

I smell the Ethiopian Yirgacheffe as I roll out of bed naked.

"Nice cock," she says, grinning like it's some kind of joke.

I throw on some clothes and follow the smell of coffee downstairs. Gloria hands me a cup of joe. After a few sips the smog starts to clear. She has the good sense to keep her mouth shut and just let my atoms reassemble into a reasonable facsimile of a human being.

"We were supposed to meet at Solley's," I say. "She never showed up, so I drove to the house. Your guys were already swarming when I got there."

"What were you supposed to meet her about?"

"What's with the inquisition?"

"I figure no one's going to notice the disappearance of a twenty-year-old case file," she says, "so I sneak it out for you as a favor. You start poking around, and all of a sudden the vic's daughter winds up dead. It's only a matter of time before some homicide dick connects the dots and goes looking for Lana's murder book. You beginning to get the picture?"

"You want your file back before it's discovered missing," I say.

"Bingo."

"I haven't copied it yet."

"Tough shit," she says.

"I want my key back."

SIXTEEN

It's almost three in the morning when I get home from FedEx Office. For the last four hours I've been feverishly flailing at the copy machine like Lucy Ricardo on the chocolate candy assembly line.

I stumble on my front steps, avoiding the fall with an awkward step that twists my ankle. I'm wondering if I should ice it as I open the door and smell coffee. Somebody's here. For some reason, Cogswell comes to mind. Then Melody walks out of the kitchen holding a steaming cup.

"Jesus, Mel. It's the middle of the night."

I should have known. Cogswell wouldn't make his own coffee.

"In case you haven't noticed, you've been wallowing in misery lately. I thought you might need this."

I actually smile, despite my mood. I have Lana's file and the copy in a box. It weighs a ton. I drop it on the side table by my door and grab the coffee. Tastes great.

"Where were you?" asks Melody.

"I needed an industrial-strength Xerox to get this finished tonight. Gloria wants to stash it back in the files before anyone finds it missing."

"Why would anyone even look? Ginger committed suicide."

"It's not just a suicide, it's a celebrity death just dripping with sex and rock 'n' roll." I feel my eyes flag.

"Ginger Strain is a celebrity?"

"Celebrity spawn. Same thing. Did you get me some background on Lana's dad?"

"Yeah. Nathaniel Strain was quite the fallen preppy. Went to expensive private schools, then Yale, on the proceeds from the metal shop his father built from scratch. He was all set to sail into Stanford Law School and finally distance himself from the working class when he got caught up in some scandal and had to drop out as part of a plea bargain. That put an end to his social-climbing ambitions."

My eyes pop open, and I realize I've nodded off momentarily, though I'm still standing. Melody doesn't notice.

"What kind of scandal?" I ask.

"Not sure. It was a long time ago. Before the web. I'd have to go to New Haven to track it down. But it involved a townie girl. Anyway, he knocked around for a few years, tried wildcatting in Texas, which is where he met Lana's mom. They got married, had Lana a year later, and divorced when Lana was twelve. The wife took him to the cleaners in the settlement."

I put my cup down and pull my copy of the case file out of the box, leaving the original by the door where I'll see it on my way out in the morning. I'm beginning to feel weak from exhaustion. I don't know if it's mental or physical, but I just want to sleep.

"Domestic violence?"

I head into my office with Melody on my heels.

"I don't know," she says. "Their statements were sealed as part of the settlement."

"Probably not," I say. "After the mother died, the county let Lana move back in with him for her last two years of high school."

"How do you know that?"

I drop Lana's file on my desk, raising an explosion of dust.

"It's what she wrote in 'Living the Dream.'" I fall into my chair and manage to stay awake just long enough to sing the last verse:

> *Livin' the dream with Daddy,*
> *Surviving the in-between.*
> *Livin' the dream of splittin'*
> *The second I turn eighteen.*

SEVENTEEN

Five a.m. Still dark. I pull into the post office parking lot on Beverly Boulevard next to the old Pan-Pacific Auditorium, where Elvis played in 1957. Thirty-eight years later, a year after Lana Strain's murder, the Streamline Moderne showpiece went up in a blazing inferno. Now it's a park. Permanence is fleeting in LA.

I park next to Gloria's car. She's leaning against it, bathed in the amber glow of the sodium-vapor security lights that make her hair look gray and disguise the color of the skirt set she's wearing. It's appropriately conservative for work, yet fits her like a glove. Even in monochrome, she looks good. I get out, and she gives me a hug and an air kiss. Doesn't want to smear the fresh lip art.

I pull Lana's file out of my backseat and put it in hers.

"You busy at noon?" she asks with her usual innuendo. How can she even think about sex this early in the morning?

I beg off. "I'm doing a load of laundry at noon."

She laughs. "Don't flatter yourself. I've got an appointment with your friend Billy Kidd. But if you don't want to do a ride-along…"

"And you want me to come?"

"I could use your observations. No one's as steeped as you are in the history and personalities of this case."

"You mean I've read the Lana Strain case file and you haven't."

"You must be psychic."

Not to mention dubious. I know she's not going to allow a potential witness or, God forbid, suspect accompany her without a damn better reason than that.

"Why are you really letting me tag along?"

She sighs. "Billy threatened to lawyer up and refuse to talk unless I'd let his official autobiographer sit in. I take it that's you?"

I'm shocked. A rock star who remembers his promises.

———

Seven hours later, I'm in the passenger seat of a mud-colored Crown Victoria, unmarked but hardly undercover. Gloria drives like she's got a light bar dancing to a siren, only she doesn't. I've got a death grip on the door pull as she roars up Laurel Canyon and swerves onto Weeping Glen. She finally slows as she snakes up the narrow street and parks in front of Billy's house.

"His daughter Sophia is going to be here, too," says Gloria. "She's looking after him."

"You talk to her yet?"

"Dumphy did. When she found the stiff."

"She tell him why she went over there?" I'm still trying to get a rope around that one. She's been estranged from her sister for two decades, then she suddenly finds her dead?

"Thought it was time for a rapprochement." Gloria strips the word of any hint of French origins by giving her native Brooklyn accent a rare break from its dungeon.

"That a guess or she say that?"

"That's a paraphrase." Some sixth sense tells Gloria that her hair needs rearranging, so she runs her hand through it. I don't notice any difference.

"She tell Dumpy why they stopped talking in the first place?"

"She said they had a big fight. She couldn't even remember what it was about, nothing big, just real emotional after their mother's death and all. Then Ginger just stopped talking to her."

"Sounds like a pattern. Ginger cut her grandfather off, too."

"One big happy family."

I follow Gloria up the redwood steps of the dome. She rings the bell, and a knockout of a woman opens the front door. Sophia Kidd. I'm slugged by a patently inappropriate desire of the sort that torched Bill Clinton's presidency.

"I'm Sophia." She has Lana's voice, like her sister did. I always thought that voice was the love child of booze and smoke, but apparently it's genetic. "Come on in," she says.

Sophia doesn't look like a Lana Strain imitator as Ginger did, but she has all of Lana's best features integrated in different proportions and with darker coloring, making her more beautiful than either Lana or Ginger, a more exotic fusion of the DNA. Her build is slighter than Lana's, slender, willowy. Her eyes are more widely spaced and almond shaped, while still sharing her mother's magnificent palette. She's wearing gym shorts, and her legs come out looking tanned and strong, her muscles well defined. Not the legs of a treadmill jogger, but of a sprinter in training. A thoroughbred.

It occurs to me that I haven't been this attracted to a woman since the first time I met Holly, back when I was a rookie cop and she was in law school. In fact, Sophia has Holly's hairdo—long, straight, and parted on one side—only Sophia's is darker, like the orange-blossom honey I used to buy Holly at the Original Farmer's Market on Third.

We follow Sophia in to find Billy slumped on the living room couch in jeans and a wifebeater, fully revealing the intricate twin dragons tattooed up his sinewy arms, their reptilian heads draped over his shoulders. Grief clouds the red crazing of his eyes like cataracts. There's a half-empty bottle of Johnny Walker Red on the coffee table. No sign of a glass.

"I'm so sorry, Billy," I say.

He doesn't seem to hear me, or else he doesn't care.

I try again. "I can't imagine what you must be going through."

He finally looks up. "My sweet Lord fucks up in mysterious ways."

He nods toward the couch, and Gloria and I sit down.

"This is Detective Lieutenant Gloria Lopes," I say.

"How do you do," says Gloria.

"Been better."

"I hate to do this right now," says Gloria, "but there are some questions I need to ask."

"Go the fuck ahead. Cain't stop thinkin' about her anyways."

Sophia takes a seat beside him and takes her father's hand. He doesn't seem to notice.

"Do you have any idea why Ginger might have wanted to take her own life?"

"She weren't the merriest old soul on the face of the planet."

"Anything specific lately?"

"Any little thing'd set her off. Honey to habanera at the flick of a mare's tail. Just like her mama."

Sophia stiffens at his mention of her mother. Though she stares at Billy's manicure, I know that's not what she sees. I wonder what she's remembering about her mother. Lana singing in the shower? Baking pot-laced brownies? Slumped against the Lichtenstein in a pool of blood?

"Ginger lived by impulse," says Sophia. "She wasn't the type to let rationality get in her way."

Billy blanches. "Lord have mercy! What right you got to bad-mouth her, Sofie? You ain't even seen her, comin' on twenty years! Least not till you found her stone cold!"

Tears well in Sophia's lower lids. "She fucked dildos on the Web! She defiled Mama's memory! You call that rational?"

"You ain't got a God damn clue what she was like."

"She was an Internet whore, Daddy! And you let her do it!"

The dog starts to yap as their voices rise.

"Don't you put that on me! Neither one of you is asked me for my goddamn permission since you was ten. That don't make her no whore. Sweet Baby Jesus, have mercy. She ain't touched a man in years."

"Like she'd tell you," Sophia says dismissively.

"For your information, it weren't no big fuckin' secret. Touchin' a man give her the heebie-jeebies. That's why she started seein' a psycho-iatrist agin."

"A hell of a lot of good it did her."

I think back on that moment when my hand brushed Ginger's leg, and she closed up like a clam. I feel strangely exonerated.

Gloria takes the opportunity to remind the combatants of our presence. "She was pretty provocative for a woman who didn't like men."

"I didn't say she didn't like 'em," says Billy. "I said she didn't like 'em to touch her. Only the Lord Almighty hisself knows what the hell was bouncin' 'round in her brainbox. She was 'bout as stable as a two-legged stool."

EIGHTEEN

I sit in my fake Eames, trying to concentrate on a handwritten transcript of Lana's answering machine messages, daydreaming about taking a nap.

Melody leans back from the computer.

"Boom-Boom Laphroig's high school buddy accepted my friend request. I suggested she friend you, too," she says.

I acknowledge this with a nod and glance out the window. The smog sits like a brown blanket over the Valley, so thick you can't even see the Van Nuys Civic Center three miles away.

The phone rings. Melody punches the speakerphone button. "Nob Brown's office."

"Is he there?" It's Holly. I start waving my arms like a flagman trying to prevent a collision. Melody refuses to lie for me, so I step into the hallway.

"Sorry," she says. "He stepped out."

"Tell him to pick up the phone, Melody."

Melody shoots me a look, but I shake my head.

"I'll tell him you called, Holly."

"I don't deserve this, Nob." The line goes dead.

Melody punches off the speakerphone. "You don't pay me enough for this shit."

I walk back into the room. "Once Jerry's on the case, I'll have to cut your pay anyway."

"I only wish there was something to cut."

We both watch a KNBC chopper buzz down the 101 to check traffic. Mel's neck is backlit by the window, a gooseneck that makes her look fragile, vulnerable. But within the frail package lies a tough broad, a Chihuahua who goes after Rottweilers. What Melody lacks in heft, she makes up in chutzpah.

She stands up and drops into her signature splits. "Lana led such a public life. How come no one ever figured out who the Asshole was?"

"The cops certainly tried. But it was a chaotic investigation. Most of the people they interviewed were so drugged out they wouldn't have known a fact if it sprang from their morning latte. And the press was all over it like the OJ trial. Everyone was jockeying for airtime. The cops logged seventy-eight confessions—seventy-eight assholes aspiring to be *the* Asshole. My personal favorite was the Baptist preacher who said the painting made him do it because 'Pop art is the devil's bullhorn.'"

She pulls an old *Time* magazine from the file. The Lichtenstein is on the cover. "That the *Dotted Babe*?"

"Yeah." Sans blood, sans corpse. "It made the covers of *Time, Newsweek,* the *New Yorker, Rolling Stone,* and *TV Guide* all within two weeks of the murder, and three months later it made *Art Forum.*"

"Lichtenstein never had it so good."

I pass her the answering machine transcript. "Put that back in the file, will you?"

"Anything interesting on the tape?" She finally moves to her work area to access the accordion file we're using to organize Lana's stuff.

"A couple folks left their first names and no call-back numbers. Maybe you can try to figure out who they are from Lana's phone bills. They're in the file."

"I guess I could do that," she says.

"The last call was from her father," I add. "He told her he was sorry he didn't beat the shit out of her the night before and, among other anatomical impossibilities, he said she could go fuck herself."

NINETEEN

I could have gone online to search the *LA Times* archives, but when you go back as far as the eighties, you have to pay for each hit, and I can't afford to buy everything that's ever been written about Lana Strain just to find the few facts I don't already know from her case file and the Web, so I'm going low tech. I'm threading 35 mm film onto the sprockets of a microfilm reader that sounds like it hasn't been oiled in about two millennia. I feel like I should be wearing white cotton gloves, as if I'm handling an ancient Macedonian burial urn.

I'm four floors underground in the Central Library on Fifth Street, but the History and Genealogy Department is flooded with natural morning light from the cavernous Bradley wing atrium. I'm scanning thousands of microfilmed newspaper pages, just as they originally appeared in the *Times* of yesteryear. I'm flooded with images from my childhood as I scroll past ads for stores and products that haven't existed in decades. The process is tedious, and six hours later I've found only three items of interest.

The first, from a long-gone gossip columnist named Liz Smith, alleged that Billy Kidd had moved back into Lana's house less than an hour after the police released the crime scene. According to Liz, Lana's father, Nathaniel Strain, had not been pleased.

The second, from an anonymous source, claimed that Billy had sent both of his teenage daughters to a shrink recommended by actress Courteney Cox, whom Billy had met while shooting a fifteen-second cameo on *Friends*.

And the third, which Billy himself told to Barbara Walters, denied the Courteney Cox rumor, claiming to have found the shrink through Lana's seamstress and best friend, Claudine Hugo.

I wouldn't describe any of these items as burning clues, and my back feels like I've been jammed inside a suitcase all day. But it had to be done.

As I head into the parking garage, I realize that my dople was the closest thing to a meal I've had since yesterday, so I crawl the Hollywood Freeway to Carnicería Argentina on Victory for an empanada fix.

Hanibal is behind the enormous meat counter braiding intestines into chinchulines when I walk in. "Hey, Brownie, how you doin'?"

"Que tal, Hanibal." I can fake Spanish when I have to.

He raves about a new Cabernet from Mendoza as he packs a dozen of his homemade beef turnovers for my freezer and heats two more for me to eat in the car.

I drive home savoring the flavor of the Pampas, feeding my soul as well as my stomach, and thinking about Lana's will. I finish the second empanada as I pull up to my house.

Melody's car is nowhere to be seen. I assume she's off either taking or teaching dance or Pilates or yoga or "movement," whatever that means. I check the mailbox, hoping for Lana's probate papers from the county, but there's nothing but catalogues, bills, and a postcard from a real estate agent I don't know letting me in on exciting news about a house sale I don't care about. Still no replies to any of the six story queries I sent out three weeks ago. I make a mental note to place some follow-up calls this afternoon.

My house is on a downslope, so I descend from the street to get to the front door. There are only eight steps but I still take them two at a time. Got to sneak in whatever exercise I can get. I've always had a naturally lean build, but lately I've been noticing some incremental waistline creep. Not enough to show, but enough to tighten my pants. As I absently palpate my key ring for my house key, I consider the possibility of squeezing in an extra swim workout tonight at Van Nuys-Sherman Oaks Park.

I open the front door and walk into an unexpected whiff of whiskey. My antennae spring up. Red alert.

I sneak toward my office, and the floor crunches underfoot. Broken glass. I freeze, an insect hitting a windshield of fear. I hold my breath and listen for someone else's, but all I hear is the ceaseless white noise of the Valley. After a long pause, I back up, trying to be silent, but with the glass on the floor, I sound like a horse chewing Corn Nuts. I've clearly lost the advantage of surprise if someone's here. I grab a fireplace poker.

In the kitchen everything appears normal, but something still feels wrong. I open the drawer where I keep my metal kitchen utensils—tongs, spatulas, slotted spoons, meat pounder, spider, potato masher, graduated graters, muddler, zester, the usual. I see my grandmother's marrow scoop with its handle of bird's-eye maple. I keep it for its sentimental value but it has a broken rivet so I never use it. Because of that, it ends up living in the back of the drawer, but now it's front and center. Someone's been in there, apparently searching. I wonder what for.

I creep up the stairs, poker raised. I feel like I'm in a film and hope it's not *Psycho*. I make the rounds of the upstairs bedrooms and bathroom without being attacked. No one's there but, as in the kitchen, someone has been. Small clues tell me someone searched every room, but as far as I can tell, nothing is missing. This wasn't a robbery.

I return to the office and turn on the light. The room looks untouched except for the smashed bottle of booze—he wasted my best single malt Scotch just when I need it. Judging by the care he took to cover his tracks, I assume he dropped it by accident.

Why would someone break into my house to search? What was he looking for? Could it have been triggered by my investigation into Lana Strain's murder? After all this time, why would anyone care enough to take the risk? And who has the balls and the skills to pull it off?

———

Scotch dries sticky. I'm on my knees cleaning the floor when Melody waltzes in. "Holy shit," she says.

"It's only a broken bottle." I wring my rag into a bucket.

"It's just such a shock to see you scrubbing the floor," she says.

"You planning to gawk? Or you planning to help?"

She makes no move to help. "What happened?"

"Somebody searched the house."

"What were they looking for?"

"I don't know. Notes?"

"The Lana Strain story?"

"Maybe. I had my notebook with me, and they didn't take the case file, but they could have slipped something out of it. I've got a call in to Gloria to see if I can get my hands on the original again to compare it against my copy."

Mel leans over without bending her knees and puts her palms on the floor, just because she can, then she reaches between her legs toward the bottom shelf of my bookcase. To extend her stretch, she reaches for the copy of *Ulysses* I read during my freshman year at Princeton. My only year at Princeton. "Stately, plump," she says then reshelves it. I'm surprised she knows the opening words of an actual book. I've never known her to read anything that wasn't measured in pixels.

"Got a suspect?" she asks.

"That's what I've been trying to figure out. I can't imagine Billy doing something like this. I guess it could have been Nathaniel Strain. But I think Gary Cogswell is the most likely. Breaking and entering would be a cakewalk for *his* boys."

"That's just great. Your pal Vlad the Impaler is probably ordering you a dople of Molotov cocktails as we speak." She glances out the window, checking the street in both directions before reaching up to pull down the window shade. No enabling a drive-by for this girl. "Thanks a lot, Nob."

I drop my rag in the Scotchy sludge and consider scooping some into a highball glass.

TWENTY

Gloria shimmies into the black cocktail dress, straightens the wrinkles, turns to the mirror, and frowns. "Too sexy," she says. Considering that the slit side almost reveals her thong, I have to agree, but I don't comment.

She's running out of black, having tried on and rejected two dresses and four skirts already. They lie in a pile on the bed beside me. I feel stiff and hot in my charcoal wool suit. The added warmth of Gloria's laptop doesn't help. I've been reading up on Bakatin, trying to winnow a motive for him or Cogswell to want to search my place.

She takes off the dress and adds it to the pile. I drill through local media sites and stumble on a reference to Bakatin's shell company, Kocibey Development.

Gloria stares into her closet with a look of intent concentration, as if willpower can levitate the perfect outfit. She selects a fifth black skirt and slips into it.

"Five-minute warning," I say.

"Don't worry. I'll do my lipstick in the car."

Gloria finds a white silk blouse and tries it on with a waist-length jacket. It's black jacquard, like the scarf that strangled a Haitian actress I wrote about last year.

I click through to a year-old blog entry from a real estate agent congratulating his wife and business partner on closing a big Chatsworth land sale to Kocibey Development. I click on the wife's name and get her contact page. I punch her phone number into my cell. Then I close the laptop. We're on the verge of running late.

"You look great," I say then regret it. I find that it's generally best to keep my mouth shut about how women look in clothes, no matter what you have to say.

"You're just saying that because you want to go."

"That's true, but you've looked great in everything you've tried on."

She does a half turn to look at herself from the back, then puts on two mismatched shoes, one with a three-inch heel and one with a six-inch. "Which do you like?" She turns first to one side then the other.

"I like the practical one."

"You're so predictable."

She kicks off the fuck-me pump and hobbles past me on one heel. I give her a swat.

"Ow!" But she says it playfully. "Don't you spank me, or we'll never get out of here."

"Three-minute warning."

Gloria panics as she disappears into her closet for her other shoe. She's a woman who rarely worries over clothes, but something about funerals stirs her inner fashionista.

On the way to Hollywood Forever Cemetery, I call the real estate agent and mention that a friend at Kocibey Development had recommended her and wonder if there were any other properties available for sale near the parcel she sold them. She tells me that there are no other vacant lots in the area, but she gives me the address of a minimall for sale a block east of the Kocibey property.

As Gloria pulls into the cemetery I call Melody and ask her to look up the minimall address on Zillow, get an address for the large parcel a block west, then run over to the Department of Building and Safety in Van Nuys to get copies of any permits that might have been pulled in recent years. I don't know what I'm looking for, so I'm casting a wide net.

The gate guard directs us to the private service at graveside where maybe thirty people stand waiting. Most of the mourners appear to be friends of Billy's, judging by their age. It's sad that Ginger had so few friends of her own. I recognize Belinda Carlisle, Axl Rose, Eddie Van Halen, and Taj Mahal.

The casket hangs suspended over the tailored hole, and beyond it stand Billy, Claudine, and Sophia, who leans against a fit, muscular man with such intimacy that he can only be Dr. Karl Lynch. No sign of Nathaniel Strain.

Lynch absently strokes his immaculate salt-and-pepper mane as if checking for perfectly combed strands gone astray. His other arm embraces Sophia protectively, a human security blanket. His hair almost matches his wide-set eyes, which are blue but so clear as to appear gray. He looks to be about fifteen years older than Sophia, but he wears the years well, looking more self-assured than age-weary. His gaze is fixed on the coffin.

Sophia glances in my direction and sneaks a half smile. If she weren't here with Lynch, I'd think she was flirting. Gloria notices but says nothing. I return Sophia's smile with a sad overtone, trying to mime my condolences.

Dumphy stands at the foot of the grave with a deputy DA I've seen around. I think his name is Mepum or Mopam or something like that. I wonder why the two of them would show up for a suicide but write it off to the celebrity angle. I've never met the DA, but Gloria once told me she'd had a fleeting interest due to his big feet but decided to pass when he'd opened his big mouth.

There had been no chapel service, perhaps to avoid the embarrassment of empty pews. Now, at the grave, a nonsectarian minister steps forward and offers a few trite homilies. It's clear that he never met the deceased. He concludes with the Twenty-Third Psalm and then asks if anyone else would like to say a few words. A man volunteers.

He identifies himself as Zeke something, Ginger's neighbor of nine years.

"Ginger," Zeke says. "What can you say? So beautiful. She had a heart as big as a blimp. Always said good morning. Always had a dog biscuit for Bertram. Always fed him and took my mail in when I was out of town. Never left her cans out after garbage day. I'm really going to miss her. I just hope that in death she finds the inner peace she couldn't find in life. God bless you, Ginger."

Zeke steps back and an obese, middle-aged woman steps forward. Her hair is so thin I can see sunlight reflecting off the sweat of her scalp. One eye is a good quarter-inch lower than the other, unhappily distorting her face to resemble Quasimodo's.

"Hello. My name is Andrea Andrews, and I'm an alcoholic."

"She's at the wrong meeting," whispers Gloria.

"I first met Ginger when we wound up in the same hospital room. I couldn't believe she'd slit her wrists, too. She was so beautiful—why would she want to kill herself? And it wasn't just outer beauty, it was inner beauty. Everybody could see it. I remember when I got out and she invited me to check out her therapy group."

Karl Lynch stiffens beside Sophia, seemingly girding himself. He's watching Andrea anxiously, like she's just pulled the pin on a hand grenade.

"She really seemed like some other person when she was there, soothing her inner child, dealing with her personal demons in group."

Andrea is noticeably shaking, fighting tears, finding it increasingly difficult to speak.

Sophia stares at Ginger's coffin almost longingly, as if wondering what it would feel like to be lying inside. Lynch turns his attention to her, touching her arm to make sure she's all right. She starts at his touch.

"We all thought she was doing so great. She was so beautiful. I mean, if *she* couldn't make it…" She breaks down, unable to go on.

A thin, balding man in jeans and a polo shirt takes her gently by the arm and leads her away. Lynch appears relieved. He puts his arm around Sophia, pulling her to him protectively, reeling her in.

Sophia stares at the coffin with a look on her face that Lana wore on her *Heart Like a Whiffleball* album. I'll never forget that album because it had "Go Down Hard," my favorite song. Billy played a mean slide solo on that song.

I glance over at Mepum or Mopam, who's now staring at me. For some reason, he makes me feel guilty for standing next to Gloria, like I've been caught out of school.

Billy clears his throat to speak. He's wearing a nicely tailored black suit, navy silk T-shirt, and black cowboy boots. His ponytail is braided and bound by the same cock ring he wore the first time we met. He looks out at the small group with the whites of his gray eyes even redder than usual.

"She was my baby girl. My sweet baby girl, Jesus rest her soul. I remember the day she was borned. They had to drag her out of Lana, both of 'em kicking and screaming, but Ginger never did seem to find her no peace on this earth. Maybe now, she'll find it in the good Lord's garden. I'll always love you, Pumpkin. May Sweet Jesus Baby God, our merciful Lord and shepherd, have mercy on your ever-lovin' sweet baby girl soul. Amen."

He bows his head, and tears rain dark spots on his shirt. Sophia pulls away from Karl and embraces her father. Billy clutches her tightly. "You're alls I got left, angel girl."

Sophia stands on tiptoe to softly kiss his cheek, and I'm embarrassed by the thought that I wish I were feeling those lips. Then Billy raises his mournful eyes. From the depths of his pain, the living legend reveals himself to be all too human.

TWENTY-ONE

After the funeral yesterday, at the condolence gathering, I asked Sophia if she'd be willing to talk to me sometime about her mother. She said she had to go to Little Tokyo today and could meet up with me afterward. I suggested Qat Haus, and she said, "You mean Little Pedro's?" I like a girl with a sense of history.

Little Pedro's was reputedly the oldest bar in LA. Its proximity to the old Parker Center made it a perfect cop stop. Around the time of the Rampart scandal, LAPD morale took a dive, and so did business at Little Pedro's. A few years later it closed. Then it became the brothel-themed Bordello. Then One-Eyed Gypsy. And now, Qat Haus. The décor is still nineteenth-century whorehouse from the Bordello days, over-the-top in a lighthearted crimson-crushed-velvet-and-gilded-wood sort of way. Though it's trendier than most LAPD hangs, the chick bartenders pour heavy, charge light, and wear burlesque chic so the bar's packed with off-duty cops.

I walk in and spot Sophia in a booth in back, sipping something pink and paper umbrellaed. Could be a Singapore sling. I slide in.

"Sorry I'm late. Traffic."

"I just got here." She's got her hair pulled back tight in a ponytail and wears red lipstick and a tight yellow blouse. Very easy on the eyes.

Aside from the bar, the place is mostly empty. Too early for anyone but an elderly man with a young woman who's either his granddaughter or a hooker. They're deep into an order of fish and chips and a couple draft beers with lime. I scan the bar and see Dumphy slumped over a shot glass, trying to get his lips on it without wetting his W. C. Fields nose. Gloria sits a few stools away, staring at Sophia like a falcon sighting its prey. There's a guy talking at her a mile a minute, but she's not paying any attention. He's a SWAT guy whose name I can never remember, but he lives nearby and got mugged by a junkie on his way home from happy hour one night. He'll never live it down.

Gloria locks eyes with me. Brrrrr. I smile a greeting across the room, but she doesn't even try to fake a civil response. She turns her back to me. What the hell is that all about?

Mindy, a barmaid who once house-sat for me when I was on a story in New Orleans, stops by. "Drink?" She's about thirty and must have that many studs in her face. I wonder how she gets through airport security.

"I'll have a Bombay rocks." Gin is the only civilized spirit to drink before five o'clock. I turn to Sophia. "You like calamari?"

"Sure."

I nod at Mindy who makes a mental note of the order and walks off. She never writes it down, and she never gets it wrong. Good house sitter, too.

"So what do you want from me?" Sophia asks.

If I tell her the truth I'll probably get slapped, so I open my notebook. "Why don't we start with your parents' divorce."

"They were fighting a lot."

"What about?" I need to pee, but I don't want to interrupt her train of thought before she even gets started.

"Me and my sister, mostly. Poppy had a unique approach to parenting that Mama didn't much like."

"What did he do?"

"He could be pretty cruel. Not that he spanked us or anything; he'd never do that. But he was a big fan of humiliation. That was his absolute favorite tool. He had this Ampex reel-to-reel recorder that used to belong to Les Paul, and one day he set it up to bug the phone when some guy was offering to take Ginger to the junior prom if she'd blow him under the bleachers. She bargained him down to a hand job, but that wasn't good enough for Poppy. He just had to teach her a lesson. So he played that damn tape at the dinner table. And to make matters worse, Grampa Nate was there, loving every second like it was some kind of soft-core sitcom instead of my sister's guts being ripped open. Mama went completely psycho, screaming at him, throwing plates, and finally smashing the recorder with a chair. I couldn't believe it. Poppy worshiped that Les Paul Ampex. Sometimes I thought he loved it even more than he loved us. And then she told him to pack his shit and get the hell out."

"How did he take it?" My bladder is getting insistent.

"He told her when she was through fucking Vern Senzimmer she could go fuck herself, if you'll excuse my French. They were both doing a lot of drugs at the time, drinking a lot, as if they needed artificial means to be crazy. And Ginger and I weren't exactly helpful. We both got Mama's drama queen gene. Between the four of us there was not a lot of sanity in residence."

My bladder's making it impossible to concentrate. "I'm sorry, you'll have to excuse me for a minute." I head off to the men's room.

Two minutes later I'm leaving the stall and almost trip on my shoelace. I put my foot on the sink to tie my shoe and hear the door close behind me. I look in the mirror and see Gloria locking the deadbolt. Her skin looks almost green, but I can't tell if it's the CFL lighting or the fact that she's already pickled.

"Hey, shailor." Drunk as a Russian poet. Whatever fragrance she's wearing clashes with the saccharine urinal-cake smell that infuses the air.

"Ladies' room is down the hall, Gloria."

"But you're not." She twists me around, jamming my back against the wall-mounted air dryer, mashing her body against mine.

"This isn't the time or the place."

She kisses me hard. Despite my discomfort, the risk of being caught excites me. She reaches down and feels my ambivalence through my pants.

"I guess your brain hasn't notified your dick," she says, "but that's not why I'm here." She gives my balls a sharp squeeze. I stifle a shout. She looks at me hard. All of a sudden she seems almost sober.

"Curb your dick, Nob. You don't want to get a hard-on for your little girlfriend out there. There's questions."

She heads out.

"What questions?"

She snaps the bolt and swings open the door to find Dumphy reaching for the handle. Dumphy doesn't seem too surprised to find Gloria in the men's room. On the other hand, surprise requires a certain degree of consciousness, and Dumphy doesn't appear to have much more than Gloria at the moment.

"What questions, Gloria?"

Dumphy salutes her and hits his forehead a little harder than planned.

She gives him the finger and marshals her balance to walk out.

"Wuz her problem?" slurs Dumphy. "I'm just tryin' to kiss ass."

"Maybe she doesn't like ass-kissers."

"You think she got those 'tenant bars without Frenchin' a shitload of starfish?"

I'm still wondering about Gloria's comment as I slide back into the booth. Sophia ordered another round while I was gone, and it's already on the table.

"You look like you've seen a ghost," she says.

"The men's room was a little crowded." I take a healthy slug of gin to clear my head. "Tell me about Ginger."

"Is that how you treat all your dates? Make them talk about their little sisters?"

I knew it was a mistake to pee. You give an interviewee time to think, and the blood rushes to their brain, leaving cold feet.

"This isn't a date. It's an interview."

"You always drink when you interview people?"

"Depends on whether I think it'll help."

"So I'm the kind of girl you need to ply with alcohol?" She looks into her drink with a sly smile and swirls it with her little umbrella.

"You were drinking when I walked in. I just went with the program."

She laughs and lifts her glass to toast. We clink, and I get back to work.

"Do you think Ginger inherited enough money to live on?"

"It's enough for me, and we split it fifty-fifty."

"You don't work?"

"I'm an artist." In other words, no.

"I earn a living making hand-carved marionettes." This woman is full of surprises. "But I do it because I enjoy it. Mama's estate was wiped out by the time I gained control, but her publishing rights earn a reasonable living. And on top of that, Ginger didn't have to pay rent or mortgage."

I ponder why Ginger was slutting it up on the Web if she didn't have to work. Was that her art form?

The calamari arrives. Sophia eyes them but isn't ready to make her move. I pick up a set of legs that looks like a deep-fried exotic flower and pop it in my mouth. The oil's so hot it burns my tongue. I grab my drink and take a swig, but I know I'm going to feel it for days.

Over her shoulder I see Gloria at the bar. She's got her back to me, but I feel like she's watching me anyway, as if her eyes have swiveled around to stare through the back of her head. She's making it hard to concentrate on Sophia.

"Why do you think your sister did the Internet thing?"

"I don't know. Maybe she just did it for kicks. Or maybe she had a boyfriend who worked there, and she did it for him. In high school she was a big prick teaser, if you know what I mean, always flirting to work the boys."

She takes the wedge of pineapple from the edge of her sling and puts it between her lips to suck the juice out. I have to look away.

"So tell me. Are you one of those writers who's driven by a passion to write?" she asks and laughs. A little too hard. I make a mental note to try to move her onto coffee but leave her question hanging.

"At the moment I'm driven by a passion to save my house from my ex."

"Ouch! I'm sorry. I didn't mean to pry."

I wave it off. No problem.

"Are you a good writer?" she asks then immediately back-pedals. "I guess that's a silly question, asking a writer a subjective thing like that about his own work."

"I subscribe to the first law of writing: you're only good if it pays off your debts. At the moment, my writing is so-so."

She laughs again.

I think about how I've not only come to bottom-feed for the likes of *Globe* or the *Enquirer* but how I've come to be glad for the gigs. It's not much of a living, but I don't live much. Since Holly left I haven't seen much point in going out in the world to enjoy life. Especially when I can be staring at a blank screen, alone in a lonely room, losing myself in some grisly homicide.

"Do you like freelance writing?" asks Sophia. "Or do you just do it because you can?"

I shrug. "The freelance market's shrinking faster than type-writer sales, but if the right story comes along, it can be a stepping-stone into books. Maybe movies."

"A story like my mother's?"

I give a "maybe" shrug and pop a calamari ring into my mouth. The squid's juicy and not too hot anymore.

"Everybody's got a theory about who killed her," she says. "What's yours?"

"I don't know yet. How about you?"

"I think my sister did it."

I choke on my squid.

TWENTY-TWO

As usual, I feel self-conscious walking into Robbery Homicide, like a guy coming home to his wife reeking of booze and cheap perfume. It's not like anyone but Dumphy knows why I quit the department, but the fact that I did earned me a gold star on a lot of shit lists.

It's late afternoon, and about a dozen detectives are packed into the bullpen, talking on the phone, interviewing wits, doing paperwork. Dumphy sits at his desk, or rather, near his desk. His sheer bulk prevents him from sitting too close.

An Asian whore sits across from him sporting a streaked-platinum shag, six-inch transparent heels, smeared crimson lip gloss, mascara streaks down her cheeks, Kleenex-stuffed nostrils, and two reddened black eyes that her heavy-handed eye makeup doesn't come close to hiding. Her gold sequined blouse is held up securely by the hydraulic pressure of her implants even with both shoulder straps torn.

Dumphy looks up when I step into the squad room. In a silent exchange of pleasantries, he raises his middle finger and I return the greeting. The least I can do. I give what I hope is a reassuring smile to the Asian vic before stepping into Gloria's converted-maintenance-closet of an office.

"Afternoon, Lieutenant."

She looks up from the file she's reading. "I saw you ogling that hooker in the bullpen."

"I wasn't ogling."

"It must have been the leash attached to her chest that was dragging you around by the eyeballs," she says. "What is it with you guys? From the second you're weaned, you're on this quest to get back on the nipple."

"And you earned your doctorate in psychology where?"

"In a thousand bars in a hundred towns." She leans back and forms an A-frame with her hands, thoughtfully tapping her fingertips to her lips. "Is there a point to this visit? Or can I get back to work?"

"What was that little hissy fit you threw at Qat Haus yesterday? You jealous?"

"Since when are you so sensitive?"

"Since you almost rendered me sterile."

She smiles. "Maybe I was a little tipsy. I was just trying to make a point."

For her, this is a magnanimous apology, so I let it suffice.

"Well, you failed. What are these 'questions' about Sophia?"

She closes the file to give me her full attention. Talking about feelings makes her nervous. Talking about murder doesn't.

"This is not for publication until I say so."

"Okay."

"Let's take a drive."

A half hour later, we pull into the parking lot of the California Forensic Science Institute. The state-of-the-art crime lab and teaching facility was designed to optimize the benefits of collaboration between the LAPD, the County Sheriff, and the Cal State LA School of Criminal Justice and Criminalistics, ending years of rivalry and miscommunications.

Gloria badges us in, and we navigate up the stairs and down the mazelike hallways. We pass a shower in the corridor that has no drain. It's in case you spill toxins, acids, or biological contaminants on yourself. They want you to be able to shower it off, but they don't want it going down any drains. Better to clean it off the floor than let it out into the world. I question the wisdom of this every time I walk by. Would have made more sense to me for them to drain it into a sealed tank. Then you wouldn't have toxins washing down the corridor and under doors. Go figure.

We reach one of the labs where she arranged to meet Edsel Martinez, a forensic chemist who was Edith Martinez until his trip to Sweden three years ago. He wears a white lab coat embroidered not just with his name but with the logo of the Edsel automobile. He's looking through a huge binocular microscope when we arrive, even though whatever he's looking at is displayed on a hi-def flat-screen right next to him. I have no idea what the object is, maybe some sort of blood cell, but the razor-sharp image is spectacular.

"Edsel, you remember Nob Brown?"

"Sure. Looking good, Nob. Even without hair gel." Edsel likes me because I've quoted him in a number of stories, but I've never mentioned his gender change, whereas most other journalists manage to work it into their lead paragraph.

Edsel hands Gloria a stapled document.

"Initial labs from the autopsy," he says, beaming with the anticipation of a father watching his child open an extravagant birthday gift.

As Gloria reads, I notice a dartboard with a well-punctured photo attached to it.

"Who's the dart catcher?" I ask.

"Werner Heisenberg," says Edsel.

"Why him?"

"He invented the 'uncertainty principle.'" Edsel pulls a dart from his pencil drawer and throws it into Heisenberg's left nostril. "I hate uncertainty."

"Heisenberg didn't create uncertainty, he revealed it," I say. "He's like the guy who found the perp while everyone else was chasing the red herring. He opened people's eyes."

"Facts are the enemy of jokes."

Gloria looks up from the labs. "How much was in her blood?"

"Enough to knock down a camel," says Edsel.

"How much what?" I ask.

"Elavil," says Gloria.

"We have no way of knowing the brand," corrects Edsel. "We just know it's a TCA, a tricyclic antidepressant."

"She must have taken it for insurance," I say, "just in case the gas didn't work."

"Or to make sure she wouldn't change her mind," Gloria adds.

"Maybe," says Edsel, "but here's the thing. We didn't find any TCAs in the kitchen, except for traces in her teacup. And there were no empty bottles or baggies in the wastebasket or compactor."

"Maybe she had them in an envelope or a Kleenex," I suggest, despite knowing they must have already covered this base.

"No." Edsel shakes his head. Something about the gesture seems odd. Then I realize what it is: no sideburns.

"What about the garbage bins on the street?" asks Gloria.

"We didn't know about the drugs at the time, and we thought it was a suicide so we didn't sift the garbage. Besides, why would she interrupt her suicide to dump a pill bottle at the bottom of the driveway instead of throwing it in the wastebasket two feet away?"

"Just because it doesn't make sense doesn't mean it didn't happen," says Gloria. She punches Edsel's speakerphone and dials nine and then a number. Dumphy answers.

"Hey, Dump. I need you to check with City Sanitation, and if the garbage hasn't been collected at the gas sucker's house, get a couple scavengers out there to look for a pill bottle or a baggie or something," she says.

"You're kidding, right? You want to put a trash team on a suicide?"

"She had Elavil in her bloodstream."

"Some unidentified TCA," says Edsel. Gloria flips him the finger.

"So?" Dumphy doesn't get it.

"So they didn't find a pill bottle," she says. "If there's none in the garbage, look for baggies, empty capsules, whatever. Catalogue everything. And do it fast before it's too late."

"Anything else, Your Majesty?"

"Yeah. Bring me a bottle of Cristal and Johnny Depp." She hangs up and turns to Edsel. "You have the pix?"

"Right here." He hands me a printout of four photos taken from different angles of the teacup I saw on the table in front of Ginger. It looks sooty from being dusted for prints. I'm not sure what I'm supposed to be looking for.

"You saw the body, Nob. Was she wearing gloves?"

Gloria's point hits me like a roundhouse kick to the jaw. There are no prints on the cup. Not even the victim's.

"It's a homicide," I say.

"Well done, Watson. Some amateur wiped the prints, and it could have been the victim's suddenly unestranged sister, aka your new girlfriend."

TWENTY-THREE

Filtered through the trees that circle the geodesic dome, the morning sun paints a Rorschach pattern on the floor. It looks like a butterfly or Dracula or the outline of a uvula against the back of the throat. Try as I might, I can't see the corresponding symmetry in the leaves outside. It's not even nine but the relentless sun has already baked off the morning dew.

Budweiser in hand, Billy Kidd collapses a few feet away from me on the sofa, head drooped back, ponytail crossing his shoulder, eyes staring blankly at the mirrored ball that hangs from the apex of the dome. He wears jeans that some chic couturier has almost shredded to get that thrown-out-of-a-moving-car look. His boots are purple suede with peacock-feather accents. And the latest Brothers CD cover is silk-screened on his lime-green T-shirt—a picture of Billy staring through prison bars with the word "Brothers" above and "In Law" beneath.

"Lord Jesus, give me strength," he says.

Gloria walks out of the kitchen carrying one of the chrome and red vinyl chairs in order to sit facing Billy. The alternative is a mud-brown wide-waled corduroy beanbag chair, which she avoids for obvious reasons. The place smells like sandalwood incense.

"We can't say for sure that it wasn't a suicide," she says. "But we have some doubts we need to eliminate."

She wiggles around until she's comfortable in the chair then asks, "Do you know anyone who might have had a reason to harm Ginger? Maybe an ex-boyfriend? A jealous girlfriend?"

"She ain't got—" he catches himself using the present tense and chokes up. "Sorry."

Gloria waits for him to compose himself.

After a moment, he resumes. "She didn't used to got no friends, really. Of neither sex. Never was much of a social flutterby."

"What about people at work?"

"Never hung out with nobody from work 'at I knowed about. She'd just go to work and come on home. Pretty much ever day 'cept Wednesday, Dr. Karl day, reg'lar as church. Side from that, she'd just sit round here, stare at the tube."

Billy pulls off one of his purple boots and lets it drop to the floor. It sounds like an anvil landing.

"Never dated?"

"I 'spect in her line o' work a date would be somethin' of a busman's holiday. Lived like a fuckin' nun, s'cuse me, Jesus."

"Don't you find that a little strange, given the kind of work she did?"

"Ever'body's strange on this planet. I leave the judgin' to the Good Lord."

"You know anyone she might have had a disagreement with?" asks Gloria.

Billy shakes his head and his ponytail slips off his shoulder, swinging over the back of the couch.

"Like I said, she was a loner."

"I understand she had a falling out with her grandfather."

"Praise the Lord, she sure as shit hated that crusty old bastard. Guess she got it from her ma."

"Do you think Nathaniel Strain could have killed Ginger?" I ask. Gloria shoots me a look, like I'm stepping on her punch line.

"I doubts it," he says. "Nate got him a set of balls the size of black-eyed peas."

"Cowards are the most likely to panic and kill in a rage," says Gloria.

"He do get ornery when he drinks, but killing his own flesh 'n' blood?" Billy shakes his head, expressing doubt.

"It's hard to believe her killer was in a rage," I say. "Drugs and gas aren't exactly spur-of-the-moment weapons."

Gloria acknowledges this with her eyebrows and a slight tip of her head.

"So you *do* think she was murdered," says Billy, his eyes tearing again. "Lordy Infant Jesus, rest her soul. She was a angel. Sweet angel from heaven. I used to lie in bed ever' night and thank the Lord for the gift of my Lana and our two little girls. My three angels. Now they's only one of 'em left on God's green earth."

Gloria and I exchange a glance and give him a moment to drown his sorrow with a long swig of cold Bud. Gloria shows a hint of her lip-curled smile, and her freckled eyes appear empathetic, but I know she's a leopard in the bush, measuring her prey before making her move. Billy grabs a Kleenex from the coffee table and blows his nose. Dropping the dirty Kleenex in an empty ashtray, he sits back again and does one of those long slow yoga exhalations.

"What about Sophia?" Gloria continues. "I understand the girls hadn't gotten along for a while."

"I couldn't say one way or t'other how they got along. They never seed each other. But Sofie's a sweet girl."

"What happened between them?"

"Reckon it's my bad. After Lana died I kinda lost myself like ever'body does, you know, gettin' liquored up, high on weed, shootin' smack. I reckon y'all know all about it. From the tabloids, I mean."

"I only read them occasionally," Gloria says, which is an understatement. She's in the habit of dropping by the market on her way home every day, unless she's got plans to eat out. She claims it's because her schedule is too unpredictable to do a weekly shopping, but I suspect it's because she needs that time in the checkout line to read about celebrity two-headed babies. Not that there's anything wrong with that. The 'bloids pay a healthy chunk of my income.

"Well, let's just say that my brain was in the 'off' position for a decade or so," says Billy. "Forgive me, Jesus. It was hard on them girls."

Billy lifts his longneck to pour some beer into his mouth without lifting his head from the sofa. I marvel at a man who can find refreshment in a morning brewski. I can't imagine imbibing before brunch time.

"How do you mean?" asks Gloria.

"Like this one time," he says, his eyes staring at the hanging disco ball as if it were a window to the past. "Ginger stoled Sofie's diary, and I caught her readin' it? She was, I don't know, fifteen? Sixteen? So I took Ginger's diary from where it was tucked up under her pilla? And figurin' an eye for an eye, I read it out loud at the dinner table while Ginger set there sobbin' her eyes out. Lord forgive me, I spewed her most private secrets out on that stained checkered tablecloth. And wouldn't you know, Sofie picked them secrets up like little switchblade party favors and passed 'em out at school. Poor Ginger comed home in tears ever' day for weeks, and it was all my fuckin' doin'."

Just when he seems to be getting maudlin, he shifts gears and asks, "You know them eighty-nine-dollar Japanese haircut scissors they sell on TV for nineteen ninety-five with a second pair for free?"

I nod unconvincingly, not sure where this infomercial is going. He turns his gaze to Gloria without moving his head. I can see the mirrored ball reflected in his eyes.

"Well, one night, Ginger took one of them scissors and just up and stabbed Sofie right in the back. Punctured a fuckin' lung."

TWENTY-FOUR

The first thing I notice is Scuba Barbie. She hangs from the overhead light on a piece of monofilament in her matching hot-pink mask, fins, shorty wetsuit, and dual tanks. Billy Kidd turns on the light, and Barbie casts a large shadow. Batman without the cape.

"Will ya look at the tits on that thang?" says Billy. "Lord have mercy. No wonder she needs two fuckin' tanks. Always wondered if Ginger'd took to Raggedy Ann instead of Slut Barbie if maybe she'da found some churchier line of work."

Ginger's room, about fifteen feet square, feels like a little girl's fantasy, frozen in time perhaps fifty years ago, long before she was even born. A menagerie of stuffed animals inhabits the canopied bed, surrounding an enormous Winnie the Pooh. Beside the bed is a vanity with a large oval mirror framed by fairy lights. The opposite side of the room has floor-to-ceiling shelves, half of them filled with dolls while the rest hold a diverse selection of children's books and young-adult romance novels.

The walls are painted pale yellow and topped by a press-on border of princesses and heroines from early Disney films—Sleeping Beauty, Snow White, Cinderella, Alice in Wonderland, Tinker Bell. I try to picture Ginger, the princess of interactive porn, inhabiting this space. Maybe in some episode of *The Twilight Zone.*

How could the woman who slept in this child's sanctum of innocence be a digital nymphomaniac? The neurotic child of rock stars, torn between two completely disparate personalities, two polar-opposite fantasy worlds. It's as if she'd boarded the train to multiple personality, but got off one stop shy, which may explain the stack of self-help books on the bottom of her night-stand. Topping the stack is *Toxic Parents*, an abuse primer I used last year for background on a matricide story. I wonder which of Ginger's parents prompted her to buy it.

"This room is not what I expected," I say.

"No shit," says Billy. "As the Lord is my witness, she'da sucked dung from a mule before she'da chucked one of these goddamn dolls. There weren't no changin' Gingerworld, no how, no way. Coulda walked in on her twelfth fuckin' birthday, woulda looked just the same, praise Jesus."

After questioning Billy, Gloria goes out to spot-check the neighbors who weren't home when LAPD canvassed earlier. Billy offers to show me Ginger's room while I wait for Gloria to get back.

"Files are yonder," he says, pointing to a cardboard banker's box under an Early American-style desk, once natural knotty pine now painted white with yellow trim.

I pull out the box and flip off the top to see stacks of files. Ginger's taxes, trust papers, investment reports, and bank state-ments. The police have already gone through them without find-ing anything of interest. I pull a few random files and take a look. As my ex-wife will readily attest, I'm no financial whiz, but I'm hoping something will jump out at me.

Billy rummages distractedly through Ginger's catchall drawer. There's a ziplock bag half-filled with change, some old barrettes, a cell-phone charger, some matchbooks, a few lipstick tubes. He holds up an eyebrow pencil.

"We had a gig in Hollywood once, left Lana's stepmom, Lynette, to sit the girls. Ole gal catched her a migraine, went and took her a sleeper, called Nate to take over. By the time we gets home, she done passed out, and Nate has them girls painted all up in raccoon eyes and hooker-red lipstick like some trailer trash on a Saturday night. Lana went right off, bitch-slapped ole Nate right on his ass." He laughs at the memory. "Fucker didn't know what hit him."

I find a journal of trust allocations signed by Cogswell. I wonder how much of the money was actually spent according to its allocation. Was that really a bedroom remodel for Ginger or did Cogswell remodel his kitchen? Camping gear for a school trip or leather pants for Billy? A winter coat or a couple grams of cocaine? New braces or new golf clubs?

The prospect of digging this all out depresses me. If there's one kind of research I hate, it's financial. The checking and cross-checking and cross-cross-checking makes me cross-cross-eyed. I decide to turn the task over to Melody.

"This could take a while," I say. "Mind if I take these home?"

"Whatever greases your mule. Want a brew?"

I'd prefer to get home, but he looks like he could use some company. "Sure."

I grab the banker's box and follow him upstairs. He pops open a couple Heine longnecks and hands me one. The financial records sit by the door. He could have refused to give me access without arousing suspicion, but he didn't hesitate. Does that mean he's got nothing to hide? Or does it mean he's already gone through them to remove anything incriminating?

It takes a great deal of skill to cover the tracks of embezzlement. My father was a CPA, a seasoned auditor and a good one, and he couldn't do it. So how could Billy? He was so bad with money that Lana wouldn't even let him administer his own daughters' trusts. That's why she hired Cogswell. A successful embezzler needs to be methodical, a knack Billy can't even pronounce. Cogswell, on the other hand, embodies it.

"Do you think Cogswell skimmed from the trusts?" I ask.

"Fuckin' A. Money don't just disappear on trees. Ain't nobody else except that scumbucket la'er."

His drawl makes it impossible to tell whether he's saying "lawyer" or "liar," but in this context it doesn't make much difference. He seals his lips around his longneck and upends it, draining half the bottle.

"He even contested the will. Tried to get me throwed out as guardian of my own lovin' daughters. Wanted Nate to do it. So I got me my own la'er to go after his God-damned thievin' ass. Fucker had him a paper trail tighter'n a second facelift."

"Why do you think he contested the will? Was he plotting with Nathaniel?"

"I doubt it. Lana had her a clause in there sayin' anybody what contested was flat cut out."

"But she wouldn't leave anything to Nathaniel anyway, would she?"

"She hated his belly for shieldin' his guts, that's a God-given fact. But she put Nate in her will just the same, just to make sure he didn't contest, I reckon. Ain't much. Hundred bucks a month. But it was enough to keep his trap shut."

"You'd think he could have made a lot more than that by hooking up with Cogswell," I say.

"They plays golf, but they ain't tight. I reckon Nate cheats and Cogswell don't like it, but Nate's always making sucker bets so Cogswell keeps him around for chump change."

"Then why try to give him guardianship of the girls?"

"I expect Cogswell had some kind of dirt on him."

Billy upends his bottle and finishes it off.

I take my second sip. "Blackmail?"

"Somethin' what give him power," he says. "If Cogswell coulda got Nate watchin' the money 'stead of me, he coulda skimmed off without needin' to go to the trouble of bush-sweepin' his tracks. Thank Jesus he lost the case, not that he didn't manage to drain them accounts anyways."

Billy opens Ginger's jewelry box and absently pokes through it. He holds up a string of pearls and looks at it in the light.

"Any idea what Cogswell might have had over Nate?"

"I'd lay money on that little pussy tail got him booted from Yale. I 'spect Nate's daddy paid her off to keep the boy's ass out of slam."

He drops the pearls back in the box and does some more index-finger prospecting.

"I heard about that. Some townie girl?"

"Not just any townie. She was his history teacher's young'n."

Alarm bells ring in my head. "How young?"

"Polanski young. Twelve? Thirteen? Nate was supposed to be babysittin' her at the time."

Billy lifts a gold half-heart pendant from the Ginger's jewelry box. Just like the one Lana wore when she was shot.

TWENTY-FIVE

Gloria sits at her desk, trying to remove a broken hinge screw from her sunglasses with a letter opener, the wrong tool for the job. This does nothing to improve her mood, which was forged this morning by water she discovered on her kitchen floor. She traced it to a drainpipe behind her sink that had been slowly leaking for weeks, ruining the subflooring beneath her cabinets and infusing the walls with the smell of rotting tuna and rancid fat. Gloria is not happy.

I sit in the visitor's chair, reading aloud from an inventory of Ginger's garbage.

"Five days' worth of newspapers—nothing clipped, no sections missing—pizza box, grocery receipt from the Canyon Store. That's that little neighborhood market halfway up—"

"I know where it is," she interrupts. "What's on the receipt?"

The faint blue print on the register tape is hard to read in the dingy light of the office. I hold it at arm's length. "Dry salami, cheddar cheese, eggs, Slim Jim, apples, Tampax, and beer. Twenty-nine seventy-six."

"Tampax must have put a crimp in Ginger's act," she says.

"Junk mail, coat hanger, dry-cleaner bag, buckie-note pad, gray with purple type, nineteen left."

"What's a buckie-note pad?"

"I don't know."

She grabs the phone and punches an extension. "What's a buckie-note pad?"

I can hear Dump's gruff voice coming through the receiver, but I can't make out his words.

"I know it's a pad of buckie notes," she says. "What the fuck's a buckie note?"

After a moment she hangs up. "It's like a memo pad with her name on every sheet, only the paper's stiffer, like thin cardboard."

"How the hell did Dumphy know that?"

She shrugs.

"You know what else bugs me?" I say. "That pendant Lana was wearing when she died. Ginger had one, too."

"So? They come in matched sets. Maybe it was the mate."

"That was my first thought. But this one was exactly like Lana's, with an outie in the center. The mate would have an innie there."

"Since when do you even notice women's jewelry?"

"I always admire your handcuffs, don't I?"

"So they both had the same necklace. Maybe it was a party favor at a family wedding."

A civie volunteer pokes his head in the door. "Your witness is here, Lieutenant."

Gloria drops her glasses and her letter opener on the desk, grabs a case file, and nods for me to follow her down the hall to interview room A. At least that's what the cops call it. The interviewees usually call it an interrogation room.

"If she says anything that contradicts something you've learned, text me," she says.

"I can't," I reply.

"Why not?"

"The keys on my phone are too small to see the letters."

She sighs. "Then just call me."

I step into an observation room about the size of a closet to watch a video feed as Gloria enters room A to question Sophia.

"I don't understand why I have to go through this again," says Sophia with a glitch of panic in her voice.

"I'd like to hear your story myself," says Gloria. "A few things have cropped up since you spoke to Detective Dumphy."

"What sorts of things?"

"A few questions I hope you can answer. Is that okay?" Gloria speaks gently, comfortingly. An assassin impersonating a nursery school teacher.

Sophia nods unsurely.

"Do you mind if we tape this? I take lousy notes." Gloria indicates the video camera hanging from the ceiling in the corner.

Sophia probably knows that Gloria will replay her answers and find little bits and pieces—a stammered word, a misspoken thought—to dissect. Maybe run it through some piece of software that can analyze her voice modulations and pinpoint her lies. But she nods her assent as they always do.

"You okay? Want some water?" asks Gloria. She likes to butter up her victims before eating them alive.

"I'm fine, thanks."

"Okay. Tell me about your sister. It must have been a shock to find her body."

"Yes." Sophia looks down as if to rein in her grief, but it's a bad acting job.

"Can you tell me what happened, Ms. Kidd?" Gloria asks.

"Call me Sophia. 'Ms. Kidd' makes me feel like I'm in the principal's office."

"Why the principal's office? Did you do something wrong?" Gloria's voice turns chastening. She doesn't expect an answer. She just wants to shake Sophia up.

Gloria leans back in her chair, tipping back on two legs to appear more informal. She smiles and softens her voice. "Just kidding. Tell me what happened."

Gloria likes to conduct interviews this way, pushing then letting up. Like reeling in a big fish. Over and over. Never establishing a consistent rhythm or tone. Always keeping the interviewee off balance, nervous. Sophia was a witness when she walked in, but now, without any accusations, Gloria has her wondering if she's a suspect.

"I...I was knocking on the door," says Sophia, "and I thought I smelled gas. This man came to help, and we went around the side and saw her through the window. We broke in, but it was too late."

"Was this man someone you knew?"

"No. He was just walking by."

"What were you doing there?"

Sophia winces as if struck by a pang of grief. "She was my baby sister."

"I thought the two of you were estranged," says Gloria. "Hadn't spoken in twenty years."

"That's why I went over there. I wanted to apologize. I wanted to fix it between us."

"Sophia." Gloria looks hurt, insulted that Sophia might think she would believe such an unlikely story. "This will go a lot faster if you'll just tell the truth."

"I am telling the truth."

Gloria sits silently, letting Sophia stew in her own anxiety.

"Look," says Sophia. "I got a call from Nob Brown wanting to talk about my mother. He said he's spoken to Ginger and wanted to talk to me, too. It got me thinking about Ginger and how much I missed her. We used to be so close, I just thought...I don't know, maybe if we patched things up, we could get that back. Be sisters again. Be tight."

I wonder if my interview request really started this ball rolling.

"Okay," says Gloria. "So you just happened to go over there to talk to her for the first time in two decades on the day she just happened to decide to kill herself. And you just happened to be living with your ex-psychiatrist who just happened to be your sister's psychiatrist, too."

Sophia flares with indignation. "Ginger stopped seeing Karl years ago."

"Is that what Dr. Lynch told you?"

"It's true!"

"She was seeing him every Wednesday," says Gloria. "They had a session the day she died."

Sophia stares at Gloria, dumbstruck. After a moment a silent tear rolls down her face. Gloria pulls a Kleenex from the box on the table and offers it to her.

"How do you know?"

"We have both their appointment books and canceled checks."

Sophia wipes her eyes.

"Why would Dr. Lynch lie to you about seeing her?"

"I don't know."

Gloria makes a big show of appearing sympathetic. "Did he know you were going to her house?"

"Why are you asking me all this?" The indignant victim confronts the bully. "I mean, she killed herself; I happened to find her. What does my relationship with Karl have to do with anything?"

Sophia's exasperation is like blood in the water to Gloria. Emotional reactions breed thoughtless revelations.

"You're living with your sister's shrink. That's irregular. He's also your ex-shrink. Strike two. He lies to you about the fact that he's still treating her. Strike three. You find her body after not having seen her in two decades. We're into a whole new inning. A whole new ball game."

Sophia glares at Gloria with those gold-flecked eyes. "Look, am I under suspicion of something? Because it feels like you're accusing me of something. Maybe I should have a lawyer here."

Her words make Gloria smile gently. I can see Gloria's wheels turning. She needs to sweet-talk Sophia now, cool her down, do whatever it takes to avoid the intrusion of meddling legal counsel.

"You're not under suspicion of anything," she says. "I'm just trying to understand the big picture. You have to admit your story raises more questions than it answers. I need you to help me reconstruct what happened to your sister."

Now it's Sophia whose wheels I see turning. She's weighing pros and cons about admitting something, and I'm rooting for the pro side.

"You can start," says Gloria, "by telling me why Karl would lie to you about Ginger."

"When I was his patient I was dealing with jealousy issues, paranoid thoughts, things like that. Maybe he was trying to avoid putting me through that again. He's a very protective, intuitive man."

"If you thought he hadn't treated her in years, why not tell him you'd decided to see her again?"

Sophia lowers her head as if the answer to her dilemma is written on the edge of the table. They both sit still for a moment. I'm thirsty for a drink of water, but the tension's too tight to get it, even though there's a cooler just behind me. I don't want to turn away, even for a moment.

Sophia finally speaks. "I saw Ginger's name in his appointment book. She'd stopped seeing him a long time ago. She must have started again and he didn't tell me. I couldn't stop thinking about it; it just ate away at me."

"So you went over there to confront her."

"Not confront her, just talk to her. Stick my toe in the water and see how it felt. The thing that drove us apart, it seemed so long ago, so irrelevant now. The last thing I expected was it would turn into something like this."

Gloria goes back on the offensive. "So you thought there was some kind of hanky-panky going on between your boyfriend and your sister."

"I didn't say that! You don't even know him! Karl is meticulous about his ethics. He would never do *anything* like that with a client. Never!"

"And yet here you are, a former patient, living with him."

"You know something? Our personal life is none of your goddamn business. I didn't commit any crime. In fact, I didn't even *witness* a crime." She closes her eyes and exhales slowly, taking a moment to calm down. "I'd like to go home now."

Gloria stares at her for a moment then waves resignedly toward the door. I leave the viewing room and close the door behind me then pretend to be wandering down the hall when Gloria and Sophia exit the interrogation room.

"Sophia!" I feign surprise. "What are you doing here?"

"Why don't you ask your friend?" she says bitterly. She follows Gloria through the bullpen toward the exit. I tag along.

Dumphy is at his desk, taking a statement from the infamous Dr. Karl Lynch. Lynch looks our way, surprised to see Sophia.

"I didn't know you were going to be here," he says.

"I didn't know you were seeing her again," Sophia replies.

His face contorts into taut furrows of concern that connect his eyebrows as if someone had raked his forehead with a fork. "This is no place for a private conversation."

Sophia starts to answer, but Gloria cuts her off. "You must be Karl."

Lynch eyes Gloria warily. His anger is visceral. "It's 'Dr. Lynch.' Who are you?"

"Lieutenant Gloria Lopes. Robbery Homicide."

"Ginger committed suicide," says Lynch.

"Not until I say so. We still have a few loose ends to tie up."

"Such as?"

"Such as why your girlfriend went over there," says Dumphy.

"It's strictly verboten for a shrink to have any kind of relationship at all with a client outside of therapy, isn't that right, Karl?"

Lynch winces at the sound of his first name, having already upbraided her for using it. He's one of those long-torsoed guys who seem tall even when he's sitting. His waist is narrow, but his shoulders are huge and his neck is thick. Far from your head-doctor stereotype. This guy pumps some serious iron, and at the moment he looks like he wants to use some of that muscle to snap Gloria's neck.

"If you've got an accusation to make, just make it…*Gloria*."

Now it's Gloria's turn to bristle at the name game. "I'm assuming you weren't having a sexual relationship with the victim. Is that a safe assumption, *Doctor*?"

"I'm not going to sit here and let you insult me with your sordid insinuations."

"I'm just doing my job; I've got a dead woman on my hands. Any idea what she might have been depressed about?"

"I'm afraid that's confidential."

"She's dead, remember?"

"She still has a right to privacy."

"That's really just a formality, isn't it?

"Is that how you treat your own professional ethics, Lieutenant?"

Gloria gives the shrink an ironic smile.

Karl Lynch looks at Sophia. "Let's go home." To Gloria, "Unless you have some objection."

Gloria just glares as he stands. Lynch has to brush past her in the narrow aisle on their way out. While he tries to pivot to minimize contact, Gloria purposely braces her back foot and leans in, ensuring a solid bump. Real mature.

TWENTY-SIX

Boyle Heights isn't the nicest neighborhood in LA, and El Tepeyac isn't the most romantic restaurant in town, but I eat there with Gloria Lopes at least once a month, because Manuel's, as the regulars call it, has been serving the best burritos around for at least forty years. If we can't find a table we take lunch back to her place, which is fifteen minutes away if the freeway's moving. Once behind closed doors, Gloria loves to explore the erotic potential of guacamole.

The lot is full, so I park across the street and reach into the back seat to grab a couple Negra Modelos from my Styrofoam cooler. Manuel doesn't have a license.

Speeding cars and low visibility from the hill make it tight to cross Evergreen. Gloria and I have to trot. The line for indoor seating snakes down the sidewalk, so we head for the takeout window. There's a line there too, but it moves fast.

I order a machaca burrito slathered with a huge side of guacamole, a chili relleno burrito for Gloria, and some taquitos to share. Enough to clog the arteries of a family of six.

A few minutes later, our forearms bulging from the weight of our food, we find an empty table on the long narrow patio.

She crunches into a taquito and moans.

"You ever hear Billy Kidd in concert?" As I say it, I feel guacamole on my lip and grab it with my tongue like a frog snatching a fly.

She shakes her head. "The Brothers were before my time."

Gloria's only a year younger than I am, so she's handing me a straight line. I resist the invitation. Gotta love her for it, though.

"He had monster chops until Lana kicked him out of the band."

"And the house," says Gloria. "In one fell swoop she took his marriage, his family, his house, and his job."

I empathize with Billy as I imagine losing my own house to Holly.

"Then two weeks later she's dead," I say. "Billy moves back into the house with his girls and gets his old job back. From the gutter to the spotlight in one easy step."

There's a thin line of sweat on Gloria's upper lip, like a clear pencil mustache. The chili relleno is beginning to get to her. Gloria wipes her lips with a paper napkin that shrinks into a sodden lump of sauce and sweat. She drops it on her tray and takes another to lay across her lap. I swallow some beer.

"You think he did it?" she asks.

"Maybe. But there's no evidence."

"What about powder burns?" She cracks into another taquito. A piece of shell falls on her lap. She retrieves it and sticks her tongue out to lick at the salt before eating it. I stare at her tongue with a pang of regret that we'd found a table instead of going back to her place.

"He tested negative, but he could have been wearing gloves."

"Alibi?"

"Home alone. Watching soap operas with the sound off and practicing his scales."

She cuts into her burrito and eats the filling without the tortilla.

"Any neighbors hear him practicing?"

"It was the middle of the afternoon. They were all at work."

"Good motive, no alibi," she says.

"You can't convict him with that."

"Nope." She pokes her fork around in the flaccid carcass of her chili relleno, looking for something to spear.

"Sophia thinks Ginger killed Lana," I say.

"Sibling rivalry?"

"Ginger liked Nathaniel Strain for it."

"The slut fingered her own grandfather?"

"She wasn't a slut, she was an exhibitionist," I reply, intending to defend her but not quite pulling it off.

"I stand corrected. You know what happens to boys who try to correct me, don't you?"

"Don't tell me."

She takes a sip of beer then looks me in the eye and licks foam off her lips. Nice and slow. I actually salivate. We men are such simple creatures.

"These chilies are making me hot. Do we have time for a quickie at my place?" She does that lip-curl smile.

"We have to be out in Chatsworth in an hour," I say, reminding her that she'd agreed to let me go with her since it was my lead she was following up.

Her smile fades. Gloria does not handle disappointment well, especially when she's horny and there's guacamole to be had.

"Look on the bright side," I say. "We're going to a porn studio. Maybe you'll get lucky."

TWENTY-SEVEN

She looks half-black, half-Chinese, close to seven feet tall, hands bound behind her back by a red rope that's wrapped around her twiggy limbs and naked torso like a boa constrictor then tied in a spiderweb configuration around her head, securing a rubber ball in her mouth. The end of the rope is hooked taut to the ceiling, forcing her to stand in what must be painful patent-leather boots, a bizarre cross between toe shoes and spike heels. The boots have eight-inch heels running parallel to their toes, so she's virtually standing on pointe.

They're called ballet boots and are designed to limit mobility for bondage and discipline submissives, or "subs." I know this because Gloria once shopped for a pair and took me along. Not that she spent the two hundred clams to buy them, or that she'd ever suffer to wear them, but she made me take a cell-phone picture to send to her dentist friend, suggesting he might buy a pair for himself.

The dominatrix is about half as tall as the black Chinese sub and thrice her girth. The dom's body is stuffed and cinched into a red latex corset like a lumpy knockwurst, her pendulous breasts hanging loose past her navel with silver studs shaped like Milk-Bones piercing her nipples. She's swinging a whip across her sub's reddened ass. I fail to see what's arousing about this, but that's just me.

The dungeon is brightly lit to allow for better video from the three hi-def cameras. Behind the cameras is a cheap banquet table set up with a platter of Costco turkey pinwheel sandwiches, some chips, a basket of fruit, assorted cookies, and an ice chest blooming with vitamin waters and Diet Green Tea with Ginseng. Over the table a hand-lettered sign reads "Craft Services," a misspelling of "crafts service" that's ubiquitous in Hollywood.

"Hungry?" asks Manny, manager of the Kocibey-owned video facility, not to be confused with the production manager of the videos themselves, whom we've come to see. Manny is square-faced, white-haired, fat, smells like an ashtray and wheezes like a prime candidate for a lung transplant, especially when he walks. He didn't give us his last name.

"I wouldn't touch a thing on that table without IV antibiotics," says Gloria with her usual tact.

I've been thinking about snagging a chip until she says this. Despite the filth that they shoot here, the place seems spic-and-span, and the food looks fresh.

The air—smoke-free and heavily conditioned—is filled with the moans and groans of female pleasure or some imitation thereof, but the dungeon is the only set we can see into as we pass through the studio.

Manny leads us down a hallway crammed with industrial steel shelves, bar-coded and overloaded with the kinds of DVDs that sully the fine art of punning. *Blue Jizzman, The Hunger Games: Snatch on Fire, Rise of the Plumbing of the Apes, XXX-Men, Pacific Rimmer*—you get the picture. The sort of wit you'd expect to find on a middle school boys' restroom wall. More DVDs are piled on the floor.

"All dead discs," he says. "Everything's online these days."

At the end of the hall is a large room that looks out over the Simi Hills to the west of the Chatsworth sound-stage facility, where the live porn feeds occupy only a fraction of the brand-new, twenty-thousand-square-foot Fun with Dick and Jane studio. The room's ceiling slants from one story at the back to almost three at the front, which is walled by large, square, steel-framed windows. It feels like a downtown loft, with a kitchen area against one wall, a walnut conference table in the center with sixteen Herman Miller Aeron chairs around it, and a half dozen Ikea workstations sprinkled around the periphery, each with a seating area for guests.

Manny points us to one of those areas, where a man who looks to be about thirty is poring over an Excel spreadsheet. He's got shoulder-length blond hair, light-brown eyes and looks tanned and fit except for a modest paunch that bulges against his purple polo shirt. He seems young to be managing a multimillion-dollar production slate.

"Sammy," says Manny. "Your three o'clock is here."

Sammy Robins turns to reveal a large strawberry birthmark down the left side of his face, roughly the shape of Italy. I note that he bears a strong resemblance to Manny. "Thanks," he says, then to me, as if hearing my thoughts, "Manny's my uncle. We try to keep it all in the family. But I suppose you already know that, being a detective and all."

"I'm the detective," says Gloria, stealing my thunder. "Lieutenant Gloria Lopes. Mr. Brown is working as a consultant on the case."

"My mistake," he says apologetically and actually seems sincere.

But Gloria doesn't let it go. "I guess you don't see many women around here with college educations."

Considering Gloria's effusive embrace of sexual freedom, I'm a bit surprised by the cattiness of her remark. But Sammy takes it in stride. He doesn't seem the type to be easily rattled.

"No offense, detective, but that's an awfully sexist assumption," he says. "A number of our actors are full-time students. One of them is working on a doctorate in psychology and another is a resident specializing in cardiology at UCLA. The girls I hire are sexually expressive by nature. That doesn't make them stupid, or even immoral. The problem with sex work is its social stigma, not the character of its workers."

"I guess the sex workers I see in my line of work are a different breed," says Gloria.

"I expect that would be true of lawbreakers in any line of work," he says.

This actually makes her smile. "Touché."

"But you didn't come here to discuss social mores. Welcome to the new and improved Dick and Jane."

"Business must be good."

"It's horrible, considering all the adult entertainment you can get free on the Internet. But we're planning to leverage our expertise into cable video romance novels."

He motions for us to make ourselves comfortable, and we take advantage, sitting in perfect unison, a miniature drill team.

"So what can I do to help our friends at LAPD?" he asks.

"We're looking into the death of Ginger Strain," says Gloria. "How well did you know her?"

Sammy's face falls into a mournful expression for a moment then morphs into slight annoyance.

"If by 'well' you're asking if we had a sexual thing," he says, "the answer is, do I look like an idiot? Rule number one in the HR handbook: you don't sleep with people you supervise. That's a harassment suit waiting to happen, even in this business. She walked in the door on time. I paid her on time. She did her job. I did my job. She had no complaints. I had no complaints. At the end of the shift, she walked out the door. That was our relationship in toto."

"What about other employees?" asks Gloria. "There must have been someone here she was friends with. Hung out with by the water cooler? Maybe went out for a drink with after work?"

"A lot of the girls, they get lonely staring at the lens, they want a little human interaction, so they do doubles. It turns the job into a party."

Party? Ball gags, whips, and torture boots? Sure, Gloria's been known to get a bit crazy with her cuffs, and a little playful spanking is not out of the question. But even she sees the downside of pain and discomfort. No gagging, no humiliation, no misdirected bodily functions. I understand some people like being treated like shit but personally, I don't get it.

"Most of the girls enjoy working the doubles shows," he continues. "It's not so much sexual as it is social. It's play time, it's camaraderie. But Ginger wasn't into that. She always worked alone. She was one of our biggest draws with her dead-rock-star shtick, but she always rode solo. She didn't schmooze with the other actors, she didn't hang with the crew, she just did her work and went home. The only people she talked to were the ones who paid for the privilege."

"What about regulars?" asks Gloria. "Did she have any fans she might have agreed to see after hours?"

"Ginger wasn't the up close and personal type. She was a very shy person off set."

Sammy is leading us nowhere fast, so Gloria asks to talk to some of the other performers and crew members. Sammy summons Uncle Manny to introduce us around, asking only that we not pull anyone off set in the middle of a show. An hour later, we've covered most everyone there and learned nothing new. Everyone pretty much echoes Sammy's description of Ginger as a lone wolf.

Our last interview is with the black Chinese sub we saw on our way in. She is now untied and eating a Snickers in her bathrobe. Manny introduces her as Jenny Demilo.

"You like doing that?" I ask, nodding toward the dungeon. "Being tied up like that?"

"The boots kill my feet," she says, "but other than that, I love it. The nastier, the better. I guess I'm just a filthy cum slut at heart."

She says this with pride and gives me an inviting look that's about as subtle as a chaser-light arrow. I grapple with my inner prude as Gloria chuckles knowingly behind me.

"Enlighten me," I say. "What do you get out of being tortured and humiliated?"

"It conditions me," she says, "for doing my rounds with the attending physicians."

TWENTY-EIGHT

We find Dumphy in his usual spot at the Qat Haus bar trying to impress a twiggy, freckled blonde from Facilities Management with his ability to shoot Wild Turkey from a highball glass without using his hands. As we head to the bar, he's already got the glass in his teeth. He swings it up like a pelican swallowing a whole fish. The trick is to do it fast and smooth to avoid spilling up your nose or down your shirt. I give him a ten. It's a well-practiced skill that I'm proud to admit I've never mastered.

Gloria grabs his arm. "Come on, Casanova. You can woo the ladies later." She pulls him off his barstool, and he follows obediently. The babe from FM doesn't seem to care. She swivels around to talk to some other lush.

We settle into a booth and order a round.

"So what's the scoop on Karl Lynch?" asks Gloria.

"He's a real piece of work," says Dumphy. "Thinks his big pecs and fuckin' PhD let him walk on water."

"Does Jesus have an alibi?" I ask.

"Not much of one," he says, scratching a bright red scar on his forehead. It looks fresh, like a scab came off an hour ago. It's the kind of scar you tell people you got from walking into a door because you don't want to admit you fell on your face. "He claims he was home all night with Sophia. They had a fight, so he fuckin' slept downstairs. He says she would have heard him if he snuck out, but I don't fuckin' believe the fuckin' scumbag."

"What else did he have to say?" asks Gloria.

"A lot of bullshit about *his* business bein' none of *my* fuckin' business."

Dumphy's attention is caught by a small pantry moth buzzing his nostril. He swipes at it, and it darts away.

"Doc Lynch claims he was in a session with Ginger," says Dumphy, his tone implying that *session* is French for *orgy*. "They was in his office from four o'clock to four fifty. The asshole even used the term 'on the dot.' Exactly fifty minutes. Calls that a fuckin' hour. Oughta bust the fucker for fraud. No wonder Medicare's outta cash."

"Skip the commentary," says Gloria, "and just tell us what he said."

"I'm tellin' you it's bullshit. Fifty fuckin' minutes." Gloria starts to object, but he puts up his hand to quiet her. "Okay. Ofuckinkay. So he says she left at four fifty. 'On the dot.'" Dumphy can't help but baste the words in irony. "Says that was the last time he fuckin' saw her. Eighteen hours later, the sister finds the corpse."

The moth returns, circling the rim of Gloria's margarita. She shields the top of her glass with her hand, and it flits off.

"No other contact?" I ask. "Phone calls, texting, e-mail?"

"He said no. So I tell him his fuckin' answering service says at eleven fuckin' seventeen they called him and got his permission to pass through a call from fuckin' Ginger. Big fat Berkeley Med School degree, president of some big head doctor ass-ociation, and he's all of a sudden gettin' pinned to the fuckin' wall by a guy had to go through twelfth grade twice and still barely got outta high school." Dumphy chuckles at the memory. "It was fuckin' sweet."

"So what'd he say?" asks Gloria. She's putting a lot of effort into keeping him on track, as if the interview left him high on endorphins, and the Wild Turkey is just reinforcing it.

"Nothin'. He starts to fuckin' cough. Goes all red in the face then says he wants to see the call log; buys himself some fuckin' time to think. Then he looks up from the log, and all of a sudden it all comes the fuck back to him how she called, but he told her it was too late and to call back during fuckin' business hours. Eleven outta ten on the bullshit meter."

The waitress sets two shots of Wild Turkey in front of him. He grabs one in each hand and slugs them down in quick succession. I'm impressed with his hand-mouth coordination. He signals for another round. He must think Gloria's paying.

"You think he went over there?" asks Gloria.

"Fuckin' A," says Dumphy. "Ginger calls, his main squeeze gets fuckin' jealous. They fight, he goes downstairs to sleep in the fuckin' den. The squeeze goes nite-nite, he sneaks out to see the porn star, calm her the fuck down, maybe get fuckin' lucky."

Two more shots arrive. He does the two-handed shuffle again.

"I gotta drain the gecko." Dumphy gets up and heads for the john.

"What do you think?" asks Gloria. She takes a sip of her drink, and a thin line of salt paints a line on her lower lip. She sucks her lip into her mouth, and it comes out clean.

"I think Karl looks good for it."

"Then the murder can't be connected to Lana's. Karl never met her."

"We all have bad hunches once in a while."

"You more than most." She can't resist a good setup.

"It all fits," I say. "Sophia goes to sleep, he jets out of there, goes over to Ginger's, finds her freaking out, realizes she's a threat to expose him. He goes into shrink mode, talks her down, tells her she needs to relax. She makes herself a nice cup of tea, he gives her a few pills to help her sleep and slips a few more in her tea to put her out."

"I hear the stuff's so bitter it makes you gag," says Gloria.

"That's what sugar is for. She drifts off. He wipes his prints off the teacup and anything else he's touched. He turns on the gas, closes the door, and goes home to his alibi. When Sophia gets up in the morning, she finds him asleep in the den, all cuddled up with his blankie."

TWENTY-NINE

I t's my mother's old-fashioned dial phone. It's pink. The numbers in the finger holes are worn out from decades of being dialed with the tips of pens and pencils. And it's ringing.

And ringing and ringing and ringing and ringing, but when I try to answer, it's just out of reach. I try to stretch, but it's just beyond my fingers. So frustrating.

The realization surfaces like the creature from the Black Lagoon: I'm asleep, and my cell is ringing. I squint in the dark at the glow of 1:53 on the screen. My ringtone is supposed to sound like an old-fashioned telephone, except it can't quite succeed with a quarter-inch speaker.

I swipe to answer. "What?" I drop the phone on the bed and pick it up again. By the time I get it to my ear he's in midsentence.

"...late, but I got me some gossip that's, uh...Oh, Lordy sweet Jesus, gonna make you cream your panties." I don't respond. I'm not sure what he wants, and I'm not sure I'm awake, and I'm not sure he's sober. "You comin' or what?"

"Okay."

I find Billy Kidd in a circular window booth overlooking Sunset Boulevard from the 24-7 restaurant at the Standard, the preferred hotel of ancient rock stars. It's the middle of the night, but the place is packed. Billy called from the Purple Lounge, where he was meeting an old friend for drinks, but the bar closed at two, so now they're here, having watermelon martinis and miso soup.

I must look like I feel because he says, "You look like you been rode hard and put up wet."

"I'm still waking up."

I recognize his friend from Ginger's funeral. She's wearing a tie-dyed earth-mother sundress under a tartan wool Pendleton shirt with the sleeves rolled up. Her unkempt, curly red hair has about an inch of gray roots showing. Billy calls my name as I approach, and the redhead stands to meet me. She looks fiftyish with lips too linear for her round face and a torso too thin for her broad hips. The whole package screams "frumpy" until she smiles. Her aquamarine eyes streamline from round to almond, her vague cheekbones become sharply defined, her narrow lips transform into a seductive bow that reveals perfect teeth, and even her pear-like shape seems to somehow deemphasize in the radiance of her spirit. It's an astonishing metamorphosis.

Billy introduces her as Claudine Hugo.

"Pleasure," I say.

"Ze plezaire is mine," Her sexy French accent completes the demolition of my first impression.

"Take a load off," says Billy. "Martini?"

I slide into the booth. "Coffee's fine, thanks."

"Suit yourself." He signals a passing waitress, and I place my order.

"We was just talkin' up the old days," Billy says. "Sweet Lordy, I've known Claudine what? Thirty years? Forty years?"

"Sirty-one. We met on ze Berlin tour, remember?"

"Oh, yeah. Damn Wall was still up. Lana hired Claudine as a personal assistant, stole her straightaway from Stevie Nicks. Man, was Stevie pissed. Still holds a grudge, if you can believe 'at. Jesus in heaven have mercy."

"I understand you and Lana were close," I say.

"Until ze day she died."

"They was best friends, man. Why in God's name you think I hauled your ass outta bed?"

"That was going to be my first question, but I got sidetracked."

"Do I look like the kinda jerkoff trusts cops? I'm betting on you to crack this thang. I want the sumbitch caught, man."

"Okay." My coffee comes, but it's too hot to drink.

"So we was in the lounge and Claudine tells me this fuckin' shit, and I figure it might be sump'in. So here y'are."

"What shit?"

"It seems that dear sweet fuckin' Lana, Lord forgive me, was having a goddamn affair on me 'fore she died, may she requiescat in pace."

I've never heard Latin spoken with a Kentucky twang before. Maybe that's how the Romans sounded.

"I sought he knew," says Claudine, "or I would not have told him."

"I thought everybody knew," I say. "It was in all the papers. The guy from Sticky White."

"Sticky White?" Billy barks a laugh. "That butt plug Vern Senzimmer weren't no affair, that was just a couple party fucks with a boy toy. Sticky White never even cut a album. I didn't give a shit about that. Even Baby Jesus knows that's just life on the road. There's only so many lays a body can turn down when they's offered up like handshakes. Lana called 'em sump pumps, praise Jesus. But what Claudine's talkin' at is an affaaaaaair, a relaaaaaationship. A thang that lasts longer'n a weekend with feelings that last longer'n a hard-on."

"Until she tossed him out like a stale baguette," Claudine notes. "He was very upset."

"Who was the guy?"

"The same scum-suckin' shit hole, forgive me Lord, what tried to kick me out of my own house after Lana died."

I have no idea who he's referring to. It must show on my face because Claudine fills in the blank.

"It was zat lawyer."

Billy nods. "Gary Fuckin' Cogswell."

I feel snakes constricting my stomach. The consigliere is back.

THIRTY

I walk into the barbecue joint, the only non-Ethiopian restaurant within two blocks, and ask for a menu. The old black man behind the counter has a rich mat of hair the color of cotton and a scraggly beard to match. He hands me a well-thumbed cardboard folio. I open it to discover more than forty-five ales from all over the world. Shocked is an understatement. I'd been considering an iced coffee but not anymore.

"You misspelled 'triple,'" I say as I read about the Allagash Curieux, a tripel ale aged in Jim Beam barrels.

"That's the way it's spelled, son," he says. "That means it's brewed in a style developed in 1934 at the Trappist abbey in Westmalle, Belgium."

I feel like an idiot. Not for my ignorance, but for my underestimation of the man. My embarrassment must be obvious. "Don't fret," he says. "It's a common mistake."

"I'll take one," I say. "With a shot of forgiveness on the side."

He chuckles as he grabs a bottle from the cold case behind him.

I don't know what this modest smoke shack is doing with such an exotic beer list, but I'm up to my ears in unexplained questions, so I don't put any effort into finding out.

I grab a table by the window and stare across and down the street at the Odessa Social Club. I take a sip of the tripel. The rich bourbon flavor is a perfect complement to the thick golden ale. Sadly, I won't be able to drink the whole thing, because it's got more than twice as much alcohol as a Guinness, and I need to stay alert.

I'm in the lull between lunch and dinner, so no one cares how long I sit, but at some point someone's going to wonder, so I pull a paperback from my pocket and lay it open on the table in front of me. I don't actually read it, but every few minutes I turn a page.

I used to take interview transcripts on stakeouts, but I once got so absorbed in my reading I missed a guy with a guitar case going into the Vietnamese manicure parlor I was watching. I only realized my mistake when I heard the gunfire. Not that I could have prevented the three shootings, but I might have been able to call 911 twenty seconds earlier, maybe saved a life. So now I bring along *The Bridges of Madison County* to eliminate the possibility of getting caught up in the text.

I'm on my fifth page flip when I see Big Ugly Guy leave the club and head away from me down the street.

I pull a picture of Cogswell from the back pages of my book to remind myself what he looks like, then slip it back in there. Cogswell is apparently camera shy. Melody had to spend an entire day looking before she finally dug up an old newspaper photo of Vlad the Impaler leaving a courthouse with Cogswell at his side. He's a short, thick guy, not fat but sort of oval shaped, pasty, sixtyish. His face looks like it's molded from dough. No cheekbones, no hard edges, lots of sag. It's a black-and-white, so I can't tell what color his eyes are, but his hair is either blond or gray, straight, and fine. I asked Jack Angel about Cogswell's eye color in the pool this morning, but before he could answer he had to take off on a fifty-meter butterfly sprint. I waited my five seconds then took off in his wake. When I got back to the wall, we were both too out of breath to talk. By the end of the workout the question had slipped my mind.

I order a pulled-pork sandwich to pass the time, and I pay up so I'll be ready to leave when I need to.

Ten minutes later a skinny black guy I've never seen before walks into the club.

My food arrives dressed with an outstanding East Carolina vinegar sauce on both the smoked pork and the cabbage slaw that comes with it. Reminds me of when Holly took me to Durham to meet her parents about six weeks after we'd started living together. We went to a Bulls game, and she made me wear her red lace panties for luck. The Bulls lost anyway, but I got lucky that night after her folks turned in. Those were great times.

The black guy leaves the club seventeen minutes after he entered.

Another hour passes. I order an iced coffee but hold onto my half-finished beer and half-eaten sandwich. At some point I'm going to have to relinquish my perch and return to my car, but a guy in a car looks conspicuous, so I'm putting it off as long as I can.

My coffee comes. I keep flipping pages.

As early-bird dinnertime approaches, the old man comes around to ask if there's anything else he can get me. I tell him no, I'm still working on my sandwich, which is something of a stretch after ninety minutes. He asks if I'd like it reheated, but I tell him I'm fine. He obviously wants to reclaim my table, but the place is still empty except for a few people who've come and gone for takeout, so I figure I've got at least another half hour before I cost him any money. As luck would have it, I don't need the time.

Less than ten minutes later, a new, silver BMW 750Li pulls up across the street. A short blond man gets out. He's facing the club so I can't see his face, but the limp, the egg shape, and the hundred-thousand-dollar ride are dead giveaways. I can't believe my luck. Less than three hours of waiting, and I hit pay dirt. I watch Gary Cogswell hobble into the Odessa and try to imagine what it would feel like to dive off a fourth-floor balcony besotted with Cuervo.

I gobble down the rest of my sandwich, cold but still good, and take one last sip of the Curieux, warm but still good. I reluctantly abandon the rest of the beer, wave to the old man, and head out through the sweet-smelling hickory haze of his converted oil-drum smoker on the sidewalk.

My car is parked on the opposite side of the street from Cogswell's, which means I'm facing the wrong direction. I drive down the street and hang a U, then pull into the curb about three-quarters of a block behind the BMW.

I don't wait long. Cogswell leaves the club about twenty minutes later. I follow him up Highland, past the Hollywood Bowl, and onto the Hollywood Freeway.

As soon as we hit the freeway our progress slows. I tail him at 10 mph past Universal Studios toward the Valley through the Cahuenga Pass, where the Second Battle of Cahuenga was fought in 1845, pretty much sealing California's independence from Mexico. On one hillside there were three small cannons and just two on the opposite hill. Both sides ran out of ammunition and had to resort to recycling the balls lobbed at them by the other. The characters in this drama are remembered only as street names today—Pico, Alvarado, Micheltorena—but back then, they battled to the death. At least to the death of one horse and one mule. A hundred and fifty years later someone dumped a headless cabby in the pass, which is when I learned its history.

Cogswell unexpectedly slides over two lanes to the right at the freeway interchange, shaking me out of my reverie. He's switching from the Hollywood North to the Ventura West or, as we say in LA, he's "transitioning." Only in California can they make a freeway maneuver sound like a lifestyle choice.

I have to move fast to stay on his tail. I flick on my turn signal, but cars are bumper to bumper, and no one's letting me in. I lean on my horn and push my nose into the next lane, wedging into the few feet between an old Ford Fairlane and a new Accord. The Accord jams on his brakes, and I see him mouthing profanities, but he chooses to drop back rather than smash into my fender. I pull a similar move to slip over one more lane and illegally zip across the painted road divider. Completing my rude transition, I cut off a Ram-tough Dodge truck to muscle my way into the flow about a half dozen cars behind Cogswell.

I pray he didn't make his sudden freeway shift in order to spot a tail because if he did, I just blew my cover. Amateur time. I should have been riding the outside lane, just to broaden my options in case he decided to do exactly what he just did. I'm starting to doubt the wisdom of that tripel ale, even if I did leave half of it behind.

I take a few deep breaths to slow down my pulse and track Cogswell's driving for signs that he's seen me. So far, so good. No sudden acceleration, no darting in and out of traffic, no swerving down an off-ramp. He's just tooling along. Maybe I got lucky. Maybe he wasn't trolling for tails. Maybe he just forgot where he was going for a minute.

Cogswell leads me off the freeway at Hayvenhurst and weaves northwest into the flats of Encino where the well-heeled homeowners trade the views of the hills for lots that are deep enough to accommodate swimming pools, tennis courts, and guesthouses. On a street I'll never be able to afford to live on, Cogswell pulls into his driveway, and an electric gate rolls open. A motion-sensing video camera swivels to watch the gate close behind him, and a brace of sizable Doberman pinschers trot after his Beamer into a six-car garage.

I drive about a hundred feet past his house and make a right turn onto another street I'll never live on. Then I turn around, drive back toward the corner to park facing his street, just close enough to the corner to be able to see his driveway.

I grab my trusty SLR and take a few snaps of the place.

As day turns to dusk I see lights go on in various rooms at various times in the house. A few cars pass on the quiet street, but no one stops at Cogswell's. The street is unlit, which makes my job that much easier since I don't have to worry about being conspicuous. I just have to worry about staying awake.

Like much of the architecture in LA, Cogswell's house is faux Spanish Colonial—exterior stuccoed to give it a whitewashed adobe facade, windows and doorways arched, and the pitched roof rippled with terra-cotta tile.

The sprawling two-story house is aglow in security lights, making it stand out against the darkening night like a stage set. I can see smoke coming out of one of five chimneys, even though it's ninety degrees out. I'm sure Cogswell's idea of warming the hearth is to hit a wall-switched igniter, fire up the gas logs, and turn up the AC. The guy must have a carbon footprint the size of Godzilla. Though I shouldn't talk. I've got my engine running to power the air while I wait. Maybe I'll buy some carbon credits.

About half past eight a red Thunderbird—one of those retro jobs they tricked out for the fiftieth anniversary—pulls up with a tall woman at the wheel. The motion-controlled security lights snap on, and I take a few shots with the Nikon. She punches a code on the security keypad to open the gate, so I know she's no casual visitor, but she parks on the drive, not in one of the two empty garage spots, so she probably doesn't live in the house. At least not full time.

She throws open the car door a little too hard, and it bounces back. She puts her arm out to keep it from closing on her. Then a pair of long lovely legs swivels out of the driver's seat. Even from a hundred yards away I think I recognize those gams. Then the rest of her gets out of the car, confirming my conjecture. It's the statuesque star of *Cheeks Asunder*. What the hell is she doing here?

She fiddles with her keychain and finds the right key. I take one last snapshot as porn entrepreneur Jane Porter unlocks Cogswell's front door and disappears inside.

THIRTY-ONE

Over the next three hours I've got plenty of time to ruminate. I know Gary Cogswell was having more than a casual fling with Lana Strain while he was working on her will. I know that just before she was killed she broke up with him and that it hit him hard. I know he holds an executive-level position with Russian mobster Vlad Bakatin. I know the Russian Mafia is heavily invested in the $12-billion-a-year San Fernando Valley porn industry. I know Cogswell appears to be shacking up with a porn heavyweight. I know Ginger generated hundreds of thousands of dollars, if not millions, for Fun with Dick and Jane Productions and was irreplaceable. I know someone murdered Lana twenty years ago, and someone murdered Ginger last week. I know that someone absconded with the bulk of Lana's estate, and the likely culprit is Cogswell.

A lot of facts but no through line.

My phone beeps. A text message. I have a love-hate relationship with those things. It's okay to get them, but a pain to send them. Maybe if I didn't know how to touch-type, it wouldn't be so bad, or maybe if my phone had bigger keys. I can read the numbers all right, but I need glasses to read the letters. Drives me nuts when people use words instead of digits for their phone numbers. 1-800-Dentist. 1-800-Flowers. 1-800-Fuck You.

I flip open my phone to see a message from Gloria: "no gc trail." I.e., no traces of calls, e-mails, IMs, PMs, or tweets to or from Gary Cogswell in Ginger's phone or digital records. If Ginger had stumbled onto some evidence that Cogswell had embezzled from her, she might have tried to contact him to demand her money back. If she hadn't called him, but somehow he found out she was onto him, he might have tried to contact her to threaten or deny. But the police found no evidence of any contact.

Without contact, it seems unlikely that Cogswell killed Ginger to stop her from revealing irregularities in his handling of her inheritance. I don't count it out, but it slides toward the bottom of my probability chart.

I turn on the radio to see if there's a Dodgers game on. There isn't. I pick up my dad's old Zeiss opera glasses. I found them in the glove compartment of his car when they hauled it out of the ravine after he killed himself in what my mother still calls "the accident." I slip the strap around my neck, as he taught me always to do, and focus on Cogswell's house. There's nothing to see. There's nothing but stillness outside the house, and all the windows are either shaded, draped, or dark.

I'm bored. I call my mother.

"Nenad! What a surprise!" She's the only person on earth who calls me by my given name. It's apparently Serbian or Croatian for "unexpected." Since neither side of my family hails from the Balkans, I have no idea how my parents came up with it, but I suspect my birth wasn't part of their master plan.

"How are you?" I ask.

"I'm doing fine for a sixty-six-year-old widow with ulcers, arthritis, cataracts, and a weak heart who lives alone and never hears from her son."

I picture her in a paisley polyester blouse and purple capris, clashing with the floral-print sofa she's sitting on in front of the TV. She's watching either Hallmark or the History Channel with a cigarette in her mouth and her bulbous feet propped up on the Queen Anne coffee table. I can hear the jangle of her junior high school charm bracelet and can picture her nervously twisting it back and forth on her left wrist. It's a habit she's had as long as I can remember, but she can only do it when her hands are free. That means she's not knitting or doing the crossword.

"What are you watching?" I ask.

"What do you care?" she replies. "Does it make any difference? Holly calls more than you." My ex-wife has lunch with my mother every Friday like clockwork. The two of them share a special bond: their disappointment in me. Their standing date helps keep that bond alive.

"Just trying to make conversation."

"I worry about you."

"I do, too, Ma. What do you hear from Teddy?"

"You mean my son with the job?"

"Yeah. That one."

Teddy is my younger brother who I talk to about once a year. My mom speaks to him every Sunday, ten a.m., but I doubt he does much speaking back. Though he teaches astrobiology, he doesn't communicate with earthlings very well. Between the two of us, Ma's pretty much given up on grandkids.

"I spoke to him Sunday. He's doing fine."

"Oh yeah? What's he up to?"

"You know. The same."

In other words, she has no idea. It amazes me that he can teach when, in my experience, he can barely string a sentence together.

"And what about you, Ma? Anything new?"

The motion detector lights go on in Cogswell's compound just as she starts telling me about some Gilbert and Sullivan singalong she went to with her friend Edna Keppler, who she's known since college when they both volunteered for Eugene McCarthy's 1968 presidential campaign.

Cogswell's gate slides open, and the red T-bird rolls out. Chances are, Cogswell's in for the evening, so I figure I'll stick to Jane, see if she's got any more surprises up her sleeve. I crank up the engine and cradle the phone to keep track of my mother's voice. When she stops talking I say uh-huh, and she starts up again. I feel conspicuous, as if driving with a phone to my ear is a full-blown felony.

"You should have heard "Tit-Willow." It was absolutely heartbreaking!"

I pass under Cogswell's security lights and pray he's not looking out the window. I keep my headlights off so Jane doesn't see me fall in behind her but when she turns at Ventura, I flick them on. In boulevard traffic she won't notice.

I slip into an easy tail. Jane's a civilian; no reason why she'd know how to spot me, even if she thought to look. I keep my eye out for cops because of the cell phone. Gloria would ride me no end if I lost a tail because I was pulled over by the Bluetooth patrol.

I tune back into my mother's monologue about Gilbert and Sullivan. "When Gilbert was two, he was actually captured by a gang of Italian brigands and was held for twenty-five pounds ransom. And that's where the *Pirates of Penzance* came from! Can you imagine?"

"Uh-huh."

Jane leads me up to Mulholland, where I promptly lose my mom along with my cell signal. I'm guessing she'll rave about the major general's song for another ten minutes before she realizes I'm gone. I drop the cell in my shirt pocket and breathe a sigh of relief.

We wind along the ridge of the Santa Monica Mountains, glimpsing breathtaking views before Jane drops down into Benedict Canyon. At Sunset she heads east past the ever-pink Beverly Hills Hotel and the mansions that once reigned over a glorious boulevard before it became a virtual highway.

At the few lonely skyscrapers that separate Beverly Hills from the Sunset Strip, the T-bird makes the hairpin left at Doheny Road then an immediate right onto Sunset Hills Road. At the top of the hill she turns into a steep driveway, goes up the drive about fifty feet, then pulls into her carport, where I can't see her anymore. I have no choice but to keep driving past so she doesn't spot me.

I park down the street and sneak back on foot. She lives in a modern house near the bottom of a long drive that snakes a quarter mile up the hill before disappearing behind some trees. It's as if Jane's house is the guard booth for the mansion up above. A guard booth worth about three mil. The house is studded with terrazzo terraces overlooking the city.

No lights go on. No sounds of doors opening or closing. No footsteps. Something's wrong. I take a step onto the driveway, and my footfall echoes between the retaining walls that flank it. I take off my shoes and climb the hill in my socks. I'm panting by the time I reach the carport. The T-bird purrs from the radiator fan and makes little clicks from the contractions of cooling steel.

I hear something and turn to see a faint glint coming at me from the shadows. Jane's Rolex? Then I see the writing branded into the wood and feel like Paul Bunyan just split my forehead. As my world fades to black I wonder, *What is it with porn babes and baseball bats?*

THIRTY-TWO

Blinding light, blurry ceiling panels, pain. I'm alive.

My head feels like it's being rhythmically whacked with a ball-peen hammer. I guess that's an improvement over Paul Bunyan's ax.

My thoughts are as slurred as a skid mark in mud. It takes a minute for my eyes to adjust to the glare of the overhead light, but when they do I see a guy in a sharkskin excuse for a suit that even I wouldn't wear. Must be a cop. The suit is dog-shit brown to match his beady eyes. His black hair is slicked straight back from a widow's peak so sharp that it looks fake, like someone painted an arrowhead on his scalp with high-gloss enamel. He looks familiar, but I can't place him.

"Can you hear me, Brown?"

"No." I giggle. Must be on painkillers.

The cop turns around and speaks to someone behind him. "You didn't tell me he's a comedian."

Gloria steps into my blurry field of vision beside him.

"You're lucky she swung for your head," she says. "Anywhere else, she could have done some damage."

"Just what I feel: lucky." I giggle again. Painkillers, definitely. Whatever they're pumping into my veins, I like it. I wonder what the pain would feel like without it. "How'd I get here?"

"She called 911 after she recognized you," says the cheap suit.

"Vajayna?"

"Good remembering," he says. "I take it you're familiar with her work?"

"What makes you think that?"

"Maybe you're a fan."

The statement is pointedly accusatory. This guy is making my drugs wear off. "Who the hell is this guy?" I ask Gloria.

"Touchy, aren't we?" he says. "Need more painkillers?"

"Will they make you go away?"

"His name's John Mepham," says Gloria. "Deputy DA."

Now I remember. He was the guy whose name I couldn't peg at Ginger's memorial, standing with Dumphy.

"I hear you got big feet," I say.

He ignores the remark. "You have anything you want to tell us that pertains to a homicide, Brown?"

"What's this have to do with homicide?" I ask Gloria. "Case you haven't noticed, I'm still alive."

Gloria takes up the questioning. "Why were you trying to sneak up on this Jane Porter, or Vajayna, or whatever the fuck her name is?"

"I was tailing her. Researching a story. It's part of my job."

"Not very good at it, are you?" Mepham couldn't resist.

I'm struggling to focus through the haze. "Is there some point to this?"

"Got a report to file, Nob," says Gloria. "Just tell us what happened so we can get out of here."

"I got assaulted with a bat. If I'm not mistaken, in Criminology 101 they call that 'the victim.'" I try to raise my arms to make little air quotes with my fingers, but I'm hit with a pain that even the drugs can't stop, so I let my inflection make the point.

"What were you doing there, jerkoff?" asks Mepham. Gloria lets a smile slip out, amused at his frustration.

In the movies, this is the moment when the journalist invokes the First Amendment and tells the DA to shove it. But, frankly, that would be a stupid thing to do. I've got no one to protect and no interest in jail time. On the other hand, it can't hurt to make the officious little shit earn his salary, so I don't say anything.

"She said you came to her office," says Gloria, "and tried to bully her into letting you talk to Ginger."

"Bully her?"

"Now you're stalking her, and Ginger's dead," says Mepham. "That makes you a likely, you ask me."

All of a sudden the psychotropic effects of the drugs are wearing off at about Mach ten.

"That makes you an asshole, you ask me," I say. No more giggling.

"How 'bout you tell us why you killed Ginger, smart guy."

"How 'bout I talk to my lawyer."

Gloria pipes in, "How 'bout you jerkwads both whip out your dicks, and I'll measure 'em." That shuts us both up.

Gloria nods Mepham out the door. He isn't happy about it, but he leaves.

"I talked to Jane," she says. "She's nervous about this whole situation. She doesn't want this in the papers."

"I'd be nervous, too, if I almost beheaded an unarmed, innocent guy."

"What innocent guy? You made threats and got kicked out of her office. Then you stalked her. You took your shoes off to sneak up on her, for Christ's sake."

"So what is that? Assault with a deadly toe jam?"

She's not amused. "How about criminal threatening, harassment, intimidation, stalking, and trespassing?"

I acknowledge the idiocy of my actions with my eyebrows. "What'd Jane tell the DA?"

"You know I couldn't tell you that if she'd said anything, but she played the emotionally distraught damsel. Refused to give a statement until she had time to recover from the shock. What about you? You distraught, too?"

"I want to talk to Jane about it before I decide."

Gloria laughs. "Sure, Nob. It's common practice for us to get the victim and the stalker together so they can work out a deal before going to trial."

"Get with the program, Gloria. It's in everyone's interest for Jane and me to agree that this whole thing was an unfortunate accident and no crime was committed. Nobody wants this to go to court. Jane doesn't want her neighbors to find out she's a porn queen. I don't want to publicize my ineptitude. Neither one of us wants the legal fees or the pain in the ass. And whether the DA decides to prosecute her for assault or me for stalking, they're going to have a piss-poor case without cooperating witnesses. So how do you suggest we play it?"

Nobody's under arrest at the moment, so Gloria and I both know there's no legal reason why I can't have a conversation with Jane. But we also know that if Gloria facilitates a powwow, the DA's going to use one of his seven-hundred-dollar Bruno Magli wingtips to give her a sphincter exam.

"You're on drugs, Nob. You're not thinking clearly. I'm telling you: do not talk to Jane." Gloria pulls a small notebook out of her purse and leafs through it. "If you do, and this goes to trial, which Mepham is aching to do, by the way, it'll look like you tried to intimidate the witness. You might as well just hand your balls to Mepham right now." She finds what she's looking for and copies it onto a napkin. "I am dead serious, you dumb shit."

She reaches out to grab my dick through the sheets and gives it a conspiratorial squeeze. "Stay away from Jane," she says, enunciating each word like a sentence unto itself. Then she walks out.

I take a look at the napkin. It's Jane's cell number.

THIRTY-THREE

'm too drugged to read, and the only TV station that works is in the middle of a twelve-hour *Bonanza* marathon. I'm reduced to watching the activity in the hallway, wishing some nurse would ramp up the action by dropping a tray.

All the patients who walk by have to clasp their gowns about them to avoid flashing the staff. It boggles the mind that these opened-back rags with their confounding string belts have not been redesigned since they were invented for the amusement of the guards in some fourteenth-century French lunatic asylum.

The gown I'm wearing has a missing belt, presumably ripped off by a frustrated patient. The worn material sports tiny red snowflakes that look like chicken pox. I'm itching to get home.

Melody sweeps into the room looking every inch the pixie. "Sorry I'm late," she says. "I had a hassle at the nurses' station with your release paperwork. You're not very popular with the staff around here."

I shrug. It hurts my head. "Just get me the hell out of here."

"They're still working on the paperwork," she says with a froth in her voice that implies it could take a year or two. "But I've got something to help you pass the time."

She hands me a manila envelope, already opened. The return address is a spoiler. Lana Strain's probate records have finally arrived from the county.

"I take it you read them already," I say.

"Good guess. They're pretty straightforward," she says as she opens the cheap fiberboard closet and takes my clothes off a coat hanger. "Billy got half as community property, she left a pittance to her father and the rest to her daughters in two identical trusts."

"Trusts?" I'm no lawyer, but I know enough to be confused. "I thought if you had a trust, you don't have to go through probate."

"You don't. Unless someone contests the will." She lays my clothes across my legs on the bed then starts to twist her torso back and forth almost all the way around.

"Cogswell." He pops up yet again. All of a sudden the blended stench of cleaning fluids and body fluids threatens to unleash the contents of my stomach. I try breathing through my mouth, but I feel like I'm inhaling toxins.

"According to Cogswell's deposition," she says, "Lana wanted to have Billy deemed an unfit parent and make Nathaniel Strain the girls' legal guardian, but she died before she could sign the papers."

"That would have given Gramps a virtual license to skim."

"The legal guardian can't get to any money unless the executor releases it. So Nathaniel would have had a pretty hard time looting the estate without Cogswell's cooperation."

"As far as I know, they never even met before the reading of the will, so why would Cogswell contest the will?"

"Why don't you ask him?" She's joking, but I'm already thinking about doing just that. I wonder what he'd do if I just went to his house and rang the bell.

———◆———

It's dark by the time Melody gets me home. I take the steps slowly.

Once ensconced in my fake Eames, I pull the napkin out of my pocket to call Jane on the land line. She answers on the first ring. Must have her Bluetooth in.

"It's Nob Brown. We need to talk."

"Why's that?"

"Because the police have their procedures, and if we don't handle this right, someone's going to get charged with something, and we'll both wind up in court and in the headlines."

She's silent for a moment and when she speaks there's a lot of mistrust in her voice. "And just how do you suggest we handle it?"

"That's what we need to talk about."

Another silence. Of all things to think about, I wonder what she's wearing.

"I'd want my lawyer there," she says.

"That's up to you."

"And we meet in my office."

"That's fine. But I'll need more than two minutes this time."

We set up a meet for the morning.

I go to bed early. I'm exhausted but I can't sleep. I'm too hyped about the meeting. Jane Porter insisted that it be in her office, on her turf. I wonder why. I have to assume the place is bugged, whether it is or not. Considering her profession, it's probably videoed.

What if I incriminate myself for some crime with nuances I don't understand, like conspiracy to evade justice or intimidate a witness or something? A conspiracy charge can be more serious than the crime you're accused of conspiring to cover up. Maybe I should bring a lawyer, too. I'm going to need someone to drive me over there anyway, since the doctor said I can't drive for a few days. I call Jack Angel.

"What do you want now, Nob?" The magic of caller ID.

"Hi, Angel. You busy tomorrow morning?"

"Why would I be busy tomorrow morning? Do I seem like the kind of guy who works sixty-hour weeks as a partner in a major law firm, serves on two corporate boards, does two days of pro bono work every month, swims four workouts a week, and tries to find time to see his wife and kids once in a while?"

"Good. Because I need you to come to a meeting with my assailant, the porn queen."

He lets a big sigh gust past those refrigerator-white teeth of his.

"You'll enjoy it," I say. "I'm hoping she'll bring your pal Cogswell."

THIRTY-FOUR

Early next morning, I log into Facebook to discover that Kate Dreyfus, who went to Beverly with Boom-Boom Laphroig, wants to friend me at Melody's suggestion. I accept then check my chat icon, but she's not online.

I check her profile and find some comments from a group composed of her high school graduating class. I click through to the group, and there's her senior class picture. Boom-Boom is big and black and hard to miss. I hover my cursor over her image and get lucky. Someone has tagged it with her real name. Josephine Barbeaux Laphroig. Looks like French-Scottish roots. I wonder if "Boom-Boom" came from Barbeaux.

I Google Josephine Laphroig and get a hit on a parenting blog. A young mother wrote gushingly about her five-year-old daughter being cured of an embarrassing stutter by a fabulous speech pathologist named Josephine B. Laphroig. I check the California Speech-Language Pathology and Audiology Board's website to verify her license and find that she's still in LA. She practices in the mid-Wilshire district. I call 411, and a robot gives me her office number. I've barely finished my first cup of coffee, and I've already accomplished something. The day is starting off well.

A little before nine, Angel's azure Jag XK rolls to a stop in front of the shredded sofa. He's wearing a natty navy-blue suit with shiny brass buttons.

"Who fragged the couch?" he asks.

"Runt." I realize I still have to call Sanitation to pick it up. I don't know how that keeps slipping my mind. "You ready for your law school reunion?"

"She's bringing a lawyer. That's doesn't mean it'll be Cogswell."

"We're going to hammer out a deal to lie to the DA. You really think she wants a legitimate lawyer involved?"

"I'll pretend you didn't say that."

There's surprisingly little traffic on the Ventura Freeway heading out to Chatsworth, so we're running early. We stop off at Brent's Deli for coffee. We grab an isolated table in the back. It's not until we're seated that I notice his brass buttons are embossed with little sea anchors. Uncharacteristically cheesy.

Our waitress looks like Dolly Parton might if she'd never had plastic surgery. Angel and I both order coffee and a side of rye toast. He's already eaten, and I'm not much for breakfast.

"So what's your game plan?" he asks.

"I'll figure that out when the ball's in play. I just want to get some face time with Cogswell. He's a hard guy to pin down."

"I'd be very careful about pulling his chain, or you might find it around your neck."

I know I should heed the warning, since Angel knows Cogswell well enough to know what he's capable of. But sometimes inquiring minds want to know a little too badly for their own good.

"I'll tread softly. His little invasion of my house has me on edge."

"You don't have any proof that he's the one who searched your house." Ever the lawyer.

"He's the only one who's got professional break-in artists on the payroll."

"Nathaniel Strain hires roughneck welders, and Billy Strain's got drug connections. Either of them could have easily found a rent-a-thief."

"Well, neither of them is going to be at this meeting, so let's focus on Cogswell, shall we?"

"This is not about Cogswell, it's about Jane Porter. This is not about your article, this is about keeping you out of court and potentially out of jail."

I nod to acknowledge my acquiescence, but we both know I don't mean it.

"Jane's obviously nervous about making a deal with you," he continues. "That's why she wants a lawyer there. I'm sure she doesn't want any media attention—it's bad for business—and there's a chance she could face charges if the DA doesn't think the assault was justified. On the other hand, she doesn't want to do anything illegal that may give you some sort of blackmail power. She's got to make sure you can't finger her for anything without going down yourself."

"Tell me something I don't already know."

"The capital of South Dakota is Pierre."

"I knew that."

"Did you know that it's the only mainland US state capital not located on or near an interstate highway?"

"You got me there."

———

At ten o'clock, Uncle Manny leads us to Jane's new office in the Chatsworth studio. In the anteroom, Jane's assistant, Robert, is watering the enormous potted fern that dominated the old office. He pops to attention as we walk in, dripping water on the new carpet, but he doesn't notice. He's wearing a black-and-white sweater-vest and black chinos today. Must be casual Friday at Fun with Dick and Jane, but Robert seems tense, the kind of tense you get when your boss is on edge. He eyeballs Angel like he's never seen a black man before.

The furniture is all the same and configured just as it was in the old digs, except in the spanking new office it looks more decrepit. Angel scans the DVD-cover art on the wall with a look of distaste, then turns his gaze to Robert, implying an unflattering association.

"Just go in," says Robert, in no mood for small talk today. He turns back to his plant and starts at the splatter on the carpet.

I do a little bow and extend my arm, inviting Angel to precede me into Jane's office. I want him to lead, just in case she's in the mood to take another swing.

We walk in to find Jane seated behind her desk beneath the *Cheeks Asunder* poster. The Sultana of Swat is wearing a pink sweat suit—no standing on ceremony for me. She's got a file on the desk in front of her with a buckie note on it. I don't recognize the name embossed on the note, but I'm proud of myself for remembering what it's called.

The place looks almost identical to the old one, except the view of the Simi Hills beats the hell out of the view of the self-storage joint on Van Nuys Boulevard. As with the reception area, they've simply moved in all the old furniture. No fancy upgrades for the porn queen.

Sitting beside Jane's desk, angled to look in our direction, making it clear that she's on Jane's team, is the closest thing I've ever seen to a female albino. She wears a bright-red, conservatively tailored knit suit on a trim frame. The red contrasts starkly with her pale skin like the stripes of a barber pole. She's in one of those ergonomic chairs whose base sprouts levers and looks like it could eject her if she were to hit the wrong one.

"Gentlemen?" She gestures toward two wannabe club chairs facing the desk. We sit without shaking hands. "I'm Hilda Priest, of counsel, Masaoka and Rosenstiel." The name on the buckie note.

I've always been wary of lawyers who claim to be "of counsel." It means they don't work at the firm, but they work for the firm. Legal guns for hire. Have tort, will travel. You wonder how much responsibility the firm will take for them when they fuck up.

"Jack Angel," says Angel, "representing Mr. Brown." I notice he doesn't ID his firm, showing a bit more respect for the impropriety of the meeting than did Ms. Albino.

Angel gives me a glance that I take to express empathy for my disappointment that Cogswell is not here. I had pretty much convinced myself that he would be, even though Jane never even hinted as much.

"I believe the ball is in your court, Mr. Brown," says Hilda.

"All right. We all know why we're here," I say, intending to avoid stating it explicitly.

"Why is that?" asks Jane.

I don't go for the bait. "Look, only you know what was going through your head when you assaulted me." I half expect Hilda Priest to jump up and object on the grounds that no assault by her client has been established. Too many middle-of-the-night *Damages* reruns. Priest says nothing, unnervingly happy to stipulate to my injury.

"As far as I could tell," I continue, measuring my words before letting them loose, "you didn't recognize me in the dark and mistakenly thought I was a prowler. You probably grabbed your bat, just to be safe. I don't think you meant to hurt me. In fact, I wouldn't be surprised if you slipped on the steep slope and struck me accidentally."

"Is that what you saw?" Jane asks.

"From my perspective, I saw nothing that would contradict that chain of events. But I was hoping you'd give me your perspective." I feel like I'm tiptoeing through a minefield and Angel's doing nothing to help.

"I've advised my client not to do that," says Hilda.

"You'd rather do it in court?" I ask.

"Are you trying to intimidate my client, Mr. Brown? Because if—" Jane silences her lawyer with a flash of her palm. The great white shark snaps her mouth shut. I can see the muscles of her jaw straining against her instinct to bite.

"Mr. Brown," says Jane. "I am frankly surprised at your interpretation of the events that brought us together today. Without detailing what happened, I will tell you that I was frightened that night. I knew I was being stalked."

"Because Cogswell spotted me on your tail and tipped you off?" A flare of surprise tweaks her eyes pretty close to the speed of light, but I see it anyway. It's all the confirmation I need.

"Because it was obvious, even to an amateur like myself. I saw you turn your lights on when you followed me onto Ventura Boulevard. One of them's out, by the way, which made you very easy to spot. Then, when I got home, you almost came to a stop when you cruised past the bottom of my driveway. It was clear that I was being followed by some rank amateur." The remark cuts to the quick. I make a mental note to fix my headlight.

"I grabbed the nearest weapon and waited to see whether you had the nerve to trespass. I get a lot of fans who see me act out a rape fantasy in a video and think it's real. They think it's what I like, what I want them to do to me. They think I want them to choke me or gag me while they rape me to make my orgasms more intense. That's the kind of person I'd expect to sneak up my driveway with his shoes off in the dark, Mr. Brown. That's who I thought I was protecting myself against. We take the threat of stalkers very seriously in my business. I don't think there's a jury on earth who would fault me for what I did under the circumstances."

"You have a lot more to lose than I do," I say. "No matter which one of us is charged—"

"That'll be you," says Hilda.

"That's a factual leap," says Angel, weighing in at last.

"It doesn't matter," I say. "Either way, if this winds up in court, it'll be all over the Internet and TV. I'll just come out looking like a green detective. It won't help my self-image, but it won't hurt my career. I'm not a private dick, I'm a writer. You, on the other hand, go from plain Jane to slutty Vajayna in the eyes of your neighbors, friends, relatives, and maybe even the IRS. Not to mention the fact that I'll have to reveal where I picked up your trail, which I'm sure won't make your boyfriend very happy."

Jane blanches, almost matching the pallor of her lawyer and confirming my suspicions.

"I can just see the headlines now," I conclude. "'Mobster's Porn Queen Girlfriend Attacks Ex-Cop Crime Writer.' That is every tabloid's wet dream."

"If this gets so much as a mention in the papers—" begins Hilda, but I cut her off.

"Hey, don't blame me for the Constitution. If this goes to court, it's public record."

"We get your drift," says Jane. "What do you want?"

"Two things. First, I know you've got privacy issues, but I want to compare the list of witnesses that the police interviewed during the Lana Strain murder investigation against your client list." Her nostrils flare in anger, but before she refuses outright, I sweeten the pot. "You don't have to let me see your records, just have your lawyer compare my list to yours and tell me if you get any matches."

"And second?" Her voice is unenthusiastic, but I get the feeling she'll go for number one if number two isn't too bad.

"I want some face time with your boyfriend."

Angel gives me a horrified look, like I've just ordered a strychnine gimlet, but Jane breaks into a smile.

"Sure, I can set up a little tête-à-tête with Gary," she says cheerfully. "But if you don't have major medical, you might want to pick some up before you meet."

THIRTY-FIVE

The porcelain teapot was already an antique in 1899 when Toulouse-Lautrec gave it to Boom-Boom Laphroig's great-grandmother before drinking himself into a sanatorium and dying at the grand old age of thirty-seven. It bears no maker's mark, but is hand painted with a red Greek geometric design around the top rim as well as the lid. It sits in a place of honor, alone on the top shelf of a built-in china nook in Boom-Boom's dining room.

"It's beautiful," I say.

"My mother told me he gave it to arrière-grand-mère as payment for a blow job. My great-grandmother was apparently famous for having the best in Montmartre."

"She was French?"

"Algerian." She takes the teapot off the shelf. "Something to drink?"

"I'm not much of a tea fan."

She laughs easily. "Don't be ridiculous. It's got a built-in strainer. Perfect for Martinis."

Boom-Boom pulls off the lid and tips the pot to show me that the inner wall has holes poked in it where the spout is attached, creating a filter so that you can steep loose tea in the pot and pour directly into a cup.

I check my watch to make sure it's after five. No problem. "A gentleman never lets a lady drink alone."

She walks into her kitchen, and I'm struck by the effortless grace with which she moves despite hips so broad that they almost don't clear the doorway. In her youth, Boom-Boom was wild, obese, and powerful. She was the sort of frenzied rock drummer you'd expect to smash right through the drumhead of her snare if her stool didn't collapse first. She's still big and powerful, but she must have lost a hundred pounds since she beat the skins for Lana Strain. Her frame is still imposing, but her padding is not nearly as thick. Her kinky hair, once Afroed out to the size of a basketball, is now pulled straight back, tight against her scalp, tied taut in a small bun. There's a touch of gray at her temples that she makes no effort to hide.

I watch her pull an ice tray from the freezer compartment of her small fridge. As she twists it out, I remember how Gloria couldn't catch a cube to save her life and wonder how Boom-Boom would do with my ice maker. Does it take some kind of advanced skills in hand-eye coordination like diving to catch a fly ball?

"My arrière-grand-mère would die all over again if she thought I wasn't putting her teapot to good use." She steps back into the dining room to grab some Gordon's gin from a small selection of bottles on a round metal Corona beer tray. She pours a lengthy splash into the pot.

Boom-Boom lives in a gray pseudocastle with fake turrets on Franklin in Los Feliz. Her small apartment is decorated with lots of textiles. The walls are covered in a pale-yellow feltlike fabric. Her couch is draped in colorful Mexican and Central American woven blankets, accented by African-print pillows. A hand-crafted shawl or afghan hangs over the back of every chair. And the floor is a patchwork of eclectic flea-market throw rugs. The stylistic discordance is surprisingly pleasing, exuding a mood of warmth, comfort, and diversity.

"You like it dry, I hope?" she asks.

"Parched."

She takes a bottle of vermouth, wets her fingertip, flicks a few drops into the gin, then covers the teapot and gives it a swirl.

She fills two martini glasses, plops an olive in each, and hands me one. We clink without toasting and each take a sip. It hits the spot.

"I'm not sure what I can tell you that hasn't been reported," she says.

"What do you know about Gary Cogswell?"

"Not too much. We rarely said more than hello and good-bye. I was just a fat-chick drummer as far as he was concerned. If you weren't a client, he didn't acknowledge your existence. Billy hated his guts."

"Why is that?"

She scratches her scalp, and a few flakes of dandruff snow onto her blouse. She brushes them off. "I don't know. Maybe because Lana slept with him. Billy didn't like her fucking people she knew."

I hand her some Xeroxed pages from Lana's journal. "Do you think she could have been referring to Cogswell here? She used a pseudonym."

Boom-Boom squints at the first page.

"Where'd you get these?"

"Billy Kidd," I lie. She seems to buy it.

She rummages in her purse for a pair of tortoiseshell readers, then scooches around to settle in on the couch. She starts reading out loud in a strong, deep voice.

"I thought about calling Hyde back but ate a whole bag of Oreos instead. Then I got depressed about the Oreos and barfed. Then got depressed about barfing and took a 'lude. Then got depressed about the 'ludes and took a nap. Woke up feeling better. Had scrambled eggs and watched *Jeopardy*. I'd like to fuck Alex Trebek."

She looks up with a grin. "Lana loved Alex Trebek." She goes back to the journal. "Hyde called five times today. He's getting on my nerves. He wanted to take the girls ice-skating. I finally told him to go fuck himself and hung up depressed."

"You'd think she's talking about someone whose name starts with H," she says.

"I don't think that was her system. For example, I'm pretty sure she called Ginger 'Kitty.'"

"For Kitty Foyle?"

"Who's that?"

"Lana loved classic movies. She named her girls after stars. Sophia for Sophia Loren, Ginger for Ginger Rogers. Ginger Rogers won an Oscar for playing Kitty Foyle."

She looks back at the pages with renewed curiosity.

"It's dated August fifteenth," she says. "What year was it?"

"Nineteen ninety-four. Just before she was killed."

Boom-Boom's eyes narrow in thought. She whispers the date, apparently trying to locate the memory. "I think that was the week we played the Greek Theater."

She resumes her reading.

"Went to the Pleasure Chest with Ducky and bought some toys. Always wanted to try a ball gag, but the one Ducky bought turned out to be flavored like Tang. Yuck. Got home exhausted. It took four shots of tequila to get the taste out of my mouth."

She looks up. "Ducky would be Vern Senzimmer," she says. "Put a condom on a boy toy you get a rubber ducky." She grins at some memory.

"I've been trying to track him down. He doesn't seem to be making music anymore."

You'd think with a name like Vern Senzimmer he'd be pretty easy to find, but I've scoured six search engines with no luck.

"He wasn't making much music back then either." She takes a sip of her martini. "Sticky White played the small clubs, but as far as I know, they never signed with a label." She returns to the text.

"Bozo got home late, and we fought as usual. We're leaving for a gig at the Cow Palace the day after tomorrow, so the girls will be on their own. I told Kitty about the Fillmore gig where

Bozo got the trots onstage and Gomer had to do a ten-minute bass solo while Bozo hit the shit house. Kitty got the hiccups from laughing."

"Bozo is Billy, Gomer is Don Patt," I say, as if it weren't apparent.

She continues. "Then Kitty went upstairs to crash, and Hyde tried to slide his disgusting hand up my crotch. I had to knee him in the balls and push him out the door on his ass."

"Does that sound like Cogswell?" I ask. "Did she ever talk about him pulling stunts like that?"

"Oh, yeah. She complained about him putting the make on her all the time, called him a dirty old man."

I had a repetitive fantasy in my teens about a concert at the Troubadour where Lana shows up to do a surprise walk-on. She starts singing "Go Down Hard" when her eyes find me in the crowd and lock there. She's singing just for me. When she leaves the stage, she wordlessly grabs my arm and pulls me back to her dressing room. She locks the door and, never taking those eyes off mine, yanks my belt open and slides it free. Then she throws it around my neck and drags me in for a torrid kiss that scorches my tongue. I'll spare the carnal details, but for the rest of the night she teaches me new, uninhibited ways to exult in the pleasures of the flesh. The thought of something even remotely like that happening to Cogswell makes me slightly nauseated.

"You lost me," I say. "You say she complained about him putting the moves on, but you told Billy they were having an affair."

"That was later. After he'd been working for her awhile. She never told me why she finally gave in, but I know it wasn't because she found him attractive."

"When was this?" I drain my glass.

"Around New Year's, I think. They were hot and heavy by Valentine's Day. I remember because Gary sent a dozen red roses, and she hid them from Billy."

She pours more gin into the teapot.

I do the math. "So the affair lasted a couple of months."

"That's about right." She swirls the teapot without even glancing at the vermouth and pours me another. She tops off her own. "Gary was not a happy camper when she ended it."

"And that was how long before she was shot?"

"I don't know. A month maybe?" She takes a sip.

"So in terms of timing, this Hyde character could have been Cogswell."

"I guess." She reaches up with both hands and scratches her head vigorously, as if her scalp were suddenly overrun with ants. A wayward flake of dandruff drifts across to the coffee table and settles on the surface of her drink.

"But she also wrote about Hyde wanting to take the girls ice-skating," I say. "That doesn't sound like Cogswell, does it?"

A little rain on the parade. She reconsiders.

"Gary barely knew the girls. Before Lana died, I doubt he could have even named them."

Boom-Boom lifts her glass and sees the floating flake. She closes her eyes and shoots the rest of her drink to get it over with, then notices I'm watching and gives me an impish grin. A little girl caught with her hand in the cookie jar.

Is Cogswell the guy she called Hyde? If so, he would have had a motive for killing Lana. Scorned lover turned obsessive. Could Cogswell have been the Asshole?

"Do you think Cogswell was still in love with Lana," I ask, "after she broke up with him?"

"Not likely. Lana's father told her Gary hated her."

"How would Nathaniel Strain know that?"

"How do you think Lana met Gary in the first place? He was at a party at Nate's house."

My glass stops halfway to my lips. "Nathaniel Strain and Gary Cogswell knew each other before Cogswell met Lana?" Visions of conspirators dance in my head.

"Are you kidding? Gary's older brother was Nate's roommate at Yale. Nate and Gary have been golf buddies for years. I'll bet they still play."

THIRTY-SIX

I guess Gary Cogswell is not as fond of reunions as his old friend and classmate Jack Angel, because I was told to come alone. And that's how I feel as I walk into the Odessa Social Club. Very alone.

I'm wearing the same old suit I had on when I met Vlad the Impaler, but this time I'm wearing a tie and leather shoes, and I spent thirteen fifty to have my suit cleaned and pressed. I was lucky to get a parking space just a few feet from the club because more than thirty seconds between my car and the door, and I'd be drenched in sweat.

It's the same time of day as it was the last time I was here, so the same stab of sunlight hits the back table at the same angle, only this time it spotlights Cogswell. He's sitting where Bakatin had been, minus the pirogies. Not even a glass of water. There's just a blank, white-linen cloth on the table in front of him. No setups, no salt, no pepper. The message is clear. He's not here to linger over lunch.

His face is the same kind of blank as the table. Cold. Unwelcoming. Unrevealing. He stares right at me. No games. No pretense. State my business and get out.

Big Ugly Guy and Bigger Ugly Guy stand up from opposite sides of the room, closing ranks to slam the castle gate. I get a sense of déjà vu and wonder if this move was choreographed. Maybe they have a practice session every morning. Maybe they rehearsed it before I walked in. They exude the stench of stale smoke, even through the tobacco cloud that fills the room. I can almost feel the pollution soak into my newly cleaned suit.

"Gentlemen, please," says Cogswell. He speaks in a soothing tone and so softly that he's hard to hear across the room, but his words hit the Ugly Twins like choke collars. It's a pretty impressive demonstration of power. The giant apes retreat to their respective posts, sliding open the human gate.

"I understand you want to talk to me," says Cogswell. He delivers his words just a notch above a whisper in a monotone that could put you to sleep. Luckily, I can depend on my nerves to keep me awake.

"You're a hard man to pin down."

"I don't like being pinned down." Beneath the poorly defined brow of that Mr. Potatohead face are two very sharp, very cold blue eyes. He waves at a chair. I sit like a well-trained dog.

"What can I do for you, Mr. Brown?" His affect is civilized, almost cordial. But all business. He strokes his tie, which I'm guessing is a $200 Ferragamo job, even though it's just a hemmed and pressed piece of machine-woven silk. His suit looks English, probably hand-tailored on Savile Row, some kind of lightweight wool, blue to coordinate with his eyes.

"I just wanted to ask you a few questions about Lana Strain. I'm working on a story."

"Mr. Bakatin mentioned that you described yourself as 'barely a writer.'" I've got to watch these offhand remarks. They come back to haunt me. "Why would you want to dig up an old-news story like hers?"

"It's the twenty-year anniversary of her death. It means a lot to her fans."

"Mr. Bakatin doesn't believe you. Neither do I. What are you really trying to uncover?"

"You think I'd be foolish enough to lie to Vlad Bakatin?"

"Don't patronize me, Mr. Brown."

"If I get lucky, I'll find out who killed her. That's a big story."

"The flip side of luck could be deadly."

"You get that from a Jackie Chan movie?" I know I should be more respectful. I won't learn anything by getting beaten and thrown out. But his emotionless monotone is getting to me.

"If I'm boring you, you're welcome to leave."

"I'm sorry. I'm a little edgy these days since someone broke into my house and smashed my unblended Scotch."

"Are you implying that I did that?"

"Of course not. But I wouldn't be surprised if you know who did."

"I know a great many things, Mr. Brown, most of which I have no interest in sharing. Ms. Porter did ask me to tell you, however, that her attorney found no matches between her subscription list and the Lana Strain witness list."

This doesn't surprise me. I knew it was a long shot. Especially since most of her subscribers probably use fake names.

"I understand you contested Lana Strain's will."

"That's a matter of public record."

"Why'd you do it?"

"As the fiduciary guardian of her daughters, it was my responsibility to look out for their interests. I shared Lana's concern that their father's lifestyle was inconsistent with the responsibilities of a legal guardian. When Lana was alive, she protected the girls from Billy. Without her, they'd be hapless victims of his prolonged absences, his emotional abuse, and his…lapses in pharmacological judgment."

Where does he get these phrases?

"Billy had two convictions for drug abuse. He was spending nine months of the year on the road. You had a willing grandfather—a friend of yours, I understand—ready to step in as guardian. There were plenty of people around who could testify to the emotional abuse. How did you lose?"

His face reveals nothing, but I can sense some invisible swelling of tension in the air around him, something on a molecular level that says he finds my question offensive.

"I'll tell you, Mr. Brown, but you will keep my name and that of my employer out of your story."

"I'm not sure I can do that. I don't know where this story will take me yet."

"I'll interpret that as a promise to do as I ask. And if some unfortunate soul were imprudent enough to break a promise to me, I would be inclined to turn the matter over to my associates for disposition."

He raises his finger about a half inch and the Uglies move at the speed of light, flanking both sides of me, snapping to attention with the precision of storm troopers. Very spry for their tonnage. Another impressive display.

"I'll keep that in mind."

His eyes search mine, as if seeking data to run through some sort of truthometer in his head. Then he drops his finger, and the goons recede into the background.

"The judge met with each girl in chambers," he says, "and asked for her opinion on the guardian issue. After speaking to Ginger, he ruled against us."

"She defended Billy?"

"Not exactly." He's not exactly forthcoming.

"Are you going to make me drag this story out of you word by word, or will you save us both some time and just tell me?"

He actually smiles. "After Lana died, Billy sent the girls into therapy. Ginger uncovered an alleged repressed memory."

"Alleged?"

"She made an unsubstantiated accusation."

"Okay, I'll bite. What was it?"

Cogswell closes his eyes and rubs them as if he's facing a difficult task, his first expression of anything bordering on emotion. Then he lowers his hands and reactivates his mask. "She said she'd been a victim of incest. She claimed it was Nathaniel Strain."

Bile rises in the back of my throat. For a moment I think I'm going to throw up. My mind travels back to that warehouse, watching Nathaniel Strain swing his head back and forth, eyes locked on that golf ball with such unwavering strength of will. I cringe at the thought of his turning that will to the task of molesting his younger granddaughter.

"How can you play golf with a guy, knowing he raped his teenage grandchild?"

"I'm not so sure he did. There were inconsistencies in her story. In fact, her sister accused her of lying about it. That's when Ginger stabbed Sophia with the scissors and the girls stopped speaking."

"What inconsistencies?"

"The allegations just didn't pass the sniff test. For example, a few weeks later she claimed to have been raped by her uncle as well. Billy's brother, now deceased."

"How do you know she wasn't?"

"Uncle Bobby was impotent. That's the kind of detail defense lawyers have wet dreams about."

"How well did you know her?"

"Jane asked as a personal favor that I see you for five minutes. I believe the sand has run out."

"Just one more—"

He raises his hand and cuts me off. Then his eyes ice up, and he says, "If I see you again, if you call me again, if I hear that you've been asking about me again, if you bother my lady friend again, or if you use my name or my employer's name in print, you will spend several excruciating hours praying for death before you are lucky enough to achieve it."

And I thought we were hitting it off.

I feel a hand in each armpit, and I'm lifted as if I weigh nothing. Then they launch me toward the door. I fly about ten feet and land hard. Both knees scrape through my favorite suit, leaving skin on the floor. I'm thinking if I had just listened to my wallet instead of my ego, I could have saved myself thirteen fifty on dry cleaning.

"Regards to Black Jack," he says, referring to Angel's law school nickname. As I limp toward the door, I marvel that such disparate men were once friends.

THIRTY-SEVEN

Gloria paints my left knee with 151 rum, the closest thing she's got to rubbing alcohol. I grimace.

"Don't be such a wuss," she says. "It's just a scrape, for Christ's sake."

"It hurts."

"Pain heightens the senses."

She's trying to sound tough, but I can hear the ache in her voice. When I hurt, she hurts. That's how close our connection is. Like Siamese twins.

We're sitting on the front steps of her Fairfax-district duplex, suffering the heat because I don't want to bleed on her carpet.

"Why are you home, anyway? Aren't you supposed to be solving crimes or something?"

"At one o'clock this morning, I got called out to a floater in Echo Park Lake, and by the time they'd gotten the scene under control, pulled him out of the water, and done the coroner bit, it was ten. So I'm taking the rest of the day off."

I'm glad she's free. It's not that my knees are so desperate for care, I just want a reality check on what I learned from Cogswell. In her private life, Gloria may not be on the most intimate terms with reality, but there's no one more clear-eyed when it comes to running evidence.

She dabs me with a little more firewater, and I cry out.

"Are you trying to turn me on?" she asks. "Because I'll spank you right here in public."

I glance across the street at the long-bearded Hasidic Jew who's sweating profusely in his black Prince Albert frock coat and black fedora. He waters a small patch of lawn and eyes us suspiciously. I glare back. Who is he to criticize me when he's breaking the law by watering midday. I wonder what passes for kosher food in jail.

She pours another splash of 151 on the wad of cotton gauze she found in her tiny cosmetics drawer.

When I was living with Holly, she used to need three five-foot shelves to hold the beauty supplies she didn't keep under the sink. Gloria makes do with a single foot-wide drawer. Pride is low on her list of deadly sins, lust being number one.

She hands me the bottle to hold as she carefully refolds the gauze to expose a blood-free surface. I take a belt for anesthetic purposes and almost gag as the rum scorches my throat. At more than 75 percent alcohol, the stuff is better suited to fueling aircraft than drinking. She swabs the other knee.

The pain takes me back to my childhood. Whenever I'd scrape a knee, my mother would sweep in like the Marquis de Sade, wielding some sort of unguent that felt like nails being driven into my flesh. The rum isn't as bad as the unguent, but it's no picnic. At least my throbbing knees are taking my mind off the impact bruise on my forehead.

Gloria seals the deal with a couple of Band-Aids and gives me a sweet little peck on the lips. "How about a little intentional pain?" She traces my fly with her fingers. I suspect she's doing it to embarrass the Hasid so he'll stop watching us. He frowns and turns away.

Sufficiently patched and somewhat apprehensive, I follow her inside. I'm wondering whether sex is such a good idea, but self-denial was never my strong suit.

At first I'm delighted to see Runt, but then he leaps up, and all ninety pounds of him slam into my chest. My head whacks the door, and my wound feels like it's been kicked by a mule wearing metal cleats. The pain bursts out in a primordial shriek. Gloria laughs. "You are such a pussy." She grabs Runt's collar and yanks him off me.

Gloria lives in a Spanish-style apartment built sometime in the nineteen-thirties. Not fancy, but it has the character of age, with handcrafted archways, thick stucco walls, and built-in cupboards and shelf-nooks whose edges have been softened over the years by dozens of layers of paint. Her selection of furniture is random, as if she has no patience for decorating. There's no consistency of style, whether it be antique, traditional, modern, postmodern, rustic, shabby, or Jetsonesque. No two chairs match or even come from the same decade. No two colors are purposely complementary. A ZZ Top poster in the style of an old pulp paperback shares the dining room wall with a reproduction of Breughel's *Parable of the Blind Leading the Blind* and a photo of Albert Einstein riding a bicycle. There's a well-worn Persian rug under the oak dining table and a bold asymmetrical Scandinavian rug under the glass-and-wrought-iron coffee table. A Mexican-tiled fireplace commands the living room. It would be a great-looking room if it weren't for the huge, stained, brown-plaid eyesore of a dog bed from Target.

In the place of honor above the mantel hangs a surrealistic oil painting of a sunset in an oven, a gift from the artist, who was saved from lethal injection when Gloria caught the actual perpetrator of the murder for which he'd been convicted. It's crooked. I walk over and straighten it.

"Don't," she says.

"Don't what?"

"Don't redecorate." She walks up to me, dead serious. "Or I'll have to truss you up and whip the cream out of you."

"Did your mother teach you to talk like that?"

She puts her arms around me and pushes her hands under my waistband, forcing my belt buckle into my stomach. She grabs my ass and hauls me into a kiss. Her mouth is warm and welcoming. Her tongue slides between my bottom teeth and my lips, but I feel it between my legs.

Then she steps back and, as only women do, crosses her arms in front of her to pull her blouse off over her head. Braless in black cargo shorts, Gloria looks fine. She grabs my head and pulls me to her nipple.

"Bite it."

I obey. As her breathing accelerates I feel her soft tongue spelunking my ear. An hour later and a gallon of sweat lighter, we lie slick and naked on the edge of the Scandinavian rug. The place smells like a locker room.

Runt snores on his bed, and I realize he's been right next to us the whole time. I can't believe he could have slept through the noise—Gloria can be very vocal. But if we disturbed him, he kept it to himself. Over the years he must have grown bored watching humans in their natural habitat.

Even in his sleep, Runt's tail wags. The metronomic precision reminds me of Nathaniel Strain's golf exercise.

"Do you think Ginger told the truth about Strain?" I ask.

"Incest victims rarely lie about that." Gloria isn't a bit fazed by the abrupt transition. Another trait we have in common. Even in the warmth of the afterglow, she's always up for dissecting a good murder. Holly used to hate it when I'd break the mood.

"Maybe she thought she was telling the truth," I say. "It's not all that tough for someone in a position of authority to plant a seed of doubt and feed it with psychotherapy. Before you know it, it's a real live memory. Look at the McMartin case, which Karl Lynch worked on, by the way."

"Why would Lynch do that?" she asks. "What's his motive?"

Her finger idly traces my abs. The two of us lying together feels good, it feels right, it feels comfortable. If we didn't know each other so well, I could imagine this going somewhere. But I suppress the fearsome thought. The power of our connection would kill us if we tried to define it as a relationship. Our intimacy is too strong for cohabitation. Confining it would be like living inside a pressure cooker, and we both know it. She rests her cheek on my chest.

"Let's assume everyone's after the money in the estate," I suggest. "In order to get it, you have to control the disbursement of funds. Disbursement requires two people: the executor to release the money and the girls' guardian to receive it. So, in order to steal any significant amount money, the guardian would have to be in league with the executor."

"Go on." She flicks her tongue across my nipple. Her mind is on the hypothesis, but her tongue has a mind of its own.

"If Nathaniel wanted a piece of the estate," I say, "he'd have to become either executor or guardian, so he'd have two choices: partner up with Cogswell to oust Billy or partner up with Billy to oust Cogswell. If I were Nathaniel, I'd try Cogswell because he's presumably less likely than the girls' father to care if they lose their inheritance."

"That could explain why Cogswell contested Lana's will, but where does Karl Lynch come in?"

"I'm getting there. Billy's not an idiot. When Cogswell tried to oust him as guardian he would have figured Nathaniel was behind it because that's the only way Cogswell could benefit. What better way to fight fire with fire than to discredit the old man? No court is going to allow custody of minors to an alleged incest aggressor."

Gloria laughs. "So Billy tried to bribe Karl Lynch to plant a memory in Ginger, hoping she'd publicly accuse her grandfather of incest? That's pretty farfetched, Nob, even for you." She checks the clock. "Shit. It's already three thirty." She jumps up and runs into the bathroom.

"Where are you going?"

"Got a date." I hear the shower turn on.

"A date?"

"Not that kind of a date."

I feel relieved. I wonder why. A minute later, the shower goes off, and she walks out of the bathroom toweling off, her hair still dry. I get up and grab my boxers from the floor.

"Okay. Maybe Billy didn't initiate the idea," I say. "What if Lynch did?"

She grabs a necklace that's lying on the coffee table and pulls it into position, turning her back to me, inviting me to clasp it. I do. She gives me a quick peck on the lips then heads into her bedroom.

"So door number two," she calls out, "you've got a psychiatrist suggesting to a patient's father, out of the blue, that they band together to plunder the girls' estate by manipulating her into believing she was molested by her own grandfather?"

She walks back into the living room in an unbuttoned, cream-colored blouse, zipping up a navy-blue skirt.

"Anything's possible."

"The guy's a psychiatrist, Nob. He stands to lose everything if he gets caught. And for what? The chance to *maybe* skim money he doesn't need from Lana's estate? It's just too loosey-goosey."

"Maybe Lynch had gambling debts and an aversion to shattered kneecaps." I can feel my logic stretching like taffy as I slip into my shoes.

She grabs a spray can of air freshener and sprays it around, adding an artificial lavender scent to the prevailing smells of sweat and Runt. The combination makes me queasy.

"You know that stuff is carcinogenic, right?"

"Spare me," she says. But she opens a window, admitting a hot breeze.

"Okay. What if it has nothing to do with the money or Nathaniel?" I ask. "Maybe it's just coincidental timing. Remember that matricide story I did last year? The fourteen-year-old pyromaniac who thought his mother was sleeping with his shrink so he killed her to keep them from talking about him in bed?"

Gloria shakes her head as she buttons her blouse. She's starting one buttonhole off, but I don't mention it.

"It's that Freudian thing," I say. "What's it called? Where the patient can't deal with the guilt over her sexual feelings for her father, so she transfers them to her therapist?"

"Let me guess: transference?"

"Right. Transference. The thing every therapist is taught to expect and trained how to deal with."

Gloria realizes her blouse is on lopsided. "Shit." She unbuttons and starts over.

"So here's Dr. Karl," I continue, despite the fact that her interest seems to be waning. "Middle-aged, handsome, but maybe not too social, hasn't gotten laid in a while, and he has to listen to this gorgeous young thing expose her most intimate thoughts, week after week. He watches her body slowly bloom into young womanhood, and as she shares her growing erotic desires, he becomes consumed with the fantasy of acting them out. She's a teenager, she's a client, she's taboo. But he's becoming obsessed."

Gloria slips into a stiletto sandal and puts her foot on the coffee table. "Lick it," she says.

I ignore the command but kneel down to strap her in. "She's in and out of therapy. After a few years, she's not jailbait anymore. The taboo shrinks, the obsession grows. Then one day she breaks down in therapy. He gives her a comforting hug. She looks up at him, cheeks flushed, wet with tears, yearning in her eyes. Transference kicks in and takes over. She pulls him into a kiss, and he can feel her heat, her lust, her defenselessness. His resistance crumbles."

"It's always the woman's fault." Gloria's sarcasm has the bite of a barracuda.

"She doesn't really want him. It's the transference talking. He knows it, but in the heat of passion he doesn't care. He has to have her."

Gloria switches feet and I strap up the other sandal as I continue to weave my theory.

"Then it's over. They're both flooded with shame, embarrassment, self-pity. Lynch knows he abused her trust; he essentially raped her. He tries to persuade her it was some sort of radical psychiatric technique, some bullshit mumbo-jumbo. Catharsis therapy, transference release, who knows? Then, to drive the point home, he makes her pay for the session."

Gloria scowls at this detail. "Only you would think of a touch like that."

"Just slipping into his shoes."

"Go on," she says. "I didn't mean to interrupt when you're on a roll."

"Ginger's a mess. She blames herself. She's humiliated, teary, emotionally charged. He worries that she'll break down and tell someone. He remembers how easy it was for him to create false memories during the McMartin case. He decides to give it a try on Ginger. He knows more about her than anyone. He knows how to push her buttons. And he knows she's had a troubled relationship with her grandfather. Nathaniel Strain is the perfect fall guy. If Lynch can make her think she was molested by her grandfather, it'll seed enough doubt and confusion to fog any future testimony she might give. Lynch brainwashes her into transferring her feelings of betrayal from himself to Nathaniel."

Gloria says good-bye to the sleeping Runt, opens the door, and leads me out.

"You've been watching too much TV," she says as she rummages in her purse for her key to lock the deadbolt.

"Yeah? Well watch this. It's ten, fifteen years later, and I start nosing around. Ginger has been repressing this stuff for two decades. But after a long hiatus, she's back in therapy. She brings up my visit, and maybe her denial cracks and the truth boils to the surface. She freaks. Lynch prescribes tranks. Later that night, she calls. She makes threats. He tells her to take a few pills to calm down, that he'll be right over. By the time he gets there, she's drowsy. He slips a few more pills in her tea when she's not looking, pockets the bottle, and waits for her to pass out."

Gloria walks to her car and opens the door but doesn't get in.

"Once she's unconscious, he wipes down the cup," I continue, "turns on the gas, and leaves. Mission accomplished."

Gloria lets this sink in for a moment then says, "You know? You're making sense for the first time since you bit my nipple."

THIRTY-EIGHT

The next day I meet Gloria at West Hollywood Park, where I leave my car so she won't have to take me all the way home. She's in no hurry today as we drive through a quaint neighborhood of small cottages built after WWII that now fetch more than a million bucks each. Lower-middle class no more. Shrewd planning and gay aesthetics have transformed the sleepy town into one of the hottest model communities in the country.

Gloria turns right at La Cienega.

"You gotta love a city that builds Restaurant Row on a street that's Spanish for swamp," I say.

No response. She's focused on weaving through traffic to slip into the left-turn lane at Melrose.

We pass Lucques restaurant in the former carriage house of silent film star Harold Lloyd. I remember the night Holly and I sat in the bar and shared a bottle of champagne and a grilled cheese and roasted shallot sandwich. We were so giddy with love that the chef sent over a complimentary chocolate tart with honeycomb. Holly broke off a piece and fed it to me. I licked the honey off her fingers and proposed.

I try to stuff the memory back into deep storage as Gloria finds a parking spot in front of a two-story Tudorish building. The lobby directory reads like a BMW dealer's mailing list: three architects, three designers, a dentist, an eBay philatelist and, of course, Dr. Karl Lynch, PhD, MD, a psychiatric corporation.

We walk into Lynch's reception area. An antique mahogany wall clock reads two forty-nine. Gloria sits down on a woven black leather chair, some sort of reproduction Bauhausy thing. I stay on my feet to check out a small but impressive collection of Yoruban fertility masks. I know what they are from a little brass plate on the wall, though I have no clue where in Africa Yoruba might be.

Dr. Karl's two o'clock patient will be leaving momentarily. As we'd hoped, there is no one waiting for his three o'clock. It's Wednesday, and he hasn't filled Ginger's slot yet.

At two-fifty on the dot the door opens, and Karl Lynch ushers out a mousy, brown-haired woman who, as she skitters for the exit, conspicuously avoids eye contact. Lynch, on the other hand, glares at Gloria. He's a study in grays with sharp-pressed charcoal slacks and an ash-gray cashmere cardigan that matches his eyes and hair. The brown shoes don't make it.

"What do you want?" he asks.

"Nice fertility masks," I say.

"I'm sure you're not here to admire the art."

"We'd like to ask you a few questions," says Gloria.

"I have nothing more to say to you."

"That's not your decision to make."

"I believe it is, unless you're planning to arrest me."

This is beginning to feel like a tennis match.

"This is not some petty crime," she says. "You're a material witness in a homicide investigation. You were the last person known to have seen the victim alive. You will answer my questions until such time as I'm satisfied."

"I'll call my lawyer then."

"You have every right. Tell him to meet us downtown in half an hour. If he's in court, I'll find you a suitable place to wait for as long as it takes him to get there." Something in her voice implies that the criteria for suitability do not include windows, freedom of movement, or even padding unless it's on the walls.

Dr. Karl ponders the choice between getting this over with here and now or calling his lawyer, canceling his afternoon patients, and chancing the accommodations downtown. It's a classic Gloria move: effective and probably unconstitutional.

As he considers, she hits a backhand smash to his ego. "Look, Dr. Lynch, if you're afraid that I'm going to beat you at some mental game, you don't have to worry. I just want to ask you about a few things we forgot to ask before."

He gives her the finger and turns into his office, but he leaves the door open for us to follow. "Make it quick," he says without looking back.

The place is painted in muted green hues, each wall a slightly different shade, probably named after plants like sage, moss, or split pea. I suspect some feng shui chose the colors for spiritual balance, but the place feels like bad karma anyway.

Lynch sits down in a forest-green leather chair with brass-nailhead-studded trim. It sits in front of his desk, facing what are apparently two client-seating alternatives: a wooden ladder-back chair and a crushed-suede sofa the color of creamy tomato soup. He picks up a leather folder and opens it to reveal a legal pad. I'm not sure if he's doing this out of habit or intending to take notes.

Gloria takes the ladder-back, sitting stiffly as if nailed to the rails. I take the sofa, wondering what Dr. Karl infers from a client's choice of one seat over the other. I assume such decisions are never random in the mind of a psychiatric corporation.

Lynch looks at me then turns his gaze to Gloria. "What's he doing here? He's not a cop."

"Mr. Brown is aiding in the investigation. He's extremely well versed in the details of the case. Is that a problem?"

He takes my measure and then shrugs. "I'd just as soon have a member of the press as a witness, I suppose. Might temper your abusive personality."

I'm flattered that he considers me a member of the press, but I keep my trap shut.

"Thanks for the free diagnosis," says Gloria. "Why don't you tell us how you got involved with the Strain-Kidd family?"

"I met Claudine Hugo in the mideighties," he says, "in a hot tub at Esalen. I was just starting out, and I'd gotten an opportunity to teach a seminar in somatic psychology there."

"Somatic psychology?"

"It's kind of Reichian. You wouldn't understand."

Gloria lets it pass. "Claudine introduced you to Lana Strain?"

"I never met Lana. She was there at the same time but for some sensory deprivation tank workshop. Claudine came to keep her company. Whenever Lana was in the isolation tank, Claudine would hit the hot tub. Our schedules coincided and we enjoyed each other's company, so we stayed in touch. After Lana's death, Billy was looking for a therapist for the girls, and Claudine gave him my number."

Gloria shifts in her chair then stiffens in a new position. I can tell that she finds it uncomfortable.

"You saw both girls?" she asks.

"Yes. It was a sort of family therapy, except Billy didn't come."

"How was it that they stopped talking to each other?"

"I can't discuss anything that pertains to our conversations in therapy."

She stiffens again. This time it's not the chair. "How is it that after they stopped speaking to each other you continued to see them separately? Isn't it a breach of ethics to see two members of the same family in individual therapy?"

"It was an unusual situation." He makes some sort of note on his pad. For his defense? "I was concerned that it could do irreparable harm to make one of them feel rejected at the expense of the other."

"You could have dropped them both."

"It was a critical time in their therapy."

"How long did you treat them?"

"Ginger stopped seeing me when she was twenty-one then came back eight or nine years later. Sophia quit therapy several years ago."

"After you started seeing her socially?"

Now he stiffens. "Well before," he snarls, every bit the alpha wolf chastening an insolent pup.

"Of course." She smiles innocently, as if her implication was unintentional. None of us buys it. Lynch writes something else on the pad.

"And the last time you saw Ginger?"

"Wednesday afternoon. At her last session."

"Was she particularly upset about anything?"

"I can't tell you that."

"Do you know if she had a date that night? Or where she might have been going?"

"I told you I won't comment on anything she said in therapy."

"Even at the risk of protecting her killer?"

"At the risk of violating her confidentiality, I'll go so far as to say that she told me nothing that might help identify her killer." He scribbles another note.

I've never seen an interviewee take notes before. I'm dying to know what he's writing. Clarence Darrow was said to have spiked his cigar with piano wire during the Scopes Monkey Trial then smoked it when the prosecution was making its case. Members of the jury were so distracted waiting for the growing ash to fall that they barely heard the prosecutor's case. Maybe Lynch's note-taking is his cigar trick, designed to distract Gloria.

"You'd be surprised at how insignificant a detail can be and still trip up a murderer," she says. "I once caught a killer who wore a shower cap to commit the crime to make sure he didn't leave even a strand of hair at the site. But we still found a few flakes of dandruff on the corpse, and that gave us his DNA."

"How interesting," he says deadpan, circling a word on his pad.

"Tell me about your relationship with Billy Strain," Gloria continues.

"He paid for each girl's therapy until she turned twenty one. That's about it."

"You didn't socialize?"

"It would be inappropriate to socialize with the parent of a patient."

"But not to shack up with a former patient?"

His face flushes. "Get the hell out of my office."

"I'm not finished."

"I am."

Knowing a lost cause when she sees it, Gloria stands and walks out.

"Nice talking to you," I say and follow her out. At the door, I stop and turn back, feeling just like Columbo. "One more question. Were you prescribing her Elavil?"

"That's confidential," he says, but the pause in his delivery answers my question.

THIRTY-NINE

I'm Googling Ginger's zip code and "pharmacy" to get a list of the drug stores closest to the Strain house when Melody walks into my office dressed like a whale. Or is she a dolphin? I know she's not a shark because she's got a spout.

"Nice outfit," I say.

"I just came from a gig for two hundred sixth graders. Dance interpretation of *Moby Dick*."

"Spouting rhetoric?"

"That's pretty rich talk for a hack."

I don't know how I'd keep my ego in check without Melody around.

"You're not going to wear that thing to work the pharmacies, are you?"

She strips out of her costume to reveal a T-shirt and shorts. I print the two-page pharmacy list and split it with her.

"Start with the closest," I say.

We take our separate cars and head out to do some legwork. I start at the Rite Aid on the corner of Sunset and Fairfax. It used to be a Thrifty that sold my dad's favorite ice cream. Brain scans have proved that humans like the taste of higher-priced food more than the same food tagged for less, but my dad had different wiring. Thrifty ice cream was the cheapest in town, and to his accountant's brain that made it taste better.

I park in back and head into the pharmacy. There's a young Asian woman behind the counter. Her name tag says Lucy Chow, so I assume she's Chinese. I wrack my brain for the name of an Asian actress and tell her that her pearl earrings make her look like Maggie Q. Lucy blushes. Good start. Then I tell her I'm picking up an Elavil prescription for my sister-in-law, Ginger Strain. She rifles through a lineup of bags in the S bin and tells me there's nothing ready. I ask if she'll check the records to make sure the prescription was received, and she taps into the computer to discover that they've got nothing under Ginger's name. Strike one.

Next stop is the pharmacy in the Ralphs supermarket down the street. The clerk is tall and Latina. I ask if she's tired of being told she looks like Sofia Vergara. Ginger Strain has no account here either. Strike two.

Melody calls to tell me she's leaving her third pharmacy with no hits. That makes strike five between us, if there is such a thing.

My sixth call is at a small neighborhood pharmacy that Google identified as the Spaulding Pharmacy, but it still has an old sign on the front that reads "Anteka Pharmacy." The pharmacist is old and male, so I skip the flattery and cut to the chase. There's nothing in the pickup box, but Ginger's name pops up in the computer.

"The Elavil's expired," he says. "She needs to get a new prescription from her doctor."

"Which one? Dr. Lynch or Dr. Whatsizname?"

He double-checks the record. "Dr. Lynch," he says. To make sure I heard right, he mimes hanging himself.

I call Gloria and tell her I've got something new. She tells me she's at Tina's and I can come meet her there if I like.

Fifteen minutes later I walk into an acetone cloud. Tina employs about a dozen Vietnamese manicurists, of whom none is available. There are five women reading fashion magazines in the cramped waiting area. I see Gloria in a chair in the back, her left foot and hand are soaking in their respective bowls of soapy water while Tina works on her right hand and an ancient fat woman squats before her, working on her free foot. I guess decades of Asian toilets have made the position comfortable for her, but my knees ache just from watching.

"Have a seat," says Gloria, nodding at a rolling stool. I draw it near and sit on it, swinging back and forth a little to check out the swivel.

It's somehow jarring to see Gloria playing the idle aristocrat, with exotic handmaidens primping her like a pedigreed chow-chow.

"You look ravishing, my lady."

"Fuck you, too," she says. "What do you have?"

"You know that Elavil bottle you never found at Ginger's house?"

"Alleged Elavil bottle."

Tina chooses this moment to let the orange stick slip. Gloria grimaces as the stick's point slides under her cuticle.

"Well, it existed once upon a time," I say, "and the label was inscribed with the words 'Karl Lynch, MD.'"

I expect her to be pleased. She's merely bored. "What a shock that her drugs were prescribed by her doctor. It doesn't take a genius to prove he wrote her a prescription. Even *you* were able to do it."

I let the slight pass. I know she's fishing for a wisecrack, but she's pissing me off, so I don't bite.

Tina finishes coating the nail on the injured finger and sprays it with an aerosol nail dryer. So much for the ozone layer.

"I think you're missing the point," I say.

"Which is?"

"The killer got rid of that bottle hoping you'd attribute Ginger's death to the gas and leave it at that."

"You think he's never seen an episode of *CSI*? Everyone knows that stuff comes out in the autopsy. Especially someone with medical training, like Dr. Karl Fucking Lynch."

"Whatever the reason, someone deep-sixed that bottle to destroy evidence, and Karl Lynch is the only person it could have implicated."

FORTY

Sophia agreed to meet me at Venice Beach, a community of contradictions. Dilapidated crack houses coexist cheek by jowl with $5 million paeans to postmodernism. Young taggers jump $500 skateboards off half walls while septuagenarian beatniks sell poems for spare change. You can buy knockoff Prada sunglasses for three bucks, but a cup of coffee can set you back five.

The place was conceived in the early twentieth century by tobacco mogul Abbot Kinney, who wanted to fulfill his dream of an American Venice, Italy. A hundred years later, only a few of his canals still exist, and they're sorely polluted. The boating lagoon has become a concrete traffic circle. And Windward Boulevard, once a grand promenade of Venetian-colonnaded nightclubs, now offers tacos and trinkets to the tourists.

As I head toward the concrete fishing pier I pass a sun-bronzed bikinied blonde on rollerblades extolling the virtues of flavored organic lubricant to an ancient shopping-cart lady. Two girls and their wheels.

I find Sophia at the end of the pier, standing at the rail near an old Mexican fisherman. She's dressed in an apricot sundress with a single shoulder strap and asymmetrical neckline. The wind presses it taut against her, outlining her flat abs, wrapping her thighs, and flapping like Old Glory behind her. She's an amazing sight. I snap a cell-phone shot of her watching the surfers bob on the gentle swell.

"Thanks for meeting me," I say.

She turns. "They're not doing a lot of surfing."

"They're waiting for outside breaks, but the surf's down. Don't hold your breath."

"The world's full of amateurs."

In profile, backlit by a cotton field of midlevel clouds, with the salty-sweet sea breeze flying her honey hair, she looks like a Vogue cover girl except healthier.

I'm still sporting a bandage on my forehead. She notices. It'd be hard not to. "What happened to your head?"

"I cut myself shaving."

It's a weak joke but she smiles anyway, to be polite I guess.

"What did you want to talk about?"

"Karl, mostly. And why you're afraid of him."

"I'm not."

"You said you didn't want anyone you know to see us together. I assumed that was because you were afraid Karl would find out."

"I don't want to hurt his feelings. He's sensitive, and he thinks you're out to get him."

The Mexican fisherman gets a strike. It looks like a big fish from the fight it puts up. We both wait to see it. The fish finally breaks the surface. It's a halibut about the size of my pinkie. I expect the fisherman to throw it back, but he just leaves it on the hook and drops it back down by the pilings. Live bait. It's a fish-eat-fish world.

Sophia turns her eyes to me, and they sparkle from the late afternoon sun reflecting off the water. "Are you out to get him?"

"I'm out to get Ginger's killer. I suspect he did it. And so do you."

"No I don't." Impatience furrows her brow. She flicks her hand as if swatting at a mosquito. "He's a wonderful man. I wouldn't stay with him if I thought he was capable of murder."

"Everyone's capable of murder. We just have different thresholds of motivation. I think Karl reached his when he seduced Ginger in therapy and she threatened to expose him."

"You've got no proof of that!" She's getting angry. I try to ease up on the gas without losing my forward momentum. I don't want her walking off in a huff.

"Look, I don't want to railroad the guy, but I'm an ex-cop, and my on-the-job training taught me that a suspect is guilty until proven innocent."

"I thought it was the other way around."

"Only in court. If you're so sure he's innocent, help me prove it. I'm not trying to judge his ethics; it's hard enough keeping track of my own. But if Karl Lynch made sexual moves on you during treatment, I'm sure you worried about him doing the same thing to Ginger."

This assumption seems to have an impact.

"I never said we had sex during treatment." A half-assed denial without much conviction. "And I didn't even know he was still seeing Ginger."

"Maybe you didn't know about Ginger, but you knew he had plenty of female patients. You must have suspected him of playing around after what he'd done to you."

Her hands start to tremble. She grips the rail to still them and looks out to sea, squinting her eyes against the descending sun. As it approaches the horizon, it appears huge, reddish-gold, and glorious. You can't beat an LA sunset over the ocean. The atmospheric distortion can be a thing of breathtaking beauty, the one and only advantage of smog.

She finally speaks. "Have you ever seen a green flash when the sun sets over the sea?"

"You're changing the subject."

"We'll have to watch for it. It's very rare, but I saw it once. With Karl. He brought me out here to ask me to move in with him."

"Were you a patient at the time?"

She turns her eyes to me, and they look deeper than the Pacific.

"No. But I wasn't particularly functional. He took me in anyway. Gave me my life back. Taught me I was worthy of love."

I pray that word won't be the death of her. In my line of work it's not unusual to care about the victims you meet, but that sort of empathy pales beside the ache I feel for Sophia. Why is that? I hardly know this woman. She's in a relationship. Is my attraction to her affecting my judgment? Could emotional bias be prodding me to accuse Karl of committing one murder and planning another? Is he really that prime a suspect? Or is that just my wish-fulfillment fantasy? My way of trying to make Sophia available? The bumpy path of this thought makes me queasy, but I continue anyway.

"If Ginger threatened to destroy Karl's career with sexual accusations, he had a motive to kill her," I say. "He had access to and knowledge of drugs, so he had the means. He slept downstairs that night, so he could have snuck out to do it. That gives him motive, means, and opportunity, the holy trinity of murder. What's to stop him from slipping you drugs, too?"

She bites her lower lip and turns her gaze back over the ocean. The sky is now aflame with the sunset, but neither one of us is in the mood to enjoy it.

"He didn't kill her," she says.

I feel deflated. I give it one more shot, hoping she doesn't know enough about police procedure and privacy rights to know I'm lying through my teeth.

"The cops have ways of digging these things out. They can subpoena his records. They can interview his patients. They can sweat it out of him. And if they catch him in a lie, they'll assume he's lying about everything. If you really believe he's innocent, it'll be much better for Karl if you help me prove it than it will be for you to sit back and let the police build a case against him."

Her gaze flits to me. I try to look sincere, like I really want to help the son of a bitch get off the hook. The deception annoys me, so I change tactics.

"Look, Sophia. If something happens to you because I can't persuade you to open up about this, I'm going to blame myself. And between my mother and my ex-wife, I've got more guilt than I can handle already. So I'm asking you: please tell me the truth."

She points to the sunset. "Here it comes," she says. We both watch the last glare of the sun slip below the horizon.

"No green flash," I say.

She stares at the blushing sky for several seconds before responding. "Buy me a drink."

FORTY-ONE

We walk up the boardwalk to the Sidewalk Café. Several parties are settling up after watching the sunset, so we're able to nab a table outside to watch the dusk disappear. The air is still surprisingly warm for the beach, despite the gusty onshore wind. Sophia orders something called a Sidewalk Slammer. I order a Guinness and some grilled Cajun shrimp to share.

"By the time I turned twenty I'd quit therapy twice," she says, "but each time I'd end up going back after a year or two. I was having a lot of short flings. I just couldn't make anything stick with a guy. It was always something different, but I was always the one to break it off. Karl said it was because of my parents. They had treated lovers like cigarette butts, and I'd rebelled against that by developing an emotional block against casual sex. I couldn't be satisfied sexually without being in love. That made me confuse lust for love, and that was drawing me into inappropriate relationships."

Our drinks arrive. Hers is blended and smells flammable. We toast before she continues.

"He said I needed to learn to distinguish between physical sensations and emotions in order to lead a healthy sex life without getting emotionally steamrolled every time. If I could make this distinction, I'd be able to recognize a healthy relationship when it came along."

I can see where this is going, and it isn't pretty. The steamroller image makes me think about Holly. In the driver's seat.

"He said he wanted to do some role-playing around it." She pauses to take a long draw on her straw. From her wince, it looks like she's tasted something off in her drink, or maybe it's the memory.

"He told me to concentrate on the here and now. It doesn't matter if anything comes of what happens, because it's only right now. Tomorrow, it'll be forgotten, lost in the past. I can't let my emotions control me. They're just voices in the wind. It's my physical sensations that are real. Let go of my mind and just feel the sensations in my body." Her recall seems remarkably detailed.

"Are you paraphrasing?"

She laughs. "It's like the first time you ever had sex. You remember every whisper, every little touch, how it smelled, how it felt, everything. This is that kind of memory."

Our shrimp arrives, lightly charred yet still juicy. She takes one and bites it off at the tail. Her smile indicates approval.

"So he tells me to imagine I'm at a party. Imagine I walk into a back bedroom to get something from my coat and find a man there. A beautiful man, a sexy man, a man I'm immediately attracted to. He's staring out the window, deep in thought. Karl says to close my eyes and imagine the man turning to me, telling me he's been watching me all night. He says he isn't sure he can control his desire for me, and I feel the same."

It sounds to me like the spiel of a nightclub hypnotist more than a therapist.

"Karl tells me to let go of my fears, to live in my body, exist only in my physical sensations. The next thing I know, we're kissing. I wanted it so bad. It felt so good. It just felt right."

I take a swig of my Guinness to wash a sour taste from my mouth. My stomach feels like someone is wringing it dry. I imagine Karl urging her to reject her feelings of humiliation, of self-loathing, of guilt. To purge the negativity that smothers her passion, that obstructs her ability to enjoy her own sexuality. To make that mind-body separation and revel in the physical pleasure for its own sake.

She takes a draw on her drink, but it's unconscious. Her mind is in another place, another time.

"I couldn't sort out my feelings. It was exciting and degrading at the same time. I was afraid to resist, because all my insecurities and paranoia were exactly the sorts of demons I'd been working to overcome. And I wanted him to want me. I wanted it so bad. But at the same time I felt so ashamed because I knew I'd started it. I tried to shut down my brain, not think about what I was feeling, turn the physical sensations into secluded little islands somewhere far out to sea."

She grabs her opposite shoulders to hug herself, and I see her hunched in Karl's arms, her feelings chaotic, cheeks slick, body shaking. I envision her stepping off the emotional cliff, snaking her arms around his neck to hold on, desperately latching onto his mouth as if the sensors in her tongue can send proof to her brain that this is all in the name of therapy, in the service of healing. I see him driven by her ardor, hastily stripping her before the bubble can burst, unpeeling her like a ripe piece of fruit to expose her last vestige of privacy.

"And then it was over," she says. She's back with me in the here and now. She grabs another shrimp but stares at it for a long time before taking a bite.

"And?" I ask.

She laughs. "I was actually thankful for the first time that it was only a fifty-minute hour, even though he let me run overtime for the first time in my life. I was still confused, but I remember being surprised at how upset he was. Even more than I was, I think. He kept apologizing for losing control. At first I thought he meant sexually, but he meant emotionally. He said he thought it would be therapeutic for me, but he hadn't realized how strong his own feelings would be. He swore he'd never done anything like this before, and that's when he told me he loved me."

She looks up at me with those eyes, expecting me to comprehend how his love had made her whole again. How Karl's actions were suddenly justified, his abuse undone. The desperate plea in her eyes reminds me of my first partner, kneeling in an alley, rolling over the man she'd just shot to reveal her vindication—a smoking gun on the pavement beneath him.

"You'll have to excuse my skepticism," I say, "but did you really believe him?"

Her face clouds.

"Look, I'm not an idiot. I know what this sounds like. But if you saw his face, if you heard his voice, if you looked in his eyes, there was no question. He made me find a new therapist. He started dating me. And six months later, he asked me to move in with him. So I think the jury's in."

I refrain from pointing out the irony of a courtroom metaphor, considering the possibility that she might soon face him in a courtroom, testifying in his murder trial. Somehow glib feels like the wrong approach to salvage the mood.

"How do you know your relationship isn't just his way of dealing with his guilt?"

"How does anyone know? Half the marriages out there could be described that way."

"Half the marriages out there aren't covering up a crime."

But she's right about guilt. Holly probably would have left me long before she did if she hadn't felt guilty about abandoning me. I think about my parents' marriage. I always suspected they married because she got pregnant with my oldest sister. Guilt was the glue that held them together. And once Dad was gone, guilt was all Mom had left.

"Don't blame Karl," she says. "I seduced him."

"It wasn't your fault. It's never the patient's fault. Karl was your therapist. He had power over you. It was his responsibility to police the boundaries. He virtually raped you, and I think he did the same thing to Ginger."

She stands abruptly, knocking her chair over. People at adjoining tables fall silent and try to hide their stares with sideways glances. She pays them no attention. Her eyes are hateful, and I feel a sense of loss, even though I know I'm right. A passing busgirl rights her chair.

"Who do you think you are?" she says.

"I think I'm the guy your sister wanted to meet at Solley's to ask me to help her expose Karl Lynch. And I think he stopped her by gassing her after slipping drugs in her tea."

"I don't have to listen to this. I need to get home before Karl does."

"So you *are* afraid."

"I just want to have a nice dinner with Karl without having to explain why I was foolish enough to trust our private history to the kind of man who could take an expression of love and twist it into an accusation of rape."

Her words make me feel like some sort of gossipmongering slime. My reaction is infantile.

"Enjoy your dinner," I say, "but don't let him near your food."

She gives me the finger and walks away.

FORTY-TWO

'm thinking about dropping by the hardware store and picking up a new flapper for my toilet as I curve around Griffith Park, transitioning from the 134 to the 5. I'm on my way to the house formerly known as hell. It's a two-bedroom box in a cheap bungalow court on Maltman south of Sunset in Silverlake. The place reminds me of a Salton Sea trailer park where I once got propositioned by a hooker who looked like my grandmother only older. The place is overdue for a major gentrification, but unless the landlord sobers up or dies it's not going to happen anytime soon.

I park on the street and walk the long driveway up the hill between two rows of five bungalows. When they were built in the thirties they were identical, but decades of tenants have individualized them with the only-sometimes-judicious use of paint, window trim, hanging plants, garden gnomes, bird feeders, landscaping, split-rail fencing, and the lone lawn jockey in front of the third unit on the right. My mother's.

The jockey was black when she bought it, but my father suggested that it might be a racist statement, even though he was hard-pressed to articulate why. Just to be safe, Ma painted his face and hands white.

When my father flew his car off a cliff, Ma was forced to sell the house where I grew up, but she kept the jockey. This bungalow was the best she could afford, an involuntary downsizing. I spent my last semester of high school sleeping on the couch before going off to Princeton. A year later, I transferred to UCLA so she could spend what was left of my father's life insurance to move, but she's still here two decades later. She likes to say it's just temporary until she can find a better place. I suspect that place will be Hillside Memorial.

I knock and hear someone walk across the scarred oak flooring inside, moving much too fast to be Ma. The door opens. It's my ex.

I've actually come because I want Holly's professional advice, and I know she'll be here for their usual Friday lunch. She's wearing a figure-hugging black jersey outfit that makes her look like Barbarella with better taste in clothes. I question the wisdom of wearing black in this heat, but I'm smart enough to keep my yap shut. She says hello.

Before I can reply, Ma calls out, "Look who the cat dragged in."

I look past Holly to see my mother lying on the floral-print sofa. She's got a baby-blue icepack sweating on her forehead, dripping into her bleached-blond hair.

"Hi, Ma. What's with the ice?"

"It's nothing," she says, implying just the opposite.

I haven't seen my mother in a few weeks. She looked drained then and looks worse now, though it's not easy to tell in the dim light that seeps under the yellowing window shades. Ma's wearing a purple muumuu with white daisies all over it. There's an abalone shell on the coffee table, overflowing with Lucky Strike butts. The place smells like the ashtray.

"She's hung over," says Holly.

"You don't get hungover from one glass of Manischewitz," she says.

"I've seen you get hungover just smelling the bottle," I say. "Why were you drinking? You know you can't handle it."

"Like you could care less how I feel," she says, sounding like she's got a sore throat.

"I do care how you feel. I just don't think it's productive for you to kvetch about it so much."

She turns to Holly. "You see how he talks to his ailing mother?"

"You're not ailing, you're hungover," I say. "Whose fault is that?"

"It was your father's yahrzeit. I guess you forgot as usual. So I had to toast alone."

This is a sore point for her. The yahrzeit is the traditional Jewish remembrance on the anniversary of someone's death. Unfortunately, I rarely remember it because the "anniversary" is on the Jewish calendar, which makes less sense to me than foie gras to a vegan. That's why we always celebrated Christmas instead of Chanukah when I was growing up. You always knew when it was coming.

My mother is Jewish, but she never practiced until my father died. His father was a Baptist who became a Mormon then lapsed and married a Catholic. Because my grandmother was religious, my father was raised Catholic but quit the church when the priest refused to officiate at his marriage to my Jewish mother.

Out of that stew three children were born. My younger brother, Teddy, who teaches at Reed College in Oregon, went Catholic. My older sister, Beth, who has a small business in Texas repairing wind instruments, went Jewish. And I, the troubled middle child, am a certified orthodox nonsectarian.

"I spoke to Jerry," I say to Holly, changing the subject and immediately regretting it.

"This really isn't the time or place, Nob."

"What's with Jerry?" asks Ma. She knows him from when he and I used to be friends. Holly gives me a warning glare.

"He's trying to sell my house out from under me, because I'm having a little trouble paying my rent exactly on time." I know it's a cheap shot, but sometimes the entertainment value is just too seductive for self-censorship.

My mother has no trouble grasping the nuances. She looks at Holly incredulously. "You would kick my son out of his own home?"

"You know I don't want to do that, Tillie. But I need the money to stay in my own place. He made a commitment."

"You should be ashamed, Nenad," says my mother. It doesn't take much to sway her vote.

"I am, Ma. And my shame is driving me to drink. Got any Manischewitz left over, or did you chug it all?"

"Go ahead and joke, Mr. Wiseacre. Meanwhile, they'll toss this poor girl in the street."

She's right, of course. It's not Holly's fault that I'm late, it's fucking Larry Flynt's. I did a story for *Hustler* about a hooker who claimed she killed her ex-husband in self-defense, even though he had his arms full of groceries at the time and she shot him in the back. She's in jail, awaiting trial, and *Hustler*'s waiting, too. They don't want to button the story until the verdict, and they refuse to pay me until then. I called my editor last week and asked for an advance at least. The trial's been delayed for seven months and still counting. He said he'll see what he can do. As Melody is fond of saying, I'm not holding my breath. Maybe I should get Jerry on the case.

"I'm sorry I brought it up," I say, and I mean it. "If my Flynt check comes in, we're home free, no pun intended."

"What about that rock and roll *mishegoss*?" my mother asks.

"I'm working on a story about Lana Strain's murder," I explain to Holly. "In fact, I've been meaning to call you about it. I could use your help."

I've always been attracted to smart women and Holly is no exception. Along with her law degree, she has a PhD in psychology, so she's the go-to gal in the DA's office on human and not-so-human behavior.

"What kind of help?"

"You're the authority on sexual harassment and abuse. I might have a victim or two."

"I'm not interested in your love life," she says.

My mother finds this hysterically funny.

"Cute. But I'm talking about Lana Strain's daughters. I think both sisters slept with their shrink."

"The *same* shrink?" she asks.

"That's right."

"Sisters?"

"They hadn't spoken in twenty years, but yeah."

"How'd they wind up with the same shrink?"

"They started out in family therapy together after their mother was murdered. The fact that when they stopped seeing him together he continued to see them both separately is your first clue about his ethical standards."

Holly takes several seconds to consider, unconsciously picking at a chip in her Pinkaholic nail polish.

"We don't get many sexually abusive therapists through the DA's office. Most of the victims are too ashamed to come forward, and if they do, they usually go straight to the state board or the civil courts. But I've tried a few."

"How'd you do?"

"Three out of five. It's tough to prove. Usually a 'he said, she said' kind of thing."

"How common is it?"

"Depends what you call common. They did an anonymous survey a few years back and one out of every ten male therapists admitted to some sort of sexual contact with a client."

My eyebrows launch. "One out of ten?"

"Don't tell me you're shocked, Nob." She breaks into a poor man's Cole Porter: "Priests do it. Cops do it. Even educated profs do it." Then she turns serious. "It's the intoxication of power. It seems to have some sort of degenerative effect on a man's ethics."

I know that women do it too, but I'm guessing it's comparatively rare, so I ignore the gender smear.

"But the man's a *doctor*," says Ma, as if beatification was the next step.

"These guys aren't thinking, they're acting on impulse," says Holly. We're talking deep-rooted mating instincts going back hundreds of thousands of years. Reptilian brain stuff. This isn't a casual poke in the hay. These are driven men who act out their own psychological stuff on troubled women who are too confused and intimidated to say no. No one's more vulnerable than a woman in an emotional crisis, especially if she thinks the man who's responsible is the only one who can save her from it."

She wipes her bangs out of her eyes, and it occurs to me that she's let them grow longer than she used to. They look good.

"And after it's over?" I ask.

"Most of these women sink into an even worse depression than they started with. Hardly any come away unscathed. Some get totally debilitated, can't hold a job, can't take care of their own basic needs. Some turn to binge eating, alcohol, drugs, even violence."

"How about blackmail? I've got a murder victim who might have threatened her therapist with exposure."

"No offense, Nob, but you're thinking like a man. These women are in too much turmoil to turn their pain into a profit center. More likely, she would have wanted to turn this guy's life into a living hell. If she threatened to go public, I doubt money would have stopped her."

"So he'd have to kill her to shut her up."

"He's already proven he's no slave to conscience."

"That's what I was afraid of," I say. "And I think the other sister knows something that can incriminate him."

"Then don't let her get near him."

"They live together."

FORTY-THREE

I fling the sheets all night. Can't sleep for worry. I don't know what I can say to get through to Sophia, but I'm determined to give it another try. I can't risk calling her if she's with Karl, so I cruise out to their Westside neighborhood just after six a.m.

California's first drive-in theater, the Pico, was closed in 1950 to make way for what has become the Westside Pavilion mall. Karl Lynch's midcentury modern home is just a few blocks due north.

Shadowed from the glow of dawn by overhanging jacaranda trees, I glide into a parking spot a few houses away and stare at the floor-to-ceiling Bauhaus windows that form the face of Karl Lynch's house. Enormous white curtains are drawn to hide the interior and encourage my fears.

I listen to KCRW for a couple hours until the garage door finally opens and Karl backs his car out. He maneuvers around Sophia's Miata to get out of the driveway and head north, presumably toward work. I stay put and watch the house for signs of life.

A few minutes later, the front door opens, and Sophia hustles out of the house, carrying a brown paper grocery bag. Her hair hangs wild, unbrushed. She's wearing gym clothes. No makeup. She seems preoccupied, intent, as if something's wrong. I resist the temptation to intercept her before she gets in her car because I want to see where she's going. I watch her place the bag gently on the passenger seat before climbing in.

In January 1928, Adolph Schleicher began work on the Samson Tire and Rubber Company, a slavish reproduction of the seventh-century-BC Assyrian palace of King Sargon II, complete with massive pillars and towers and heraldic griffins and bas-reliefs of Babylonian princes carved into a 1,350-foot-long stone facade. The tire plant, like Sargon's palace, covered twenty-three acres of land, and its entrance was guarded by giant winged bulls with human heads. Today this majestic palace houses an uninspired outlet mall called the Citadel and overlooks one of LA's ugliest byways, the Santa Ana Freeway.

I'm guessing that's where Sophia's headed as she merges into the right-hand lane to exit at Atlantic Boulevard. I'm wrong. She heads northeast, away from the mall, through the unimaginatively named City of Commerce, apparently searching for a street number amid the boxlike cinderblock buildings. She finally turns into the parking lot of a U-shaped one-story structure with glass-brick windows and aluminum lettering that reads "Service Evidential Laboratories, Inc."

I'm familiar with the lab. Its founder and fearless leader, Dr. Selena Service, is a well-known figure around the LA courts, a frequent defense witness in high-profile criminal trials.

I pull up in front and watch Sophia pass several empty parking spots to find one in the shade. It's only nine thirty in the morning, but the heat is already oppressive.

I wait for her to cross the lot and walk in the back door before I head in the front. I'm waiting at the closed reception window by the time she winds through the building to find it.

"What are you doing here?" she asks.

"You took the words right out of my mouth." I nod toward her grocery bag.

"You followed me."

"I'm worried about you."

She thinks on that for a moment. The last time we spoke we didn't part on very friendly terms, so I assume she's trying to decide whether to hold the grudge. Finally, she turns her attention to the sign on the reception window that tells her to "Ring Bell for Service." An intentional pun.

The receptionist tells us to wait. A few minutes later, Dr. Selena Service opens the door to the inner sanctum. She introduces herself to Sophia and gives me a friendly nod of recognition, then she leads us into the back. Sophia hasn't asked me to join her, but I follow her in, assuming she'll squawk if she doesn't want me.

Selena Service was the star center on her college women's basketball team called, inappropriately enough, the Cal Tech Beavers. Almost six five, she sweeps down the lengthy lab corridor, her stride hard to match. Sophia has to do a little skip every third step just to keep up without breaking into a run. Service's mane of long curly platinum-blond hair is tightly constricted by a hair band with bobbles shaped like a pair of silver dice. Her hair seems to explode from the band like a shotgun spray. Flowing in her slipstream is an audacious scarf, tiger-striped in neon orange and green, wrapped around her neck to offset the refrigerator white of her immaculately ironed lab coat.

"We don't get many civilians in here," she says over her shoulder, "mostly lawyers, PIs, and the occasional consumer advocate." She speaks almost as fast as she walks. "Some of the things we've found in fast foods...well, I guess nothing shocks me anymore since I found human thyroid in a cube of vegan cashew cheese."

Dr. Service leads us into her office and points to a lone reception chair, lime-green upholstery with wooden arms whose lacquered finish, after years of rubbing elbows, is down to its last flakes. "Take a load off."

Service sits behind her desk as Sophia, still absorbing the thyroid revelation, takes the proffered chair. I lean against the door jamb, trying to look casual as Sophia sets her grocery bag on Service's desk.

Service looks at me. "You here on a story, Nob?"

"Right now I'm just along for the ride. Sophia came on her own."

Service points to the bag. "So what is it? Powder or pizza?"

"I'm sorry?" says Sophia.

"Most civilians either find white powder in their kid's bathroom and want to know if it's cocaine or Desenex, or they puke from takeout food and want to sue Dominos."

"I just want to get this analyzed." She pulls a ziplock bag and a Tupperware container from her grocery bag. A croissant and some coffee.

"You're looking for something like botulism, salmonella?"

"Not exactly. I doubt it would be…" She has to search for the word. "…biological."

This surprises Dr. Service. "You think somebody tried to poison you?"

"I expect to prove he didn't," she says, glancing at me. "But I need to be sure."

"You poor thing," says Service.

———

I walk Sophia out of the lab.

"What made you suspicious?" I ask.

"You. At the beach."

"You didn't taste anything off in the food?"

"I didn't even try it. The timing was just too strange. He never brings me breakfast in bed."

"Do you have a place to stay tonight?"

She looks at me bewildered, like the thought had never occurred to her.

"I can't just leave Karl. What am I going to tell him?"

"You can't stay there with him. You think the man tried to poison you."

"No I don't!" Her voice softens. "I just have to be sure."

"You can't go back there. The man's job is to see through people. He'll know you're hiding something."

Her inner conflict finally buckles her. She buries her face in my chest. I can feel her tears soak through my shirt. I pull her close and suffer a pang of guilt for enjoying the feel of her body under this circumstance. After a minute, she pulls away self-consciously.

"Sorry," she says. I don't reply, giving her the moment to compose herself. She finds a Kleenex in her purse to blow her nose.

"This whole thing is probably me just being paranoid," she says. "I'm not going to destroy my relationship for nothing."

End of discussion. She bites her cuticle. I bite my tongue.

FORTY-FOUR

Leaving me thoroughly frustrated, Sophia drives off to her studio to paint puppets or whatever the hell she does.

When I get back to the office, Melody is thumbing the digits for Boom-Boom Laphroig. I'd left her a note to make the call and find out if Boom-Boom has a number for Don Patt, the Brothers' bass player.

As I check my inbox I hear her introduce herself. Within two minutes they're chattering away as if they were long-lost roomies. How do women do that?

I've been expecting an e-mail or letter or summons from Jerry, but so far nothing. Is that promising news? Or is he just waiting for the right moment to pounce? My only hope is that Holly can't bring herself to hurt me anymore, no matter how badly Jerry wants to drop the anvil. She is already tormented over breaking my heart. I'm sure she's afraid of compounding the burden. God bless Holly's mother, the Mistress of Guilt.

My deep thoughts are interrupted by a positive indicator: Mel is jotting something down.

She hangs up. "Got him. Boom-boom doesn't have a number, but a friend told her Don Patt was working at Ciacotti's Hardware."

This is a stroke of luck. The place is only five minutes away.

"I've got a yoga class," she says. "If you want to wait till I get back, I'll go down there with you."

That suits me fine. I'm in a section of Lana's journal where she writes about Patt. I want to finish it before we meet.

Melody heads out, and I find my Post-it bookmark in the journal. My readings haven't revealed any clues, but I've gleaned quite a bit about Lana's feelings toward the people in her life, at least those whose code names I've deciphered. She could be painfully blunt.

She despised her father but couldn't bring herself to cut off all ties with him, apparently because she didn't want to dishonor her late grandmother.

She put up with Billy because she liked his guitar work and "incidentally," she noted, because he never hit her. She didn't have much to say about him as the father of her daughters except that the girls loved his grilled cheese and bacon sandwiches. In the sack, she thought he was selfish and inept.

Claudine seemed to be the only person whose company Lana actually enjoyed, despite the tiresome occasions when Claudine tried to steer her toward a healthier lifestyle. Lana suspected that Claudine had the hots for Billy, but she didn't think anything would come of it. Nor did she care.

Lana used the word "oafish" to describe Boom-Boom Laphroig, which struck me as an odd word for a rock star. But Lana loved Boom-Boom's rhythms and artistic choices. Lana also thought having a black drummer gave her blues more authority, even though Boom-Boom grew up in a small mansion in Beverly Hills, the daughter of a plastic surgeon and an interior designer, the surgeon being her mother.

Don Patt was the weakest musician in the band, according to Lana. She also suspected he was gay, even though she once walked in on him getting head from their bus driver's wife. But because Don never came on to Lana, she assumed he couldn't be attracted to women. She had a sizable ego, at least sexually.

I always thought Patt was pretty good. I saw him rip out an unbelievable solo when the Brothers played the Hollywood Bowl in '91. I'll never forget how Lana heated up that cold October night. The next day I spent a half hour constructing a protective cardboard sleeve so that I could keep my ticket stub pristine forever. I still have it in my safe deposit box.

The only person Lana mentioned having any respect for was Gary Cogswell. She thought he was both smart and shrewd, which she considered key assets to her continuing success. Aside from Claudine, he was the only person she trusted. Lana depended on him to bring order to her chaotic life.

For the sake of expedience, she put up with his frequent sexual overtures. She couldn't blame him for trying, seeing as how her multiple sex partners seemed to be chosen by the luck of the draw, but she didn't find him attractive enough to give him a tumble. She called him Humpty Dumpty behind his back.

Humpty's luck changed when Lana found herself simultaneously negotiating a new recording contract and planning her estate. Cogswell was buried in a multimillion-dollar corporate lawsuit at the time. Ever the savvy businesswoman, she seduced him to reclaim his focus. As soon as the trusts were set up and the contract signed, she broke it off. He responded like a rejected teenager, but if she cared, I have yet to read about it.

Lana wrote surprisingly little about her daughters, leading me to believe she didn't afford them much time or attention. She rarely mentioned family outings or referred to her feelings for them, their grades, their boyfriends, their triumphs or disappointments. Lana was preoccupied by her own needs, and family wasn't one of them.

It bothers me to read Lana's private thoughts, not so much because I feel like I'm trespassing, but because she was so petty and cruel. It hurts to see the woman of my dreams exposed as a small-minded bitch who I'd hate to spend time with.

FORTY-FIVE

Ciacotti's Hardware has been on Ventura Boulevard forever. It should be a historic site, a cultural landmark. For the last few years it's been a dungeon in there, because they turn the lights off to save money when no customers are in the store, which is most of the time. But such economy is no match for economies of scale. Home Depot and Lowe's have finally trampled Ciacotti's into the ground, as they have most neighborhood hardware stores. When Melody and I approach, we see a sign on the window announcing a going-out-of-business sale. A sad state of affairs.

We walk in to find Don Patt minding the store, easing the hospice patient through its final days. Lana described Patt as "a Harley jacket on a Schwinn." He still sports the anorexic biker look: greasy hair, dirt-encrusted nails, acne-scarred skin, jail tattoos scattered across his arms, and a dark-brown front tooth, long deceased. It worked a lot better onstage than it does behind the counter. Patt must be in his forties but he looks a lot older. I try to give people the benefit of the doubt, but after the doors close next week, I can't imagine anyone hiring this guy for anything except highway cleanup.

Patt takes a drag on the butt of an unfiltered cigarette then drops it on the floor and steps on it. The smoke drifts into one eye, and he squints in response.

"What can I do you for?" he asks. "Whatever ya want, gonna be half price. Goin' outta bidness sale."

I tell him I need a toilet flapper, and he walks over to a wall switch and flicks on the bare fluorescent bulb over the plumbing aisle. He moves knowingly down the aisle and brushes his hand across an array of flappers, causing the packages to swing on their display rods like little doggie doors. Even in this tiny store, where most of the goods have already been picked over by bargain hunters, there are six different flappers to choose from, all standard size.

This has always mystified me. Why is there more than one style of flapper? They all do the same simple thing: flap over a hole to seal it. Isn't there an ideal shape and material? In a world where physics has defined the optimal automotive silhouette, toilet flappers are still all over the map. Some are flat, some conical, some almost globular. Hasn't anyone put these things through a wind tunnel?

"What's the difference between them?" I ask, assuming Patt's intimacy with the store grants him some sort of expertise. I wouldn't be surprised if he sleeps in the back at night.

"Well," he says, "this one's fifty cents more than the others. With the sale, that's only two bits."

"Somehow, that doesn't make my choice any easier."

"It's a toilet part," says Melody. "Just pick one."

Melody loves hardware stores even more than I do. She claims it's endemic to her sexual orientation. But she's champing at the bit to get out of this one. Don Patt is making her nervous. She wants me to get on with the interview and get the hell out. But I'm afraid to push it. He seems like the kind of guy who's easily spooked. I want to ease him into a conversation.

I pick the flapper that appears to have the least amount of dust buildup on the theory that it's had less time to decay from the smog. We head back to the counter.

Patt rings me up on an old-fashioned mechanical cash register. Two ninety-five. I hand him a twenty. He starts counting out ones to give me change.

"Had a guy come in two days ago," he says, "pulled out a wad of hunerds fatter'n a twin-bearin' mare. Wanted change, like I'd have it here. I like to took my peacemaker, whack him on the head." He gestures toward a two-foot crowbar hanging on a hook behind the counter and gives Melody a big grin to showcase that long-dead front tooth. What a kidder.

I notice a photo on the wall behind the crowbar. It's a group shot of the Brothers. Early eighties, from the looks of it.

"That you?" I ask.

He turns to look, as if he doesn't know what I'm talking about. "In my heyday."

"That's the Brothers of Libation. I saw you in concert at the Bowl in '73. You're Don Patt, right?"

"Used to be." He taps a Camel out of a soft pack.

"I knew you looked familiar. I loved you guys."

"Them was the days. Didn't need no talent in them days, just calluses, guts, and a broken pool cue, if ya know what I mean."

He lights a kitchen match with his thumbnail and fires up the cancer stick.

"That's illegal in a place of business, you know," says Melody, ever the guardian of public safety.

"What they gonna do? Shut me down?" He sucks deep then blows two streams out his nose.

"My name's Nob Brown. I'm a writer. Could I ask you a few questions about Lana Strain?"

His perpetual frown becomes a grimace. "Fuck no. I been shat on by enough writers to flood a cesspool."

"I just want some background."

"What part of 'fuck no' don't you understand?" He takes his crowbar off the wall and smacks it on the counter. Melody jumps, moving toward the door.

"Okay, I hear you," I say. "No quotes, no questions about the band, no questions about Lana."

"Then we's done."

"Can I have my change?" I nod toward the stack of ones he's still holding in his hand.

"You wanna come on over here and git it?"

"Let's go, Nob," says Melody. She's had enough.

But I'm determined to get something more than a toilet part out of this.

"Look, you can keep the change if you'll just help me out with something that has nothing to do with you or your band."

His eyes narrow as he tries to figure my angle.

"I'm trying to find Vern Senzimmer. I'm hoping you can help me out."

"Who the fuck is Vern Senzimmer?" he asks.

"Sticky White?"

He bursts out in one of those surprise laughs that comes of a long-forgotten memory jetting to the surface. It seems to break the tension. "Fuckin' Sticky White, man."

"So you remember them?"

"Total asshat of a band. One of them boys put me in the hospital on Mercer Island one night. Fucker got behind me with a beer bottle when I wasn't lookin'."

"Vern Senzimmer, by any chance?" asks Melody.

"Now I remember him. He was the scrawny-ass bitch. He'd never have the balls. It was that tight-ass brawler played drums. What the fuck was his name?"

"You wouldn't have any idea how to get in touch with any of them, would you?" I ask.

His face suddenly clouds with suspicion. "You a cop?"

My glance flicks to the crowbar. "I told you I'm a writer. I'm doing a piece on Lana. I understand Senzimmer had some kind of thing going with her."

He lets out a guffaw that segues into a hacking smoker's cough. "Little shit hops her once, thinks he's a fuckin' rock star. Truth is, he was just in the tight pants at the right time. She'd fuck a drape if it was hung."

"You have any idea how we can reach anybody from Sticky White?" asks Melody.

"Try lookin' down the toilet." He blows a perfect smoke ring then blows another one through it. Then his brow clenches as if he's had a second thought. "Lasky might know."

"Who's that?" I ask.

"Moe Lasky. He's an old barker used to book gigs for a shit-load of Seattle bands. If he didn't book Sticky White, he'll sure as fuck know who did."

He starts hacking again. I wait until he gets his lungs under control. "How about a number for Lasky?"

"If I had one, it'd be twenty years old. But you could call any club in Seattle. I reckon they'll know him if the fucker's still breathin'."

FORTY-SIX

Melody hits the phone as soon as we get back and starts calling Seattle clubs. Everyone knows somebody who knows somebody, but no one knows anybody directly. She follows Moe Lasky's trail like a rat in a maze, hitting several dead ends, backtracking, and winding in circles. She finally connects with a friend of a friend of a friend of an ex-partner's friend who visited Lasky last year in a retirement community in Big Lake, Washington, about an hour north of Seattle.

It turns out that Moe's still there, and his brain still works. He digs up a number for the third ex-wife of Brigs Long, former manager of Sticky White. The ex is no longer in touch with Brigs but gives Mel the office number of their son, who's a CPA in Milwaukee. The son has a current number for Brigs but won't give it to us. Mel flirts him into calling Brigs for us. About a half hour later the son calls back with an eight-year-old number for Senzimmer that may or may not still be good. I call it and hit the jackpot.

Senzimmer agrees to a four o'clock meeting this afternoon in Long Beach. If I hit rush hour traffic, the forty-five-minute drive could take me two hours. There's no predicting rush hour anymore, so I don't know why I look at my watch, but I do. It's quarter to three.

I change into clean clothes while Melody plugs the address into my GPS. When I walk back into the office, she's bent over with arms wrapped around her calves, stretching her head through her legs. A human pretzel. She manages to hand me my phone from this position. I shudder as I take it.

The freeway is flowing pretty well, and the cruise to Long Beach is uneventful, except for a green Toyota that almost does a lane change into my lap.

I get off at Cherry Avenue and open my window. I'm still three or four miles from the shore, but I can already smell the sea breeze. It's a beautiful day with the temperature approaching only eighty along the coast.

The address I have for Senzimmer is just south of Fourth Street on Junipero Avenue in a tranquil neighborhood just a few blocks from the beach. It turns out to be a fairly large Spanish-style church called Our Saviour's Lutheran.

Clouds are actually rolling in for the first time in two weeks by the time I park in front. It's hot, but the air feels slightly muggy for a change. I walk toward the entrance and find a huge Pacific Islander, looks Tongan or Samoan, pruning a gorgeous burst of flame-orange birds of paradise with the concentration of a topiary artist. I ask him how to get to the courtyard, and he rises to his full height, dwarfing me. He must outweigh me by two hundred pounds. He raises his long hedge pruner, which looks like a nail clipper in his massive hand, and uses it to point me in the right direction. Without a word, he goes back to his gardening.

As far as Google is concerned, Vern Senzimmer dropped off the planet around 1999, so I have no idea what he'll be like. I do know that a church is the last place I would have expected to find him. His last known address was Tehachapi State Prison, where he did time for selling heroin to a fifteen-year-old crack whore working out of a porta-potty on Skid Row. The only pictures I could find of him were from a few years earlier, at the height of his dubious rock career, before his decline into serious drugs, and even then he looked like a speed freak with pneumonia. So my expectations are low as I round the corner and see him, but nothing has prepared me for what I find.

"You must be Nob Brown," says a man who looks like a stranger wearing Vern Senzimmer's eyes. This version of Vern is healthy, stocky but fit, about fifty pounds heavier than any Vern I've seen in a photo. The new Vern's chestnut eyes are clear and bright, his skin tanned and glowing. He seems robust, vigorous, friendly. He's sitting on a brick half wall that surrounds a sprawling tree, some sort of pepper or willow, I'm guessing. Holly would know.

Senzimmer jumps up and gives me a firm, amiable handshake then gestures around the pastoral courtyard. "Beautiful, isn't it?"

I see the obsessive hand of the Samoan in the perfectly manicured hedges that surround the brick walkways, flower beds, and patches of lawn.

"Very peaceful," I say. "Do you work here?"

"I'm not that pious," he says. "But I do coordinate four meetings a week here. AA."

"I take it you've renounced your former lifestyle."

"For twelve years, seven months, and sixteen days so far."

"But who's counting?"

He laughs. "Have a seat, Nob. Can I call you Nob?" I shrug my assent. He gestures toward two nearby benches placed to form a conversation corner, and we settle in.

"You said you wanted to talk about Lana."

"I'm writing a story about her. It's gotten a little out of hand." I pull my reporter's notebook out of my pocket and flip it open.

"So I've read. It's so sad about Ginger."

The scent of some sweet flower floats by on a wisp of sea breeze. Gardenia? I seem to recall the same smell floating from a scorpion bowl of rum punch I once shared with Gloria at a Chinese restaurant. This was early in our friendship, before my marriage to Holly, when we were trying on a romantic relationship. It never did fit right. We tried a number of alterations but they just drove us apart. It wasn't until we gave up that our relationship really clicked.

"I sent a condolence note to the house," Senzimmer says, "but I didn't know if Billy was still there."

"He is."

"He got it, then. That's good. I feel bad about what I did to him."

"What did you do?"

"I slept with his wife."

"From what I understand, you weren't the first, and he didn't care."

"She slept around, sure. We all did. But with me and Lana it was different. We had something going. It wasn't just recreational sex; it was a thing, you know? Something that might have had a future. It was okay with Billy if Lana had a zipless fuck, but having a regular lover was different. Like cheating. I really have to reconnect with him, make amends."

Admission and apology. Two steps down, ten to go. Not to criticize AA. Senzimmer is clearly in a better place now than he was when he was in Sticky White or when he went upstate. But I tend to mistrust dogma, no matter how positive it may be. Especially when there's a Higher Power invoked.

"Were you still seeing her when she was killed?"

"We broke up a couple months before. I think Billy gave her an ultimatum."

"According to the tabloids, she dumped Billy for *you*."

He smirks. "I don't mean to burst your bubble, Nob, but in the tabloids, truth is just a four-letter word."

"I see your point," I concede, though it's something of a sore one. I take pride in the veracity of my reporting when I write for the 'bloids. But I've been screwed by so-called editors more times than I'd care to count and, of course, it's my byline that takes the licking.

"What was she like?" I ask.

"She'd swing with the wind. Be one person one minute, another the next."

"Mood swings?"

"Not like that. Like she couldn't decide who she wanted to be, so she tried out different personalities." He frowns as if unhappy with his own description. "She used to dress up like old movie stars, you know. Used to make me do it, too. We'd play roles."

"What do you mean?"

"She'd dress up like Myrna Loy in the *Thin Man* movies and dress me up, too. We'd be Nick and Nora Charles. Or we'd put on golf outfits like Spencer Tracy and Katherine Hepburn in *Pat and Mike*. We'd party a little then have sex, all in character."

I'm having a hard time seeing Lana Strain role-playing classic movie stars. It is so far removed from my own Lana fantasies.

"I never saw Lana as the classic movie type," I say.

"She was a total freak for the Golden Age. Just look at her girls. Both named for Academy Award winners."

Boom-Boom Laphroig had told me about the names, but I hadn't put it together as an obsession. I flash on the crime-scene photo.

"Did she ever wear a black dotted swiss halter dress?"

"She loved that dress," he says. "Marilyn Monroe was supposed to wear it in *Some Like It Hot*, but it never made the cut. Lana picked it up at some charity auction. She'd wear it with these red stiletto heels and those old nylons with the sexy seams up the back? Then she'd put on this big blond wig."

I flash on the crime-scene photo and remember the blurry thing on her vanity that looked vaguely like a human head. A wig stand.

"She'd make me wear a tweed double-breasted suit, and I'd be Joe DiMaggio. Or I'd put on a tux and be JFK. She'd whip us up some martinis and cocktail wieners, and we'd have a little party. Then she'd sing me "Happy Birthday" and start a slow peel of that dress...man, could she sizzle."

I rarely envy other men, but I'm doing it right now.

"Was this role-playing thing something she did with everyone?"

"I don't think so." He looks pensive. "We'd been together a couple weeks before she suggested it to me. Most of the guys she had were one-night stands. Wham, bam, thank you, Sam. If he was good, she might keep him around a few days, but that was it."

"So if she was dressed up the night she was killed, you think she was expecting a lover she knew pretty well?"

"That would be my guess."

"And when you'd do this role-playing, would she already be dressed when you got there? Or would the two of you get dressed together?"

"Oh, she'd be dressed and ready to play. It was like everything she did—the music, the drinking, the drugs, the sex—there was nothing halfway about it. I'm sure she spent hours on that makeup."

I try to remember her makeup from the crime-scene photo, but very little of her face was visible through her hair. I make a note to recheck the photo and the autopsy report.

"Ever see her wearing a gold half-heart necklace with a jagged edge?"

His brows indicate a positive hit. "Never saw it on Lana, but her father had one like that."

"Nathaniel Strain?"

"Yeah. He showed it to me once at some weird art opening on La Cienega, some friend of the family. It was really bizarre. The artist did this kind of surrealist stuff with taxidermy. A sheep with a pig's head, a snake with eight dachshund legs, you know."

Actually, I don't. But I nod anyway. I'm struggling with the notion of Strain wearing one of these pendants like some smitten twelve-year-old.

"There was this one piece," he continues, "had a pelican in flight with its beak impaling the heart of a bull. Nathaniel dug out his broken-heart pendant and made some lame joke about it."

"He was wearing it?"

"It was on his keychain."

I remember the gnat of a clue that I just couldn't snatch that day in Strain's office. It was right in front of me in the photo of the young Nathaniel Strain showing more pride in his vintage MG than in his granddaughters. He was holding his keychain aloft, and I'll bet my left ear that that pendant was on it.

Lana had one. Ginger had one. And now Strain has one. Three pendants, two murders. Is there a connection? If these pendants have any meaning, Strain is the only one left to ask. But the last time we spoke, he threw me out of his office. If I want another shot at him, I'll have to beg his forgiveness. That has all the appeal of a French kiss from a camel.

FORTY-SEVEN

The next day I meet Sophia for lunch at Sri Siam in Van Nuys. When it opened twenty-five years ago, it was only the second Thai restaurant in the Valley. It's tucked into a cheap minimall on Vanowen and the atmosphere, to be kind, is basic. But the food sings.

"Your friend Lieutenant Lopes doesn't like me very much, does she?" Sophia asks.

"What makes you think that?"

"The way she acted when she questioned me."

"It's tough to tell with Gloria. She's known for picking some pretty unusual ways to show her feelings. Makes her hard to read sometimes."

"It's easy to see she likes you." She twists her chopstick wrapper into a paper stick. I always wonder why Thai restaurants give you chopsticks. In Thailand they eat with a fork and a soup spoon.

"We go back a long way."

"I think she might be in love with you."

I choke on my own saliva. "Love is a complicated thing for Gloria. She doesn't believe in monogamy, but she has a hard time dealing with the outcome of that. She's got a boyfriend, by the way. And he's not me."

"What makes him a boyfriend if they're not monogamous?"

"He's monogamous. It's just that she's not."

"And he's okay with that?"

"He knows about it."

"What about you?" She glances up at me. I notice a little freckle in one of her eyes.

"I'm okay with it."

"I meant, is love a complicated thing for you, too?"

I don't know where she's going with this, and that makes me nervous. She's diving into some untested waters.

"Not if I can help it."

The air is suddenly flush with exotic scents, and I turn to see our kai jiew pork omelet arrive.

"Did you know Vern Senzimmer?" I ask.

"I knew the name from that night my mother kicked Poppy out, but I never met him."

"I met him yesterday. He told me your grandfather has one of those gold pendants like your mother had."

Instead of replying, she takes a bite of omelet.

"So did your sister," I add softly.

She freezes, hands hovering over her plate. Something crosses her face that looks like grief then she turns to stare out the window.

"Did Karl know about your grandfather? About the pendants?"

I presume Strain gave a half-heart pendant to each of his victims as an initiation into his secret club, a reminder of her vow of silence, a symbol of their grim bond.

I also presume he didn't pass up any opportunities.

"Your grandfather gave one to you, too, didn't he?"

Sophia's chopsticks start to tremble. She puts them down on her plate. I take her reaction as an affirmation. She looks me in the eye and transmits her pain like a broadcast. I long to say something analgesic, but only platitudes come to mind. The noise of the restaurant recedes into the background as we retreat together to a private emotional space carved out by her tacit revelation.

An irritating sound shatters the moment. Sophia erupts in a flurry of motion, rummaging in her purse for her ringing cell phone. I'm annoyed that she's taking this call, as if she's depriving me of some sacred experience. She says hello then listens. Stunned, she drops the phone back in her purse.

Her face is a blank, but tears start to brim, causing the afternoon sunlight to flare off her cheeks. "They found drugs in the coffee he gave me."

FORTY-EIGHT

Sophia comes back from the restroom looking like a different person. Her eyes are still red, but her nerves are settled, her tears are stanched, and her face is no longer streaked with mascara. I've ordered her a Thai iced coffee that now sits at her place beside her half-finished Singha. She sits down and eyes them for a moment, trying to decide whether to spike her mood up or down.

"You okay?"

She nods and reaches for the beer.

"Do you want me to call Gloria?"

"No police. Not yet. It could have been some sort of accident."

"Sophia, it was no accident. He did the same thing to Ginger."

"You don't know that. Maybe somebody's trying to frame him."

She clings to denial like a drowning woman to a sinking raft.

"Somebody who had access to your morning coffee?"

This penetrates like mercury poisoning. She hangs her head.

"I guess I need a place to stay." She considers her options. "Maybe I could stay with you for a few days?"

A small inappropriate thrill shivers my timbers. "Me?"

"If it's okay."

"I've got plenty of room, but don't you want to stay with someone who's, you know, maybe a closer friend?"

"To be honest? I don't know if I can face any of my friends right now. They'll all be thinking 'I told you so,' but they'll be too sensitive to come out and say it. I really don't want to deal with that kind of two-faced shit. At least with you, there's no bullshit."

"What about your dad?"

She gives me a look that requires no words to express how absurd that would be.

I give her a sheepish smile. "You're welcome to stay. Mi casa es su casa." At least until Holly takes it away.

———

Freshly showered and still buttoning my shirt, I rush downstairs to answer the bell. Sophia had swung by her place to throw a few things in an overnight bag, so I expect that she's at the door, but I eyeball the peephole just to be sure. She's waiting, chewing on her ponytail. She hears me twist the deadbolt and drops her hair as I open the door. She gives her head a twist to pull her ponytail off her shoulder and it disappears behind her back.

"Iced coffee?"

"Sounds good."

I take her bag and put it at the foot of the stairs then lead her into the kitchen and get the coffee out of the fridge.

"What did you tell Karl?" I ask.

"I told him Poppy was having a lot of trouble dealing with Ginger's death, and I was going to move in with him until he could get it under control."

We go into the living room and settle in on the couch.

"What if Karl calls your dad's house?"

"He and Poppy don't get along. If Karl wants to talk, he'll call my cell."

She stares out the window at the view. Her green-gold eyes are reddened by tears, reflecting a hailstorm of emotions. For some reason an image comes to mind when Lolita lets Humbert Humbert licks an annoying speck of dust off her eyeball. I imagine the briny taste of Sophia's tears.

She's sitting close enough for me to smell the apricot shampoo in her hair. I imagine her in the shower, working the lather, water streaming a sheen down her body. I want to kiss her. What the fuck is wrong with me?

I try to think about baseball, but it won't take my mind off her lips. She parts them just a bit, her eyes searching mine, and it occurs to me that she's thinking the same misguided thing. Her desire couldn't be clearer if she had "Kiss me" scrawled on her forehead.

"I'll make up the bed in the guest room," I say and get my ass off the couch before my dick leads me astray. Shame isn't as good as a cold shower, but it works better than baseball.

FORTY-NINE

That night I get home from a grueling three thousand meters in the Van Nuys pool to find Melody and Gloria sitting on my moonlit deck, drinking my beer, probably disparaging my reputation.

Runt comes running, and I brace myself to knee him in the chest before he can thump mine. After a couple attempts, he gives up, and I give him a hearty but civilized ear ruffling. He finally gets over his need to greet and goes back to sit by Gloria, eyes peeled for dropping food.

I open the fridge and find some duck mole empanadas left over from an experiment I tried last week. Worked out pretty well. I stick them in the oven, pour myself a glass of five-dollar Malbec, and join the odd couple outside.

"Where's Sophia?" I ask.

"She's taking a nap," says Melody.

Gloria raises her glass in a mock toast. "You go out with the chick on one date, and she's already living in. Pretty swift work, Studly."

"I never go on dates. I can't write them off." I sip my Malbec.

"I stand corrected," she says. "You're living together after only one tax dodge. She planning to file charges against her boyfriend anytime soon? Maybe get a restraining order?"

"I don't know. We only talked for a few minutes before she went off to nap."

"Depression sleep," says Melody. "That's what happens when your therapist tries to kill you."

245

"He hasn't been her therapist in years," says Gloria.

"Good point," I say. "He raped her when he was her therapist then dumped her as a patient and tried to cover his tracks by trapping her in a relationship then waited until she was in love with him before trying to kill her. Much less traumatic that way."

"Exactly," she says, skirting my sarcasm. Gloria wipes her brow with the back of her hand to squeegee off a sweat slick. It's been dark for an hour, but it's still in the high eighties. At least she's dressed for the weather in her canary tank top and old denim cutoffs. Melody's wearing four or five layers of clingy bodywear in blacks, whites, and grays, all variations on the basic leotard with names like *jazz suit* or *body hose*. One of them is long-sleeved, another long-legged; between them all she looks like she's wearing a thin patchwork wetsuit. My body temperature spikes just looking at her. She's not even breaking a sweat.

We look out over the Valley floor to see millions of shimmering lights throwing off every color from ROY to BIV, as my high school physics teacher used to say. The brilliance of the light pollutes the darkness of the sky, causing visibility problems for local astronomers, but tonight the stars shine brightly.

Runt suddenly perks up. There's something on the hill below the house. Maybe a raccoon or a coyote. I pray it's not a skunk. Runt sits stock-still, ears erect, brow furrowed. One hundred percent concentration.

Gloria shifts her attention from Runt back to me. "So let me guess. You think he put downers in her coffee, just like he did Ginger. Because he was trying to kill her, just like he did Ginger. Am I right?" asks Gloria in her trap-setting voice.

"Why not?"

"The guy's a grade-A sphincter, that's for sure. But the asshole's got brains. I have a hard time seeing him try to reenact the exact same murder with a second victim when he knows we already suspect him of the first."

"On the other hand," I say, "if he's already a suspect, she's a huge threat if she can incriminate him. And if she dies, he's going to be a suspect no matter how he kills her, so he might as well use a method he's comfortable with."

We hear a rustling sound in the bushes, and Runt jumps to his feet with a little growl. The humans all fall silent, straining to hear it again. The hill is pitch black so we can't see what's out there. I consider getting a flashlight from the kitchen, but it's too much trouble. Runt trots over to the railing and peers down. After a few moments of silence, the rest of us go back to our conversation while Runt stands guard, hackles raised. He doesn't bark, but he goes in and out of a growl so soft that it seems more to bolster his self-confidence than to scare off an intruder.

A light flares on the hill, and Runt starts barking his head off. A flame flies through the air, a bottle breaks, and with a chilling whoosh my deck is ablaze. It happens so fast we don't even have time to stand. The fire splashes across the far side of the deck, so none of us is ignited, but within seconds the flames stream up the wall of my house.

I run for the hose and find it tangled and disconnected. The flames roar louder as I grope for its coupling. Gloria pulls a gun from her purse, jumps the rail, and disappears in the shadows. Melody rushes into the house. Out of the corner of my eye I see the flames shoot higher than my roof. I spot the end of the hose and frantically screw it onto the nib. I turn the valve on with one hand while I'm still connecting the hose with the other, and at last I see water shoot out. I aim the stream full blast on the fire and use my thumb to broaden the spray. The accelerant fire doesn't want to go out, but at least my efforts seem to be slowing the spread of the flames beyond the splatter pattern of the gasoline or whatever it is. Runt is barking himself hoarse, but that doesn't seem to be damping the fire, either.

Melody reappears with the small fire extinguisher I keep in the kitchen. She lets out a blast of some sort of foam designed to put out grease fires, but it doesn't seem to have any effect. Just as I'm starting to panic, the extinguisher chemistry finally kicks in. The fire coughs a few times, gasping for breath, then finally dies out.

"Does that get me a raise?" she asks.

"No."

"Typical."

Under the deck I see small drips of fire on the hill. I point the hose through the new gaping hole in my deck and drown them out one by one as sirens approach. Everything but my adrenaline appears to have been extinguished, but just to be sure I turn on my sprinklers to water the hill. Gloria lets out a shout from below and, a moment later, climbs onto the deck soaking wet, gun in hand, no perp.

"Thanks for the shower," she says.

"See anybody?"

"Too dark." Her shins are scratched up from the bushes, but other than that she's okay. Runt comes up, tail wagging, and gives her a lick.

My nerves won't cede control to my brain, so I still haven't fully absorbed what just happened. It occurs to me that if we hadn't been sitting right there, my house would be history. As the smoke is still clearing, I wonder what Jerry would have to say about that.

Melody snaps me back to reality. "Jesus! He could have killed us all!"

FIFTY

t seems like forever, but firefighters arrive within seven minutes of the conflagration with a pumper and a hook and ladder.

A few months back, LAFD sent me a threatening notice about brush clearance. It irritated me at the time, but tonight they are forgiven; their intentions have been validated. If they hadn't made me clear the brush, the hills would be alive with the sound of combustion. The whole neighborhood could have gone up.

Sophia managed to sleep through the fire, but the arrival of the trucks wakes her up. She wanders out of the house yawning. "What happened?"

"Someone threw a Molotov cocktail," I say.

She tries to make sense of this as the LAFD checks for live embers lurking on the hill or in the eaves. Someone scrapes a few char samples from the deck and seals them in a glass jar to take back to the lab and ID the ILR, copspeak for ignitable liquid residue.

After the firemen leave it feels like the air has been sucked out of the night. Runt lies passed out in the middle of the kitchen, having barked himself into a stupor. The rest of us need a massage and a shower but settle for a beer. The half-finished Malbec tastes like someone spiked it with liquid smoke.

We settle back into our respective seats, trying to ignore the damage to the deck and the house, at least until daylight makes it unavoidable.

"Cogswell?" asks Gloria.

"Or Karl," I say.

"Karl would never do this," says Sophia.

"But he would try to poison you," I say. Sophia has no response.

"I like Karl for Ginger's murder," says Gloria, "but Cogswell strikes me more as the firebomb sort, and I think he's a prime for Lana's murder."

"What about Grandpa Nate?" asks Melody. "He's got access to industrial chemicals and workers with strong arms for throwing."

"I wouldn't put it past him," says Sophia.

This guy really knows how to curry the love of his granddaughters.

"And we can't rule out your dad," says Melody. "He had a lot to gain by Lana's death."

"But not by Ginger's," I point out. I still find it hard to believe that mere coincidence could explain how both mother and daughter were murdered.

"Poppy didn't do it," says Sophia. "He couldn't have. Violence is against every religion he ever tried."

"Maybe the arson's unrelated," says Gloria. "I can name several people who would not only love to see Nob go up in flames but would gladly douse him with gas and flick the Bic."

Between my six years as a cop and seven as a writer, I've pissed off a lot of people, including many card-carrying psychopaths.

"Like Sonny Meadows," Melody says to Sophia. "He's a guy Nob busted for robbing and raping an eighty-five-year-old blind woman. He pleaded down to assault with intent to commit rape and only got eight years. With good behavior he could be out by now."

"Or Kurt Crandal," says Gloria.

Sophia looks to Melody, who says, "Kurt and his brother Booger, whose real name escapes me, broke into a batting cage and tied a security guard to the backstop in front of the ninety-mile-an-hour hardball machine. They cracked a Coke machine for quarters and launched pitches at the guy until they ruptured his spleen, broke both knees, and rendered him sterile."

"Booger had Down syndrome, so he got off with a hand slap," adds Gloria, "but Kurt drew a dime in Quentin. I wouldn't be surprised if he was out by now, either."

"And to be fair to the opposite sex," I say, "it could have been Renee Shoenfeld. She cracked her mother's skull open with a family-size jar of gefilte fish. Her lawyer argued that Mamma drove her crazy with verbal abuse and bad cooking. I dubbed it the "burnt brisket defense," and it caught on. Renee got sent up, and I started getting anonymous death threats postmarked California Institution for Women. They had to be from Renee since the Manson girls are the only other inmates I know of there, and they'd have no reason to take a sudden interest in me."

"Let me do a cage count," says Gloria. She calls Dumphy and tells him to check status on all three.

While we wait to hear, a smoke detector pierces the night. It's screaming from the house. Some ember wasn't found, and now the house is going up five minutes after the fire department drove off. I run into the kitchen, followed closely by the others. Black smoke streams from the oven. I throw it open to see the empanadas turned to charcoal. Bad news for dinner, good news for the house. The four of us release a collective breath, even though I'd spent four hours making those damned empanadas.

Dumphy comes back to report that all three cons are still in their cages. Renee was supposed to have served her sentence by now, but she stabbed a guard with a chicken-bone shiv and bought herself an extension. And the other two never managed to internalize the concept of good behavior so they got no time off. With those three off the list, we're back to the Strain family saga.

Gloria points her finger at me like a recruiting poster. "I don't want you here alone, just in case your friend comes back for a second try. You're sleeping at my house tonight." She realizes her lapse and turns to Sophia. "You, too."

"I'm not going anywhere," I say. "No one drives me out of my own house."

"Except maybe your ex-wife," says Melody.

FIFTY-ONE

Gloria decides to spend the night on the couch. I climb into bed, hoping she won't try to sneak up to my bedroom after Sophia drifts off in the guest room. She doesn't.

The next morning Gloria and I head over to Karl's office. He isn't happy to see us.

"Talk to my lawyer." He starts to close the door. Gloria jams her foot in it.

"Where were you last night?"

"I have nothing to say to you."

He shuts the door, but we've got what we came for. No scratches on his face or forearms, so he was either wearing long sleeves, gloves, and a ski mask in a heat wave, or he wasn't tossing flaming bottles at my house last night.

We head back to the car to drive home and tell Sophia she was right.

"I spoke to the arson team this morning," says Gloria. "The dirt on your hill was too loose to hold any footprints, so that was a dead end. They haven't found any witnesses in the neighborhood. There were no prints on the bottle. And they haven't gotten to the residue yet."

"I'm sure he used gloves."

"Or she."

"Have to have a pretty good arm for a she. A liter of liquid has heft, and that toss was a thirty-foot line drive."

"I'll arm wrestle you anytime."

"I don't care how strong you are, you still throw like a girl."

"Fuck like one, too. Or don't you remember that far back?"

"What next?" I ask, pushing her back on track.

"Maybe we can drag a confession out of Cogswell," she says.

"And maybe spareribs can clear a clogged artery."

The thought of approaching Cogswell again is about as alluring as a frat house toilet stall after a binge party. It also means that we'll have to check up on his proxies, the Ugly twins. Something else to look forward to.

I'm suddenly hit by one of those realizations that's so obvious I feel like a fool for not having had it before.

"Whoever threw that firebomb must have killed Lana," I say, "because Ginger's murder doesn't give anyone a motive to try to silence me. You're already investigating Ginger's murder. Getting rid of me wouldn't change that. But Lana's case is different. It was on ice. He was home free until I started searching under rocks. I must be getting too close for someone's comfort."

"I hate to say it, but you could be right."

She pulls into a parking spot near the Odessa. Cogswell's BMW is parked in a red zone in front of the club.

"That's his Beemer," I say.

"Let's go."

"He told me if he saw me again, I'd spend several excruciating hours praying for death before he'd answer my prayers."

"You want to wait in the car?" She's annoyingly amused.

"Not on your life."

She leans over and kisses me gently on the lips, no tongue this time. "Don't worry, lover. I'll protect you."

As we get out of the car, I feel my scrotum tighten up, trying to protect my yáytsa. Big Ugly Guy is sitting on a folding chair by the front door. He sees us from a half block away and stands, obstructing the entire sidewalk. He takes a step sideways to block the entrance.

"Closed for private party," he says.

I keep my yap shut but notice he's got no scratches on his face.

"I don't give a shit," says Gloria. "This is our invite." She sounds confident and flashes her badge. If she's as scared as I am, she's a better actor. "We're going to talk to Gary Cogswell one way or another. The question is whether I'm going to have to tow his car out of this red zone to get his attention."

BUG's face is immobile except for a little twitch of his lip, as if he's trying to hide his disgust while watching a geek bite the head off a live chicken. It takes a moment for the power of the badge to mold his decision and another for the decision to migrate from his brain to his mouth.

"Wait here," he says and steps inside. We hear the clack of a deadlock, just to make sure we don't jump the gun. We're left standing on the street, staring at the door like two dogs waiting for a handout. After minute or two the bolt clacks in reverse, and the door swings open. Big Ugly Guy nods us in.

The lights are brighter than the last time I was here, and the first thing I see is Bigger Ugly Guy in a Bozo suit, complete with clown makeup and a big red ball for a schnoz. My jaw nearly drops off my head. If he has facial scratches, there's no way to see them.

The place is filled with balloons and streamers hanging from the ceiling. A stereo blasts Barney or Big Bird or some equally saccharine creature. There are probably two dozen five-year-olds running around a ring of chairs, screaming at a pitch that could shatter crystal. One of them, a skinny blond girl with an enormous nose, wears a plastic tiara. I'm guessing she's the birthday girl.

The music suddenly stops and they all drop into chairs. All but one. The birthday girl has squeezed into the last chair just a heartbeat ahead of a chubby, redheaded boy.

I hear a roaring laugh and look up to see Vlad the Impaler having the time of his life. "You are outski, Nicolas," he bellows.

The freckled, frustrated boy sucks up his disappointment, shrugs, and takes a seat at one of the tables on the periphery of the action.

I notice a group of thugs in the corner exchanging bills and realize they're betting on the kids.

The insipid music starts again, and Bigger Ugly Bozo pulls a chair out of the circle as the action ramps back up.

Our chaperone nods for us to proceed toward the back. Vlad doesn't bother to acknowledge our presence as we pass. I see Cogswell in the same old spot, the Odessa's excuse for a conference table. He does not look pleased to see me. There's a half-eaten slice of pizza on a plate before him, and an empty demitasse. I wonder if he had a dople. There's also a bottle of twenty-five-year-old Macallan single malt Scotch. Just like the bottle Angel brought to my bachelor party before I married Holly. It was unbelievably complex and smooth, and I thought I'd finally found my drink. Until the next day when I tried to buy some. Five hundred bucks a bottle. If you can find it. I'm disappointed to see that there's only one shot glass on the table, and Cogswell is already using it.

"You can go back to the door, Petya," says Cogswell. So the goon's got a name. Reminds me of Petya in *War and Peace*. When I read it in college, I was shocked when he died. I remember learning that the name comes from the Old Greek "Petra," which means "rock." As I watch him lumber toward the door, I wonder if his parents had any idea how prophetic that moniker would prove.

Gloria and I take seats across from Cogswell, and I let her do the talking.

"Gary Cogswell?"

"And you would be?"

She flashes her badge. He takes it from her and scrawls her name and badge number on a napkin before passing it back.

"What can I do for you, Officer?" Against the rigidity of his icy blue eyes, his rubbery face seems overly animated as he actually gives her a friendly grin.

"It's Detective, actually, and I'd like to know where you were around eight o'clock last night," she says.

"May I ask why?"

"I'd like to hear your answer first."

He smiles again. "Lieutenant, really. You're speaking to a lawyer. Surely you don't expect me to answer a question like that without knowing the context."

Now she smiles. "Is that because you have something to hide, Mr. Cogswell?"

"It's because I see no reason to voluntarily surrender my Constitutional right to privacy without a compelling reason."

He picks up his fork and knife and cuts himself a bite of pizza. I can't remember the last time I ate pizza with utensils, assuming I ever have. He's clearly more fastidious than I, but then he's got more of an investment to protect in his blue English suit, the same one he wore last time. A different tie, though. Blood red instead of pale yellow. I wonder if there's any significance to the choice.

"Someone threw a Molotov cocktail at Mr. Brown's house last night."

"Aside from the fact that Molotov hailed from my current employer's native land, I fail to see what that has to do with me." He looks at me for the first time. "I'm relieved to see you unharmed, Mr. Brown."

"I'm sure your heart's aflutter," I say. He smiles. I'm glad I was able to amuse him.

"Mr. Cogswell, I know you're aware that Mr. Brown is writing a story on the murder of Lana Strain."

He nods while chewing another piece of pizza, unwilling to speak with his mouth full. He's careful to lean over his plate with every bite and to chew with his mouth closed. My grandmother would have loved this guy.

"So I'm sure you understand," she continues, "why we're checking alibis on everyone involved in that case, especially those who knew of Mr. Brown's inquiries, such as yourself."

"And your two palookas," I add.

He turns those blue crystals toward me and allows another hint of amusement to curl his lips.

"You have such a way with words, Mr. Brown. No wonder you're...how did you put it? Hardly a writer?"

"I believe I said 'barely.'"

He ignores the correction and turns back to Gloria. "I wouldn't normally dignify this imposition with an answer, but to minimize the impact of this intrusion on my goddaughter's party, I'm going to make an exception. The fact is, Petya, Isaak, and I were all here last night, blowing up balloons, putting up streamers, assembling party favor bags, and making banners for this celebration."

The image of egg-shaped Cogswell or either of the whale-sized Ugly Twins trying to haul their oversized butts up on these spindly chairs to hang streamers just doesn't ring true. But the story came to him so easily and with such confidence that I know they already contrived to back each other up, so there is going to be no cracking of alibis here.

Besides, the speed with which the arsonist took off down the hill and the minimal trampling of the landscaping makes it hard for me to believe any of these three did it. The fact that they have a ready alibi implies that they were up to something unsavory last night, but I suspect it had nothing to do with my bonfire. That's not to say that Cogswell couldn't have sent someone else out to do the deed, but we aren't about to find that out by asking him. I guess Gloria comes to the same conclusion, because she stands up and gestures for me to follow.

"Thanks for your time," she says. "Maybe I'll see you in court sometime."

He responds to her double entendre by throwing me a malicious scowl, a clear reminder of the torture-death threat that ended our last tête-à-tête.

FIFTY-TWO

The cops have already canvassed Ginger's neighborhood, but some people clam up when cops come around, so I decide to rerun the task, maybe find someone who saw Karl's car that night. I take Melody with me in case we run into any women home alone. Mel's presence makes them more likely to open the door. It's also more effective to have two sets of eyes and ears to pick up signals from an interviewee, to make sure you don't miss an important follow-up question, or to make sure no one blindsides the back of your head with a hammer.

Nobody's home directly across the street from Ginger or at the house on its downhill side. Moving uphill, the first house has an old Honda Civic parked on the apron. The front door is sandblasted to look like something rescued from a New Mexican ghost town, and there's a weathered cowbell hanging beside it with a heavy wrought-iron skeleton key for a clapper. I clang it twice.

A silver-haired woman in a black unitard opens the door. Her face is more wrinkled than not, like a dried apple, but her eyes sparkle with life, and her body is hard and lean. Behind her I see a wall of mirrors in the living room with a ballet barre mounted across it. No furniture. Two girls who look to be about five years old practice moves at the barre.

"Yes?"

"Sorry to bother you, ma'am. My name's Nob Brown, and this is my associate, Melody Elvenstar."

She brightens at this. "Like fairy stars?"

Melody blushes. "My parents were in a spiritual phase when they picked it."

"Each of the seven points of an elven star represents a gateway to the higher self. Your parents gave you a great gift in that name."

Terrific. A witness who believes in fairies.

"Ma'am, we're sorry to bother you," I interrupt, "but we're looking into the tragic death of your neighbor, Ginger Strain. Would you mind answering a few questions?" I nod over her shoulder at the two girls. "We can come back later if it would be more convenient."

"Are you with the police?"

"No, ma'am. I'm a writer. But I'm working with the police. We all want her killer brought to justice. Ginger was gracious enough to grant me an interview a few days before she died, and we were supposed to meet again the day her body was found."

"So you were fated to become involved," she says and, buried deeply beneath my empiricism, some part of me agrees. She turns and calls out, "Why don't you girls have your snack now. I'll be out front for a few minutes." Then she steps out onto the porch and closes the door behind her. "My neighbor's girls. I give lessons."

She and Melody sit on an old wooden porch swing suspended by a rusted chain. I hook my butt on the porch railing opposite. She introduces herself as Rose Gold, former high school dance teacher now retired along with the high school dance program. I ask her how well she knew Ginger.

"Oh, I knew her since she was a little girl. I gave lessons to both the girls." She smiles at the memory. "They were such sweet girls. At least they were until Lana was..." She lets her silence fill in the missing exposition as her wrinkles seem to slump in a moment of mourning.

"Then you knew Lana, too."

"Oh, yes. I've been here forty years. Lana was away a lot, and there's not a lot of street life on a street without sidewalks, but we'd see each other now and again. Watering and so on. It was hard on the girls with their parents on the road so much."

For some reason it hadn't occurred to me before that with Lana and Billy in the same band, the girls would have been left parentless whenever they were on tour.

"Who looked after them?"

"Billy's mother sometimes, until she died. Sometimes a lovely French girl. I think her name was Claudine. Billy's brother once or twice. And they had a nanny when they were babies."

"What about Lana's father?"

Rose stares at Ginger's house, trying to summon a vision. Finally she says, "Not that I remember."

"Were you home the night Ginger was murdered?"

"Oh yes. I don't get out much in the evenings. My night vision is gone, so I can't drive after dark anymore." She glances sadly at her beige Civic. It doesn't look like she drives all that well before dark either. The driver's side door sports multiple scrapes, a rear taillight is broken, the front fender on the passenger side is so banged up it seems corrugated, and the hood, an incongruous forest green, is a junkyard replacement. Rose and her car have clearly shared some adventures.

"Do you remember seeing or hearing anything unusual that night?"

"As I told the police, there was nothing that I can think of."

"No one coming or going?"

"I don't spend a lot of time looking out the window. I usually have dinner in front of *Newshour*, then I catch up with my Facebook friends for a while, and if I'm not too tired by then, I'll settle in to read by the fire."

"Your Facebook friends?"

"Oh my, yes. I've got my Pilates group, my dance group, my hiking group, my spiritual group, and my book group. It's a chore to keep up with them all."

"Do you remember anything at all about that night?"

"No. I really don't. Sorry."

"Well, thank you for your time," I say.

As Melody and I head down the steps, Rose has an after-thought. "You might ask Will. He mentioned something about some car."

We turn back in unison and Melody asks, "Will?"

She points down the street at the house two doors down from Ginger and Billy.

"He does gardening for most of the neighbors. Has done for thirty-odd years. Comes and goes through our yards as he pleases. I'll see him out there in the middle of the night some-times. He goes through everybody's trash and probably peeks through windows, but he's always there when you need him. There aren't many secrets around here that Will doesn't know."

"Did he talk to the police?" I ask.

"Goodness, no. He hid up in the hills somewhere while they were around. But you just tell him I sent you over. He'll let you in."

Between the two of them, the squirrel appears cleaner. Will's face is smudged with mud, and his hair comes down below his shoulders in wannabe dreadlocks that look like they're coated with bacon grease. He's probably close to sixty, but his hair is jet black and his thin arms roped with muscle. His nose looks like a pig's snout that's been sunburned and mottled from what looks like a half dozen liquid nitrogen scars, as if he's been one-upping skin cancer for years. His nails are long and blackened from gar-dening and rummaging through trash cans for the salvageable junk that now litters his yard—broken chairs, lengths of scrap lumber, old lamps, a plastic birdbath, a Hoover upright with a plant sprouting through a hole in its bag, the dome from an old-fashioned streetlight.

The squirrel perches on Will's shoulder, as calm as a frenetic creature can be. Will hands a Brazil nut to the squirrel, who sits absolutely still except for its feverish chewing that extrudes a fine mist of nut dust on Will's ragged, stained black-and-green-plaid lumberjack jacket.

Will doesn't look me in the eye when he speaks but he invites us in when I tell him that Rose sent us.

We walk into a great room that, like the yard, is filled with piles of junk that presumably can't survive the elements outside. In the midst of the mess, like a child's secret fort, is a cozy seating area around a cast-iron potbellied stove. Will's got a fire going, using tightly rolled newspapers for logs, as if the summer heat needed help. He sits on an old sofa covered with a ragged serape and an army-surplus wool blanket. Melody and I sit on once-discarded lawn chairs that Will has repaired with a clear bias toward function over style.

"We understand you saw something the night of the murder," I begin.

"Nex' mo'nin'," he says, "budappenat nigh'," by which he means he saw it the next morning but it happened that night.

He's got what they call a "yat" accent, as in "Where y'at?" Not regional, just unintelligible. A lot of dropped syllables and slurred consonants. The way he runs his words together, he's hard t'unnerstan'.

"Scrape mall, lef pain."

"I'm sorry. I didn't quite get that."

"Scrape mall. C'mon showya."

That last part I understand. We follow as he grabs a flashlight and leads us outside to the street. He points the light at the rock retaining wall that fronts his house to illuminate a six-inch paint scrape. *Scraped my wall,* he'd said, *and left paint.*

"Warntair nawt fo. Sort'n mawnin whena come dowfada pape." It wasn't there the night before. He saw it in the morning when he came down for the paper.

"You're sure?"

"I spected fweeds jessfo sunoun." Another few questions, and I manage to deduce that he *inspected for weeds just before sundown* on the night of the murder. His yard may look like a junkyard, but Will does not tolerate anything sprouting between the rocks of his precious wall. Neither was he pleased to see its natural beauty scarred with paint, especially in a color as conspicuous as turquoise.

FIFTY-THREE

We wind across Mulholland from Laurel Canyon to Woodcliff to avoid rush hour traffic while enjoying the view. But I don't notice the view. My foot's on the gas and my mind's on fire. Sophia, of the turquoise Miata, has been lying to me.

"Could you slow down a little?" Melody's got both feet up, bracing herself against the dash.

"She's been lying the whole time."

Will noticed the scrape hours before Sophia found the body. That meant she was there sometime during the night. So she lied. It should be as simple as that. But it's not. I don't simply feel like a fool, I feel emotionally betrayed.

"Get a grip," says Melody. "You're acting like a cuckold."

"A cuckold?"

"What do you want to do? Barge in and confront her? Think with your big head for a change. You don't want to tip your hand until we think this through."

"What's to think through? She lied to me."

"You are such a crybaby. She lied to everybody, including the police."

She's right. I'm letting my emotions lead my actions, like I did on the force. When the fuck am I going to learn my lesson? I ease up on the gas and take a deep breath.

"Maybe we should grab a coffee before we head home," I say.

She lets out a sigh of relief. "That's the Nob we all know and sort of love."

I head down Beverly Glen and manage to find enough cells to reach Gloria. She's just leaving the Van Nuys courthouse, where she testified against a gangbanger who shot up a laundromat, killing three women but missing the guy he was gunning for by ten feet. The target shot back and didn't even hit the drive-by car. If the city really wants to cut down on innocent bloodshed they ought to run an after-school program to teach gangbangers how to shoot straight.

After her day in court, Gloria is in no mood for coffee, so we meet up at Pineapple Hill—Gold Rush saloon décor, stiff drinks, big screens, and free popcorn. It's early, so there are only a few guys in the bar watching a Dodgers game and a mid-fifties couple making out in the back of the lounge. I'm guessing Jdate.com, since he's wearing a yarmulke.

We grab two red-velvet loveseats across a coffee table by the fireplace, and a good-looking waitress appears like magic. It's a few minutes short of the cocktail hour. I order a Bombay. Gloria asks if the Cabernet comes out of a box and when the waitress says no, she orders a glass. Melody wants a club soda with lime.

The waitress leaves, and I fill Gloria in on our conversation with Will.

"What would Sophia have to cover up?" she asks.

"Maybe she's still protecting Karl," says Melody.

"He tried to kill her," says Gloria. "What's to protect?"

"It could be she just doesn't want to admit she lied to us," I say. "She originally lied to protect Karl. Now that motive is gone, but she's afraid to change her story. She thinks it would complicate things."

"Did it ever occur to you," asks Gloria. "that maybe Karl went over there in her car to throw off potential witnesses?"

This thought makes me wonder why I had been so quick to accuse. I've spent plenty of time looking into Sophia's eyes, and I've seen empathy, warmth, and honesty. On the other hand, I'm not always the most objective scholar when it comes to reading women.

We decide that our best shot at the truth is for me to talk to Sophia alone. Gloria agrees only if I promise not to mention the paint scrape. She wants to keep that as a surprise, if necessary, for official questioning on the record with Sophia's lawyer present. Without the paint scrape to rattle Sophia I don't have much leverage, but if I time it right, get her all cozy and trusty, lay on the charm and oil her jaw with a little wine, she might confide any secrets she's keeping.

<hr />

There's no open space in front of my house, so I park a few houses down. As I walk back, I pass Sophia's Miata and see the fresh scrape on the passenger-side fender. I might have seen it before and not even noticed. Without context it's a minor blemish, a scratch, not even a dent. But now it practically screams at me.

I find Sophia lounging on the living room couch, staring out the picture window. She's wearing a loose white button-down blouse and a retro aloha skirt, midnight blue with white hibiscuses. Her lips are backlit against the gray sky, and their silhouette in profile is crisp and inviting. But her brows spell trouble.

"What's wrong?" I ask.

She turns her gaze to Senzimmer's book on the coffee table. "What's that?"

"Research for my piece on your mother."

"I mean the drawing."

She's talking about a piece of scratch paper I'm using as my bookmark. The part that sticks out of the book reveals the little sketch I drew the morning after Gloria showed me Lana's half-heart necklace.

"My mother had a pendant like that," she adds.

"They come in pairs. Any idea who has the other half?"

She shakes her head then puts both hands behind her neck, drops her chin, and throws her long amber locks over her head to hang in front of her face. Then she throws her head back, sending her wavy hair flying behind her. Finally, she shakes her head like a terrier. Some sort of preening, I guess.

"She hated that necklace," she says.

"She was wearing it when her body was found."

"That's impossible. I tried it on once when I was a kid, and she got so mad she flushed it down the toilet."

"Whoever gave it to her must have broken her heart."

"I doubt it. My mother was the one who always did the heartbreaking."

"Maybe she was in love with a married man."

"My mother wasn't capable of love." Her sadness drifts through the room like an acid- rain cloud, making me feel heartless for planning to trap her into revealing the truth about where she was on the night of the murder. My deception wells up like puke in my throat.

She's lying on her side against the back of the couch. I sit on the edge before her, hip to hip.

"Okay," I say. "The truth is, I feel something going on between us."

"Me, too."

"I don't think it's healthy. You've been through too much, too fast. You shouldn't trust your emotions right now, and I shouldn't react to them."

A wisp of shame crosses her face. "I don't believe in ignoring my feelings," she says, barely audible. There's a fear in her eyes. A fear of another loss. I feel the urge to hold her, to comfort her.

Her eyes are sucking me in again. *She may have lied to you.*

She puts her hand on my cheek, a languid touch alive with promise. *On the other hand, maybe not.*

I'm afraid of losing my way if we kiss, but of losing her trust if we don't. I'm still debating when she decides for me. Her kiss feels like a jolt from a stun gun. Deep, unbridled, charged with longing. She rouses feelings I haven't known since my first date with Holly, but in their wake I'm awash with guilt. My motives are unclean, a mishmash of truth and lies. How far am I willing to let this go? Am I cad enough to sleep with her in order to lure her into telling me the truth?

I pull away. "I can't do this," I say. She grabs my head and pulls me back in.

FIFTY-FOUR

The morning sun wakes me from a dream about Sophia's lips. They were the size of a small canoe, and I was cradled naked between them, feeling as if I were afloat in a soft, warm paradise. If I could repeat this dream in an endless loop for the rest of my life, I would die happy.

I open my eyes and feel disoriented. *Where's my clock radio?* Then I realize I'm under an afghan on the living room rug. Sophia lies beside me, her hand across my groin as if owning it even in sleep. To my relief, we're both clothed, at least partially. We'd kissed and begun exploring each other's bodies. By the time we fell asleep it felt as intimate as sex, but we didn't cross that line. I suspect it was because neither one of us was willing to test that emotional minefield for the time being.

Her lips look just as soft as they were in my dream. I remember losing myself in them last night and feel a pleasant stirring sensation under her hand. I watch her eyes twitch beneath her lids, and I question my doubts about her.

Sure, her car scraped Will's wall that night, but why would she have gone over there? It makes more sense that Karl drove it there while she slept. The vanity plates on his mustard Porsche read "PHD KARL." That's the sort of detail that sticks in a witness's mind. If he was worried about one of Ginger's neighbors remembering his car, he'd be much better off taking the Miata with its generic, forgettable license number.

I slip out from beneath Sophia's arm and trudge to the bathroom to brush my teeth and empty my bladder. When I return, she lifts her face to me curiously, as if trying to read the morning-after mood.

"Morning, sweet lips," I say.

She smiles. "Morning, Nob."

I give her a little kiss. I'm minty fresh, but she still tastes like the morning after. It's a raw, honest taste that says she's not afraid to reveal the person behind the curtain. Not the taste of a deceitful woman.

She yawns and follows me into the kitchen, unselfconscious, breasts playing peekaboo with her half-buttoned blouse. I set up a pot of coffee then sit down to watch it drip through. She pokes her head in the fridge and, as she bends over, her hibiscus skirt drapes like falling water over her perfect ass and looks like something I can imagine staring at every day. Is that where I want to go with Sophia? If so, it's not going to happen until we stop lying to each other.

"You have to tell me the truth."

She gives me a quizzical look.

"About what happened that night," I continue.

She lets out a sad sigh and comes around behind me to wrap her arms around me. She lays her head on mine. It's a loving gesture, but I'd rather be able to see her eyes. "Can't we just forget about all that for a little while?"

"That's not an answer."

She moves to sit in the chair beside me and puts her hand on my forearm, stroking it, looking sad.

"After last night, do you really think I'd lie to you?"

"I don't know."

Pain contorts her face.

"After last night, I'd hope you could trust me," I say. "Your car was at Ginger's that night." I'm sure Gloria wouldn't approve, but technically I haven't mentioned the paint.

Sophia is shocked by the bald statement, as if I'd slapped her.

"I want to know why," I say.

She searches my eyes for compassion but finds only accusation. Her protective facade finally crumbles. She doesn't know how I found out, but it's clear that I did. Denial is no longer an option.

"I'm sorry," she says softly.

"When you find yourself in a hole, stop digging." It's a Will Rogers quote, but she doesn't look like she needs the citation.

"I was afraid to tell you," she says. "I was afraid for Karl."

"So he did go over there."

She falls silent, weighing whether to tell me or how much to tell me or maybe whether to sink a knife in my chest instead.

Finally she says, "We both did."

I'm floored. "Why in the world would he take you with him?"

"We were in the middle of a fight that night when Ginger called. That's what started it all. I didn't know who he was talking to, but it was obviously a patient who was in crisis. Karl said he'd be right over. I begged him not to go away angry, but he just grabbed his keys and left. I had this panic that he was never coming back, so I went after him."

"You had no idea where he was going?"

"Not until he turned onto Weeping Glen. Then I realized he must be going to see Ginger. It made no sense. I thought he'd stopped treating her years ago. But the door opened, and there she was in her nightgown, throwing her arms around him, sobbing. I watched him hug my sister, then lead her inside and close the door like he was closing it on me."

She leans over and lays her head on my shoulder.

"What did you do?" I ask.

"I had to get out of there. I had this insane fear that he'd look out the window and see my car. That he'd realize I'd followed him and hate me for it. So I guess I drove home; I don't remember much until I crawled into bed, and the fog just sort of lifted and I realized he was cheating on me."

She gets up to pour some coffee for us both.

"When Karl finally pulled into the driveway I heard his car door open, but he didn't slam it shut like he usually does. He was trying to be quiet."

I nod to let her know I'm on the wavelength. She puts a cup of hot coffee in front of me and sits back down with her own.

"Then I heard his shoes crunch the gravel outside. The front door opened. The stairs creaked. The bedroom door brushed across the carpet. He was trying not to wake me." She snorts at the irony. "As if I could sleep."

She takes a sip of her java.

"I said, 'I'm awake' and turned on the light, you know, so he wouldn't have to go into the bathroom to undress. He held out his hand for me to see that it was trembling and says, 'The guy was ready to kill himself.' Can you believe it? The 'guy'? He had this elaborate story made up, and I just let him keep winding more coils around his own noose until I couldn't take it anymore. I went into the bathroom and sat on the tub and felt sorry for myself."

She looks into my eyes for a minute, maybe trying to gauge my reaction. I try to look empathetic but keep quiet. I don't want to bump her off track.

"Karl asked me for a sleeping pill, so I opened the medicine cabinet, pulled out the pills, and poured out a handful. I looked in the mirror, and all I could see was pain. It would have been so easy to just swallow them right then and go lie down beside him. Let him find me dead in the morning and realize I'd found him out. Let him live with *that* guilt for the rest of his fucking life."

"But you didn't."

She gives me one of those politely affirming smiles just in case I think I'm being insightful in stating the obvious.

"When I came back with his pill," she says, "it was pretty obvious I was still upset. He told me he thought I was being unfair to him." Her eyes flare at the memory. "It made my stomach cramp. Me being unfair to him? 'This is what I do,' he says.

'I'm a psychiatrist. My patients have crises. Usually at night. Please have some compassion.' Compassion?! That was the last straw. I started screaming about how I knew where he went and who he saw and what a complete shit he was for fucking my sister, if you'll excuse my French."

She takes another sip, and her soft lip curls around the edge of the coffee cup. I look away to keep my mind on her story.

"Then he started in on how he was just trying to protect me. How he knew I'd be upset, that I'd react 'inappropriately.' *He's* fucking a client who also happens to be my sister, and he's accusing *me* of being inappropriate!"

She takes a moment to let some of the rage evaporate. "The next morning, I went back over there to confront Ginger. That's when I found her body."

"Why didn't you tell all this to the police?"

"Even after all he's done, I still love him. I was afraid they'd blame Karl for her suicide."

"It didn't occur to you that if Karl and Ginger were sleeping together, he might bear some responsibility for her death?"

She closes her eyes and takes a deep breath. "I still love him."

I know I shouldn't, but I feel dejected. She takes my hand in both of hers and lays her face on it.

"Can you forgive me for lying to you?" she asks.

I have an urge to kiss the top of her head, but my feelings are so tangled I'm afraid of sending the wrong message. If only I knew what the right one was.

The words that come out of my mouth are the same ones Holly used when she left me. "Forgiving is easy; it's trusting that's hard."

FIFTY-FIVE

Lana Strain was born in Langtry, Texas, hometown to Roy Bean, who gained prominence as the "hanging judge," though he was probably just a notary public with an inflated ego. Nathaniel Strain drove his wife to drink then used that as his excuse to take custody of the girls when he divorced her. Lana was twelve when the family of three relocated to Southern California and moved into the home that Nathaniel still owns in what was then the overwhelmingly white, middle-class, Republican town of South Pasadena. Not much has changed in South Pas since then except for its political bent and the closing of the historic Rialto Theater where the hapless writer was murdered in Michael Tolkin's *The Player*.

Gloria slows at the end of the Pasadena Freeway where it morphs into the treelined streets of South Pasadena.

"If Lana flushed it down the toilet," says Gloria, "how did it wind up around Lana's neck?"

"I think her killer put it there. It meant enough to Lana to make her hate it. And it meant enough to her killer to make him replace it."

"So whoever gave her that necklace killed her?"

"That would be my guess."

"Why would a killer place a clue on his victim that points to him? I think it's more likely that Sophia made the whole thing up."

"Why would she do that?"

Gloria glides to a stop in front of Strain's Craftsman-style house on a parcel staked out to pay a poker debt in 1888, the year the city was incorporated. At least that's what it said in one of the Lana Strain biographies I read.

"I don't know. To cover up for somebody? To frame somebody? To send us on a wild goose chase?"

"She'd never do that."

"You worry me, Nob. When your little head gets involved, your big head tends to suffer."

She leads me up Strain's gravel path and rings the front doorbell. The street is dead at eight on a Saturday morning. The door opens, and Strain's bug eyes peer suspiciously through the steam from his Pearl Harbor souvenir coffee mug. He's wearing a maroon flannel bathrobe and black leather slippers. Dapper. His bushy eyebrows rise at the sight of me.

"Nathaniel Strain?" asks Gloria, knowing full well that he is.

"Yes?"

"Detective Lieutenant Gloria Lopes. I believe you know Mr. Brown. May we come in?"

"What's this about?"

"Just some routine questions, sir. About your granddaughter's death."

He rolls his bulbous eyes in my direction. "What's he doing here?"

"He's helping with the investigation. If that's a problem, Mr. Brown can wait in the car."

"I'm an Eli," he says. "We don't abide Princeton men."

"How do you know where I went to school?" I ask.

"At Yale we learned to do our homework."

"Is that how you learned where I live?"

His jaw twitches. He's nervous. But I can't tell whether it's because he's feeling guilty, or because he can sense that I've made an accusation but can't figure out what it is.

"If you two are finished," says Gloria, "I'd like to proceed."

"I already talked to some other detective."

"I'd like to hear for myself if you don't mind."

Strain doesn't send me packing, but he gives me one last glower before leading us into a warm, airy den. There's another photo of the vintage Morgan convertible on the wall, but none of his family. Below the windows on another wall, a built-in bookcase runs the length of the room, filled entirely with golf trophies and hundreds of old *National Geographics*. Is there some law against throwing those things away?

He points us to one of a matched set of flowered sofas and seats himself on the other to face us across a broad glass coffee table.

"Please make this quick," he says.

"I'll be as brief as possible," replies Gloria. She does nothing to disguise the disdain in her voice. "When was the last time you saw Ginger?"

"I don't remember precisely. It was probably four or five weeks before she died. She'd broken off relations between us, but we ran into each other at a family friend's birthday party.

"Did you talk to her there?"

"I said hello. She just walked away."

"Was Sophia there?" I ask. I wonder if she'd told me the truth about the last time she'd spoken to Ginger. Gloria strafes me with a glare for interrupting her line of questioning.

"If she was I didn't see her."

"This falling out with Ginger. What was it about?" asks Gloria.

"I don't know. She'd go off on these delusional tangents, and there was no reasoning with her."

"What sorts of delusional tangents?" Gloria is setting her trap.

"Every sort. Spacemen, weird diets, human rights for lab rats. I don't remember anything specific."

"Oh, come on, Mr. Strain. You can't remember that your own granddaughter accused you of incest?" Snap!

There's a lot of activity under Strain's skin as he forces himself to maintain control. His pupils dilate, eclipsing the steel blue of his eyes, just like last time. He takes a deep breath before answering.

"No one took her seriously. She was always on the verge of a breakdown."

"An emotional breakdown is hardly unusual for an incest victim," says Gloria. "In fact, it can validate the accusations."

"You have no right to come into my home and accuse me of such an abomination."

"I haven't heard you deny it."

"Of course I deny it."

They stare at each other for a beat. I take the opportunity to find an excuse to look around. "May I use your restroom?"

"First door on the right." He seems irritated at the interruption.

I wander into the hallway and hear Gloria say, "Where were you Thursday night around eight o'clock?" She's asking about the firebombing.

I notice there's no alarm panel near the door. You'd think someone whose daughter was murdered would be a bit more security conscious. Unless he did it.

There's nothing of much interest in the hallway. Some English foxhunting prints on the walls. Nothing personal. I pass the bathroom door and peek into the next room.

A guest bedroom disguised as a shrine to Lana leads into the bathroom I'd just passed. It's obvious that this was once Lana's bedroom. I can feel her presence in the ceiling light made of Indian glass beads and the window shade pull in the shape of a Fender Stratocaster. But the walls are filled with objects that postdate her life in this room. Nathaniel has covered the walls with Lana's album and CD covers, music reviews, magazine covers and posters, including the swimming pool poster I had over my bed. It lacks only candles to be a full-fledged shrine.

I walk through into the bathroom. Small. Maybe eight by ten. Yellow tile floor with a black border. Claw foot tub. No shower. Frosted-glass, double-hung window behind the tub. Wooden Venetian blinds pulled up. Heating vent in the ceiling. Pedestal sink with a built-in bevel-mirrored medicine cabinet above it. Old Sloan-valve tank toilet. Not exactly low flow, but I flush it anyway for the sound effect.

I return to find Gloria dangling Ginger's pendant.

"It started with Lana," Nathaniel is saying. "I gave her one when she turned thirteen, to celebrate her coming of age."

My veins ice up.

"When Sophia turned thirteen, I gave her one, too, sort of a family tradition. And then Ginger the next year. I always thought that was the one thing the Jews got right, that celebration of the coming of adulthood."

"I guess the tradition took a turn for the worse," says Gloria, "since somebody put one on Lana to celebrate the coming of death."

"Maybe she just happened to be wearing it," he says.

"Your guess is as good as mine," she replies.

They glare at each other like divorcees at a custody hearing. I'm not sure which one dislikes the other more, but there's so much animosity in the room I half expect the windows to blow out. Strain's patience is wearing thin. I furtively unstrap my watch and slip it into my pocket, thankful that, unlike everyone else I know, I don't use my cell phone to tell time.

Nathaniel stands. "If you're quite finished, Detective Lopes, I have constructive things to do."

I feign embarrassment. "Oh! I left my watch on the sink. Sorry."

I rush out of the room before anyone can respond and quick-step back into the bathroom. My gaze lands on a heating vent in the floor by the toilet. A second heating vent. An odd redundancy in such a small room.

The sound of movement in the hall horsewhips my heartbeat. Turning to the task at hand, I unlatch the window then walk back into the hall strapping my watch onto my wrist.

FIFTY-SIX

I'm a half block from Nathaniel Strain's house, watching his car for the second night in a row. Melody begged me to let her come, but it's too dangerous. I told her she should go home and charge up some power tools. She gave me the finger.

Last night I followed Strain from work and sat around from about six to nine then gave up. Tonight, to save gas, I just showed up at his house and waited for him to get home, which he did about an hour ago, the same time as last night. He's got to go out sometime, but I'm only giving him two hours to do it tonight. I've got my own life to live.

I know he's at work during the day, but my chances of being seen by a neighbor are higher. At night there's less risk, but I've got to find my opportunity.

My cell rings. It's Gloria.

"They IDed your accelerant," she says. "It was just gasoline. Could have come from anywhere."

"Did I rate super, at least?"

"Just regular. The bottle is interesting, though." She won't just tell me, she has to bait me first.

"I'm listening."

"What do I get?"

I see Strain come out of his house. He's dressed in a dark suit.

"What do you want? A box of Crackerjacks?"

"A tongue-lashing would be nice. Maybe with Pop Rocks."

He gets in his car and pulls onto the street.

"Just tell me what the hell you know."

I start my engine and follow.

"It's a Macallan bottle. Twenty-five years old."

I can still see the Macallan sitting in front of Cogswell as I follow Strain up Fair Oaks into Old Town Pasadena.

"No prints, but at five benjies a bottle, there aren't many people around who buy the stuff."

"At least not many who might have a reason to firebomb my house. Cogswell drinks the stuff, by the way."

"That's of passing interest but not what I'd call a conviction on a plate."

"I suspect he wanted to make sure I knew who sent the message. I just wish I knew what the hell he's afraid I'll find."

Strain pulls into a valet line at the Green Hotel. From the dress of the others in queue, it looks like he's going to some sort of formal dinner. Maybe a charity event or an awards dinner. "I can only imagine two possibilities," says Gloria. "Either he killed Lana or he embezzled from her estate."

"I think Nathaniel Strain killed Lana."

"If you're right, and that's a big if, that leaves embezzlement. But the statute's already run out on that, so I think embezzlement is unlikely. Maybe we should get together, talk this thing out."

When Gloria uses the phrase "get together," it has only one meaning. The prospect of blowing off a little tension later tonight sounds pretty good, but a whisper of guilt keeps tickling my brain like I'm being untrue to Sophia. This bewilders me, considering that we're not in a relationship, and I'm not even sure I trust her anymore. I tend to lose interest in women I don't trust.

I watch Strain walk into the hotel as the valet drives his car away. Opportunity knocks.

"I can't right now," I say.

"Why not?"

I hang a U-turn and head back toward South Pas to do a little breaking and entering. "You don't want to know."

The ground is muddy, but at least there are no cacti or rosebushes beneath the window. I pull a pair of cheap, oversize galoshes over my amphibious shoes to prevent identifiable footprints, and I slip on some latex gloves before touching anything. Foresight. My mother would be proud.

Strain's guest bathroom window is perhaps a foot higher than it needs to be for anyone short of a circus acrobat to pull himself through, so I have to roll the recycling bin over to climb on. I'm not surprised to find the window unlatched the way I left it; Strain probably doesn't use his guest bath much. But the window doesn't want to open. I ram the bottom of the frame with the heels of my palms. It barely budges. A neighbor's dog starts to bark. Great. I ram it a few more times and rip the palm of one of my gloves, but I finally inch it open it far enough to slip through.

I contemplate the hole in my glove before going any farther. My fingertips are still covered, but the oils of my hand will be left behind through the tear, and I know they can tell a lot about the residue with something called desorption electrospray ionization, a process I once wrote about for *Popular Science*. But I'm not sure they can use it to ID me, and I figure no one's going to waste that sort of resource on a modest little B and E anyway.

I slide through the window into the bathtub. Before getting out of the tub I feel around in the dark to drop the blinds and find the light switch by the door. I pull out of my shoes, leaving them in the galoshes in the tub before stepping out in my socks. No mud prints in the house.

I tread softly up the stairs to the master suite directly above. I'm not sure what I'm looking for, but in the back of my mind is the unlikely hope of finding the gun that killed Lana.

The bedroom is an innocuous space painted beige with white trim and furnished with modest antiques that could have been handed down from Strain's parents. The bed is immaculately made, implying a military past that I know he doesn't have. I guess he's just anal. A black cardigan sweater hangs from a wooden valet stand near the closet with some loose change, golf tees, and cufflinks in the tray. A thick putter leans against the wall by the bed. I wonder if he keeps it there for practice or protection.

I walk through into the bathroom. It's got a black-and-white checkerboard floor with a big shower beside a separate tub. There's a small tile-shaped bronze floor strainer about five feet from the window wall. But the floor is perfectly flat. There's no point in having a drain if the floor isn't angled to flow into it. I kneel down and peer through it, but all I see is darkness. Then I notice that the strainer is not grouted in. A hidey-hole? I keep my gun in one. Why shouldn't he?

I pull my Leatherman from my pocket and loosen the two retaining screws. The strainer lifts out easily to reveal a square piece of cardboard beneath it, painted black. I lift it out to find that there's no drain underneath. I'm looking right through the ceiling vent into Lana's bathtub below. This is not what I expected but it makes perfect sense.

> I've seen his eye glint through the wall,
> Just where the vent holes show it all.
> Love's in his eye, it caught the light
> Some asshole's watching me tonight.

FIFTY-SEVEN

I check my watch for the tenth time. Holly is six minutes late. Minutes that seem like hours. I feel as nervous as a teenage virgin handing fifty bucks to a Tijuana pimp.

We're supposed to meet at CBS Seafood, just around the corner from Phillipe's, which claims to have invented the french dip sandwich. Holly chose CBS because the food is good and she can walk from her office, even though the dim sum is much better in the nearby San Gabriel Valley. That's where we always went for Chinese when we were married. That's where I taught her to use chopsticks.

CBS is packed at lunchtime, of course, so I got here early to grab a place in line. Now it's almost my turn, and Holly's not here yet. They won't seat me without her. The place is loud and chaotic with dim sum carts cruising like bumper cars. I doubt they'll be able to track my place in line if they call me and my party isn't ready. These are the little moments in life that torture me most. Give me a firebombing any day.

They shout my name. I panic. Holly bursts through the door. I feel like the governor just called off my execution.

"Been waiting long?" No *sorry*. No hug. All business.

"You're just in time."

We follow the hostess to a table in the corner, and I hope we're not so remote that the carts won't come by. "Thanks for agreeing to have lunch."

"I'm booked all day. Lunch was the only time I could do it," she says to smother any thoughts I might have that she's actually glad to see me.

Her hair is a mess from the wind on the way over. Her white silk blouse is disheveled, partly untucked from the hurried walk. A mist of sweat coats her brow, and her lipstick is splotchy. She still looks beautiful.

"Just to get it out of the way," she says, "The whole thing with the house is on hold for a few weeks." No *how are you*s. No *good to see you*s. No *the worst mistake I ever made was divorcing you*s.

"I'm trying to get the money together—"

She raises her hand like a traffic cop to stop me. "I don't want to talk about it. I just thought you should know. Trudy called Jerry out of the blue, and he's gone off to Tobago to see her."

"Jerry went to see Trudy?"

I can't believe she'd want to see him since he kicked her ass out of the house and sicced the IRS on her to drive her out of the country. And I can't believe he'd want to see her since he thinks she's a smack whore. If *they* can reconcile...I slam the brakes on that train of thought.

"She cleaned herself up. At least that's what she says."

"And he believes her?"

"He wants to believe her. He's been miserable since they broke up."

If I'm lucky, he won't come back and Holly will find a more rational lawyer, maybe even one with compassion.

A dim sum cart pulls up, and I let her order the first round. She points to some har gow, some shui mai, and some golden-brown dumplings I can't pronounce, much less spell. "I take it this has to do with Lana Strain's daughters being abused by their shrink."

"That's just one piece of the puzzle. I want to ask you about another piece. Involving incest."

According to her eyebrows, Ms. Get-down-to-business is suddenly Ms. Concerned.

"After Lana was killed, the girls went into therapy," I explain. "An alleged witness told me that soon after that, the younger girl, Ginger, accused her grandfather of molesting her. That's what estranged the two sisters."

She tries to pick up a shrimp dumpling with her chopsticks, but it slips away.

"How old were the girls?"

"Thirteen and fourteen."

She tries and fails again to grab the slippery dumpling. I reach over with my chopsticks and pick it up for her, dipping it into her sauce and holding it up for her to eat. She looks wary for an instant, as if I'm trying to seduce her, but then takes it in her mouth. As she savors the shrimp, I savor the intimate moment.

"How reliable is your alleged witness?" she asks. I can tell she's pressed for time because she talks while she's still chewing, and she hates when people do that.

"Not very. But I found something last night that may substantiate the story. That's what I wanted to ask you about."

"Go on." She has less trouble grabbing the big crab dumpling and taking a bite out of it.

"I found a spyhole in the house Lana grew up in. It looked down on her bathroom from the floor above. Her father was spying on her in the bathtub."

She chews on this as she chews on the dumpling.

"So I'm wondering," I continue, "if this guy is a voyeur, does that increase the likelihood that he's an incest abuser?"

"Well, it certainly doesn't make it less likely. I'd think most incest aggressors would be drawn to voyeurism given the opportunity, especially with young victims, which is not to say that most voyeurs would necessarily be drawn to incest. But if an adult goes to the trouble of installing a spyhole into his young daughter's bathroom, that implies several things: a propensity for acting out sexual taboos, an attraction to young girls, a problem with impulse control, and an antisocial personality disorder."

"I'll take that as a yes." I eat my last shui mai and signal a passing cart. The dim sum lady pulls up, and I order some fried minced shrimp wrapped around sugar cane spears.

"There's another thing," I say. "He gave her a pendant when she turned thirteen. One of those hearts cut into two interlocking pieces to make matching pendants that complete each other. He also gave one to each of his granddaughters when they turned thirteen."

"To seal the deal," she says.

"I think so."

As the dim sum lady serves us, I recall Boom-Boom reading the entry in Lana's journal: "Hyde tried to slide his hand up my crotch. He's so predictable." She wasn't talking about Cogswell, she was talking about Nathaniel! Jekyll and Hyde. The man who became the monster, the protector who became the Asshole. So many of her journal entries suddenly make sense.

"So if we assume Ginger was telling the truth and Nathaniel was an incest aggressor," I say, appropriating her jargon, "what are the odds that he molested Lana as well?"

"I'd take that bet in a heartbeat. And I'd add the other sister to the list."

"Her name is Sophia," I say.

I feel a pain in my gut and doubt it's the dim sum. I take a sip of water, less to quench my thirst than to take a moment to refocus my thoughts. If Lana and both of her daughters were molested by Strain, any or all of them could have threatened to expose him. That gives him motives for killing both Lana and Ginger. The two murders might be connected after all. And Strain is the only suspect with motives for both.

"If Lana was molested," I ask, "how come she never told anyone about it?"

"Most children don't. They're sworn to secrecy by the aggressor. They believe it was their fault for acting too sexy, that they'll be blamed for breaking up the family if they say anything. The aggressor makes it their special secret, an exclusive club that only they belong to, a secret bond that only they share. So the victim never says anything."

"Not even to her mother?"

"Even if she did, there's a good chance her mother wouldn't believe her. These women often turn a blind eye or accuse their daughters of lying or even accuse them of being seductive, of bringing it on themselves."

"What kind of mother could do that to her own daughter?"

"Denial is a powerful force in any family dynamic. Especially when the alternative is to lose your husband—maybe put him in jail—and perhaps end up out on the street."

I take this in as I bite into a sugar cane shrimp. I offer a bite to Holly. She eyes me for a moment then reaches over and takes her own. I guess there's an intimacy limit.

"So if you're an incest victim," I say, "and you've got this deep, dark secret, what happens when you have daughters of your own and grandpa comes to visit?"

"That's the big question, isn't it? You said the girls were thirteen and fourteen when Lana was killed. They were just coming into puberty. Maybe that's what turns Strain on. Lana might have seen signs that he was getting interested in the girls, or that she was already too late. He could have killed her to shut her up."

"What would be the point of killing Lana when the girls could still testify against him? Ginger actually made a public accusation against him."

"Nobody took incest accusations seriously in those days. And after the murder of her mother it would have been easy to write it off as a symptom of post-traumatic stress."

"Okay. So then twenty years later she's in therapy again, and it resurfaces. But this time she's not an unstable teenager, and this time the psychological environment is more receptive. Maybe she even remembers something that implicates her grandfather in Lana's murder. She confronts him, and he has to kill her, too."

Holly shrugs to acknowledge the possibility as she licks some sugar cane juice off her fingertips. I am bitten by longing.

"The thing is," she says, "incest victims often become part of a cycle of abuse. When someone they love betrays them like that, they learn to take the abuse in order to get the love. They come to associate the two. Love and abuse. Humiliation and pain become familiar territory, home turf. They confuse violence for passion. Healthy relationships feel unnatural to them. They can't settle in. Abuse is all they know, what they understand. It's what makes them feel comfortable. It's a cruel irony, but that's how it works. So they gravitate toward abusive men."

This idea crystallizes for me. "Like Dr. Karl Lynch," I say.

FIFTY-EIGHT

Runt has been barking his head off for a good two minutes before Gloria finally comes to the door. "Who is it?" I wonder why she doesn't just look through the peephole. She sounds like I woke her out of a hangover in the middle of a REM cycle.

"It's me," I say, thinking my father would have corrected my grammar.

She opens the door stark naked, one hand holding up the edge of her sleep mask for a visual verification, as if she doesn't believe me. Then she drops the mask back over her eye and, without a word, turns around and trudges blind back into her bedroom. I hear her flop onto the bed. At least Runt seems glad to see me. I close the door and follow her in.

"Long night?"

"Remember the floater in Echo Park Lake?" Her voice sounds like she's talking through a comb and wax-paper kazoo. "I was up all night catching the guy who did it."

"*Allegedly* did it," I say.

She responds with her middle finger.

"If you want to fuck, I'm too tired to help but knock yourself out." She pulls her mask down as she falls back on the bed. She's shamelessly naked and blindfolded, looking absolutely delicious and oh so submissive for a change. Her breasts lie flattened and soft on her chest like two pancakes, each topped with a sweet dollop of strawberry jam. Another dotted babe.

My mouth waters in a Pavlovian reaction, but as tantalizing as she looks, I'm not tempted. Once again thoughts of Sophia intrude. I feel like my emotions are circling the nuthouse, looking for an entrance. Gloria starts to snore.

"I just want to talk," I say. "But I need you awake."

She rouses herself to say, "Not gonna happen."

"Nathaniel raped them, Gloria. All three of them. From age thirteen until they were old enough to refuse."

It's amazing how the right words can wake the living dead. Gloria rips off her sleep mask and stares into my eyes, to see whether I'm serious or just trying to get a rise out of her.

"Those broken-heart pendants were his initiation gifts," I add.

She sits up, grabbing the sheet to pull across her as if her nakedness is suddenly inappropriate. Ugly news inspiring empathetic modesty.

"Why would he put one on Lana after he killed her?" she asks.

"I don't know. Maybe Lana discovered one of the other pendants and realized he was victimizing the girls. She confronted him, and he panicked and shot her. Then he put the pendant around her neck as a warning to the girls to keep their mouths shut about the incest."

"But then the girls would know he killed Lana. Why incriminate himself like that?"

"He didn't think the police could figure it out without the girls' cooperation. No one else knew what the pendants meant."

"That's still taking an awfully big risk."

"Unless the girls already knew he was guilty. Maybe one or both of them saw it happen."

"Then twenty years later, out of the blue, Ginger decides to threaten to turn him in?"

"It wasn't out of the blue. It was after I started asking questions. She tells Dr. Karl about our interview, he digs a little, and boom! She wakes the sleeping monster."

"It doesn't smell right," says Gloria. "I need some coffee."

She gets up, tying the sheet over her shoulder like a toga. As she leads me into the kitchen, the sheet drags behind her, mopping a faint trail through the dust on the hardwood floor.

"It stinks," she says. "Ginger and Sophia were both interviewed ad nauseam by the investigating officers. They've been interviewed by dozens of reporters and writers over the years. No offence, Nob, but what makes you think you're so special?"

"My smile?"

"It's certainly not your dick." Ouch.

She dumps some canned grounds into her Mr. Coffee, then adds a pinch of cinnamon and a pinch of salt to make a pot of what she calls her "Chief's Special" coffee. Arguably the worst coffee I've ever tasted.

"If you're right," she says, "and Ginger was shocked into remembering or moved to reveal what she knows, whatever rattled her cage had to have been a lot heavier than a couple softball questions from you."

"How about being raped by her therapist," I say.

FIFTY-NINE

Jack Angel naked is a wondrous thing. Like one of those Greek statues of an Olympic athlete, only black. How does he do it? I'm in pretty good condition, and Angel's easily got twenty years on me, but in the shower he still makes me look like Will Farrell.

"How do you stay in such great shape?"

"Picking cotton."

"Is that joke politically correct?"

"Not if you make it," he says with that thousand-dollar smile. I try to puzzle this out.

We're trying to cool off in the hot showers after a killer butterfly set. Everyone else is already getting dressed except for the gap-toothed homeless guy sitting on the handicapped shower bench singing "Bad Romance" to himself, as if Lady Gaga didn't already live in an alternate universe. His legs are swollen like tree trunks—I'm guessing cirrhosis of the liver.

Angel borrows my shampoo without asking.

"You ever know anyone who committed incest?" I ask.

"I represented a victim two months ago." He lathers his silver head.

"Why did she need a defense attorney?"

"It was a he. Molested by his father. He tried to burn his own house down. With his pregnant wife in it."

His shower stops and, eyes shut to avoid shampoo, he feels around like a blind man for the timer valve.

"I hate these damned things," he says as he punches it on with his palm.

"Was the wife okay?"

"She got out in time. I lost the case, but I got him off light." He rinses off and the lather flows down his body like bird shit on one of those Greek statues. "Incest is a very persuasive mitigating circumstance."

"I can't even imagine a father doing that to his own child, no matter what the gender."

"No comment on the limits of your imagination," he says.

We head into the locker room to dry off. As usual, we both have trouble seeing our combination locks in the dim light and look like idiots fumbling to get them open.

"Nathaniel Strain molested Lana at thirteen then molested both her daughters when they reached the same age."

"How could Lana have ever left a girl alone with that man, knowing what he was capable of? Makes you wonder."

Angel retrieves his hanger from the cage guy. They keep a few extra hangers back there for patrons who need to dress for work, but Angel brings his own. You can't trust just any hanger to keep your suit crisp. I pull my clothes from the locker where I stuffed them, preferring the convenience of the wrinkled look.

"That client I told you about?" says Angel. "His grandfather molested his father, too. They passed it down from father to son, generation to generation. According to the expert testimony, it's more common than not." He pulls on his navy-blue boxers.

I feel a cloudburst of sadness. "Jesus. You'd think for the victim the mere thought of doing it to someone else would be repulsive."

"The incest did a real job on my client. He couldn't put two thoughts together. Everything scared him. Everyday life was impossible for him to handle. The smallest little thing over-whelmed him. Waitress says they're out of rye bread? He loses his appetite and won't talk unless we leave. Flat tire? He cuts it open to check for a bullet. When unexpected things can assault your peace of mind like that, repetitive behavior becomes very seductive."

"He have any kids of his own?"

"The wife was pregnant with their first when he started the fire. In fact, I think that's why he did it. He was afraid of what he'd do to his own kid."

SIXTY

Sophia's car is parked in front when I get home, so I expect her to be in. I walk into the house calling her name. No reply. I strain to hear sounds that might explain the lack of response, maybe water running in the shower or a loud radio. Nothing. Maybe she went for a walk.

I drop my swim bag by the door and walk into my office to find her. She's sitting in the fake Eames chair, wearing a pillow-case over her head secured by a thick collar of duct tape around her neck. Her arms and legs are lashed securely around the chair. Cogswell is standing behind her.

The hair on the back of my neck rises like vestigial hackles. I sense someone behind me, but he grabs my arms before I can turn.

I twist hard, but his hands are like vices tightening down to my bone. From the force of his grip I assume he's one of the Ugly Twins. The smell of stale smoke confirms it. But the tobacco scent is barely noticeable above the more powerful smell of sweat, the cologne of fear. That must be mine.

"What the fuck!"

Someone reaches out from behind me and puts his hand over my mouth. I manage to sink my teeth into his flesh. One point for the good guys.

I'm jerked off the ground in what seems like an effortless lift. Then Isaak, the bigger one, steps forward, sucking his thumb like a baby. He slaps me with his other hand. Hard. His eyes are wild, reddened, seemingly bloated, as if elevated blood pressure is pumping them up. His eyebrows seem to be bristling with static electricity. Apparently, he's got a low tolerance for pain, at least for his own.

Cogswell puts his finger to his lips, signaling me to be quiet. He doesn't want me to say anything that might ID him to Sophia. He must have surprised her from behind and thrown the case over her head before she knew what hit her. Technically, he's already guilty of kidnapping. That's three to eight years right there. But if she can't finger him, he won't have to kill her. So I keep my trap shut.

On the other hand, it doesn't bode well that he seems unconcerned about me seeing him.

Cogswell nods toward the door, and they drag me outside to my deck. At least it's mine until Jerry gets back from Tobago. Cogswell follows us out and closes the sliding glass door behind him.

Isaak takes out a huge buck knife and slices a piece of fabric from one of my deck chairs to wrap his thumb. It'll cost eighty-five bucks to replace it. Another chore for my list.

"I thought I told you to leave me alone," says Cogswell. "Instead, you bring me to the attention of the police. Are you averse to verbal communication, Mr. Brown? Because it is not in your best interest to force me to seek alternative modes of communication."

"What is your problem? I'm just trying to write a story about Lana Strain. Until you started throwing your muscle around, you were barely a footnote."

He nods to Petya and Isaak. The bigger one hoists me over his shoulder, and before I know it I'm being dangled by my ankles over my deck railing into the darkness. Though my head is only four or five feet from the slope, I'm hanging right in front of a structural post. Chances are, I'll land headfirst on the corner of a concrete footing and split my skull wide open. I wonder if they planned it this way or just got lucky. I imagine my brain bursting out of my fractured cranium and bouncing down the hill like a loose soccer ball.

"Are you getting the message yet, Mr. Brown?"

"Do you really expect me to carry on a rational conversation like this?" For a beat, all is still. The vehicular river-roar of the Valley sweeps up the hills, giving texture to the silence. An owl hoots nearby. I wonder if Petya and Isaak are just going to drop me and be done with it.

"I'm not a very patient man, Mr. Brown, and right now, you're making me late for dinner. Jane hates it when I'm late."

"You're welcome to leave anytime." My voice sounds choked from the pressure of the blood rushing to my head.

More silence.

"Look, Cogswell. Did it ever occur to you that maybe all of this intimidation is a big fat waste of time?"

"It occurred to me that you're risking your life to stay on this story," he replies. "Why would someone who's barely a writer do that if you haven't uncovered something explosive enough to make a big sale?"

"Any sale is a big sale for me. I'm in the hole to my ex-wife." If I weren't upside down, I would have swallowed my pride instead of choking on it. But I'm guessing a divorce settlement is something a lawyer can identify with.

Bad guess. "Bon voyage, Mr. Brown."

They let go. As I start to fall, I'm seized by fear. My brain freezes and my elbows lock in an autonomic spasm, some naïve primal attempt to survive the sharp concrete with nothing worse than a couple of broken wrists. Instead of seeing my life flash before my eyes, I see a replay of my brain being jettisoned from my skull.

Then my ankles jerk, and I'm dangling again. I'm suddenly flooded with consciousness. My brain defrosts from the realization that he let me go and caught me again a few inches later. I was in free fall for only a fraction of a second, a fleeting dip of my toe in the icy waters of death. I hear the Slavs chuckle at their little joke. Funny guys.

They haul me back onto the deck and throw me at a chair. I knock it over and feel a pain where my palm breaks my fall. Beats falling on a concrete corner. I right the chair and climb into it. Cogswell puts his foot on my chaise lounge and leans on his knee. He's trying to look tough, but the Pillsbury Doughboy just can't pull it off.

"Shall we start over, Mr. Brown?"

Possible replies are bouncing around like pachinko balls in my head as I search for the most likely to get me out of this alive. Finally, I decide to just lay it on the table.

"I've got to wonder why you want me off the story so badly. Correct me if I'm wrong, but I don't think you had Ginger killed."

"We don't kill nobody," says Petya.

I can't figure what I know that he's so desperate to hide. He's taking a huge gamble tonight. Kidnapping and assault are not lightweight charges.

"So what are you so afraid of?"

Cogswell nods to Petya who gives me a slap on the ear, snapping my head to the side like a rubber ball on an elastic paddle string. The pain is excruciating. My ear rings, and I feel so dizzy I have to close my eyes. I try to turn my head to look around, but my neck won't move. Serious whiplash. It takes a minute for the vertigo to subside.

"Mr. Cogswell's not afraid of nothing," says Isaak.

I open my eyes to find the barrel of an automatic about an inch from my right eyeball. I don't know what make or model it is, but I recognize the thick barrel of a silencer when I see one.

Then, as if we're not all tense enough, Sophia walks out of the house.

Cogswell looks up, as surprised as I am. The duct tape collar is still around her neck, but she has managed to free herself from the chair and rip the pillowcase apart at the seams to hang down over her chest and back.

"Leave him alone, Gary. Just go."

I see the barrel lift away from me to point at her, and I react without thinking, leaping up and tackling Cogswell head on. I hear a thud and realize the silenced gun has gone off. I pray the bullet didn't hit Sophia.

I have a vague sense of two enormous bodies rushing toward us, but our forward momentum carries us through the fire-weakened railing, sending us hurtling into the darkness. I see the gun glint in the moonlight as it flies into the bushes and hear something that sounds like an explosive wheeze as I land on Cogswell and knock the wind out of him. From the loud thuds behind me I know that his thugs have jumped down from the deck, but the sound of crackling brush tells me neither one of them landed on his feet.

I push off Cogswell's gasping chest and cry out for Sophia to run. Then I tear down the hill as fast as I can, thrashing my way through the thick brush. I hear the distinctive clack of an automatic being chambered and a rasping "No!" from Cogswell. I guess his boys don't have suppressors on their guns, and he doesn't want to attract attention. After all, he knows as well as I do that this won't be his last chance.

SIXTY-ONE

I stumble onto the street with no plan. Small lacerations from blind bushwhacking bleed down my face. I taste it trickling into my mouth, the flavor of desperation. I don't hear anyone behind me, so I'm assuming they decided to call it a night. They'll surely retrieve the silenced gun before they leave, because it's got Cogswell's prints on it. That could take a few minutes. But after that they'll be heading out, so I've got to get off the street.

My neighbor Teri lives a half block away. With three Rottweilers to manage security, she doesn't bother locking her wooden gate. I make a beeline for her house and slip quietly into her front yard. As the gate latches behind me, I hear growls grow into vicious barking. Four hundred pounds of dogs barrel toward me, fangs gleaming in the dark, reflecting the moonlight. I cower with my back to the gate and brace myself for the impact. By the time they recognize my smell, it's too late to stop. They slam me against the fence then trample me as they jockey for position to lick my face. I'm the guy who feeds them when Teri goes out of town. I quiet them down as quickly as I can, knowing that Cogswell's gang has heard the noise but from the street above will have no idea where it's coming from.

I position myself in front of a gap in the redwood to watch the street for Cogswell's car. The Rottweilers lose interest in me and play-fight with each other for a minute before lying down to pant out their adrenaline. I try to wrangle my jangled thoughts.

I hope Sophia escaped unscathed. After I went over the rail with Cogswell I heard his two goons jump down from the deck, so she should have had time to get away. Unless she was frozen by fear. Or tried to hide in the house. Assuming she ran, where would she go? How will we reconnect?

And what will Cogswell do next? He's been bruised, humiliated, and infuriated. He also committed some serious felonies and left behind two witnesses who are motivated to get even. He can't let this slide, and neither can Vlad the Impaler. A heavy gloom washes through me as I contemplate just how deep is the shit I'm in.

"Move and I'll blow your head off."

I freeze. The dogs stir.

"Teri, it's me."

"Nob?"

I turn to see her framed in the kitchen doorway, her diaphanous nightie backlit to reveal every nuance of her two-hundred-pound frame. She's holding a pistol that I recognize as one of her ten-year-old's toys. Chrome-painted plastic.

"Go back in the house," I whisper. "I'll explain in a few minutes."

"But—"

I shush her and turn back to my crack in the fence. She does as I say. A moment later, the house goes dark.

About ten minutes later, I see Cogswell's Beemer come down the hill. There's not enough light to see the passengers clearly, but from the density of the shadows in the car, it looks like Petya and Isaak are with him. I have no way of knowing whether Sophia is there, too.

I head into Teri's house to find her sitting in the dark. She has pulled a dining room chair up to the front window to watch through a crack in the curtain, hoping to see whatever it was that I was looking for.

"Were they in that car?" she asks.

"Yes."

"Who are they? What's going on?"

"They're involved in a story I'm writing. Things got out of hand."

"They came to your house?" By which she means to ask, *You brought bad men to our neighborhood?*

"Yes. I'm sorry. I didn't think they'd come. I'm still not sure why they did."

"Should I call the police?"

"I'll take care of it. Thanks for your help. I've got to go."

I'm antsy to get out of here. I have to find Sophia.

SIXTY-TWO

I figure it's safe to go home, but not to stay there too long. I hope to find Sophia waiting. Her car is still parked in front. I walk into my house calling her name. No answer. Déjà vu.

I search the house. No Sophia. Her purse is still in her room.

I try calling her cell phone. It rings in the house. I follow the sound into the guest bath. It's plugged into a charger on the counter next to her hair dryer.

I go outside and call her name, hoping she's hiding out somewhere within earshot. No answer. I walk the street for a block in each direction calling her name. No answer. I try neighboring streets. No answer. I pass a woman with a basset hound wearing socks on its ears to protect them from dragging on the ground. She asks if I've lost my dog.

By the time I get back to the house I'm close to panic. All I can think about is saving Sophia. In fact, that's pretty much all I've thought about since I met her. I hope that's not what attracts me to her, but I fear it may be.

Lacking any leads to follow, I call Billy. He hasn't heard from Sophia but will tell her to call me if he does. I don't tell him she's in danger, but I mention that Cogswell's looking for her, too, and she doesn't want him to find her, so don't help him out.

I call Claudine. She hasn't heard from Sophia in years, but she has a number for the studio where Sophia makes her marionettes. I call it and get voice mail.

I put up a pot of coffee then go to the hall closet and pull out the terra-cotta drainpipe I use for an umbrella stand. Beneath it is a five-inch-square patch I cut out of the oak flooring. I push on one side of the patch and the opposite edge levers up a quarter of an inch, just enough to get a grip. I pull out the square, reach into my hidey-hole, and pull out my Chief's Special. I'm not big on guns, but sometimes you just can't settle your nerves without a snub-nose .38 in your waistband.

By the time I get back to the kitchen, enough coffee has dripped for me to pour a cup. I pull the carafe out of the machine, but there must be a few grains of grounds caught in the drip valve because the coffee keeps leaking onto the black metal warmer plate. Each drop goes up in smoky steam as it hits, smelling of burnt coffee, leaving a little spot that looks like a bloodstain. I pour fast and jam the carafe back in before the thing self-destructs.

Next, I call Melody to tell her not to come back to the house until I tell her the coast is clear. The last thing I need is for her to get caught up as a hostage by Cogswell in order to lure me out of hiding.

"I told you not to mess with Vlad," she says, "but do you listen to me?"

"It's not Vlad, it's his lawyer."

"Same difference. How are you going to find Sophia?"

"I don't know. She doesn't have her cell phone."

"Well, I'm around if you need some help or a place."

"Thanks."

I'm not sure where I'm going to stay until I figure out a way to deal with Cogswell, but my house isn't an option.

It would be a pain to move in with Melody because she lives in a tiny studio apartment, so one of us would have to sleep on the floor, or we'd have to squeeze into her standard double Murphy bed, which isn't much more comfortable. More important, it won't take much for Cogswell to learn that she's my assistant, so I should steer clear of her for her safety as well as mine.

Holly isn't in the running either, for the same reason, even if she'd have me.

Angel is a possibility. As far as Cogswell knows, he's my lawyer, nothing more. But if, god forbid, Cogswell found out I was there, it would endanger Angel's wife and kids. I could never forgive myself if something happened to them because of me.

My mother's place is out of the question for every imaginable reason, not the least of which is I'd rather face Cogswell than have to listen to her kvetching all day.

I don't have the money to move into a motel or short-term rental.

That leaves Gloria. I get exhausted just thinking about living round-the-clock with her creative libido, but at least she's equipped to take on the potential danger. I give her a call. She tells me to come on over and bring my dick. I could have done without the coda.

I throw some clothes in an overnight bag, grab my swim bag and a few paperbacks from the pile by my bed, and head out.

On the ride over, something's bugging me. Something Melody said that roiled my subconscious. Some fleeting thought that never got a chance to slow down for a tête-à-tête. I replay our conversation.

I told you not to mess with Vlad, but do you listen to me?

It's not Vlad, it's his lawyer.

Same difference.

I can't hook it. This is happening more and more. Am I growing senile? My phone startles me out of my reverie. I don't have my headset on, so I scoff the law and answer by hand.

"Nob?"

"Sophia! Thank god! I've been worried sick about you."

"Well, don't stop now," says a voice that ices my spine. It's Cogswell.

SIXTY-THREE

"You can't go up there alone," Gloria says. "I can have a SWAT team rolling in ten minutes."

"No SWAT. No guns," I say, feeling the press of the Chief's Special against the small of my back. "He'll want to make a deal. It would be too dangerous for him to kill me now. He knows we're working together on this. He's got to assume I told you about his visit. He's too exposed."

I hear a whirring sound through the phone line and realize she's grinding down Runt's claws with her electric minigrinder. She does this once a week.

"Cornered animals are irrational," she says.

"Cogswell doesn't do irrational. Logic is his animal instinct. It's what he falls back on."

"That's why he hasn't killed her yet. He needs her to lure you in so he can kill you both."

I exit the 134 at Forest Lawn Drive and head toward the back entrance to Griffith Park. Cogswell told me to go straight to the merry-go-round and wait there for his call.

I get caught behind a garbage truck doing about five miles an hour. I have to control the urge to blow my horn.

"I'll tell him I already told the police he tried to kill me. He'd be writing his own death sentence by killing me now."

A motorcycle speeds by me so close that I think his jacket's going to catch on my side mirror. He shoots around the garbage truck causing an oncoming car to swerve onto the shoulder.

"Only if we can prove it," she says. "These guys have a lot of practice getting away with murder. On the other hand, if he doesn't kill the two of you, either one of you can testify against him on the kidnapping charge. It's a calculated risk."

I hear Runt yelp in the background. Gloria swears, and the whirring stops. She must have hit the quick of a claw. I imagine her reaching for the styptic powder while lying on top of Runt to keep him down.

"At least let me meet you up there. It's stupid to go alone."

"Stupid is my middle name." It just comes out. I'm not sure what I mean. Another one of those just-barely-a-writer moments. But I don't want any police presence. If Cogswell wants to kill me, there's not much I can do about it in the long run. In the short run, I don't see how setting up a shootout is going to help.

"Besides, there's no time," I say. "He said I had to be there in exactly thirty minutes." I check my dashboard clock. I've got two minutes left. I try to peer around the garbage truck to see if I can pass, but he's too wide. I try to calm down. The truck slows to a stop at a stop sign. I cut around him and see a car at the opposing stop sign. I slam into a left turn in front of him, blasting my horn to make sure he sees me. He blasts his horn in return but doesn't move.

I can see the merry-go-round in the moonlight now, just down the road, but the seconds are ticking like hatchet blows. I swerve into a right turn through another stop sign and stomp on the gas to climb the hill fast. I swing into the parking lot on the dot and grab my phone in expectation. My finger hits a key and the phone lights up to show me that I've got no cells. Not a single bar.

In a panic, I throw the car in gear and screech around the parking lot, staring at my screen, praying for a cell. Nada.

Now what?

I shut off my engine and drop my head on the steering wheel in frustration. I feel like banging it. Instead, I hear Melody's voice.

I told you not to mess with Vlad, but do you listen to me?

It's not Vlad, it's his lawyer.

Same difference.

No it's not!

I jam the car back into gear and screech down the road heading for the 5 Freeway.

Stupid *is* my middle name! How could I not see it before?

I drive out of the park with the reckless determination of a kamikaze pilot, almost hitting a golf cart crossing the road as I check my missed calls. Why the hell is a cart here after dark? There's one call from a blocked number that must have been Cogswell, but there's no message. I'm not surprised. Either a message or a return number could be used against him in a court of law. But if he thinks I'm going to sit on my ass and stew in my own fear until he decides to call again, he's in for a nasty shock.

SIXTY-FOUR

I rush through the door like a freight train and run smack into a human wall. How do they move so fast? Only this time it's not Petya and Isaak, it's two other lugs. The Ugly Twins must still be with Cogswell. And Sophia. Somewhere else.

Before I can even open my mouth I feel the cold circle of a gun barrel on the back of my neck and a hand slipping my .38 out of my waistband. I didn't even remember it was there, but I guess these guys can smell them. Just to be safe, he pats me down.

I strain to see into the back of the room, but there's no sign of Vlad the Impaler. One of the Slavic monoliths has a plastic cigarette dangling from his mouth, some sort of quit-smoking device. He's wasting his time in here. The secondhand smoke is thicker than a Code Purple smog alert.

"I need to see Mr. Bakatin," I say.

He takes the fake coffin nail out of his mouth. "He don't need to see you."

I see the bartender/barista watching us intently and call out to him. "Leon! Remember me? Mr. Bakatin had you make me a dople. He knows me."

The thugs look over to Leon for some kind of sign. He reaches for a phone and punches a number. The place is silent as a shark, but he speaks into the receiver so softly that I can't hear a word. Time stands still. After a moment he looks up.

"He's busy."

"Tell him I can prove he's being double-crossed. If he doesn't think what I have to say is worth his time, he can have my yáytsa after I'm finished."

Leon says something into the phone then smiles and hangs up.

"He told me to sharpen my knife," he says, then smiles as if savoring the prospect.

The human wall responds to some hidden signal and opens up. At the same moment, Vlad Bakatin steps through a door in the back and sits down at his usual table. I head back to join him. This place is beginning to feel like a second home.

"You got balls, Mr. Nob Brown," he says as I take my seat. "We'll see if you gets to keep them."

"Believe me. I didn't come here for fun. Gary Cogswell came to my house tonight with Petya and Isaak. Did you know that?"

His face is impassive. This is a guy who'd kill me at poker. I just hope that's the only thing he'd kill me at. But I find it encouraging that his lack of response invites me to continue.

"They tried to kill me and Lana Strain's daughter. Then they kidnapped her when I escaped. It didn't make sense. I asked myself, 'Why would you send Cogswell and two goons to take a huge risk to stop a story about Lana Strain, a story that has nothing to do with you?' And then *bang*, it hit me. You didn't send him; he's operating behind your back. And you have to figure a smart guy like Cogswell is not going to do something that stupid unless the alternative is even worse. He's got to be hiding something from you that he's afraid I'll write about."

I haven't thought this thing all the way through, so I'm winging it here, but I've still got his interest, so I must be on the right track. Vlad still says nothing, but he doesn't stop me either.

"So I ask myself, 'What do I know about him that you don't?' It's got to have something to do with Lana Strain. If he killed Ginger, that could be a problem, since she was a golden egg, and

I know you've got a stake in Fun with Dick and Jane through Kocibey Development."

His eyes narrow. He's not happy that I know this.

"Look, it's public record. Anyone can find out. If you're worried about it, just pay your taxes. There's nothing illegal about Dick and Jane."

"Just tell me vat you know."

"Well, I don't think he did it, because he's got no motive. So what else could it be? He was nervous about my story from the start. He broke into my house to search for my notes after the first time I came here. Why? Because he looted Lana Strain's estate when he was her lawyer. Only Cogswell could have embezzled from her daughters without getting caught. But if that was all it was about, he'd have nothing to worry about. The statute of limitations has run out. He wasn't afraid of the law, he was afraid of you. He knew that if you learned about his history, you might double-check your own books, and he'd get caught with his hand in the cookie jar."

The Impaler smiles. "You are full of theories, Mr. Brown, but vere is the facts."

"How about the fact that your consigliere has been sleeping with your porno partner behind your back?"

"Jane vould not give Cogsvell time of day."

The way he says it makes me realize he's been sleeping with her, too, and he thinks she's been faithful.

"She's not fucking him for his body, she's doing it to keep him in line. Jane's in a perfect position to skim cash from Fun with Dick and Jane, and Cogswell's in a perfect position to cook the books so you don't find out. It's a match made in heaven."

"Is just cheap gossip."

"I followed her to his house." I actually followed *him*, not her, but I figure the little white lie couldn't hurt.

"He is attorney for company. It could be business meeting."

"Why hide it from you if it's business?"

Vlad says something to one of his thugs in Russian. The thug's reply is impassioned, as if he's defending Cogswell or, more likely, Petya and Isaak. Vlad looks increasingly persuaded. Finally, he turns back to me. "Boolsheet."

"I watched her let herself in the gate with a code. Is he the kind of guy who gives his security code to business acquaintances?"

He resumes his discussion with his thug, seemingly reasoning something out. I've been assuming these guys are all muscle, including ear to ear, so I'm impressed that Vlad is considering the guy's opinion. I don't know what they're saying, but it doesn't look like the gist of it is leaning in my favor.

"He's got a good friend of mine," I say. "I want her back."

Vlad moves a finger, and his thugs grab me and lift me out of my chair. I panic for my yáytsa.

"I can give you proof!" I blurt.

Vlad nods and they drop me back in the chair. I land on my tailbone and let out a yelp.

"What kind proof?" His eyes sharpen with suspicion.

I reach into my jacket pocket and feel four hands constrain me like an iron maiden.

"They're just photos," I say. Vlad flicks an eyebrow and his hoods let me go. I slowly extract the printout I'd made for just this purpose and hand it to the Impaler. It has six shots in sequence.

"It's Jane," I say, "letting herself into Cogswell's house. Check her key ring. You'll find his key."

SIXTY-FIVE

I have the air conditioner on full blast, every vent pointed straight at me. The temperature in the car is probably in the low sixties. I'm still drenched in sweat.

Why hasn't Cogswell called?

I try to conjure the gentle rhythm of Sophia's breathing as she sleeps, the quiet purr of her latent snore, the sweet gust of her breath on my neck, the silky warmth of her skin against mine, but instead I see her in some backseat, crammed onto the floor, bruised, aching, and scared, her wrists duct-taped behind her tightly enough to make her hands throb from loss of circulation, her head filled with visions of a painful death.

Call, damn it!

In theory the Odessa is only fifteen minutes from Gloria's, but in traffic it is taking twice that long. I went through a half dozen doples before hitting the road, and now I feel like I'm peaking on speed but stuck in a tar pit. I finally pull up in front but keep the motor running for the AC while I spring open my sunshade and wrestle it under my visors to cover the windshield. I spend another minute glaring at my cell phone, willing it to ring. The proverbial watched pot.

Gloria's not home, so I get her hide-a-key from the garage and let myself in. Runt pretends to be a watchdog for about half a second then runs up with his tail wagging, whining with excitement. I knead him with both hands behind his ears, and he flaps them for me.

The place is hot but not lethal. Gloria has her thermostat set to "Oldsmobile," as she calls it, by which she means eighty-eight. Hot enough to conserve energy but cool enough to keep Runt from slow roasting on days like this. I turn it down to "trombones." Seventy-six.

I want to jump in a cold shower to rinse off the sweat, but I'm afraid he'll call while I'm in there. I settle for filling the sink with cold water and dunking my face a few times for as long as I can hold my breath. On the fourth dunk, my cell finally rings.

I swipe my face with a towel so I don't short out my phone. Then I answer.

"Don't you care about the girl?" he says.

"You sent me to a place without cell service."

"Bullshit. We checked it out."

"Your boys must not have AT&T."

"What does it take to get through to you, Brown?"

I wish I knew what he wants me to say, but I don't. Between the pressure of the situation and my worry for Sophia, it's tough to think straight.

"Just tell me what you want," I say.

"I want to tell you to your face."

"So you can kill us both? I don't think so."

"Why would I want to kill you both?"

"I don't know. But you already tried once."

"If I wanted you dead, that's what you'd be."

"I think you tried and failed. I'm not willing to give you a second shot."

"Do I have to send her ear in a box?"

The thought of Sophia listening to his end of this conversation hits me with a wave of nausea.

"Somewhere public," I say.

"Fine. But I won't bring the girl."

"I'll want to talk to her on the phone."

"Arclight Hollywood. Forty-five minutes. Just you."

I wonder if he knows I'm only ten minutes from there. I don't tell him. We agree to meet in the bar and hang up.

I wish Bakatin had returned my gun, but he hadn't. I'm sure Gloria's got an extra stashed somewhere. I could call her and ask, but I'm afraid of spilling the beans. The last thing I need is the cops showing up at my meet. I'm better off unarmed anyway. What am I going to do with a gun? Pull it out in a crowded theater?

It's just short of eleven p.m. when I order my iced coffee. The Arclight Cinema bar is dead, but the adjoining lobby is busy. Both privacy and witnesses, the perfect meeting place.

The bartender puts a straw in my iced coffee and slides it in front of me. Tough guys don't use straws. I leave it on the bar and drink from the glass. Appearance may not be everything, but right now it may be all I've got.

I pick a semicircular booth with a view of the entrance and sit at one end. That way I've got a quick exit if I need one.

Cogswell limps in right on time. Petya walks at his side but a half step behind like a dog on a heel. No sign of Isaak. Must be with Sophia.

Cogswell slides in across from me, but Petya shoves me into the booth and sits down in my spot to cut off any possible escape. So much for the best-laid plans. I hope I'm the man, not the mouse.

"Where's Sophia?"

"Unless I intervene, she's in her last resting place." He nods at his ape.

Petya's huge hand reaches under the table and frisks me from the waist down. He slams me into the table to frisk me from behind. I'll have the memory etched across my chest tomorrow in black-and-blue. He manhandles my front and sides to make sure I'm not wired. The waitress approaches, but Cogswell waves her off. She looks at me, worried, but I give her a nod to signal that I'm okay. She turns tail uneasily.

"You came to my house to talk," I say. "Things got out of hand. The girl wandered off. You found her and gave her a lift home. That's all that happened if you just let her go."

Cogswell laughs. "Ever the comedian."

"I'm serious."

"You could be dead serious if I give the word."

Petya takes a drink of water, and it goes down the wrong pipe. He starts coughing. It feels like a small earthquake in the booth. I want to hit him on the back to help out, but if he gets the wrong idea, the situation could sour fast. Cogswell and I wait him out in silence until he gets over it.

"I want to talk to her," I say.

"Go ahead." He sweeps his hand magnanimously toward Petya who pulls out an iPhone and redials a number. My nerves are on high alert as Petya says something in Russian then hands me the phone.

"Nob?"

The surge of relief at the sound of her voice is more powerful than I expect. It makes my voice come out whiny. "Sophia, are you okay?"

"I'm okay, but—" The line goes dead.

"Now I talk and you listen," says Cogswell.

I throw the phone down, hoping it'll shatter on the slick Formica. Petya's hand shoots out to grab it, but he's too late. It bounces off the table with a satisfying crack and launches onto the carpet, landing at the feet of Vlad the Impaler. Cogswell looks confused by Vlad's presence.

Then Vlad tosses my photos of Jane on the table.

Cogswell's potato face pales at the sight. He knows he's a dead man.

SIXTY-SIX

I lean against the shower door, enjoying the sight of Sophia toweling off.

"How are you feeling?" I ask.

"Better." She shakes her hair and sprays me with water. "I'm just tired."

She grabs her snifter off the sink and takes a sip of Hennessy.

"You really think my grandfather killed Mom?"

"I do."

She shivers at the thought and wraps a towel around her hair.

"Great family legacy," she says.

"Too bad we can't prove it."

"I don't think he did it."

She moves into the bedroom and climbs into bed. I grab the sheet to cover her, but she's down for the count before the linen lands.

I go down to the office and call Gloria to unload. She's less than ecstatic about my handing the scales of justice to Vlad the Impaler to deal with Sophia's kidnapping, but Gloria appreciates that Bakatin managed to get Sophia back safe and sound. Moreover, if the police were to officially know about the kidnapping, they would have had to learn about it from me or Sophia, and neither one of us wants to be diagnosed with the terminal illness of "mob informant." So Gloria lets the matter drop.

The next morning I find Sophia in the kitchen, pacing like a tiger in a circus cage. She's been up for two hours, waiting to go over to Karl's and pack up her clothes, but she can't show up until he heads off to work. The anticipation is killing her. She's got the oven timer set for nine o'clock, and when it dings she's out the door in seconds.

I grab a couple slices of organic twelve-grain whole-wheat bread and make a sandwich out of some leftover roast beef in the fridge. Rare, of course.

The phone rings. I answer.

"You must be busy," she says.

"Too busy to call my mother. You through now?"

"A mother's work is never done."

"How've you been, Ma?" I bite into my sandwich. As I swallow, I think I see something move on the bread. I stare at it, waiting to see if any of the twelve grains come alive.

"Fine. As always. Nothing ever changes here in my lonely cell."

"Good. That's good. At your age, change is usually a cry for medical attention."

I regret the joke as soon as I say it. I try to avoid comments that might remind her of her medical history. Not because of the cancer but because of my father. He had been an auditor for the city controller for eighteen years until my mother talked him into accepting a better-paying job with a big accounting firm. A few months later, they discovered a tumor in her breast. My father hadn't been at his new job long enough for his benefits to kick in, so we were uninsured. My mother's medical bills ate all their savings in a matter of months.

Then I got into Princeton. My father was so damn proud. The prospect of telling me I couldn't go because he'd fucked up must have agonized him. That's when, in a desperate display of bad judgment, my father "borrowed" money from his new employer. Two months later he got caught and drove off that cliff.

I force my thoughts back to Lana's murder, shoving my father's memory back into its cubby before it blackens my mood. He got nailed, charged with embezzling, and drove his Chevy off the levee. I was sixteen at the time.

Ma felt responsible for his death and went into a deep depression. She eventually got past the cancer, but she never got past the self-blame, no matter how many sobbing in-laws assured her it wasn't her fault.

But today she's too focused on guilt-tripping me to let a medical crack faze her.

"That's how you talk to your mother?"

A seed is definitely crawling on my bread. Fucking organic maggot. I drop the sandwich in the sink and ram it down the drain with a dirty spoon. I'm desperate to hang up so I can run the disposal, but I can't tell my mother I'm eating live food because I know she'll use it against me for the rest of my life. I stand, hand poised above the switch, waiting for the conversation to end.

"Look, Ma, I really can't talk. I'm working."

I briefly consider sticking my finger down my throat then decide that it's only protein.

"Working is something you do with a scalpel or, God forbid, a shovel. Why don't you get a real job like your brother?"

"We'll discuss this later, okay? I gotta go. Love ya."

I hang up and hit the disposal switch. As the mechanical vortex devours my sandwich I wonder how long a seed critter can survive in a bellyful of stomach acid. The thought gives me heartburn, reducing his chances.

My appetite gone, I take a legal pad out on the deck to organize my thoughts for the first draft about Lana's murder. I've got to produce a story whether or not I can prove who killed her.

Two hours later I drive over to Gloria's. She answers the door in black fishnet stockings, a red lace thong, and matching garter belt. Her intentions are about as subtle as a *Bootylicious* centerfold. But she's pulling on jeans. What's wrong with this picture?

"Dumphy just called," she says. "Shots fired at Karl Lynch's house."

SIXTY-SEVEN

For once I don't care that Gloria is driving too fast. I just want to get to Sophia. I flash on my mother speeding to the hospital after my dad drove off the cliff. The not knowing is torture.

Two neighbors called 911 to report gunshots. A squad car reached the scene a few minutes ago, but they're waiting for backup before approaching the house. No one knows who or what is inside. We're on the freeway with full siren and flashing gumball. Gloria sticks close to the shoulder so she can carve her way around traffic clogs. At this rate, we're about ten minutes away, a minor miracle.

We pull up to the house to find a couple unmarked rides and five black-and-whites, lights dancing. Cops crouch shielded behind the cars, guns drawn, trigger fingers tense. They're watching Dumphy approach the front door. He looks even bulkier than usual, swathed in a Kevlar vest beneath his LAPD windbreaker. The area is roped off with yellow tape, alive with red and blue flashes and jittery cops, but silent as a leopard poised to pounce.

Gloria orders me to stay in the car and keep my head down; then she gets out and runs, hunching for cover, toward a group of men in cheap suits huddled in a circle behind a vanilla Crown Vic.

Dumphy tiptoes up the two front steps, favoring a far edge over the middle to minimize creaking. He presses his back against the wall of the house next to the front door before pressing the doorbell. I assume the cops have already tried phoning but got either no answer or no satisfaction.

The front door opens a crack, and Dumphy speaks to someone out of view. My car windows are open, but the conversation is inaudible. After a moment, he enters the house and the door closes behind him. A chorus of murmurs erupts from the cops, a low-pitched hum of anxiety. The uncertainty is driving them nuts. I don't know who can hear what over their radios, but I don't see anyone who appears relieved about what's going on inside.

I picture Sophia, lying on the floor, limbs askew, a warm crimson slick growing slowly beneath her. My fear constricts my chest, making it difficult to breathe. My heart is running a two-minute mile. I'm driven to act but there's nothing productive to do. So I sit in the car, peering over the dash. And I sweat.

Gloria is deep in conversation with the suits when their attention is suddenly drawn to the house. The front door opens, and Dumphy steps out holding an evidence bag with a gun in it. He gives the all clear and points to Gloria, who rises and heads for the house. There is a universal release of tension. I get out of the car and try to follow Gloria but a uniform steps in my way.

"You'll have to stay back," he says.

"I'm with her."

"Not that I've heard."

I call out to her, but she doesn't look back as she disappears into the house with Dumphy. Two paramedics follow them in. I can't shake the sinking feeling that the woman I was hoping to fall in love with is lying dead on the floor of that midcentury modern coffin.

The ME's wagon pulls up, and an investigator from the coroner's office heads into the house. A minute later, the paramedics file out looking grim. The seconds tick to minutes.

Finally, Gloria steps out on the porch and motions for me to join her. The cop lets me pass. As I head toward the house, a lab tech comes out and says something to Gloria. They head back in together.

I mount the steps, but a uniform makes me wait outside. From inside I hear a beep, then a robotic time stamp from a few hours ago. They're listening to a voice-mail message on a speakerphone. I hear the voice of an elderly woman.

"Mrs. Lynch, this is Esther over at Evidential Labs? I'm afraid I made a mistake and charged you for a bacterial on that food sample, but we only screened for inorganic compounds. Sorry about that. I just wanted to let you know we'll be crediting the difference back to your card. So…I guess that's it. Bye."

I get a bitter taste in my mouth as my stomach churns. If Karl picked up this message, he would have known Sophia was onto him. Did he come home to finish the job the spiked food had failed to do?

As I turn this bleak question around in my mind, Gloria steps outside again. "Sophia's okay."

I exhale for what seems like the first time in an hour. My eyes tear up.

"Before you crack open the champagne," says Gloria, "she's under arrest. She shot him, Nob. She shot him dead."

SIXTY-EIGHT

A squad car takes me back to Gloria's to pick up my Acura. She won't let me go with Sophia to the station, because I might do or say something that could taint a potential case against her.

On the way to Gloria's, I call Billy and tell him about the shooting.

"Jesus Effing Keeeeerist," he says. "What the fuck?"

"It's a mess. You've got to get her a good lawyer then bail her out."

Big sigh. "I'll call Al."

"Is he a criminal lawyer?"

"Ain't no kinda lawyer. He's my ex-manager. But he reps rappers these days, half of what gets shot, t'other half of what gets busted for the drive-bys. He deals with this shit all the time."

I hang up to let him get on with it.

The cop drops me off at my car, and I drive straight to jail, don't pass go, don't collect $200. I don't care what Gloria says, I need to be there for Sophia. I'm not sure why, and I'm pretty sure it's a bad idea, but I head over there anyway.

The station is a zoo, as usual. The desk sergeant, Franco Drago, was a groomsman at my ill-fated wedding. He tells me that Sophia is still in interrogation with some detective I've never met and some DDA I've never heard of. He patches me through to Gloria, who's watching Sophia on the video feed.

"I thought I told you to go home," she says.

"What's your point?"

"Go home, Nob." She hangs up. I guess she's not going to invite me to watch.

Three hours later, Billy shows up with two guys in tow. One is a wiry Jewish guy who looks Irish. Must be Al. He's got curly red hair that he wears in a short Afro, what Melody calls a Jewfro. He's sporting a tie-dyed shirt that almost reaches his knees, gray sweats, and sandals. The other guy is in a white summer suit and could be Clark Kent's double. Must be a lawyer. I'm across the room, so I don't hear what they're saying, but several people recognize Billy, and there's a lot of nudging, pointing, and even smiling going on. The magic of celebrity lifts the general malaise of the waiting area, if only for a few moments. Meanwhile, Al leads the charge with an intensity that makes Sergeant Drago sit back to protect his eardrums. I'm not sure why they brought Clark Kent since the mouthpiece doesn't say a word.

Twenty minutes later, Sophia walks out, a free woman. She looks exhausted and unhappy as she hugs her father and Al. Then she sees me and her tear-reddened eyes light up like Vegas after a blackout. Coming here wasn't such a bad idea after all.

She grabs Al's hand and leads him across the room to meet me. The lawyer and Billy follow. I get a hug, too, then she says, "Nob, this is Uncle Al." And to Al, "This is my friend Nob Brown." *My friend.* I guess that's what I am, though the words sound foreign coming from her lips.

"So you're the famous Nob Brown," he says. "I hope you'll be kind to our little Sophia. She's been dragged through a trainload of shit."

"Nob's been there for me, even when I wasn't," she says. "He kept warning me about Karl, but I didn't listen."

"It weren't your fault," says Billy. "The jackass was tryin' to shoot you. You did what you had to do."

She starts to cry.

The crudeness of a gun seems so unlike Karl, the MD/PhD who tried to stage a faux suicide. Guns are loud, they're messy, they lack subtlety.

"She wrestled the gun away from him," Al explains. "Thanks to you, Nob, she had those lab results, so the police had reason to believe her when she told them he was trying to kill her. *Kaynahorah*."

I recognize the word from my childhood. My mother used to say it a lot when she still had good news to report. It's a Yiddish prayer to keep the evil eye from spoiling good news, from yanking the rug out from under you. I hope it works.

We part ways with Billy and Al, and a half hour later, we're back in my kitchen.

"It's okay," she says, answering an unspoken question. "You can ask me."

I hand her a cup of coffee and take a seat at the table. "I wasn't sure you wanted to talk about it."

"It's not like I can stop thinking about it." She holds out her coffee. "But if you want me to tell you what happened, you'd better put a little Cognac in here."

I grab a bottle of Hennessy and pour a taste into her cup. Sophia takes a sip, savors the flavor, then takes another before beginning.

"I knew Karl had patients all day, so I thought I'd have several hours to pack my things."

She tips her cup and takes an unexpectedly loud slurp. She makes a cute apologetic face. Her cup had been full so I hadn't given her much Cognac, but it seems to be relaxing her anyway. Probably a placebo effect. But I can still hear a tremble in her voice.

"I was in the living room," she continues, "when the front door banged open, and Karl charged in. His eyes were all red and bugging out, and he was just out of control. I'd never seen him like that. I didn't know what to think. I kept asking him why he wasn't at work, sort of just babbling, but he wasn't listening anyway. He was screaming: I was trying to ruin him, I was paranoid, what the hell was I doing at a forensics lab—"

I interrupt. "He heard the message from the lab?"

"I guess so. He didn't actually say."

She takes another sip. I top off her coffee with a little more Cognac then pour a few fingers into my own cup. She closes her eyes and takes a deep breath to muster strength.

"I've never been so scared in my life. He demanded to know what I'd done, so I told him they found Nembutal in the coffee he made me, and the police already knew about it. I thought maybe he wouldn't hurt me if he knew he couldn't cover it up. But he was so out of control, I don't know if it even registered. He went for the Chinese desk, and I panicked. That's where he kept his gun. I grabbed a lamp and smashed it over his head. He had the gun then he dropped it then I tried to grab it but he pushed me into one of the art cases and it crashed over and things were crashing and breaking everywhere and we were both trying to get the gun and somehow I ended up with it. So I pointed it at him, thinking it would make him stop."

Her lips quiver, and her eyes tear. She takes a sip to compose herself then continues. "But he didn't. He tried to grab me, and the gun just went off."

SIXTY-NINE

hear a knock and wake up to find that my bedside light is still on. The clock reads two a.m.

"Yeah?"

The door opens to the visage of an angel. Sophia's wearing one of my old baseball jerseys for a nightshirt. Slinky polyester that comes halfway down her thighs. If she has on anything underneath, it's not apparent. Luckily, the team was too cheap to print their name on the shirts. I don't know that I would have kept mine if it were emblazoned with the words "Master Batters."

"Sorry," Sophia says. "I saw your light and thought you were awake."

"Come on in."

"I couldn't stand being alone."

I scooch over to give her room to sit on the edge of the bed.

"I couldn't stop thinking about Karl," she says. She grabs her shoulders and shivers. "Do you mind?" She lifts the edge of the blanket, seeking permission to climb under it.

"Help yourself."

She crawls under the covers and nestles in on her side so that we're face to face. We're not touching, but I feel her warmth and wish we were. I think about baseball but only because of her silhouette in my jersey.

"What he did to me in therapy was awful, but he tried to make up for it. I truly believe he loved me, I really do."

I don't quite know what to say, or what she wants me to say, so I play it safe. "I think I understand."

She smiles. "Are you trying to play therapist now?"

"I'm trying to keep my negative opinions to myself."

"I know you didn't think much of Karl, but you didn't know him. He wasn't some sort of monster; he just lost it. I know what it's like to be overwhelmed by paranoid fantasies, and I think that's what happened to him."

"Just an innocent victim of emotional problems? Driven by his inner demons to kill Ginger and try to kill you? Poor Karl."

She laughs and pulls the sheet up under her chin as if she's cold. It makes her look like she's huddled in a sleeping bag, like we're kids having a sleepover.

"I'm not saying it wasn't his fault," she says. "I'm just saying I understand how you can love someone and try to kill them at the same time."

I wonder how this understanding affects her stages of grief. For that matter, I wonder how they're affected by the fact that she pulled the trigger.

"Do you think he loved you when he put drugs in your coffee?"

"Haven't you ever loved and hated someone at the same time?"

I think of Holly. "I take the Fifth."

I roll onto my back with my hands clasped behind my head. She snuggles up tight against me, her head on my arm. She swings her leg across mine. It's confirmed: she's wearing nothing beneath the jersey. I feel her pubic warmth on my thigh. If she moves another inch, she'll feel my reaction.

"When I first moved in with Karl we went for STD tests and when we both passed, I went on the pill. We opened our last box of condoms for one last Trojan fling to celebrate our commitment to monogamy. Cut to seven months later. He was shaving in the bathroom, and I happened to notice the condom box in his bedside drawer. A dozen came in the box and we'd only used that one so there should have been eleven left. I got this sudden urge to count them. Talk about paranoid."

"It's not paranoid if it's true," I extend my arm around to hug her to me. I feel her warmth against my side through the soft jersey. She kisses my chest, and I feel it in my groin.

"I never found out for sure. He walked out of the bathroom just as I dumped the box on the bed, and he flew into a rage. He couldn't believe I'd stoop so low. He accused me of sabotaging myself and all the work I'd done in therapy. He started ranting about me trivializing his love and trashing our relationship and how without trust we've got nothing and I was terrified that I'd destroyed everything and it was over. I just wanted to melt in his arms and have it all go away. But at the same time I felt like his tantrum was just a big cover-up. Why make such a big deal of it unless it was true, unless he was cheating on me."

"I can't imagine cheating on the woman I love."

"I can tell." She snuggles closer and her knee brushes my family jewels. I shudder and she feels it. She lifts her head and looks at me with those autumn eyes. "Why didn't we make love the other night?"

"I thought you might regret it in the morning."

She traces my lips with her finger. "Maybe I regretted the missed opportunity." She retraces my lips but with her tongue this time. I can barely breath between the sexual promise and moral haze.

"I didn't want to take advantage," I say. "I'm not sure that's changed."

She straddles me and can feel my arousal overruling my concern.

"I'm a big girl," she says and slips out of the jersey. She's the most beautiful sight I've ever seen.

SEVENTY

"Is she as good a fuck as me?"

"As I," I correct her, "and she sleeps in the guest room."

The end of my deck and the wall of my house look like the raw face of a strip mine as Gloria and I sit with our backs to the ruins having coffee and cold pizza. I feel like I'm in a war zone. The to-do list is growing: fix the toilet, get a new couch, rebuild the deck, repair the deck chair, pay off the ex-wife, replace the smashed bottle of Scotch, and solve the two murders.

The morning is mild for a change, midseventies with a few scattered powder puffs of clouds in a clear blue sky. LA has some of the worst air in the country, but we've cut pollution by two-thirds since 1955, which is nothing short of a miracle. When I was a kid, we had days that were so smoggy they'd have to close the schools. That doesn't happen anymore. Today is a poster child for environmental progress.

Runt whines. Gloria tosses him an arc of stale pizza crust. He snatches it in the air. Runt is not one to let food fly by. He keeps his snout skyward so the crust won't fall out of his mouth as he chews.

"I wasn't asking how she sleeps, I was asking how she fucks."

"Give it a rest, Gloria. This routine is getting old."

She smirks. "Listen to Mr. Sensitivity over here. I just want to know where I stand. I know you're a monogamous kind of guy, so is your dick available these days or not?"

I glance nervously toward the house. I'd hate for Sophia to overhear this conversation. But I'm pretty sure she's still asleep. We had a long night, not that I'm complaining.

"You're just jealous."

"Why should I be jealous? You in love?"

"Of course not." I feel like I'm lying, and I don't know why.

"I know. Because you're still hung up on Holly." The accusation stings, like I was a college swim coach accused of staring at camel toes.

"Besides," she says, "Sophia just killed her last lover. You don't want to be next. She's a basket case. She's numb, she's susceptible, she's breakable, she's damaged, she's an emotional depth charge. I know that you're dumb enough to make a move on a woman like that at a time like this. I just wonder if you're crass enough."

From any other woman this would be an insult, but I know Gloria well enough to hear it as an expression of her love. She's worried about me. I have an urge to let her know I appreciate it, but she's sparring, and I don't want to give her an opening.

"She's spent a lifetime getting fucked over by men she trusts," I say. "Do you think I want to join the list?"

"Very chivalrous of you. But if her last relationship is any indication, she can edit her own list."

"It was self-defense, Gloria."

Gloria gives me the eye. "Did Sophia tell you how she happened to shoot him?"

"They fought for the gun. It just went off."

"What are the odds of an unintentional gunshot putting four bullets in a guy?"

Something clenches in my gut and migrates to my face.

Gloria reads me like a neon sign. "I guess your girlfriend forgot to mention that little detail," she says.

"How did she explain it?"

"She said it was reflex. Not like a muscle twitch, but mental. Like some kind of survival instinct thing."

"I can see it. Fight or flight. She was cornered. He closed in, fear took over, she pulled the trigger. And kept pulling it until he fell."

Gloria's abdomen lurches in a silent guffaw.

"You don't buy it?"

"Got no way to disprove it," she says. "Besides, it's not up to me, it's up to the DA. But I've yet to see a case where multiple gunshots didn't spell out intent."

SEVENTY-ONE

Karl's house looks the same, except there's a remnant of yellow crime-scene tape knotted around the mailbox post. Sophia unlocks the front door then stands back.

"You go first," she says.

I can actually see a rapid pulse beating in her carotid artery, but despite this her face is pale. The memory of Karl's death is a fresh wound that she's afraid of reopening. I step ahead of her into the house.

I was here just after the shooting, but I never set foot inside. I expect to see some blood on the living room carpet, maybe an overturned chair, but I'm not prepared for the chaos. The room looks like it was decorated by a grenade launcher. There's debris everywhere from a huge overturned display case of glass art. Sheet glass, blown glass, etched glass, stained glass, fused glass, leaded glass, molded glass, in thousands of shattered shards of every imaginable color. Chairs are strewn about, an antique red-lacquered Chinese desk is overturned, lamps lie on the floor, and over everything is a patina of fingerprint powder. The powder, too, is multicolored, though all in the gray scale, each selected to contrast with the shade of the underlying surface or object.

Sophia follows me in, and I hear a little gasp. I'm guessing the last time she was here, her nerves were overloaded, and her eyes were so fixed on Karl that she tuned out the collateral damage. It won't take much to persuade a jury that this was a life-or-death battle, if it comes to that. She's going to need a shovel to clean this place up.

I notice a clear spot on the carpet, heavily stained with blood where his struggle ended. Sophia sees it, too, and rushes past. I follow her up the stairs.

The bedroom is large and painted eggshell white. The bed is a low platform with built-in nightstands and lights. Two walk-in closets obviate the need for dressers. A flat-screen TV is mounted on the wall. And through the open bathroom door I see a built-in vanity cluttered with makeup. No need for much furniture. Aside from the bed, there is only a blond leather lounge chair with a Memphis-style side table.

"Make yourself comfortable," says Sophia. She pulls a large suitcase from her closet and opens it on the lounge chair. She heads back into the closet to start selecting clothes to pack. I sit on the bed, presumably on Karl's side, judging by the *Journal of Behavior Therapy and Experimental Psychiatry* on the nightstand. I look across the bed and see a pile of paperback mysteries on Sophia's side, a Chelsea Cain on top.

She walks in with an armload of folded sweaters and puts them in the bottom of the suitcase.

"Can I help?" I ask.

"I'm fine." She disappears back into the closet.

I look out the window and feel calmed by the scenery. The neighborhood is tranquil, wooded. Across the street a teenage boy practices free throws through a hoop mounted on his garage. The familiar bounce of the basketball is a comforting sound. An old woman wrapped in a stylish wool coat walks a miniature schnauzer on a retractable leash. Even the dog appears placid.

Sophia looks like a Stepford wife packing for a long vacation; her domesticity seems unnatural in this house of lingering death. I indulge a fleeting fantasy of what it might be like to live here with her. Let Holly have my house. Let Jerry deal with replacing the deck and repairing the office window. I'll just move uptown with Sophia and help her forget.

She walks out of the closet, holding a stunning pair of high heels covered in what looks like emerald-green Thai silk. She wraps them carefully in T-shirts before packing them.

My eyes wander to Karl's bedside drawer. A square box of Kleenex, too tall for the drawer, wedges it six inches open. I peer in, and the famous box of condoms stares up at me like a movie prop.

"Count them," Sophia says. I look up to see her watching with a strained expression, a jewelry box in her hands.

"Does it matter anymore?"

"I want to know."

Karl is dead, but she's still jealous. I wonder if she'd feel better knowing they're all accounted for or if it would assuage her guilt to know he cheated.

I grab the box and dump the contents on the bed. There are eleven. Her expression relaxes, even though it proves nothing and changes nothing. She goes into the closet and comes out with a stack of panties. She drops them on the chair and starts rolling them into cylinders to pack.

My eye falls on a dust pattern inside Karl's bedside drawer. Highlighted by the oblique angle of the sun through the window, it looks like a key ring except it's got a crescent bisecting the center. A trigger guard. Karl had kept a gun in the drawer. The thickness of the dust made it clear that the gun had been left untouched in that drawer for a very long time. And the crispness of the pattern revealed that it had been removed only recently.

He went for the Chinese desk, and I panicked. That's where he always kept his gun.

SEVENTY-TWO

It's about three o'clock in the morning. I can see that Sophia is having nightmares from the way she grimaces, the way she twitches, the way she kicks off the sheets. It's been a hot night. The moon streams through the window and falls across her at an acute angle, making sharp planes of the shadows, a cubist painting across her breasts and up her neck.

Why do any of us do what we do? Why did my father? He had a life. Maybe he was in financial trouble, maybe even facing a few years of jail. But he had a wife who loved him, three kids he was proud of, plenty of friends, marketable skills, and a mean hook shot. What made him decide to take a flier off that cliff?

I had a woman who loved me, who I loved, who I would have died for, killed for. I had a job I was proud of, where I could do some good for the world and still earn a pension. What made me sabotage all that? I didn't have to quit. I could have fought, yet I didn't feel like I had a choice. You don't rat out the guys who cover your back in the field. I was protecting a twisted code of honor, a false god, but that realization came too late. Never again.

I gently kiss the top of Sophia's head and the musky scent of her hair warms me like the smell of fresh-baked bread. I wonder about my attraction to a woman who shot the last man she loved. While he was unarmed. Four times. And probably lied about how she got the gun.

He may have been a sociopathic opportunist, an emotional saboteur, a chainsaw slayer of trust and self-esteem, but his guilt should have been judged by a jury, not by a jealous lover.

On the other hand, Sophia's psychological ingredient list was top-heavy with mitigating circumstances.

I watch her head bob gently on my chest as I breathe. She looks so peaceful, so angelic. It had to be self-defense. Maybe she didn't lie. Lynch could have had two guns, one in the bedroom and one in the living room. That's certainly possible.

Sophia's eyes flutter half-open and look into mine. She smiles contentedly. She feels safe with me. I want to kiss her but don't want to fully wake her. She needs a rest from reality. Her eyes close and she falls back to sleep. A barely conscious moment devoid of guile. I'm warmed by the kind of feeling that could be mistaken for love. Unless it is. The thought isn't soothing.

I can't stop thinking about those four shots. After all that Sophia has been through, Ginger's death could have easily pushed her over the edge. Sophia could have been temporarily insane. I try to reenact the murder in my head, but there's a problem with the script. If she was packing her clothes, what was she doing in the living room?

"Sophia, wake up."

"Wuz wrong?" she mumbles, eyes at half-mast.

"How many guns did Karl have?"

"What?"

I sit up abruptly, pushing her off my chest onto her back. "Did he have more than one gun?"

"What are you talking about?"

I grab her by the shoulders, pinning her to the bed. "Just tell me!"

"You're scaring me."

I back off. She snatches the sheet to shield her nakedness, eyes open wide.

"Tell me about the second gun."

"What second gun?"

The disappointment on my face must have spoken volumes.

"Baby, what's wrong?"

"What's wrong is you brought the gun downstairs before Karl got home and waited to shoot him as soon as he walked in. You killed him in cold blood, and you've been lying all along."

She slaps me hard on the same side Petya hit. It hurts like hell, and I feel a headache start to bloom. At least she's finally awake.

"I really wish you hadn't done that," I say. "What's the point of feigning outrage when you know I'm right? I saw a dust impression of the gun in Karl's bedside drawer. He didn't keep it in the living room, but you lied about that because you'd have a hard time arguing self-defense if the police knew it was all premeditated."

"You bastard! I trusted you!"

She takes another swing at me, but I catch her hand. "Stop playing the shocked little innocent. It doesn't wash. You never trusted me. You lied to me from the first day we met, and you're lying to me now!"

"He was going to kill me!" Sophia bursts into tears. "He was afraid I'd tell the police that he went to Ginger's the night she died."

"Bullshit."

"It's true!" She pulls herself up and crushes her lips into mine as if lust will slap some faith into me.

I shove her back down onto the bed. "What else did you lie about?"

Her eyes flit away for a microsecond before staring back at me. If she were under interrogation, that would be a tell. It's so quiet I think I hear her heart pounding. Or maybe mine. I can smell the salty tears on her cheeks. She finally takes a deep breath, girding herself for something tough. I hope it's something resembling the truth, but I don't expect it.

"I want to trust you, Nob, you've got to believe that. But trust scares the shit out of me. I can't take getting burned again."

She grabs me around the waist and hugs me there. I don't push her away.

"You can trust me," I say. At this point I'm thinking she doesn't have much choice, but I don't say so. Her timing seems suspiciously convenient. "Tell me what you're hiding."

Her eyes search mine, looking for some sign. Then resignation wins out. "Karl didn't drug Ginger. And he didn't turn on the gas."

"Who did?"

"She did it herself."

This is the last thing I expect to hear. "That's not what the cops think."

"She left a suicide note. I can show it to you."

I open my mouth but nothing comes out, like my brain is flashing *tilt*. She hangs her head and takes a deep breath. Then she gets up and walks out.

I couldn't have been more surprised if she'd told me she'd killed Ginger herself. The police already ruled suicide out because of the fingerprints, or lack thereof. There was no explanation for the drugs—no bottle, no baggie, no paper packet, not even a tissue with residue. And there was no note. Until now.

Sophia comes back with a piece of paper in her hand. She hands it to me, but I motion for her to drop it on the bed. If it's got any prints besides Sophia's, I don't want to compromise them.

It's a piece of bone-colored stationery. "Ginger Strain" is embossed across the top in dark plum, and across the bottom, her address. The handwriting has that same calligraphic style I noticed when I browsed through Ginger's address book. If this isn't Ginger's writing, it's an amazing facsimile. The message is short and simple.

Dr. Karl treats me like shit, and he knows me better than anyone. So what's the point?

"Where did you get this?" I ask.

"I went back over there later that night, after Karl fell asleep. I was going to confront her, but she didn't answer the bell. I snooped around and found the back door unlocked. She was already dead, still holding the pen. That was under her hand."

341

I expect her to continue but she doesn't. I look up from the suicide note. She's staring vacantly into space.

"And?" My voice snaps with impatience, kicking her back on track.

"I knew exactly what she meant. I felt her pain. And I realized I couldn't keep stuffing my own pain anymore. It was like a fog lifting. I looked at Ginger's body, and I saw my own lying there. We were interchangeable. It became so clear. The charade was over. I couldn't keep pretending that Karl's betrayal wasn't killing me inside. Ginger died because of him, and I knew that his love for me, our whole relationship, was a lie. My therapy was just another sexual conquest for him, another exercise in dominance. He made me think I was sexy, I was loved, I was willing. But the truth is he raped me. Just like he raped Ginger. Only she found a way to end the pain once and for all."

She stares out the window as if watching a funeral pyre. "I knew he had to be stopped, but I didn't know how. I sat there with her body for...I don't know. It seemed like hours. Could have been five minutes for all I know. And then it just"—she gestures with her hand as a fairy might wave a magic wand—"came to me. One of those 'ah-ha' moments."

She stands and grabs one of my shirts from on top of the laundry hamper. She puts it on to warm herself. I take a tissue and move Ginger's note to my nightstand where it will be safer. Sophia comes back to bed.

"I took her pill bottle and wiped her prints off her cup so the police would think someone tried to fake her suicide. Then I turned the gas back on, locked the door, and went home."

"Why go back the next day to find the body?"

"I knew my relationship with Karl would make them wonder what I was doing there, raise difficult questions."

"You went back just to implicate Karl?"

"Yes."

"Did you drug your own food, too? So we'd all think he was trying to kill you?"

"He did kill me, Nob. Just like he killed Ginger. He killed us with betrayal. He sucked us dry, he bled us out, he emptied us. He took what little life our grandfather left behind, and he crushed it. God only knows how many other women he did it to."

Now that the truth is out, she looks deflated, vulnerable. An abandoned child in an adult costume.

"I'm not proud of what I did. And I'm not happy about it either. I still loved him, no matter how much I hated him. But I knew he'd just keep on destroying other women's lives if someone didn't do something about it, and I didn't see anyone else stepping up."

Her eyes are all the more hypnotic in her sadness. She sits back and hugs herself, and I know she wants to be held; I just don't know if I can do it and stay clear-headed.

"You were a cop, Nob. With my mental history, you know no court would ever take my word against his about what happened in those sessions, at least not beyond a reasonable doubt. He would have walked away scot-free. What would you have done?"

"I probably would have confronted him and killed him with my bare hands," I say. "But at least that would have been a crime of passion."

"Does it really make a difference?"

"Hell yes, it makes a difference. You didn't kill him in a rage, Sophia. You orchestrated it step by step. You staged Ginger's suicide to frame him for murder. You faked your own poisoning to lay the groundwork for an alibi. Then you shot him and rigged it to look like self-defense."

Her eyes tear again. "If I had just confronted him, I'd probably be the one who got killed. Who would stop him then?"

I try to balance what she did against why she did it, but the scale keeps bouncing. I can't begin to imagine the depth and breadth of the suffering that drove her to do it. The hurt and betrayal of her grandfather's incestuous pedophilia, the turmoil of her parents' explosive separation, the shock of her mother's murder, the long estrangement from her only sibling, the treachery of Karl's seduction, the agony of his subsequent philandering, the blow of discovering her sister's corpse, and finally the chaos and guilt surrounding Karl's shooting. With all she's been through, it's little wonder that the trauma of being bound and kidnapped had such little impact. But does any of that give me the right to withhold what I know from the police?

"I'm not sorry I did it," she says. "I'm just sorry I lied to you."

I pull her close enough to feel her heart racing. She's not crying anymore. Maybe she's all out. Or maybe the truth has set her free. I just know that I ache for her.

"It feels strange to finally have someone to trust," she says. "It feels good."

She turns her face to mine, and I see her lips quiver again. I want to quiet them with my own, but I'm afraid to. Afraid it'll push me into a decision I'm not ready to make.

"Karl always told me I had to get those self-defeating demons out of my head," she says. "I think they're finally gone."

That's when the doorbell rings.

SEVENTY-THREE

I could really use my gun right now as I make my way to the door. I turn to find Sophia behind me, her eyes wide with fear. My first thought is that Cogswell and his boys have come back, though I doubt they'd use the bell. I motion for Sophia to take a seat on the sofa and be quiet, then head into the hall to peek through the peephole. To my surprise, it's a cop.

He's about my height but probably half my weight. His LAPD uniform drapes off his shoulders like it was on a coat hanger. If there's a body in there, it doesn't make much of an impression. He's Latino, name-tagged Ramirez.

"Sorry to bother you at this time of night, sir, but we've had a report of shots fired in the neighborhood. Have you seen or heard anything unusual?"

"No. Nothing. You'd think I would have heard a gunshot."

"It may not have happened today. Your neighbor found a bullet lodged in his refrigerator door."

The shot that went off accidentally when Cogswell and I went over my railing.

"Looks like it came through his window screen," he says, "from this general direction. No one seems to have heard it, and he was away for a few days, so we don't know when it was fired. Have you heard or seen anything?"

If I tell the truth, I'll have to implicate Vlad, which would be not only suicidal, but ungrateful. I could say that my own gun went off while I was cleaning it, but they'll want to see it, and I can't produce it. I could just deny any knowledge, but if the bullet pierced my neighbor's screen, the lab may be able to nail the trajectory and figure out that the bullet came from my deck. There's no good answer to the question.

I make a face like I'm having cramps. "Can you talk to some other neighbor and come back later?" I clench my teeth. "I've had the trots all night. I've got to get to the pot."

He backs away like I've got TNT strapped to my chest. "Sure, mister. No problem."

I close the door fast.

Sophia comes out of the living room. She heard the whole exchange. She puts her arms around my neck.

"You didn't turn me in," she says. She kisses me, her tongue hungry for mine. I can't help but savor the pleasure for a moment before rejoining the real world.

"I've got to call Gloria." I pull my cell from my pocket. Panic twists Sophia's brow as I hit Gloria's speed dial.

"What are you going to tell her?"

"Ramirez is going to come back sooner or later. I'd much rather talk to someone I know and trust."

I reach Gloria in Glendale, where she's investigating the severed head of a Salvadoran gangbanger that was found in a Dumpster behind an Armenian grocery on Pacific. She says she's just winding up there. An hour later I hear her pull up outside. I expect her to knock, but when she doesn't, I peek through the curtains and see her on the street talking to Ramirez and another uniform.

When she finally comes down the steps, I open the door before she can knock.

"Officer Ramirez is very concerned about your bowels," she says.

"I've had a miraculous recovery."

She walks past me into the living room where Sophia sits sipping a Pernod and soda. I have no idea how Pernod snuck into my liquor supply, but that's where she found it.

"Drink?" I ask Gloria.

"I'm on duty. So why do you need a homicide detective for a property crime?"

"The shot was fired from my deck."

"Why didn't you tell Officer Ramirez?"

"I had to go to the pot."

She gives me one of those looks you give to a child who denies eating the cookie through chocolate-covered lips.

"It's a delicate situation," I add.

I grab a glass. She's on duty but I'm not, even if it's four o'clock in the morning. I don't want to take the time to get ice, so I pour myself a snort of the Glenlivet neat. Nothing like an unblended Scotch in the early hours to focus the mind.

"I wasn't sure Ramirez and company would be up to it," I continue.

"I'm listening."

I grab another glass and pour a shot for Gloria. "On duty" means she won't ask for a drink, but if it's in front of her, she won't waste it. The woman's got a unique take on ethics; what can I say?

"It was Cogswell." Her interest perks up. "The gunshot was an accident."

"Accident?"

I hand her the unblended. She takes it without comment but thanks me with that coy curl of her lip.

"He was showing me his gun. I accidentally tripped and fell into him. It went off."

Clearly skeptical, Gloria looks to Sophia, who sits stock-still, eyes glued to me.

"Why make me drive over here to lie to me?" asks Gloria. "You could have just as easily lied to Ramirez."

"If Cogswell finds out I told the police, he'll send his thugs back, and the next shot won't be accidental."

"Your friends shot a Sub-Zero, Nob. If we were in Beverly Hills that'd be a capital offense."

"I know what you're thinking, but you're wrong. You're thinking you can't let this slide because it's tied to Ginger's murder. But the gunshot had nothing to do with that."

"And you know this how?" Her eyes narrow along with her focus, her bullshit detector on full blast.

I hear Sophia take a sharp breath behind me. I don't hear her exhale. I've hit the moment of truth, and she's scared that I'll tell Gloria that she tampered with the scene. I know Sam Spade would let the broad swing for it, but this is murkier than that. I think of the pain Nathaniel inflicted on Sophia. I think of the pain Karl inflicted on Sophia. Am I going to be the next to betray her? The only alternative is to turn my back, and that strategy hasn't worked out very well for me in the past.

"Ginger committed suicide," I say. "She left a note." It hurts to see the trust drain from Sophia's eyes.

Gloria bursts out laughing. I'm not sure what kind of reaction I was expecting, but this wasn't it.

Sophia lets out a hysteria-tinged snicker. "What are you talking about, Nob?" Then to Gloria, "He doesn't know what he's saying."

"That's not unusual," says Gloria.

Sophia turns back to me. "I was just kidding about the note. You know that, right?"

Gloria looks to me for an explanation.

"I can show you the note," I tell her. "I'm sorry, Sophia, but you dealt the cards. The hand's got to be played."

Sophia's green-gold Lana eyes turn as cold as a reptile's. "I trusted you."

"A lot of people trust me. Because I don't tell lies." Which is a lie, in and of itself.

SEVENTY-FOUR

The sun is just rising as I throw some beans in the grinder. Gloria slips into some latex gloves before taking the suicide note out of the ziplock bag I'd put it in for safekeeping. She holds it obliquely to the light to see if there are any visible stains or prints. The lab will find latent prints with ninhydrin or superglue fumes, but beyond Ginger's and Sophia's, I doubt they'll find any surprises.

I made Sophia tell Gloria what happened at Ginger's that night. Now Sophia leans back against the kitchen wall, arms crossed dejectedly, eyeing me like a battered wife watching her husband guzzle down the bottle of Wild Turkey.

Gloria slips the note back into the bag and lays it on the table.

"This paints a whole new portrait of Karl's murder," she says.

"It doesn't have to," I say.

"What are you suggesting? I should let her go because you think her ass is hot?" Her gaze swings at Sophia like a tire iron. Sophia reacts like she's been smacked.

"I'm just saying she tampered with evidence relating to Ginger's suicide," I say. "That doesn't necessarily have a bearing on Karl's death."

"Sophia alleged he tried to kill her to cover up Ginger's murder," says Gloria. "If Ginger wasn't murdered, Sophia's claim of self-defense sort of loses its oomph, don't you think?"

I think about the dust impression from the gun, but I keep it to myself. The police had their shot at the house. If they didn't find it, less power to 'em. Besides, with no chain of custody, I doubt it would be admissible anyway.

I pour the grounds into the coffee machine. "Have a cuppa, hear me out before you do anything precipitous."

"Like making an arrest?"

Gloria's thoughts are running parallel to mine, she just doesn't know it yet.

"Do you think the public would be any safer if Sophia was locked up?"

Gloria doesn't bother to answer. I pour her a cup of coffee and set it on the table then lift the bagged note and put it on the counter where it can't get spilled on.

"No matter what you think, you'll never make a murder case stick," I continue. "But even if you could, justice would get screwed."

"Is that so?" She's playing hard to get.

"I don't think Karl deserved to die for his sins, but I don't think he deserved much better than that."

"I should let her loose because she killed a jerk?"

"Karl's is not the only corpse here, Gloria. Sophia shot him; there's no disputing that. But no matter what happened that day, she'd already served a sentence before she even committed a crime. Will justice be done if she's punished twice? Last I heard, double jeopardy is unconstitutional."

"That's absurd," says Gloria. Even Sophia looks dubious.

"It's relative. Karl raped Ginger just like he did Sophia, and Ginger killed herself over it. The man was her therapist. What if he drove her to suicide to cover up his own crimes? Wouldn't that be murder? He's hardly an innocent here. But even then, he didn't start it all. Nathaniel Strain is guilty of that. He's the reason Sophia and Ginger were in therapy in the first place. He's the reason they were susceptible to Karl's abuse. He's the reason Ginger was neurotic enough to kill herself. And he's the reason Sophia was angry enough to pull the trigger."

"You're really reaching," says Gloria.

"Nathaniel Strain is the root of all evil here. He raped his own daughter when she was thirteen. He raped his own grand-daughters when they turned the same age, and when Lana found out, he killed her to shut her up."

"You can't prove that, Nob."

"You know it's true. The man's a multiple incest aggressor and a murderer, and he's free as a bird. You going to let him get away with it?"

"Sometimes the bad guys get away with it. That's the price of a free society."

"The man is a monster, Gloria, and he's run out of family to victimize. How many other pubescent girls has he abused who've never come forward? How many others are out there right now that he hasn't gotten to yet? We've got to bring him down."

Now I've got both Gloria's and Sophia's interest.

"What do you expect me to do?" asks Gloria. "Gun him down in the street?"

"There's nothing we can do about Lana's murder. But we can nail him for incest if Sophia testifies. She's the only eyewitness who's still alive. Ginger's teenage accusations will back her up, and she may give the courage to other witnesses to come forward."

Gloria finally catches on. "But if Sophia gets tried for Karl's murder, or convicted of tampering with evidence, any defense attorney worth his salt will shred her on the stand."

"Like a block of Parmesan," I say. "So who are you going to take down, Gloria? Sophia or Nathaniel? Because you know you can't have them both."

"You are such a son of a bitch," she says. I'm pretty sure she means it as a compliment.

SEVENTY-FIVE

We're cramped in a van a block from Strain's house watching a balding technician named Ramsey tape a wire to Sophia's stomach. We're all concerned for her safety.

The Nathaniel Strain incest sting isn't a Robbery Homicide case, so Gloria enlists the aid of a friend from Sex Crimes, a detective named Sheryl Bane, who takes over the case but lets Gloria run it with her. Sheryl is every pedophile's worst nightmare, a pit bull who chases them down and chews them up. She's flat-faced, black-haired, and about my height but could probably out-bench-press me if push came to shove.

"I don't like you going in there alone," says Sheryl. "The man's a filthy pig scumbag child molester."

"He's never hit me, he's never hit my sister, and he never hit my mother except in self-defense."

"He shot her in the head," I point out.

"I don't think so," Sophia replies. "Didn't you see her shrine in his house? He loved her. She was his only daughter. He wouldn't hurt her, and he won't hurt me. I've got to do this."

"Well, you don't have to do it alone," says Gloria. "I'm going in with you."

"He'll never admit it in front of a witness," says Sophia.

"I still don't like it," says Sheryl. "You get hurt, it's on my watch."

Sophia fixes her with a hard eye. "For the first time in my life I'm the hunter instead of the prey. I'm doing this."

We all fall silent as the technician finishes up and straightens her blouse. She's wired and ready to go.

With a troubling brew of excitement and trepidation I watch her walk down the street. Then she turns the corner and disappears.

Ramsey turns up the volume, and we can hear Sophia breathing as she approaches her grandfather's door. She sounds pumped up, like she's been jogging, even though she's only walked a short block. The fidelity is crystal clear, but the prevailing sound is the rustling of fabric against the mike. To minimize that interference, Ramsey instructs Sophia to keep still once she gets inside, but that's only possible if things don't get out of hand. There's no telling how Strain will react to Sophia's visit, but a physical confrontation isn't out of the question.

Sophia stops, and we hear a distant chime—the doorbell ringing inside the house. Distant footsteps, the clack of a deadbolt, the creak of the door, like the sound effects of a radio play.

"What are you doing here?" Strain sounds surprised.

"We need to talk." Sophia sounds determined.

The door closes and the bolt clacks shut. She's locked inside the lion's den.

"What is it?" He sounds worried, a grandfather concerned that his granddaughter has come to him in trouble.

"It's this." We hear a faint metallic clink. Her half-heart pendant hitting the glass coffee table. "The police said Mama was wearing one when she died. Did you give it to her like you gave me mine, Grampa Nate? Did you do her, too?"

"What's the point of dredging all that up? It's gone. She's gone."

"Just answer me."

"What's past is past."

"Not to me. I live with it every day. With the feeling of your filthy fingers and your slimy tongue and your stiff prick. I was only thirteen, you son of a bitch. Is that how old she was when you fucked her? Is that how you like them?"

"I don't know what you want me to say after all these years." He's wily, not giving an inch, but I can hear his irritation heating up.

"How about you're sorry, you piece of shit?"

"Don't you talk to me that way!"

The plan was to try to get an admission without pissing him off, but she pulled the gloves off early. It's making me nervous. I've seen how little it takes to set him off. I remember thinking how close he was to smashing his one iron though my skull.

"Are you going to admit what you did? Or do I have to go to the police?" Oh, no.

"And tell them what? That you lied to them when Ginger made those charges all those years ago? Why should they believe you now? It'll be your word against mine."

"You killed my mother. How about that? Did she threaten to tell the cops how you raped her and then raped her daughters? Is that why you did it?"

Gloria and I exchange an anxious glance. Sophia is pushing him too hard, just like I suspect Lana did before he killed her.

"You ignorant little bitch. You want an apology? Look in a mirror for it. Everything I did was something you wanted, something you asked for. Tarting around in those short skirts, tits sticking out like a fuck-me ad. You were nothing but a little slut, just like your mother!"

"How did she get that necklace around her neck, you son of a bitch? She flushed the one you gave her down the toilet. I saw her do it."

"Shut your mouth, Sofie." His voice is pure menace.

"You shot her, then you put one of your little golden hearts on her to mark your goddamn territory."

The van fills with an awful sound, part scream, part smack, muffled by the scraping rasp of fabric on mike and crashing furniture. He hit her.

I don't hear anything else as I wrench open the door and flee the sound chamber into the night. Gloria calls my name then hits the ground running behind me. As I turn the corner and sprint for the house, I hear the harsh explosive crack of a gunshot.

I bound up the steps and launch my full body weight into the door, hoping to smash the bolt through the jamb. It holds firm, smacking me back like a brick wall. For a split second I think I'm going to lose consciousness, but it clears. I hear struggling inside, then the frightful boom of another shot.

"Get back!" I step aside, and Gloria blasts the lock with her Glock 22.

The door swings open. Strain wheels in our direction, gun in hand. Gloria shouts for him to drop his weapon, but he raises it. They fire at the same time. I feel something smack into my chest and realize it's a bullet that just blasted through Gloria's body. She goes down hard. She's got a hole the size of a golf ball in her back. *Please God, don't let her die!*

I collapse to my knees, my tears salting her wound. I try to stanch the flow but her blood gushes through my fingers. Strain is still standing, blood spurting from his neck. I cough up blood of my own. We're all drowning in it. Blood, blood, and more blood.

SEVENTY-SIX

Strain's hand shakes as he swings his gun toward Sophia. She dives for it and wraps her hands around his, struggling for the weapon. She's been clipped in the left leg, but she can still use it. I hook my arms under Gloria's and drag her outside, out of the line of fire. I see Sheryl run down the street and shout, "Officer down!" She lunges for cover at the sound of a gunshot in the house. I pray that Sophia wasn't hit. I've been praying too much lately, especially for an atheist. If Gloria makes it, I swear to God I'll start believing.

I hear sirens approaching. Gloria's eyes are open, staring at me, struggling to stay focused. As she fades, I feel my heart start to dissolve. The Siamese twin thing again. If she goes, I go with her.

"Stay with me, Gloria."

"Do you love me?"

"Of course not."

She almost smiles. "Liar."

I hug her tight with my shirt wadded between us to compress her entry wound and my hand clamped tight against her exit wound, but it feels like a losing battle. I rest my cheek against her head. Her hair is soaked with my tears.

"Stay with me, Gloria."

Sophia comes out, breathing hard, stained with her grandfather's blood.

"He's dead," she says.

Three squad cars screech up, and all hell breaks loose.

I feel like I'm trapped in an oil drum bouncing down a mountainside as the ambulance careens through the streets. The siren screams. Every time its modulation bottoms out, I can hear the siren of the ambulance that carries Gloria. They won't tell me if she's dead or alive. At this point she's probably both, like Schrödinger's cat. They tell me the bullet is lodged in my chest muscle, just above my heart, probably not deep enough to cause serious damage. If Gloria's body hadn't slowed it down, it would have killed me. I just hope it didn't achieve in her where it failed in me.

We swerve to a stop and the doors fly open. As the EMTs pull my gurney out I see the back of Gloria's ambulance. Empty. Doors wide open. Too much blood on the floor.

I've lost my temper in public, and I've cried in sappy movies but, unlike my mother, depression is not part of my repertoire. Until tonight. I stare at the TV, but my mind is trapped in the operating room where they've been trying to stitch Gloria's shredded chest back together for three and a half hours. Lung. Arteries. Trachea. Muscle. Ribs. Life's blood. They're keeping her alive with machines, because her body can't do it on its own.

Perry Mason's deep-set eyes bear down on a hapless witness. "In that case, Mrs. Longstreet, why did it take you almost an hour to make a ten-minute drive?"

Ten minutes feels like an hour to me at the moment.

The witness starts sobbing. "I didn't mean to kill him!"

I try to shift my body on the bed, but my hospital gown is pinned by my weight and fights the move. It takes an effort to lift my butt in order to free the gown, and the effort hurts. It's just a small annoyance, but I feel like Sisyphus pushing the rock uphill.

Keep breathing, Gloria.

The door opens a few inches and Holly peeks in, worry etching her perfectly sculpted brows, trying to see if I'm awake.

I switch off the TV. "Any news?"

"She's still in surgery." Not what I want to hear, but at least she's still alive.

Holly walks in, gnawing at a cuticle.

"I used to worry every day about you getting shot," she says. "When you left the force, I thought, *At least he's leaving the violence behind.*"

"Sorry to disappoint you." I resist saying *again.*

"I didn't mean it like that." She goes back to her cuticle.

A scowling nurse walks in, drops a tray on my table, and leaves without a word. The Salisbury steak and gravy looks like sewage from a Goodyear plant. I eye the small plastic cup of orange juice, wishing it were beer.

"Want some?" Holly leans over me to reach for the juice. I smell rose water and woman. The scents are not strong, but they have a powerful effect on me.

"I don't want anything on that tray."

She straightens up, and her scent recedes like a fog burning off.

"You have to eat."

I'm too tired to crack wise, so I ignore the remark. My neck aches from the indentation my head made in the pillow. I reach to flip it and get another stab of pain.

"Let me help you," she says leaning over me again to lift my head gently with one hand and grab the pillow with the other. I get another whiff of her as the soft skin behind her earlobe beckons just inches from my eyes. I remember loving the taste of that spot. That's when Melody walks in.

Holly lowers my head and steps away fast, as if caught cheating.

"I've been watching the operating room door," says Mel. "No one's coming out smiling."

"Fuck," I say. "She wouldn't be in there if I'd just kept my mouth shut."

"You didn't know he had a gun," says Holly.

"I knew he'd shot Lana," I say.

"You didn't know for sure," says Mel.

"Yes I did."

———

Like a dog, a hospital never really sleeps, even when it appears to. It may dim its lights and limit its activity at night, but it's still alert, prepared to leap into action. The nurses go out on covert patrol as opposed to full maneuvers. They lock the visitors out, keep the noise level down to a low roar, and distribute sleeping pills. Mine's in a little cup on my water tray, untouched. I need to stay alert if I'm going to sneak out.

I'm attached to an IV that's delivering saline solution or something, don't ask me why. I have to unhook it. I can't just tear off the white surgical tape without ripping the needle through the top of my hand, so I have to hold the needle in place with my other hand while I pick at the tape with my teeth. I endure a couple minutes of slow torture as I worry the tape off my arm, uprooting my arm hair follicle by follicle. When it comes free, I pluck a tissue from the small box they charge insurance companies two bucks for. On my bill, it'll be eight bucks. The hospital expenses for this story are digging my financial hole into a vertical mineshaft.

I pull out the needle and use the tissue to compress the exit wound. To counteract my impatience, I force myself to watch the clock for two minutes to make sure the bleeding stops before I toss the tissue. Mission accomplished.

I lower the bars on my bed and twist myself out. When my feet hit the floor, my chest feels like a round of birdshot has hit it point-blank. I take a moment to let the pain subside and my head stop swimming. My legs wobble, but they hold me up.

My heart monitor communicates wirelessly with the nurses' station. It's on wheels, so I assume it's got battery backup. I just hope the battery is charged. It has a power switch, but if I turn it off some nurse might notice that it stopped, so instead I pull the plug. It gives a single beep then keeps monitoring on battery power. I grab the pole and wheel it into the hallway. No one seems to be running in my direction. So far so good.

I head for the elevator. As soon as the doors close, I rip the monitor leads from my chest and sides, and when I get to the fourth floor I leave the monitor in the elevator. By the time they figure out whose it is, I should be done.

The ICU is hopping. People everywhere. I'll only have a minute before I get caught, so I have to move fast, which in my condition isn't easy.

Then I catch my first break. I see Gloria right away. She's parked on the near side of the ward. She's got a breathing tube in her nose. I hobble over to her bed and see a nurse's face across the room snap up to stare at me. I head for Gloria, and the nurse heads for me. I glance at Gloria's monitor but can't decipher much. Then I look at her face. She's looking back. I take her hand and feel a weak squeeze of recognition.

"If you die on me, I'll never sleep with you again."

Her lips do that curl. "Liar," she mouths. Then her eyes flutter shut.

SEVENTY-SEVEN

I lean against the new handrail on my deck and try to recall what it felt like the night Gloria got shot. I was hit, too, but that's not what comes to mind when I think of that night. It's been more than a year, and I've been interviewed about it so many times that my glib descriptions have begun to repaint my recollection. Blurred memories have flooded the once-uninterrupted landscape of my past, turning it into an archipelago of isolated highlights, each one a bar saga of its own. The first crime-scene photo. Ginger's work. Ginger's death. The missing fingerprints. Billy Kidd. The gold necklaces. Karl's murder. The contemptible grandfather. The ballistics report that proved Gloria was shot by the same gun that killed Lana Strain.

I padlocked myself to my keyboard for two weeks to wrestle this thing onto paper for *Playboy*. Then Chuckles sold the piece as a book, and I had to chain myself down for another seven months.

Now that it's published I'm hoping to land some better assignments, but so far I've been spending so much of my time promoting the book that the only thing I've had a chance to get off the ground was five hundred words for the *Journal of Cleaner Production* on the impact of a drowned body's decomposition on surrounding water quality. I researched it at the Japanese tea garden of the Donald C. Tillman Water Reclamation Plant in Van Nuys, where they found Gary Cogswell's body floating with the koi.

The doorbell rings. I'm not expecting anyone. I'm not expecting any packages. Melody has keys. Jerry never came back from Tobago, and Holly's paid up anyway. Angel would have called first.

The bell rings again as I walk through the house toward the door.

I doubt it's Sophia, since she hasn't spoken to me since the shootout. Billy tells me she's become a recluse in the house she inherited from Karl after the DA decided the shooting was a clean self-defense. She spends most of her time painting, mostly in shades of black. The picture I took of Sophia on the Venice pier still wallpapers my cell phone. Maybe I'll change it someday.

I look through the spyhole. Gloria has a bottle of wine in her hand and a pair of cuffs hanging from her belt loop. A deadly enough combination. She's still laying off the gin to give her lung a break. Don't ask. It's the same brand of logic that governs her love life.

She spent three weeks on the breathing tube before they thought she was strong enough to breathe on her own. Another week and she called me to pick her up from the hospital. They sent her home with one of those breath exercisers where you're supposed to keep three Ping-Pong balls in the air, but instead she made me use my own techniques to make her breathe hard. Respiratory therapy wore me out.

I open the door. "Aren't you supposed to be at work, Lieutenant? I know I am."

"What's the point of getting shot if you can't get a mercy fuck on your day off?"

"It's the middle of the afternoon, Gloria."

She reaches out and caresses my neck, giving me that smile of hers.

"All work and no play makes Nob a dull boy."

"But productive."

She slams me against the wall where I stay pinned by the horns of this dilemma. She kisses me hard and sure. She knows I'll come around.

ACKNOWLEDGMENTS

I would have never been able to write this book without my father's forever appreciated, retroactively beloved, constant and irritating corrections of my grammar and usage. It was he who taught me the beauty of language.

Invaluable guidance of Kristen Weber and Mark Haskell Smith saved me from plunging into the structural abyss. Early readers who encouraged this effort despite all odds include Tom Rosenstiel, Ira Ingber, Dan Burstein, Jeff Kalban, Clair Carmichael, my talented compadres in Clair's and the above-named Smith's workshops, and my beloved Oxnardian critique group.

Getting accolades from friends and family is a gimme. But when you send a baby manuscript into the cold hard world, getting accolades from total strangers is exponentially more heartwarming. For that I'd like to thank Ann Collette, who saw something in my writing that prompted her to propose to me when she agreed to be my agent. And to my intrepid publishers Lee Goldberg and Joel Goldman whose raucous enthusiasm is every author's dream. Let us hope their passion for this book looks like foresight in hindsight.

And most importantly, I'd like to thank the two women in my life who not only never wavered in their support for what must have seemed the acme of folly, but gave brilliant, insightful notes that doubtless saved me from enormous embarrassment. Karina and Zoë, I love you to death, and live to do so.

ABOUT THE AUTHOR

Craig Faustus Buck is a writer of many faces. His journalism has appeared in hundreds of publications from the *New York Times* to *Sports Illustrated* to *Le Monde*. He has coauthored several nonfiction books, including *New York Times* #1 best seller *Toxic Parents*. He has written for and produced scores of network television series, pilots and movies, including an Academy Award-nominated short film. His short story "Dead End" was an Anthony Award finalist, and many others have appeared in anthologies and magazines. He is currently at work on a sequel to this book, tentatively titled *Go Down Screaming*.

CPSIA information can be obtained at www.ICGtesting.com
Printed in the USA
LVOW12s1612050615

441362LV00005B/628/P